For Mary, I-
this book as
writing it

STREETS

A NOVEL
BY
R. GIAN SANTE

PublishAmerica
Baltimore

First printing

ISBN: 1-4241-2494-8
PUBLISHED BY PUBLISHAMERICA, LLLP
www.publishamerica.com
Baltimore

Printed in the United States of America

For Jane, who lived on
and came back from
the streets

PROLOGUE

Henrietta Castle sat at the makeshift desk, eyeing the blank screen on the laptop computer. Ordinarily when she wrote, the words flowed effortlessly, smoothly. Not so with this manuscript, this was different.

What started as an exposé of an unconcerned society on the treatment and neglect of homeless people—or Streeters, as they were known—developed into a book-length work of nonfiction that would read like a blood and gore horror novel.

Hank, as her friends called her, decided the only way to get unbiased information about street people was to become one of them…to see the dark side of society through their eyes.

She forced herself to live with that multitude of unwashed, unpressed, purveyors and guardians of body lice, missing teeth and smelly breath.

The inhabitants of the streets had metamorphosed from easily identifiable, sterno-swilling men, referred to as bums, who staggered through the skid-row section of downtown Philadelphia, into ever growing numbers, which included women and children. Skid Row no longer had physical boundaries and Streeters, disbursed like dandelion seeds on the wind, popped up unwanted, in every section of the city.

One thing was certain. Gathering the information necessary to pen the pages changed Hank's life and almost caused her death.

Someone malevolent and sinister began a methodical resolution to the ever ballooning problem of Streeters, with the process of elimination by murder.

Streeters were fair game for the maniacal killer and Hank Castle was no exception.

CHAPTER 1

Henrietta Castle stood in front of the gas-log fireplace eyeing the neat row of awards, testament to her achievements as a freelance investigative reporter. The only problem with being a freelance writer was that she was never sure where she would be at any given time. She poured two fingers of cognac, sat on the sofa, propped her feet up on the cocktail table and went through three weeks of accumulated mail. She paged through the latest copy of the *National Post Magazine* until she saw her likeness staring back at her from page ten. Recognition in the prestigious publication elicited a feeling of pride. Her series of articles on the problems of alcohol and drug abuse as they related to teen suicides had won her the coveted Pyle Award from the Society of American Journalists.

She took her cognac to the large picture window overlooking the Benjamin Franklin Parkway. A mixture of snow and sleet blanketed the area and glistened in the trees, giving them a fairyland appearance. Two women clung to each other to stay in an upright position as they staggered up the Parkway battling the elements. Each woman carried a shopping bag that Hank came to recognize as the symbol of street people. Hank thought about the thousands of people like her, who never gave a second thought to the homeless, wandering the streets of all major cities. Aloud, she said, "Maybe that's where my next story is coming from. Nobody seems to want to write about it." She picked up the phone and punched in seven digits.

The voice at the other end answered, "Stockheim, here."

Hank smiled at the soft, familiar tone of his voice, and said, "There are three things in this life that are eternal, death, taxes and Wally Stockheim, editor extraordinaire."

"Hank." Stockheim laughed. "Only you would dare to talk to a high-flying guy with such disrespect. How've you been, sweetheart?"

"I'm fine, Wally."

"Really?"

"Yes, really."

"Your old job is still waiting if you want it, I miss that unique style. You've come a long way, baby. I saw the article on you in the *National Post*. You made it big and I'm proud of you. It's nice to know that others are finally appreciating your talents." Wally Stockheim had recruited her from the University of Pennsylvania when she was a senior. At the end of her first year on the *Journal*, under Wally's tutelage she received the Philadelphia award for journalism.

Her voice rang with excitement, as it had when she was a cub reporter. "I have a great idea for a solid story but I want to freelance it."

"What have you got in mind?"

There was a brief pause, and Hank said, "Street people. Why the problem? What are the authorities doing to correct it?"

"Street people? Come on, Hank, it has been tried…many times. You know that."

"Yes, Wally, but it has never been tried from the inside."

"They'd spot you before you could get a foot in that nonexistent door."

"Not if I'm one of them. Will you run the story when I get it?"

There was a pause. "How do you want to handle it, a weekly byline?"

"No. I'll give it to you all at once. It will take months to get what I need but in the end, it will be complete and exclusive."

"Hank, have you thought this thing through? The street is a tough place for a man and it can be impossible for a woman. I don't like the idea. I've seen what can happen on the streets." He paused. "It's less than a year since you were released from the hospital. I don't want to see you become a statistic."

"Old worry wart. There are women and children living on the streets because they have no choice. It's just as dangerous for them." Hank fingered the telephone cord. "I had a nervous breakdown, Wally, but I'm fine now. If you don't believe me you can ask Dr. Thornton, he'll verify that I am as solid as gold. Jeremy Thornton would never have released me if he wasn't convinced I could handle stress. Being a reporter isn't what I do for a living…it's what I am. You know that I have never been a quitter and I can't start now." The silence on the other end of the phone made her smile. "You know how I hate statistics so I'll avoid the possibility of becoming one."

Stockheim sighed. "Okay, but I don't like it. I'll send over the standard contract. Need up-front money?"

"No thanks."

"How will I reach you?"

"I'll get in touch with you when I can, which won't be often."

"Okay, Hank. Take care of yourself."

Hank put the phone back on its cradle and went down the enclosed fire-tower stairs of the apartment building to the basement and unlocked the door to the residents' storage area. A fluorescent light flickered eerily above her head as she rummaged through a footlocker and came up with two pairs of old jeans. The size ten denims were frayed but answered her need as did the extra large flannel shirt that had belonged to Julian Grant. She tried to push the thought of him from her mind but it persisted. Doctor Thornton said when painful memories intruded into her life, she should face them, deal with them. The more she tried to avoid them the more they would pursue her.

She took a deep breath and fingered the material of the blue and red plaid flannel shirt.

When she and Julian were newlyweds, they had gone to the Poconos to ski. At night they sat around the fireplace in the main lodge with other young couples and talked and drank and laughed. Those were the happy days. She was convinced nothing could alter their relationship. Julian loved that flannel shirt; he even wrapped it around her when she came out of the shower. He carried her to the bedroom and made love to her until dawn. Theirs was a relationship based on love and trust...she thought.

She pressed the shirt against her face. She had loved the scent of him, of musk and aftershave. Two years after their vacation in the mountains, love was only a word in the dictionary but no longer in Julian's vocabulary. Emotionally, he distanced himself from Hank and collected an odd assortment of friends. He succeeded in destroying her trust; first by his affair with a sixteen-year-old girl, then with a nineteen-year-old boy.

At twenty-six, Hank was a has-been. The last time she saw him was in the home they shared in Gwynedd. Julian, a young girl and two boys were engaged in a daisy chain of sex on the floor in the living room.

Hank called the police. Julian's anger was provoked and he beat her into unconsciousness.

On August 8, 1988, he was represented in the divorce action by his attorney. Although he continued to live in the Philadelphia area, Hank never saw him again.

Hank stared at the flannel shirt in the flickering light and pressed it to her face. She realized this piece of material had once sustained her during the painful months of separation and divorce from Julian Grant. This thing, that was once an amulet, this cherished talisman of enchantment of the early days of their marriage, was in reality nothing more than a worn piece of fraying flannel with a musty smell from being stored in a mildewed old footlocker.

There, she thought, that wasn't so bad. The pain attached to the memory of Julian Grant was gone, thanks to Doctor Thornton, he taught her to stand on her own. She had survived. The overhead light in the basement dimmed to a spectral dullness. Hank thought she heard a muffled, deep-throated laugh. Suddenly, her senses were honed to razor-sharp awareness. There was an unfamiliar pounding that started in her chest and worked its way into her throat, making it difficult to swallow. She made her way to the door and frantically pushed the bar until it gave way under the pressure of her body just as the ghostly shadow of light died. When she reached her apartment, her trembling, uncoordinated hands had difficulty mastering the simple task of unlocking her door. She was short of breath and more than a little frightened. She took out her canvas tote bag and thought about what she would take with her. She purchased a winter coat from a secondhand store. She decided to spend the first few days observing the street people, their attitudes, how they walked, what they said and how they said it. Her experience as an investigative reporter made her somewhat of an expert on body language. She had to learn the lingo of the street people and that would be more difficult. Key words that set them apart and allowed them to identify one of their own from frauds like her.

There was a knock at her door and she looked through the peephole to see who it was. Wally Stockheim was stomping the snow from his boots. She unlocked the deadbolt, slid the chain from the latch and threw open the door.

She smiled at the red-faced man standing in the hall. "I'll bet you didn't go home last night."

"Are you kidding? In this city, three snowflakes fall and the whole goddamn city comes to a grinding halt, couldn't even get a cup of coffee. Would you believe the coffee shop in the Journal Building is closed? The goddamn mensch who runs it lives in the apartment house across the street. The storm is so bad he can't walk fifty yards?"

Hank grabbed the Cossack hat from his baldhead and smoothed the gray fringe of hair around his ears. "I haven't had breakfast yet either. Join me. Coffee's just about done. You pour and I'll fry the eggs."

* * *

The rain and sleet had stopped but the cold, harsh dampness persisted. A new cold front moved in. Going to a shelter for the night was out of the question. The list of names for beds was filled before noon. Hank Castle opted for space at a side street entrance of a department store.

Ordinarily, the cloak of night was welcome because it provided a protective mantle for street people but the darkness that settled on the city this night carried with it a sense of peril, an unseen menacing presence. It was a feeling Hank couldn't shake. By ten o'clock, downtown Philadelphia was deserted. She settled into the alcove, putting layers of newspapers under her. She pulled a moth-eaten olive-green woolen blanket out of the dirty, stained canvas tote and wrapped it snugly around her. She had to do something symbolic to keep out the fear...the fear more than the cold. The blanket served both purposes. She sipped some of the cheap brandy she had bought at the state liquor store and settled back against the darkened alcove. She heard the familiar shuffle of a Streeter as he claimed his share of space in the same doorway. It was too dark to see his face. He grunted as he settled down and covered himself with many thicknesses of newspaper. Hank locked her canvas tote bag securely in her arms then fell into an uneasy sleep.

She awakened before dawn with a full bladder. Disgruntled that she had to leave the comparative warmth inside the blanket to find a toilet, she mumbled obscenities to some unseen presence, folded her blanket and tucked it under her arm. As she moved out of the area she bumped the other occupant of the alcove. He showed his annoyance by mumbling a few obscenities of his own, grunted and turned his back to her as he rearranged the layers of newspapers on top of him.

Half asleep, Hank stumbled through city hall courtyard. "Shit," she said to the howling, cutting wind as it tore at her aching body and assaulted her with razor-sharp ferocity. "Pick on somebody your own size."

She found an unheated toilet facility in the subway station and wasn't happy about the necessity of baring her bottom to relieve herself. As she left the deserted, dimly lit subway, the feeling of impending disaster took hold again and shook her into animal awareness. Her coat collar was turned up and pinned in front. She pulled her nose and mouth into the warmth and protection of the collar and shuffled back to her sleeping area. The derelict in the corner of the alcove had not moved.

Hank hunkered down inside the blanket to capture her body heat. A feeling of foreboding alerted an instinct that she hadn't used since her days as a crime reporter and sleep refused to return. In the dim reflected light from the streetlamp, she saw a stream of dark liquid oozing its way from the alcove, down the sidewalk toward the curb. Her first thought was that her shared space rival had urinated. She mumbled, "For chrissake, just because people treat you like a pig doesn't mean you have to act like one." Then she noticed a dark stain on the newspapers that covered the man's upper torso.

Her heart pumped wildly. Hugging her canvas bag to her chest, she backed up until she was against the door of the department store, her eyes fixed on the continuous ooze of dark liquid that now reached the street.

Hank pressed her body against the display window inching out of the alcove. In her haste to escape, she slipped in the exuding stream and almost fell.

"Blood!" She gasped as she backed away, "It's...blood." She pressed the back of her hand to her mouth to stifle the scream that became trapped between her throat and lips. She scanned the area for signs of other Streeters. It was deserted. The silence of the night was amplified to a deafening roar.

Terrified, she ran looking over her shoulder, afraid of what was behind and painfully aware of what might be ahead.

She didn't stop until her labored breathing made it impossible to continue. The cold air burned the back of her dry throat as she gasped for breath. She pulled her face into her collar and tried to calm her breathing.

The headlights of an oncoming car seemed to be her salvation and she stood in the street waving her arms in a vain effort to stop the vehicle. The driver swerved, narrowly missing her and sped off. In her frustration, Hank raised her fist and shouted, "Bastard." In the overhead light across the street, she saw a public phone. She walked around the outdoor phone stand debating whether or not to call the police. Aloud, she said, "I don't have to give them my name," trying to reassure herself. Blowing on the tips of her fingers, Hank lifted the receiver and punched in the numbers, nine, one, one. She gave the information quickly and concisely, then hung up and moved away from the area. She was unable to control the shaking of her body and the brandy did nothing to alleviate the cold or the fear. She stood against the side of a building for whatever protection it afforded. One question kept prodding and nagging at her. Why would anyone want to kill a derelict?

The flashing blue and red lights of patrol cars told her the message had been relayed. To her surprise, Streeters began emerging from unseen places. Some glanced at the backs of the police, turned and walked away. Others approached cautiously taking a step, then stopping, another step and stopping but always moving forward. Watching Streeters converge on the area, she dared to venture back and stood on the periphery of the gathering crowd. The police cleared the area for fifty feet in both directions and the crime laboratory personnel began gathering whatever evidence they could. Seeing the body again made her cringe.

Hank didn't notice the casually dressed man watching her, until he was standing beside her. In the shadows, his face seemed devoid of eyes. He nodded toward the victim and said, "Did you know the victim?"

Too terrified to speak, she merely shook her head.

"What's your name?"

That question unsettled her. "Who wants to know?" she asked, trying to keep the fear out of her voice.

He didn't smile but she detected amusement in his voice as he pulled out a leather case from his inside pocket and flipped it open. "I do, detective Andrews."

She squinted at the leather case but before she could get a good look at it, he put it back in his pocket.

"Well, Detective Andrews, if that is in fact who you are, let's walk over to the streetlamp where I can get a good look at that identification you flashed so quickly."

It was clear he thought her actions amusing. He took her arm, led her under the nearest streetlight and slowly removed the identification from his pocket, flipped it open and put it into her hands. "You can read?"

Hank didn't miss the sarcasm. "I'm homeless...not stupid." She noted his name was Storm Andrews. *Strange name,* she thought and handed back the leather case.

"What's your name?" he asked again, the amusement was gone from his voice.

"Hank," she mumbled.

"Hank? What the hell kind of name is that?"

Her eyes shot warning sparks. "What the hell kind of name is Storm Andrews?"

"A complete one, now what's the rest of your name, Hank?" He took hold of her wrist with a vice-like grip. "Hank? That is what you said, isn't it?"

"Street people don't have surnames and Hank is short for Henrietta."

"Well, Henrietta...you had better have a surname. I don't give a damn what names you use among yourselves. What you choose to call yourself is your business. When a crime is committed and you are questioned, you give me whatever information I want. Understand?"

Hank studied his features under the streetlight and did a quick mental analysis. Good looking, in a rugged sort of way. Probably on the shorter side of six feet, dark wavy hair that needed cutting and he definitely needed a shave. The all-weather coat stretched across obviously broad shoulders was unbuttoned and revealed a turtleneck fisherman beige sweater over dark trousers. She looked away before answering his question. "Castle," she said softly.

"What was that?"

"Castle," she shouted.

"Castle," he repeated and nodded and studied her under the streetlight. "Castle…as in citadel?" His tone was mocking.

She tilted her chin. "Or as in propugnaculum, if you prefer." She saw a flash of white teeth.

"I always go with my instincts, Hank. Something told me you were out of place here. What are you doing living like a bum on the streets? Where's your home?"

Hank pulled back. "The last I heard, this was still a free country. What I'm doing on the streets is none of your damn business. Look around you, Detective Andrews; this is where I live, here under this streetlight. I live over there, in that doorway or if you prefer, I live in Fairmount Park." It was obvious Hank was ready for battle. Her tone was soft but her eyes were defiant. "Look at us, we're part of your rotten society whether you like it or not." Without realizing it, she had moved closer to him until his lips were on a level with her eyes. Aware of him now, as a man, she backed away again and stumbled against the fire hydrant behind her. Her feet went out from under her and his arms reached out, caught her and set her securely on her feet again. She stepped out of the protective circle of his arms and backed away. "Now, Lieutenant, if you've finished with your stupid questions, I would like to find a place to sleep before the sun comes up."

"Thanks for the promotion but I'm only a sergeant. I think I can find a comfortable bed for you tonight. Nine-one-one got a call from a woman about the murder. The voice sounded educated. Frightened but educated. Did you make that call?" He waited for a reply.

"No," she lied. Her chin jutted forward. "I'm inclined to think the educational standard among street people is higher than that of the police department."

"Okay, lady, you had your chance." Roughly, he spun her around and pulled her arms behind her. The cold metal circlets around her wrists almost caused a panic within her. She had always hated having her hands tied, figuratively and literally. He shoved her toward a parked car.

"My bag."

Detective Andrews looked back and saw her canvas bag leaning against the fire hydrant under the streetlight. He opened the backdoor of the car, put his hand on top of her head, forcing it down as he gently pushed her into the car. He slammed the door and walked back to pick up the bag. He threw it onto the seat beside him as he slid behind the wheel.

"Where are you taking me?"

"Headquarters. You won't be such a smart-mouth there."

"What are you going to do, beat me with a rubber hose?"

He watched her through the rearview mirror. "Today our methods are much more scientific. We use truth serum." He almost laughed at the terrified expression on her face.

Detective Andrews ushered her into a small room, which served as an office. He unlocked the cuffs and left the room. Minutes later, he returned with two cups of hot coffee. He told her to hang her coat on the rack in the corner and to sit in the chair beside the desk. When she obeyed, he handed her a cup of steaming coffee.

"All right, Henrietta, alias Hank, where do you live?"

"I told you where I live."

"Tell me again."

"I live on the streets...of this fair city."

"How long have you lived on the streets?"

"Three weeks."

"Where did you live before that?"

"What difference does it make?"

"A lot. If you live on the streets and have no visible means of support, I can book you as a vagrant. Are you on welfare?"

"No."

"Why not?"

"You have to have an address to be on welfare."

"How do you support yourself?"

"I have some money."

"How much?"

"That's none of your business."

"You just made it my business. You might have gotten your money by killing a poor unsuspecting bastard then robbing him."

"Wh...What? That's ludicrous."

The amusement in his voice returned. "Why not?"

"Because I'm not a murderer," she shouted...then, softly, "That's why not."

"I don't know that. You're no different than any other bum on the street. Ah, I beg your pardon, you're no different than any other homeless person."

"Different *from*," she corrected.

He took the correction with a smile. Not a bad smile at that, she thought. The door opened and a uniformed officer came in with her canvas bag and a small paper sack. The canvas bag went on the floor and the paper sack on the desk. Andrews reached inside the sack and pulled out two sandwiches and asked, "Corned beef on rye or ham and cheese on whole wheat?"

At the mention of food she began to salivate. "Corned beef, please."

He handed one of the sandwiches to her. Unwrapped the other one for himself, raised it to his mouth and almost demolished half of it in one bite. He put the canvas bag on the desk. "Empty the contents of the bag onto the desk, please."

She took another bite of sandwich before she started. She stared at the contents. A pair of panties, a blouse, a sweater, half of a roll of toilet tissue, a comb with three missing teeth, a used, thin bar of soap, a blanket, a toothbrush, a bottle of aspirin, a small jar filled with white powder and a half empty bottle of cheap brandy. The realization hit her, that these would have been all of her worldly possessions if she was really one of the homeless. The thought sickened her.

Andrews picked up the jar and the bottle of brandy. "What's in the jar?"

"Baking soda and salt." She saw the doubtful expression on his face. "I use it to brush my teeth."

He opened the door and handed the jar to an officer. "Have the contents analyzed." He returned to Hank and held up the bottle. "You a boozer?"

"No." Her anger had a razor-sharp edge.

He put the bottle on the desk. "Don't get uptight. I'm only trying to figure out why you're on the streets."

"I'm on the streets because I don't have a place to live. That's why they refer to us as homeless." *Idiot,* she thought.

"Do you have a record?"

She looked puzzled. "You mean have I ever been arrested?"

"That's the general idea," he said.

"No."

"I keep getting the impression I know you from somewhere. It couldn't have been social, so it must have something to do with the Department. Don't lie to me, Hank. If you have any priors, I'll find out."

Her nostrils flared and her eyes shot angry sparks at him. "I told you I don't have...a record and I know we've never met before because I always remember bad manners."

He studied the stubborn tilt of her chin. "Do you hate all men or just cops?"

"Let me give you a mini lesson on street people, Detective. We have very little respect for the police and absolutely no trust in a system that plagues and rousts us."

"I'm not impressed." He threw his empty Styrofoam cup into the wastebasket. "I think the majority of street people are out there because they're incapable of coping with everyday problems. They like freedom from responsibilities. They enjoy being a burden on society. They take pleasure in making the working-stiff feel guilty because he has some comforts that he worked damn hard to get. Most of your Streeters are too lazy to go to work and earn their way like everybody else. So they lay a guilt trip on the rest of us. In essence, they're saying, feel sorry for me. Feed me. Take care of me."

A flush of embarrassment crept over Hank's face, burning her cheeks.

The door opened and another plainclothes detective filled the doorway. His eyes narrowed as they traveled over Hank. He didn't try to disguise the contempt he felt. Without taking his eyes from her face, he said, "We've got a match on the voice."

Andrews nodded. "I thought we might." He shifted his position so that he was looking at the new arrival. "Detective Mike Shaye, this is Henrietta Castle, alias Hank."

Shaye sat on the corner of the desk forcing her to look at him. "You're the one who called about the murder, aren't you?"

Hank struggled to show a calm she didn't feel. "Why would I do that?"

Shaye pulled out a cigarette, lit it and blew the smoke in her face. "Why not? Maybe you get your kicks from seeing a frenzied crowd."

Something about Shaye awakened a revulsion in her that she couldn't squelch. "Sure," she said, "or maybe I think the police department isn't smart enough to carry out an investigation without fucking up." *My God,* she thought, *I don't use words like that.* She looked away quickly before they could see her embarrassment. She was startled at the sound of a soft laugh, almost musical in sound. It bothered and confused her. The sound was coming from Storm Andrews, which embarrassed her even more. She was ashamed that her intelligence had dropped to such a low ebb that she had to resort to vulgar language to get her point across. She was a journalist and her whole life was words. How could words fail her now?

"We've been taping your voice since you got here and made a comparison with the voice on the nine-one-one call. As Mike said, we got a match. Now do you want to tell us what you know about the murder?"

"I didn't kill him. I don't even know him...at least I don't think I knew him. I didn't see his face."

"Apparently, neither did the killer," Mike snapped. "He was stabbed in the back."

"But...why?" Hank stammered. "What could anyone possibly gain by killing a Streeter? It couldn't be to rob him. Street people don't have anything worth stealing."

"Nothing that we know of," corrected Storm Andrews.

Hank turned slowly until her eyes locked onto Andrew's face. "Are the police actually investigating the murder of this leper? This pariah? An ostracized outcast of your precious society? I'm surprised, Detective Andrews."

Shaye covered the distance to her chair in two steps, grabbed a handful of Hank's sweater and pulled her to her feet in front of him. "That mouth is going to get you in trouble. As far as I'm concerned, you and your kind are nothing but trash."

Hank stared, unblinkingly, into Shaye's ice-blue eyes. "Take your filthy hands off me, you ugly bastard." Her voice was low and controlled.

Instead of backing off, he deliberately grabbed both breasts and squeezed.

Storm Andrews was out of his chair like a bolt of lightning but not fast enough to get between them.

Gut reaction brought Hank's knee up hard into his groin.

His hands released her breasts and formed a protective cup around his testicles as he fell to his knees in front of her. He retched in a vain effort to vomit the lump that formed in his belly. His complexion turned purple from his effort to breathe. "I'll get you, you fuckin' bitch."

Hank's anger spewed like a volcano. "You depraved bastard, if you ever lay a hand on me again I'll make sure your name hits national headlines telling how Philadelphia's...finest...treats female detainees. It's called police brutality, you simple-minded jackass."

Shaye tried to get up but fell back against the desk. Storm Andrews stepped between them and knelt beside Mike. "You okay?"

Shaye was grimacing and holding his testicles with both hands. "Leave me alone with this whore and I'll get a confession out of her in ten minutes."

"Cool it, Mike," Storm said in low tones, "Internal Affairs is breathing down our necks as it is." He stood and faced Hank.

Hank's left breast throbbed but she stood her ground and glared back at him.

Andrews forcefully sat Hank in a chair. "If you ever pull a stunt like that again I'll put you in a cell and throw the key away. Now, what made you call in the murder to nine-one-one? The victim would have been found in the morning anyway."

Hank felt like she was walking on a picket fence. "I guess I hoped he was still alive. Don't ask me why I called, I don't know. If I thought I would end up here I would not have made the damn call. I'm sorry now that I did."

Storm Andrews picked up a pen and began writing. "Tell me everything you know about the victim. Do you know his name?"

Hank shook her head. "I don't know. I didn't see his face when he came to the store entrance, it was dark, some time after ten o'clock.." She related the events as they took place, leaving out nothing.

"Was he still alive when you went to find a restroom?

"Yes."

"How do you know that?"

"He turned over as I was leaving. He cursed me for disturbing him. I guess I made too much noise. Anyway, he covered himself with his newspapers."

"When you got back, how did you know he was dead?"

"I didn't know he was dead. I knew he was wounded. I could see the blood trickling down the sidewalk."

"It was dark. How did you know it was blood?"

Hank could feel the panic mounting in her chest. It was like being in quicksand. The slightest movement, the smallest word could get her in deeper. "It wasn't running like urine, it kind of oozed down the pavement. When I stood up to get a better look, I slipped in it and I knew it was blood. That's when I ran to the nearest phone and called."

"Did you see anyone else in the area?"

"I don't think so. Maybe, but I don't remember. I was scared. It could have been me. What if I hadn't gone to find a toilet?"

Andrews stood up. "In all probability the victim would still be alive too." He saw the confused expression on her face. "It's only conjecture but as long as there were two of you, the killer probably would not have attacked. This killer is using a knife, not a gun. You have to get close to your victim to stab him. The killer would be taking an unnecessary risk with the two of you there. When you left to find a latrine you made it easy for the murderer to get his victim…or her victim, as the case may be."

"How many women do you know with the strength of a man, Detective?"

"It doesn't take that much strength to plunge a knife into the back of a sleeping victim."

Mike Shaye glared at her from the floor with his back propped against the desk. "What the hell do you care?"

"In spite of what you think, Streeters care about other street people. Nobody can tell you about it. You have to feel what they feel…the cold, the hunger, the abuse, the contempt. Just like the look on your ugly face, Shaye."

Shaye's upper lip twisted. She couldn't tell if it was a sneer or a smile. Hank hoped it was a sneer. She thought, *What a terrible burden to carry through life, if a smile looked like that.*

Hank stood up. "Book me or let me go. You can't hold me for no reason."

Shaye said, "Why don't you call your attorney? There must be lots of lawyers living on the streets. Smart asses…just like you."

The sneer on Shaye's face infuriated her but she was not going to allow him to intimidate her any more than he had already. "Don't make fun of street people, Detective, you never know what's in your future. One day you may be forced into being one of us."

"Put your shit back in your shopping bag and get the hell out of here." Shaye struggled to his feet, felt dizzy and sat on the edge of the desk.

"How am I supposed to get back?"

"You know so much about your rights, you must know you have the right to walk back. Since you have no home, we can't very well drop you off there now, can we?"

"You know, Shaye, the police department is the wrong place for your kind of hate. You belong in a compound with skinheads with a swastika painted on your armband." She turned to Storm Andrews. "That," she pointed toward Shaye, "is the kind of hate that ends in murder. He's crazy."

It was snowing when she walked out of the police station and Hank pulled up the collar of her coat. A car pulled up in front of her.

"Get in, Hank. I'll take you back where I picked you up."

Without replying, she opened the car door and got in. They rode in silence. When they got back to the murder scene, the crowds had dispersed and there was only a partial chalk outline where the body had been, most of it was covered by drifting snow. That particular entrance to the store was cordoned off with yellow plastic tape with black lettering that spelled out *police crime scene*.

Hank reached for the door handle.

"Be careful out there, Hank. Last night the victim was male but that can change. We don't know what we are dealing with."

She tried to study the expression on his face but it was five thirty and still too dark. "Thanks for the ride…and thanks for the sandwich and coffee."

CHAPTER 2

It was almost noon when Hank entered the Salvation Army shelter for hobo stew, a doctored version of beef stew, substituting frankfurters for beef with potatoes and carrots. It was thin, more like soup than stew. She sat at a long table, her canvas bag on the floor between her feet.

The woman beside Hank mumbled to herself as she stared into her bowl. Her auburn hair, like her face, was lifeless. She looked ill. It was difficult to judge her age. Hank thought she was probably in her early thirties and painfully thin. The man on the other side of Hank was elderly and seemed to inhale his food. She turned back to the woman. "Are you all right? You look sick."

The woman's lips stretched slightly in an effort to smile. "I think I'm okay. I'd give anything for a couple of aspirins."

Hank dug into the canvas bag and opened the side zipper. "I'm Hank," she said, producing a small bottle of generic aspirin and offering them to her.

The woman shook out two aspirins and handed the bottle back to Hank.

"Why don't you take two more for later, just in case the first two don't work?"

Thanks, Hank. I've got a headache that won't quit." She picked up her cup of now cooled tea, using it to chase the aspirin down her throat. "I'm Maxine, Max for short. Would you like to have my soup and sandwich?"

"No, thanks. Put the sandwich in your bag and save it for later. Are you sure you can't eat the soup?"

Max shook her head and winced from the pain.

Hank turned to the man next to her. "Do you want this soup?"

He grabbed the bowl from her hands and emptied it into his own and continued to eat without interruption. He huddled over his bowl to assure himself that the food wouldn't be snatched away.

"You're welcome," Hank said as she turned back to Max. "At what point do you cease being human and become part of the animal world?"

Max laughed. "There are more animals in that white-collar world out there," she looked toward the outside, "than there are in the streets. Here we steal because we're hungry. Out there, they steal because they're greedy." She met Hank's gaze and Hank thought, *There it is, the hurt, the anger and desperation that seems to be part of this way of life.*

"Where have you been sleeping nights?" Max asked.

"Wherever. Last night it was a doorway. Well, I slept there for part of the night. Tonight? Who knows?"

"Do you know where the Azalea Gardens are on Kelly Drive?"

Hank nodded. She knew this woman was not from the area. Natives still referred to Kelly Drive as the East River Drive.

"Try there," Max whispered confidentially. "You are fairly well hidden by the bushes and you don't feel the cold as much. I stay there most of the time."

"It's a long way from a toilet. Even if I'm lucky enough to sleep six hours, I only have a four-hour bladder."

Max grinned. "You can do a lot of things behind bushes."

Hank said, "I guess anything is better than interrogation at headquarters all night."

Max gasped, "You mean…?" Her voice trailed off.

Hank nodded. "Last night I shared the doorway with the murdered guy and was dumb enough to call nine-one-one. I'm still not sure how the cops knew I made the call. They took me in. That's the last time I do a stupid thing like that. From now on the cops can find their own dead bodies."

Painful as it was, Maxine opened her eyes to look at Hank. "You're new to the streets, aren't you?"

Hank stared back. "How did you know that?"

"You haven't lost your sense of humor yet. Generally cops are bad news for people like us. There are some sadistic men on the force." She thought a moment then continued, "But there are also a lot of nice cops."

"I think I met one of each last night." Hank still felt the ache in her left breast.

Max said, "Once in a while we have the misfortune to be rousted by one of the bad ones. They pick up one of the woman on a vagrancy charge but instead of going to the precinct they take her to the park and rape her." She smiled. "Police vans are not always used for the purpose for which they were originally intended."

"Why don't the women report it to police headquarters?"

"Sure. Report a police rape to the cops? You're dreaming, Hank." She rubbed the back of her neck and closed her eyes again. "It's strange the cops didn't pull in more people for questioning last night. You can bet they would have turned this city inside out if the victim had been a member of the police force."

"Yeah, I got the impression it's a close-knit brotherhood."

Max said, "Most of them are good, hardworking cops. It's the few renegades that make it look bad for the others."

"The detective who pulled me in last night gave me a sandwich and hot coffee. He didn't have to do that. The other detective made me feel like shit."

Max raised her head quickly and winced from the pain. "You want to know what shit feels like? Go into the department stores and before you get fifty feet inside the door, somebody has called security." Max bit her bottom lip, then continued, "I'm not saying we're angels. God knows there are some street people who would steal the dentures right out of your mouth, but generally we go in the stores to get warm in winter or to cool off in summer. It takes a lot of guts to be on the streets."

Hank liked this woman. She thought, *If you got beyond the ragged clothes, she has an almost ethereal quality. When she talks there's sadness, not in what she says but in what she leaves unsaid. She would have been the perfect model for a painting of the sorrowful Madonna.* They picked up their bags and walked out together. The sun broke through the gray skies and a small patch of blue appeared. They walked several blocks when a malodorous bearded man approached them.

He leaned close to Maxine. "Watch out, Maxie, there's a storm warning up."

She reached out and touched his arm. "Thanks, Benny, we'll be careful. This is my friend, Hank."

The odoriferous man grunted acknowledgement of the introduction and shuffled away.

Hank looked puzzled. "What storm warning? It's clearing up."

"The storm warning refers to a homicide detective. His name is Storm Andrews. Benny was saying that Andrews is pulling in people for questioning. He seems to be a fairly good cop but his partner, Mike Shaye, is bad news. A real predatory animal."

Hank nodded. "I met him last night. He reminded me of gargantua."

Max watched as the man in front of them tossed a newspaper into a trash container. She retrieved it. Hank looked over Max's shoulder at the headline. *Victim Claimed by Mad Slasher.* Max shook her head. "Damn. The next couple of weeks will be hard on us. The mayor will demand that somebody be charged with the murder, just to get himself and the cops off the hot seat."

Hank scanned the article. "The murdered man's name was Martin Higgins."

Maxine's face went pale and she took the newspaper back and read the account of the slaying.

Hank asked, "Did you know him?"

"I talked to him once or twice. Didn't seem to be a bad sort. He sat beside me at the kitchen a couple of nights ago." Max's eyes held a mischievous glint, "Boy, that's scary, I ate with him and you slept with him and now he's dead."

"I didn't sleep with him."

"Okay, he slept with you, or at least he slept in the same doorway. You know what I mean. Do you really think the cops will investigate the murder of a Streeter?"

Hank shrugged. "I doubt it but they have to go through the motions. I didn't see much interest generated at the police station last night but then again, I'm no authority on police procedure. It would be a different story if the murdered man lived on Society Hill or in one of the Father, Son, Holy Ghost houses."

"What's that?"

"Those houses on Pine and Spruce Streets. They're called that because the houses have six rooms, two rooms on each of three floors. The houses were condemned then some smart builders bought them for next to nothing, gutted them and made them into smart townhouses. I guess it's convenient for men who burn the midnight oil...or cheat on their wives."

Max looked at Hank out of the corner of her eye. "What a perfect setup. You can certainly tell God is a man. He looks out for his own."

It seemed strange to hear such bitterness coming out of the mouth of someone who looked like a saint. When they reached the park they brushed the snow off the first bench they saw and sat down. Hank picked up the paper and read aloud. "*The body of Martin Higgins, age forty, was found in the doorway of a downtown department store after an anonymous telephone call to the police. The victim was identified by an outdated driver's license, which gave his address as New York City. It is thought the victim is one of many homeless people living on the streets of Philadelphia. An autopsy revealed eight stab wounds in the victim's back. There was a note beside the body but police would not comment on it.*"

Max moaned, "Rest period is over. Look to your left."

Hank looked over her shoulder. A patrol car was slowly cruising the area.

"Maybe I'll see you tonight at the Azalea Gardens," Max said as she picked up her bag and headed west.

Hank spent the rest of the day wandering about the streets of busy downtown, studying the faces of everyone she passed. None of the people she saw looked like murderers. She asked herself, *What does a murderer look like?* Aloud, she said, "Probably like everybody else, that's why the cops haven't caught him."

* * *

It was one of the coldest Decembers on record and Hank pulled her nose and mouth into the protection of her coat collar. There was a small state liquor store in the next block and she fingered the five-dollar bill in her pocket and decided it was a necessary expenditure. She brought the pint of cheap brandy to the counter.

The man behind the register said, "That will be four dollars and twenty-five cents."

Hank handed him the five-dollar bill. He threw the three quarters across the counter and pushed the bottle in its brown paper bag toward her. Their eyes locked and she could see the disdain in his expression.

Evening began to cloak the city. A light snow started falling again, gently at first then heavier, in swirling patterns. The Azalea Gardens were out for the time being and Hank made her way to Sansom Street looking for an empty doorway that would offer some protection against the wind and snow. Most of the protected areas were already occupied by other Streeters, and some were kind enough to offer to share space in already crowded quarters, while others blocked the area with their arms to indicate they were not willing to share the space.

Between Sixteenth and Seventeenth Streets she found a spot that was protected and unoccupied. She settled down and wrapped her blanket snuggly around herself when she saw a form covered from neck to ankles in a moth-eaten threadbare cloth coat approach the doorway. Since Hank did not indicate any opposition the newcomer hustled into the opposite corner of the protected area, carefully put some layers of newspapers down and sat on them. Her gray, wrinkled face was partially hidden in the turned-up collar. She dug into her plastic shopping bag and pulled out a blanket that looked almost as bad as the coat she wore. Her hands were gray like ashes hardened from the harsh weather and she pulled the blanket close around her body, ignoring Hank's presence.

Hank pulled out the brown paper bag, broke the seal on the bottle of brandy and lifted it to her lips. The heat from the alcohol warmed its way into her shivering body.

The veteran Streeter came to life and lifted her head out of the coat collar. To Hank, she looked like a turtle stretching its neck out of the shell testing the atmosphere for signs of danger. She studied the bottle in Hank's hand and moistened her lips with the tip of her tongue. Hank took another swallow and offered the bottle to the half-frozen woman.

The veteran Streeter hesitated only briefly before snatching the bottle and downing a mouthful. She closed her eyes briefly and nodded. "Thanks," she said.

Hank nodded. "It takes the edge off the chill."

The Streeter looked in her shopping bag. "Trade ya half a sandwich for another swig."

Hank passed the bottle back to her. "Keep your sandwich."

The old woman accepted the bottle and took another gulp, smacked her lips and handed it back to Hank. "Who should I be thankin'?"

"I'm Hank."

"Thanks, Hank, I'm Molly. These poor ole bones pick up the chill and don't defrost till summer." She turned and faced the wall and before long, Hank could hear the muffled snore coming from under Molly's blanket.

Hank lay on her side with her knees tucked under to conserve as much body heat as possible and pulled the blanket under her chin. As soon as her body heat was entrapped in the blanket she felt the comfort of twilight sleep engulf her. She thought she saw a shadow in the doorway and squinted into the dimness of gathering night. No one was there and she wasn't anxious to disturb the newly created warmth. She pulled her head and neck under the blanket and sank into a deep sleep. She dreamed she was in the park, running from something...or someone wearing a black cloak with a hood. It seemed to be gaining on her and she felt the panic rising from her wildly thumping chest into her constricted throat. Hank tried to scream, but as often happens in dreams, no sound escaped her lips. The black-robed figure had caught her and was shaking her like a rag doll.

"Hank, wake up." Molly was shaking her into consciousness. "Get your things. We gotta get outta here."

In a half stupor, Hank struggled to open one eye. "What's wrong?"

"Across the street." Molly nodded in the general direction.

Hank pulled the blanket away from her face and glanced in the direction Molly indicated. Across the narrow street, at a forty-five degree angle, in the doorway of another building was a bright patch of crimson in the stark whiteness of the snow. The snow continued to fall.

"What is it, Molly?"

Molly was busy collecting her things. "From here, I'd say it looks like blood. "I'm not goin' over there to see it up close. Let's go before the cops turn this place into their personal playground." Without another word, Molly headed toward Seventeenth Street, away from what appeared to be a corpse on the other side of Sansom Street.

Hank scampered to her feet, not bothering to fold the blanket, and she stuffed it into the canvas bag. She pinned her coat collar so as to cover her nose and mouth and headed toward Sixteenth Street, half walking, half running. She looked into a doorway near the intersection and saw Maxine snuggled in the corner of the protected area. Hank stopped and shook her.

A look of fear crossed Maxine's face until she recognized Hank, then she smiled. "You scared me, Hank, is something wrong?"

"Get your things together, it looks like another murder. Hurry, Max."

Max covered her mouth with her hand and whispered, "Where?"

"Across the street, halfway up the block."

Maxine's eyes were large with fear as she tried to comprehend what Hank was saying.

"Hurry, Max. We've got to get out of here before the cops come."

"Who...who is it?"

"I don't know. All I saw was the blood on the snow. For all I know it could be a dead animal but I'm not waiting around to find out. I've had one experience with the cops and I'm not about to have a repeat performance. Coming?"

Max was on her feet, blanket over one arm and shopping bag over the other. "Let's go, Hank."

They made their way north on Sixteenth Street to Chestnut Street, then east on Chestnut and crossed over Broad Street. They finally stopped when they reached Tenth Street and huddled together in the doorway of a small shoe store and wrapped their blankets around them. Max looked sick. Her face was drained of color in spite of the cold.

"Max? You okay?"

"Just tired. I didn't get much sleep last night."

"The cold?"

"No. It was just a night filled with memories best forgotten. I think I was asleep but I feel like I was awake...like I was seeing things through somebody else's eyes. It was a weird feeling that I can't explain. I'll be like a zombie for the rest of the day."

Hank offered her some brandy but she shook her head.

"Hank? How did you know about the body?"

"Do you know Molly?"

Max nodded.

"We slept in the same doorway. This morning she woke me when she saw the bright patch of blood in the snow. She told me to get out fast. She went one way and I went the other. That's when I saw you."

Max smiled. "I'm grateful you stopped. Do you think the victim is a Streeter?"

"Probably. The body was in a doorway just like the last one. It could have been somebody coming out of a bar. Maybe he got mugged. Whoever did it was quiet. I didn't hear anything. We'll find out soon enough." Hank blew on her fingertips. "I would give anything for a cup of hot coffee right now."

"The day shelters will be open soon. I feel like I'll never be warm again." Max's teeth chattered so that her words came out in staccato tones. Hank moved closer and put half of her blanket around Maxine. The heat from their bodies and the additional blanket helped stop the shivering. Max rested her chin on her knees and closed her eyes. At eight fifteen, Hank suggested they head for a shelter. Max was happy to go where she would feel safe and warm.

Word had already spread that another derelict had bought it on Sansom Street. The victim was Kenneth Wooster.

"Did you know him, Max?

She nodded. "A good man, a gentle man. He helped me when I first came to this city. He went out of his way, actually. Showed me where the shelters were, checked on me to be sure I was eating. Protected me from the not-so-nice men." She sipped her hot tea. Hank looked toward the entrance and saw Mike Shaye standing in the doorway.

"Don't look around, Max. Mike Shaye is here. You and I spent the whole night in that doorway on Tenth Street with Molly. We weren't on Sansom Street at all. I'll find Molly so she'll tell the same story…just in case we're picked up."

"Do you think they suspect us?"

"They suspect everybody. Especially me. I was in the wrong place when both murders were committed."

"I was there too, and so was Molly. They can't think all three of us did it."

Hank took a sip of her watered-down coffee. "No sense giving them a bone to chew on. As far as anybody is concerned, the three of us were together on Tenth Street." When Hank turned around again, Mike Shaye was gone.

The snow was still falling when they left the shelter. Hank asked, "Where will you be sleeping tonight?"

Max looked up at the swirling snow. "I think I'll put my name in for a bed in the shelter for tonight. What about you?"

"I don't know. I have to find Molly first. Where can you go to get out of the weather?"

"The library. It will be dry and warm and I will be among friends." She laughed at the puzzled look on Hank's face. "Books. Books have always been my friends." She hesitated. "They never betray you." Embarrassment brought a flush to her cheeks. "I'll help you find Molly. With both of us looking, it shouldn't take too long."

"No. You go to the library and I'll see you tomorrow morning at the shelter."

It was mid-afternoon and Hank had checked almost all of the subway stations in the area. The snow was heavier and blanketed her footprints as soon as they were made. She tried to keep her hands in the torn pockets of her coat but they were chalk white from the cold and ached. There was only one more place to look and that was the train station at Thirtieth Street, where SEPTA, the city transit and AMTRAK shared facilities. The station was teeming with humanity. Office workers, students from the University of Pennsylvania and health care workers from several of the area hospitals all crowded around the ticket counters for transportation out of center city. Hank searched the corners and alcoves looking for Molly. She found her sitting against the wall behind the news stand. She pushed her way toward the wall. Molly moved over when she saw Hank.

"I've been looking all over for you, Molly."

"What happened?"

"Nothing yet. Mike Shaye is on the prowl. You and Max and I spent the entire night in a doorway on Tenth Street, near Chestnut. We were all there by about ten o'clock."

"Does Maxie know this?"

"Yes."

"Good move. Let's not give that big ape anythin' to hang on us. Do you know who it was that got it last night?"

"Ken Wooster, I think. At least that's the scuttlebutt around the shelter."

Molly's reaction was much the same as Maxine's. "There's lots of others that would probably deserve it, but not Kenny." She shook her head. "What a waste. Why would anybody want to kill him? He was a good man. Oh, he mighta flirted some but he never meant nothin' by it. I doubt if he used that pecker of his for anythin' but peein'. I think he was sweet on Maxie. Always went outta his way to do things for her. How did she take it?"

"She was depressed."

"Yeah. Well, there went her knight on a white charger. She's still pretty. Maybe somebody else will look after her." She looked directly at Hank. "She needs protection, you know. Maxie's fragile and I think she can break. It's hard to believe she's been on the streets for seven years. That's a long time for one so frail." She laughed. "Hell, seven years on the streets is a long time for anybody."

"Are you going to stay here for tonight, Molly?"

"You bet. I'm not about to give up a warm place to sleep for some watered-down chicken soup. What about you?"

"I'm hungry, so I'll probably go to the soup kitchen and take my chances on finding a place to sleep."

"You could try gettin' into one of the hospitals. Usually in bad weather, there are a lot of accidents and the emergency rooms are crowded. Nobody pays much attention to who comes and goes. If you get in, head for the fire exit and go down. You can probably find a place to sleep under the stairs. You gotta be outta there when housekeeping starts with their buckets and mops at seven o'clock. If you don't hit the same hospital too often; nobody'll say nothin'."

"Thanks, Molly."

Hank decided to go back to the warmth and safety of her own apartment. She started in that direction when she had the uneasy feeling she was being followed. She changed direction and headed for city hall. She stopped under one of the stone arches that led into the courtyard. The driving snow made it impossible to see but she knew she was being followed. She pressed against the wall under the arch and waited. Mike Shaye came lumbering out of the snow like a giant grizzly. She was partially hidden but not enough. He pulled her out into the open. "You really get around, don't you, Hank?"

"A moving target is harder to hit."

"Always a smart ass." His eyes were bloodshot, like he had been drinking. "Where were you last night?"

"What's it to you?"

"Don't give me any of your shit." He moved menacingly close and she could smell the booze on his breath. "Where were you last night?"

Hank's stomach started churning. She recognized the feeling as the beginning of fear. She was already convinced he was crazy. "Why do you want to know?"

"There was another murder last night." He moved closer. "Now...where were you?"

She knew better than to taunt him. "I was on Tenth Street. Now get out of my face, Shaye."

He was big but he moved fast. He grabbed a handful of her coat and lifted her off the ground. At the same time his fist connected with her right eye. His face was so near that their noses almost touched. "Where on Tenth Street, Hank?"

"Put me down, you sonofabitch." She suddenly realized her situation was hopeless. There was no traffic, no one walking the streets and she was alone with a man totally out of control and filled with hate.

He pulled his fist back again and Hank shuddered as she closed her eyes.

A voice said, "Put her down, Mike." There was a pause. "I said put her down."

Shaye released her coat and she dropped about a foot, slipped in the snow and hit the back of her head against the stone wall.

Someone touched her face. She looked into the granite gray eyes of Storm Andrews.

"That's a nasty bump," he said. "How do you feel?"

She looked to where Shaye was standing, then back at Storm Andrews. "If you're looking for a murderer among the Streeters, you're looking in the wrong place. Try the police department. Try that bastard." She pointed with a reddened, chapped finger. "He probably committed both murders. I told you he was crazy."

Andrews stood up and looked around him. "How did you know there was another murder?"

She nodded toward Shaye. "He told me."

Andrews looked at his partner. Shaye nodded and walked away. Storm helped her to her feet. "You're not winning brownie points by taunting him, you know."

"I can't help it." She brushed the snow from her coat. "Keep that creep away from me. He's crazy. I wouldn't put it past him to have committed those murders. Do you see the way he looks at street people? That, Mister Detective, is raw hate."

"I think you are imagining things. I admit he doesn't have much love for Streeters but I don't think he hates them."

"No? Then you don't know your partner as well as you think you do."

"What makes you such an authority?"

"When you live on the streets, you see raw emotions that you would never see otherwise. Hate, contempt, revulsion, disgust, you name it and we see it. We experience it and we hope we can forgive it. Now, what do you want, Andrews?"

"How about if I take you to dinner?"

She nodded. "Police headquarters again?"

"A little restaurant I know, not far from here. Hungry?"

"Starved." She looked down at her clothes and pulled her collar up.

"It's okay. My car's across the street." He took her arm and steered her through the snow. The streets were deserted. Hank felt like they were the only people on earth. The lack of activity gave her an uneasy feeling, like a disaster had hit the city. It was eerie. The only sound was the crunch of the snow under the tires. The windshield wipers didn't help much and the snow was packing up on either side of the blades. He pulled onto the sidewalk of a small restaurant, which Hank must have passed hundreds of times without ever seeing it. It was strange that so quaint a place as the Achaea was under her nose but it took a cop to introduce her to it. He held the door and let her pass. They were greeted by an elderly, well-dressed man who embraced Andrews. They laughed and slapped each other on the back. He introduced the man as Nick Andros, Uncle Nick. They sat in a booth near the back of the restaurant and Uncle Nick brought two glasses filled with a caramel-colored liquid. Storm smiled his thanks. He handed one glass to Hank and raised the other and touched her glass. "To better days," he said, and sipped the liquid. "It's okay, it's Metaxa. A little potent but it will warm you."

She sipped the liquor and smiled. She put the glass down and blew on the tips of her fingers, blue from the cold.

Storm reached over and took her hands into his. "They're like ice." He rubbed her hands between his and studied her face. He withdrew one of his hands and turned her face so that he could see her eye. "That's quite a mouse you've got. How did it happen?"

She pulled her hands away and turned her face toward the wall.

"Did Mike do that?"

"Would you believe me if I said yes?"

He took one of her hands again and continued to rub it. "Yes. I would believe you."

She felt the tears sting her eyes. "Don't worry about it. It's not the first shiner I've had and probably won't be the last."

"I'll make sure Mike stays away from you."

"Are you going to keep him away from all the bag ladies? I wasn't kidding, his hate makes him a dangerous man."

Uncle Nick returned with their dinner of roast lamb with egg and lemon sauce, artichokes and salad riffled with feta cheese and black olives. As far as Hank was concerned, all conversation stopped and all of her concentration went on the food. She was aware that he was watching her. "What?"

"There's no need to bolt your food. Nobody's going to take it away from you."

She was conscious that her mouth was packed with food and yet she kept shoveling in more. She laid the fork down and chewed what was in her mouth and swallowed. "Sorry, I guess I was hungrier than I thought."

He was studying her in the dim light of the restaurant. "You're a real enigma, Hank. I know I've seen you before. Sooner or later it will come to me. I know for sure you're not a Streeter. You don't circle your plate with your arms to protect the food from being stolen. Before you began, you unfolded your napkin and laid it in your lap. You used your salad fork for the salad and picked up the dinner fork for the main course. In spite of what you say, you don't belong out there. I can't understand why you are punishing yourself. I'm sure you have a good reason but I don't believe you're a Streeter." He put his napkin on the table and lit a cigarette. "You have to know how dangerous it is. A murderer has killed twice. Both times his victim were men and indications are, there will be more carnage. There's no way of knowing if this executioner will continue to target only men."

"You think it's a serial killer, don't you?"

"I'm afraid so. He is establishing a pattern."

"What kind of pattern?"

"He selects lone men. Always while they sleep. Stabs his victims in the back, not once but many times, then repositions his victims so that the blood will run downhill. This killer isn't trying to hide his crimes. If anything...he is challenging the police."

"But why?"

"Good question. So far the reasons are known only to the killer."

"Do you think he will strike again?"

"Absolutely. I'm looking for a common denominator. That's what makes me think the killer is also a Streeter."

Hank gasped. "I can't believe a Streeter would do that."

"Only another Streeter could possibly know what the common denominator is. Only another Streeter knows the secrets of the street people."

Hank swallowed a mouthful of food. "You're wrong. Street people know very little about each other. Conversations are never personal. Nobody talks about where they came from and the reason why they're on the streets is known only to the individual. They will share their food and shelter, they will even give blood to save another Streeter. The one thing they won't share is their lives prior to being on the streets and another Streeter will never ask. I think the killer hates street people. Probably somebody who is constantly being reminded of a bad time in his life; just by the sight of a street person."

"What makes you say that?"

"When someone stabs another human being that many times, there's a lot of anger, a lot of hate, a lot of hurt that won't stop."

Storm was quiet for a moment. "Interesting theory. You just narrowed our list of suspects down to about a hundred thousand people in this city alone. If we're importing the killer from another city, think of the permutations."

Hank laughed for the first time in days. "I think my theory has just as much merit as yours, Detective Andrews."

"Call me Storm. You should laugh more often, it's a nice sound." He laughed. "You're also very pretty when you blush."

They stood to leave, he dropped some ten-dollar bills on the table, got her coat and held it while she struggled back into it.

"Where can I drop you?"

"That's not necessary. You've been very kind. Thank you for dinner."

He opened the door. "Look at that snow, it's a blizzard. I can't allow you to walk around in this. Where are you going tonight?"

"Drop me at the nearest hospital." She laughed. "You look so funny." She pulled her collar up to cover her ears. "Hospitals are warm and dry. The cleaning people won't be around until morning. I'll be gone by then."

"Why don't you just stay at a shelter?"

"I didn't get my name on the list early enough. There are too few beds in the shelters for the number of homeless people. There is also a limited number of times you can sleep in a shelter. If you use up those times in the beginning of winter, you have no shelter on the really cold nights. It's not as cold when it's snowing as it is after the snow stops and the wind cuts you to the bone and the temperature drops to zero."

The ambulance area was packed with vehicles transporting injured people to the emergency room. Automobile accidents were claiming a lot of victims as Molly had said. The activity level was hectic. She smiled at Storm. "I won't have a problem finding a place to sleep."

Their eyes locked for a moment. "Thanks again." She slid out of the car and followed a group of family members into the waiting area then quickly looked for an exit and went down the stairs to a utility room, where she made herself comfortable. Again she had the feeling she was being followed. She put her head down on her arm and winced from the pain below her eye. She thought she heard someone on the other side of the door. She strained to listen. Nothing.

As sleep overtook her, she thought about Max and Molly and Storm Andrews. The last face she saw in her mind was that of Mike Shaye...filled with hate.

* * *

Storm Andrews paced the ten-foot width of his office. He stopped in front of the victim chart on the wall, staring at the paucity of clues in the two slayings. He examined the note found with the first victim, forty-year-old Martin Higgins, on January 10. It was a verse from *Julius Caesar. When beggars die, there are no comets seen; the heavens themselves blaze forth the death of Princes.* Storm hit the wall with his fist. "What the hell is that supposed to mean? Is the killer saying that the death of a street person is insignificant?" He smoothed out the copy of the note left with the body of forty-one-year-old Kenneth Wooster on January 11. It was a quote from John Bright. *The angel of death has been abroad throughout the land; you may almost hear the beating of his wings.* Obviously, the killer was taunting the police. Was this clever murderer saying he was close enough to be detected? Storm wondered if age was a factor or was it just coincidence that the two victims were in their early forties? He marked the information on the chart.

He sat at the desk and looked up a number for the forensic psychiatrist the police department used.

Pamela McGowan, M.D., had been instrumental in aiding police to solve a difficult case by developing a psychological profile of a rapist-killer. She was also helpful in talking to law enforcement staff when they were feeling undue pressures during investigations. He punched in the number. "Doctor McGowan please." He listened, then said, "No, this is police business. Ask her to call Detective Andrews."

The door opened and Mike Shaye blew in like a tempest. "Why is it that the weather forecasters can predict the weather for every city in the country, except for Philadelphia? Damned snow is crippling this city." He saw that Andrews was unshaven. "You sleep here last night?"

"It was easier than trying to get home. Sit down, Mike, we've got to talk."

Mike sat on the edge of the desk. "What's up, buddy?"

"Why are you harassing Hank Castle?"

"That tramp is bad news. I've got a gut feeling. When I saw her I thought, that black widow spider is going to chew up my friend and spit him out. There's something wrong with her, Storm, there's a volcano inside her and I don't think you want to be around when it starts to spew."

"You may be right, Mike, but it's not me that I'm concerned about. It's you. You've lost control. Twice now you opened the door for a charge of police brutality. What is it about this woman that sets you off?"

The expression on Mike's face was all the answer he needed. Storm nodded, "Of course, Claire. She looks like Claire. She even walks like Claire. But, Mike, she is not Claire. Just because your ex-wife turned out to be a tramp doesn't mean all women are whores. You're punishing Hank because your wife was a nympho and went to bed with half of the Department." Storm picked up a file folder from his desk. "Hank hasn't registered a formal complaint yet but she might." He threw the manila folder into Mike's lap. "There are thirty complaints over the past two years from women accusing you of using unnecessary force during arrests or while they were in lockup. That's only the ones with the guts to register complaints. I'm worried about what you might do. You've allowed your hate to color your logic. Claire's been gone for three years. It's time to let go and get on with your life." He stared at his partner. "Mike, I'm going to recommend that you see a psychiatrist. In the meantime I want you to stay away from Hank. Internal Affairs is still looking into the charges against you in the Laurel case. They're breathing down our necks, Mike. It's important that they know you are getting professional help. I have a call in to Doctor McGowan."

"For chrissake, Storm, can't you send me to a male shrink? Damn broads are taking over the whole fucking world." He pulled out a cigarette and lit it. "You're throwing up a smoke screen because of this Castle broad. Storm, you didn't hear a word I said. She-is-dangerous. She might even be lethal."

"I hear what you're saying but she is not my problem, you are. Hank isn't the one losing control…you are. You're stalking her and I want it to stop. You've been carrying this hatred around, nurturing it and now you think all women are rotten."

Mike turned away and walked to the window. Storm knew Mike was angry because the back of Shaye's ears had turned purple-red.

"Mike, I just don't want to see you throw away everything you worked for because of a woman…any woman."

"Okay, buddy." Mike Shaye turned around and faced Storm. "Do me a favor and protect your back. Between the two of us we might strike a happy medium. I don't trust anybody and you trust too many people. I'm not sure which one of us is crazy." Mike thrust his hands deep into his pockets. "You're right. She does remind me of Claire and that might have something to do with the way I feel. But there's more to it than that. She's a disaster looking for a place to happen."

Andrews reached over, picked up a copy of *The National Post* and began paging through the magazine. Mike picked up the file of complaints that fell to the floor when he stood up. He scanned the contents quickly, then said, "Hank has taken up with two other bums. One toothless old hag called Molly and a scatterbrain called Maxine."

"Well, well, well. What have we here?" Storm flattened the magazine out on his desk. There smiling up from the page was the face of Henrietta Castle. The magazine stated she had done a series of articles for the Associated Press and was honored at a dinner in New York City.

Mike Shaye looked over Storm's shoulder at the face of Hank Castle. "Why the hell didn't she tell us she is a reporter?"

* * *

Snow was still falling in the morning, when Hank left the hospital. The only thing moving was a disgruntled snow removal crew trying to open the emergency routes. She had gone only a few blocks when her shoes and socks were soaked and freezing. She headed for her apartment. She entered through the tower stairs in the rear of the building, walked up to the fifth floor and let herself in. She kicked off her shoes and peeled off the sopping socks and clothes and threw them in the washer. She let the water run in the bathtub. In the closet she found a pair of Totes boots. She scuffed them and tore off pieces from around the top to make them look used. At least she would have something to keep her feet dry. She refilled the brandy bottle with Courvoisier from her liquor cabinet and put hot coffee in a thermos and tucked them into the canvas bag. She was ready to go back.

When she closed the tower door and started down the stairs, she felt uneasy. With each step down, the specter of fear clutched at her throat, choking her. She lifted her hand to her throat trying to tear away at the unseen menacing presence that filled her with panic.

She stumbled and held onto the railing with both hands. Her canvas bag tumbled ahead of her onto the basement floor. Her eyes scanned the dimly lit area. She saw nothing but she knew she wasn't alone.

She gathered the things that had fallen out of the canvas bag and was amazed to see the brandy bottle and thermos were still intact. She was less than ten feet from the door leading to the outside and safety. She dashed for the door and pushed on the release bar but nothing happened. The pounding of her heart grew louder. She wasn't sure but she thought she heard a faint, odd kind of laugh. Déjà vu? Was this her dream repeating itself in her consciousness? If she turned around would she see a black hooded figure coming after her? She could no more stop herself from turning around than she could stop trying desperately to open the door.

Finally, she looked over her shoulder…there was no black hooded figure and everything was as it had been when she entered the tower stairs. But the fear was still there. Frantically, she pushed against the release bar with all her weight. Slowly, the door creaked open a few inches. She pushed harder, bracing one foot against the doorjamb and pushed with all of her weight against the door. The snow had drifted and piled up against the outside of the door but fear gave her the shot of adrenalin needed to find the strength to clear the passage. She stumbled outside and pushed the door closed with her back. She waited and watched for the door to open again, knowing her pursuer would be relentless in the chase.

The wind blew snow from all directions and soon the arc created by the opening of the door was covered over.

She was alone.

CHAPTER 3

The shelter was unusually quiet. Fear had penetrated the delicate balance between resignation and resistance and threatened to tip the scales. The murders seemed to whip the weaker ones into mental submissiveness.

Maxine was standing in line talking to a man Hank had not seen before. Max gasped when she saw Hank. "What happened to your eye?"

Hank shrugged her shoulders, "I lost an argument with a door."

Max shook her head. "Hank, meet Ned, our poet laureate. Ned, this delightful person is Hank."

Ned made an elaborate gesture at a bow and kissed Hank's hand. She held on to his hand, turned it over and returned the kiss. Blue eyes twinkled and he stood ten feet tall, in spite of his five-foot-eight frame. His smile was contagious. He said,

"Jenny kissed me when we met,
Jumping from the chair she sat in;
Time, you thief, who love to get
Sweets into your list, put that in:
Say I'm weary, say I'm sad
Say that health and wealth have missed me,
Say I'm growing old, but add,
Jenny kissed me."

Hank smiled, she liked him.

"Henceforth," Ned said, "I shall call you Jenny." There was challenge in his voice when he asked, "Can you identify the poem?" They passed through the line and carried their cups of hot tea to a table and sat down.

Hank said, "Like most people, I've heard the poem countless times but for the life of me, I can't remember who wrote it."

Max laughed. "It was Leigh Hunt."

"Of course," Hank said, "I should have remembered."

Ned took her hand again, "Jenny, my dear, meet with us often and I will refresh your memory as well as your spirits."

He was right. By the time they left the shelter, her spirits, if not soaring, were considerably higher than when she entered.

Max and Hank walked together holding on to each other for support on the ice that was still a base coat on streets and sidewalks.

Max looked concerned and touched Hank's eye. "Who hit you last night?"

Hank smiled. "Not to worry. Everything is fine now. Where are you going today?"

"To the library again. By this afternoon the streets department should have cleared some of the streets and if the merchants want to do business, they will clear off the sidewalks. My feet are wet already." She looked at Hank's feet in the Totes boots. "Where did you get boots?"

"Somebody left them in the waiting room at the hospital. When nobody claimed them, I did. Besides, they were beat up. I'm glad I had them, it was a long walk over from the hospital this morning."

"You slept at the hospital? How?"

"Molly told me how to do it. I could never sleep in the train station like Molly. I'll bet she can sleep on a picket fence."

Max laughed. "Must be the sign of a clear conscience. I wish I could sleep like that. There was a young girl with a baby in the bed next to me at the shelter last night. Poor kid, she cried all night." Max's eyes had a faraway look. "Memories are never as vivid or as sad as they are in the dark." They stopped at the corner. "See you," Max said as she picked her way through iced-over footprints toward the library.

Hank supposed that Max's place among the Streeters would be difficult to put on paper. There were so many facets to her personality. Some were contradictory but most were simple and straightforward. She seemed to know all the women and most of the men by name. Hank watched Max walk away and thought, *She's a throwback from an era long gone. She belongs in a castle, a fairy-tale princess waiting for Prince Charming.* As she turned the corner onto the Chestnut Street Mall, she collided with another Streeter, lost her footing and landed on her rump in the wet snow. Instead of helping her up, the Streeter growled, "Watch where you're goin'."

Hank felt an arm under hers, helping her to her feet. Molly glared at the man. "Damn you, Franz, at least you could help her up. You ain't got no manners, no how."

"If she was watchin' where she was goin' she wouldn't be sittin' on her ass in wet snow," he grunted and continued on his way.

"You okay, Hank?" Molly asked as she tried to brush off the wet ice chips.

"Thanks, Molly, I'm fine." She brushed the wet snow off the back of her coat. "He was right, I wasn't watching. I probably bumped into him and not the other way around."

"He still shoulda helped ya up. He's got no call to leave you sittin' in the snow. The seat of your coat's all wet. In ten minutes you'll be shiverin' with the damp."

"It's okay, Molly...really. I slept at the hospital last night. It was great."

"I shoulda gone with ya. The station was noisy. The trains stopped runnin' for a couple of hours and people got backed up in the station. It was around one o'clock before it quieted down. Did you see Maxie?"

"I saw her at the shelter. She was with Ned."

Molly frowned. "Yeah. The poet," she said in a flat tone.

There were no pockets in Molly's coat and she tried to tuck her hands up into her sleeves. Her knuckles were a chapped angry red.

"You look chilled to the bone."

"I am. Sure wish I had gloves." She blew on her numb fingers.

Hank reached into her bag and pulled out the brandy. "I don't have an extra pair of gloves but maybe this will help."

Molly's eyes brightened. She didn't bother to look around. She reached for the bottle and took several swallows before handing it back. "Thanks, that helps."

Hank remembered she had a pair of black wool gloves in her storage locker and made a mental note to look for them. A section of newspaper blew around her legs and she retrieved it. At the left of the page was a picture of the latest victim. The headlines seemed to create their own icy fear. *BODY OF SECOND HOMELESS VICTIM FOUND FROZEN ON SNOW-COVERED STREET.* Hank read aloud: "*The body of Kenneth Wooster, age forty-one was found yesterday morning on Sansom Street. The victim had been stabbed in the back, similar to the murder of Martin Higgins, the previous night. Mr. Wooster was identified by his Social Security card. There was another similarity between the two murders, a note was left beside the body but police have not revealed its contents. The last known address for the victim was Chicago. Inquiries are being made to Chicago police.*" The rest of the story was continued on page five, which Hank did not have.

She crumbled the paper and tossed it into the nearest trash container. The notes referred to in the article aroused her curiosity. *Why would a killer leave a note? Unless he wanted to get caught or was convinced he would not be caught. Is he taunting the police? I hope I live long enough to get the whole story,* she thought. The murders were a bonus as far as Hank's story was concerned.

Tension was mounting among the Streeters. None of them believed a street person was responsible for the crimes. Hank decided to go back to her apartment once a week to record everything that happened, so she would have reference material catalogued when she began to write the book. The decision made her expedition to the streets more tolerable, knowing that once a week she could spend a comfortable night in her own bed.

The next three weeks were uneventful. The Mad Slasher, as the newspapers dubbed the killer, had not struck again and the Streeters were beginning to relax. The end of January and the beginning of February were mild, almost spring-like. Nature fooled the mere mortals into believing that the harsh winter was over as buds appeared on trees and bushes. Molly, Maxine, Ned and Hank sat in Fairmount Park enjoying the warmth of the sun.

A Streeter waved when he passed and Maxine returned the wave. "Top of the morning to you, Terry. Ash Wednesday?"

The Streeter nodded and smiled and wore the ashes on his forehead like a ribbon of honor. "And the balance of the day to you, Max," he said.

Maxine smiled back. "He has a marvelous brogue," she said.

Hank turned her attention to Ned, who was fingering the buds of a forsythia bush. His eyes twinkled when he smiled.

"There is a pleasure in the pathless woods,
There is a rapture on the lonely shore,
There is society, where none intrudes,
By the deep sea, and music in its roar:
I love not man the less, but Nature more."

"Byron's 'Childe Harold's Pilgrimage,'" Hank said.

Ned smacked his knee, pleased to have the poetry identified.

"The way you was grinnin', anybody'd thunk you wrote the damn thing." Molly elbowed Ned's ribs.

"Whenever poetry is recognized it honors the poet and gives satisfaction to those who have committed it to memory."

Hank studied this sensitive man, who was obviously well educated. A good guess would be that he was a teacher of literature at one time or another. What could have driven him to the streets? How many poems had he memorized? Here he was spouting poetry to a trio of street people and delighted that he found at least a few who would not laugh at the ancient practice of storytelling in rhyme. He had begun a quote from Shakespeare when a scream for help came from the bushes about fifty feet away. For a moment they looked like a tableau, frozen in time. Then the spell was broken. They ran toward the scream. Ned was the first to plunge into the bushes, followed by Hank, Max and Molly. Ned was pulling a man to his feet. Under him lay a young girl, her panties torn and lying on the ground. The man had a full erection and fought desperately to recapture his prey. Max knelt beside the girl, holding her, comforting her. "It's okay. We won't let him hurt you. It's okay."

They heard the wail of a baby on the ground about ten feet away. The baby was wrapped in an afghan. Hank hurried to pick up the baby, rocking it and crooning.

Ned held the man on the ground by sitting on his chest.

Molly walked over, shook her head and punched him in the face. "Damn you, Duke, if you got to get your ashes hauled don't pick on a little girl who can't defend herself."

"Get the fuck off me, Ned, before I split your head open."

Molly grabbed him by the hair and pulled his head back. "You ain't listenin' to what I'm sayin', Duke. If you want some ass go get it where you usually get it and leave this kid alone. If we ever catch you chasin' her again, I promise you won't have anythin' left to screw with. Do you get my meanin'?"

Duke threw Ned off his chest and pulled up the zipper to his pants. "God damn you, Molly," he said as he wiped his nose on the back of his hand and noticed that his sleeve was bloody. How would you like it if I busted you in the tits?" He picked up his cap from the ground, looked at the frightened girl and said, "I'll see you around, kid." He stopped when he saw Hank. He squinted, "Hey, Suzie, you look different than you did last night. I liked you better the other way." He winked.

Molly shook her head, "Bastard, her name ain't Suzie and you'd better get the hell outa here."

Hank was outwardly calm as Duke walked away but something inside was churning like a whirlpool out of control.

"That's a bad one." Molly said as she watched Duke walk away. "Guess we better keep an eye on the kid."

Max asked the girl if she wanted to go to the hospital. She refused.

"Is my baby all right?"

Hank looked at the baby and smiled. The baby took hold of Hank's finger. "She's fine. What's her name?"

"Iris."

Ned took the baby and handed her to the girl.

Max walked over to the girl. "Now I remember you. You were in the bed next to me at the shelter the night of the big snow."

"Yes, I was there, I'm Bridget." She appeared to be about eighteen and Iris looked to be about nine months old. The girl looked ill but the baby looked healthy enough, except her legs and feet looked odd.

Max said, "Some of us will be spending the night in the Azalea Gardens. Do you have a place to sleep tonight?"

"Yes. The people at the shelter have been very kind to me. I haven't had to spend too many nights on the street."

"You're welcome to be with us whenever you want company." Molly touched the girl's face with a tenderness that surprised every one...except Max. Hank felt they wandered into a secret place of Molly's past where emotions she thought were dead were on display, and she looked away before Molly realized her vulnerability was showing.

Ned walked to the shelter with Bridget and the baby. Molly, Max and Hank went to the soup kitchen for a hot meal, then to the Azalea Gardens.

Hank looked at the bushes with their promise of spring and agreed this was much better than the concrete doorways of department stores. "I'll be glad when daylight saving time begins again. I hate it when it gets dark early. What happened today made me realize how vulnerable we are with a maniac loose in the city."

Max and Hank put their blankets under the bare bushes. Molly put hers down across the footpath from them. She grinned, "I snore loud."

They sipped brandy to lessen the chill before bedding down. Hank put her head on the canvas bag and closed her eyes. She could hear the slow, even breathing of Max and soon came the monotonous buzz of Molly's snoring.

The trauma of the rape in the park awakened memories Hank thought were dead. Involuntarily, she winced, the memory still very much alive and painful.

It had been a sweltering, muggy August afternoon. Hank was five years old, playing on the back porch with cardboard cut-out dolls. Bruce Dickinson staggered out and planted his feet wide apart to give himself balance. It didn't help much. He weaved his way to one of the rocking chairs and collapsed into it. He tried to focus on what Hank was doing. He wore a sleeveless undershirt that accentuated his hairy chest and arms. His disheveled copper-red hair sat like a dead animal on his head. A heavy stubble of beard confirmed a three-day growth. He held a cylindrical package tied with string.

"Here's a surprise for you." His slurred speech was punctuated with a loud burp. Bruce Dickinson had married Alma Castle when Hank was four. Hank held the package, doubtful that it was for her. Since he married her mother, he had never given either of them anything. All he did was take.

Hank didn't trust him. She eyed the package suspiciously. "What is it?"

"Open it and find out." He watched her study the package. "Go on," he prompted, "It won't bite."

Hank tugged at the string until it fell away from the crumpled brown paper wrapping and stared at the cardboard cylinder, then looked at him. "What is it?"

"A kaleidoscope."

Hank turned it over in her hand. "A what?"

"A kaleidoscope," he repeated.

"Oh," she said, more confused than before.

Bruce Dickinson lifted her into his lap and told her to look into the tiny hole at the top. "Hold it, and twist the bottom, like this." She saw the loose bits of colored glass fall into different patterns. "You have to look up at the sky. The light makes the colors brighter and prettier."

She tilted her head back so that it was supported against the matted hair on his chest.

With a quick motion, he lifted her dress and tugged at the elastic on her white cotton panties. She felt his thick fumbling fingers explore her private places. "Stop it." She tried to pull away from his vice-like grip. Her voice echoed her panic. "Mommy said nobody should ever touch me there."

"Yeah? She likes it well enough," he said as he held her against him with one arm while he continued his exploration with the other hand. His breathing was loud, uneven and rapid and his breath smelled like a mixture of beer, whiskey and cigarettes. She felt something hard probing against her backside. She thought it was the kaleidoscope until she saw the cylinder roll down the steps to the trash-littered yard.

"No!" she screamed and pulled free of his grip. He lunged forward, narrowly missing her, and fell face down on the rough wooden floorboards. His lips were slack and slobbering. His eyes had a strange look she hadn't seen before. She ran down the steps, across the yard to the back gate, barely supported on one hinge, and into the woods behind the low-rent project housing as fast as her legs would carry her. She could feel the vibration of his heavy footsteps behind her coming closer. As she entered the tall, heavy brush, she glanced over her shoulder. He had stopped, looking at the overgrown weeds in front of him. She found the old hollowed-out tree trunk lying on its side, which was where she hid when he was drunk and beat her mother. He stopped some distance away from where she was hidden, parting the weeds and cursing. He kept rubbing the bulge inside his pants.

"Where the hell are ya...ya little bitch?" He swayed and steadied himself against a tree. "Come and see what I got for ya," he said, as he pulled down his zipper.

Hank held her breath. His ankle-high, grease-stained boots had come menacingly close to the edge of the hollowed-out log.

"Come back here, ya little bastard." He staggered toward the full-leafed maple tree and weaved like a tree ready to be felled. She could see him through the weeds. She watched as his hand disappeared inside the open zipper and pulled out something long and hard. The tip of it looked like a dark purple bulb and he held it in his hand, squeezing it. Then he began pulling on it and she saw the same look in his eyes she had seen on the back porch minutes earlier. His hand pushed and pulled at the object, slowly at first, then faster. It was then that Hank realized the other end of the object was attached between his legs. Saliva oozed from one corner of his mouth as his eyes got wider. All of his concentration was on the thing he was punishing in his hand. Then his eyes rolled upward and almost disappeared behind his eyelids.

She saw a milky substance spurt from the end of the thing he held. His hips jerked and his fingers seemed to squeeze the last of the milky stuff out of the tube. His fingers relaxed and his body shivered from head to toe. The sound of his breathing slowly grew quiet. His eyes opened and he watched as the thing he had been pushing and pulling got smaller and smaller. Then it disappeared back into his pants. He closed the zipper, looked around and retreated along the same path he took to get there. Hank stayed inside the tree trunk until she was sure Mama had come home from work.

Hank shook her head as she pushed the memory back into the past and drifted into a troubled sleep.

In the pre-dawn hours, Hank wasn't sure if she dreamed it or if someone was standing over her, peering into her face but she was too sleepy to look or care. When the first light of morning insisted she open her eyes, she rolled over to see Maxine sleeping contentedly about ten feet away and Molly was just rousing herself on the other side of the path. Hank sat up holding her back. "Apparently part of me was sleeping on the dirt and part of me was on the blanket. The part on the dirt is letting me know it wasn't a good idea."

Molly walked behind a tree. Hank heard a rush of water hit the dirt. Hank still couldn't go any place other than a restroom.

Max rolled over and rubbed her eyes. "It can't be morning already."

"Wanna bet?" Hank said as she folded her blanket.

Max stretched. "I must be a night person. I could stay up all night and sleep all day. At least I think I could. I've never tried. Where's Molly?"

"Taking a pee. Damn, wish I had a cup of coffee."

At eight thirty they were standing in line at the shelter waiting to get in for some hot cereal and tea. Hank lifted her arm and put her nose to her shoulder. "Wow. I have to find some place to take a shower. Even I can't stand me."

Max laughed. "If you ask at the shelter, they will probably let you use the upstairs shower."

Ned came into the shelter, his eyes searching. Max waved to him and he made his way to the table where they were sitting. He sat between Hank and Max. "Bad news."

Max turned pale. "Not another murder?"

"Afraid so."

"When?"

"Probably last night some time."

Max looked alarmed. "Do you know who it was?"

"No. Couldn't get close enough to see or hear anything but I'll tell you one thing, Mike Shaye is on the warpath. The killer is making the police look like monkeys."

Hank laughed. "That's not hard to do. If you hold up a mirror and the reflection looking back at you is hairy all over with black beady eyes and has a long tail like a monkey, then I guess you're a monkey."

Ned laughed but Hank wasn't feeling funny. She was scared. She had a taste of how nasty Shaye could be and Hank knew she would do everything possible to stay away from him.

Max was visibly shaken. "God, does this mean the police will be taking us in for questioning?"

Ned put his hand on her shoulder. "I doubt it. We had nothing to do with the murder. Where were you last night?"

"On Kelly Drive at the Azalea Gardens."

"Then you have nothing to worry about. The murder happened over on Chestnut Street around Twenty-Second. You were nowhere near that area. I spent the night at the Thirtieth Street station and I don't remember seeing anybody that I knew. Hell, I'm not going to let it upset me. I guess we'll find out who it was soon enough."

The first thought that came into Hank's mind was whether or not there was another note that the police wouldn't reveal. The group left the shelter together, going their separate ways, but they agreed to meet later.

There was nothing about the murder in the morning paper and Hank assumed it probably happened after the newspaper went to press.

At six o'clock Hank met Max and Molly at the shelter. No one had seen Ned since morning. A man in a torn navy peacoat stopped to talk to Molly. It was clear she was agitated. Probably more than agitated, she was damned mad.

Molly looked at Hank. "The cops packed Ned off in the wagon and are holdin' him."

Max looked shocked. "What for?"

Molly pushed her bowl away from her. "Suspicion of murder."

Max shook her head. "No, it can't be. We've got to help him. He can't stand being confined."

Hank could see Maxine's agitation mounting and she turned to the others. "We have an alibi because we were together. Ned was at the station and chances of anybody going to the police to clear him are slim. If I go, you two still have an alibi. You were together at the Azalea Gardens. I'm going to tell them I was near Ned at the station last night. Maybe they'll let him go. If not, I'm going to call the Public Defender's office. Do you know where they took him? Well, no matter. I'll go back to the precinct where they took me. Wish me luck."

It was a long walk to the police station and by the time she got there a light drizzle had started. It had turned cold again.

The uniformed officer at the desk bellowed when he saw Hank. "You again? What the tell do you want?"

Strange how an attitude could make you feel contaminated, she thought. "I want to see Detective Andrews."

"He's busy. What do you want to see him about?"

"Last night's murder."

His name-tag, identified him as Timothy O'Toole. His eyes narrowed. "What murder?"

"The one my friend Ned is being held for."

"Who's Ned?"

"Don't play games with me, Officer O'Toole. If I can't get anywhere with you, maybe the newspapers can." She turned and headed for the door.

"That short fuse is going to get you into trouble some day."

She recognized the voice without turning around. "My fuse is short only when bullies pick on defenseless women or innocent men."

His eyes held hers captive and she prayed he could not read her thoughts. Ned's freedom depended on her.

Storm Andrews held the door open and waited for her to come in. She saw him flinch when she passed. Her body odor had ripened.

"Have a seat. I'll be right back."

She glanced around the room as she unbuttoned her coat and was about to sit down when Mike Shaye walked in.

"What the hell are you doing here?"

"None of your damn business."

The door opened again and Storm Andrews came in with two cups of steaming coffee and handed one to Hank.

"Black, right?"

Hank nodded. "I understand Ned was picked up."

Storm Andrews took a sip of his coffee. "Is that his name?"

"It's the only name any of us know."

"Okay, so what's your point?"

"I know he couldn't have done it."

"You know shit," Shaye said through clenched teeth.

Hank ignored him and kept her eyes on Andrews. "Ned slept at Thirtieth Street Station last night. So did I. He couldn't have committed the crime."

"How do you know a crime was committed? It wasn't in the papers."

"We have our own network. It's far better than the local paper. By eight thirty this morning most of the Streeters knew somebody had bought it."

Storm put his cup down and sat on the corner of his desk, facing Hank. "How well do you know this Ned?"

"I don't know him well at all but I do know he couldn't have committed the murder."

"He's known as *the poet* on the streets. Isn't that right?"

Hank looked bewildered. "Yes. So?"

"As a matter of fact, we hear he spouts poetry all the time. Have you ever heard him?" Storm lit a cigarette.

Hank was confused by this line of questioning. "What does his poetry have to do with the arrest?"

"Just answer my questions, Hank."

"I'm not answering any more questions until you tell me why."

"It seems that our serial killer is also a poet."

Hank felt her heart stop but her thoughts were going at the speed of light.

"That's what you've got? You're accusing a man of murder because he can recite poetry? Do you know how many colleges and universities there are in Philadelphia and the surrounding communities? Each school has its own English department, which includes literature. Are you going to question every professor and every student of English simply because they know poetry? Ned could no more kill another human being than I could."

"In my book, that alone makes him a prime suspect. I think you could kill a man and enjoy it," Shaye sneered.

Hank tried to stay calm. "You know, you really should stop smoking. It's bad for your health. I would hate to see you die from lung cancer before somebody has a chance to put a bullet through your thick skull."

He turned his head ever so slightly in her direction and the malevolent stare unnerved her.

"Mike, why don't you run down that lead that just came in," Storm urged.

Shaye didn't shift his gaze and his lips formed the word *Whore.*

Her eye contact with Shaye didn't waver either and her lips formed the word *Asshole*.

He picked up a folder from the desk and walked out.

"Stop goading him, Hank. He doesn't like you much to begin with and I'm not always going to be around to stop him."

She took a deep breath. "What about Ned?"

"He's not being charged, if that's what you're concerned about." Andrews was flipping the pages of a magazine with his thumbnail and studying her.

"Is he free to go back with me?"

"I'll let you know as soon as we get the results of the polygraph." His eyes settled on her clenched fists. "I wonder how well you would fare in one of those tests."

"Book me and we can find out."

"You know what you remind me of Hank? One of those television news hawks, you're pushy, ill mannered and rude. You walk around with a chip on your shoulder just daring somebody to knock it off. Some day…somebody will."

She felt her face flush. "Yeah? Well, don't judge me, Mr. Detective, until you've lived part of my life."

"I don't buy that shit, Hank. You can still get what you want without being hard and bitter. I'm not your enemy. You are."

His phone rang. It was only then that his eyes left her face. He didn't say anything; he just listened then hung up the phone. "You can pick up your friend. The polygraph was negative."

"It wouldn't have been admissible in court anyway." She buttoned her coat.

When she reached the door, Andrews said, "Incidentally, Ned is a nice guy, sensitive, intelligent, considerate. He's been on the streets a lot longer than you. I found none of the bitterness in him like I see in you." He turned his attention to the magazine in his hand. "Now get out of here."

When she reached the front desk, Officer O'Toole was finishing a phone conversation. "Will do," he said and hung up. "They're bringing Ned back from lockup. Sit over there and wait."

She sat on a bench near the door watching the activity in the station. A heavy mahogany door opened and Ned came into the room accompanied by a uniformed officer. The officer put his hand on Ned's shoulder and smiled at him. "You take care, Ned."

"You too, Officer." Ned saw Hank and smiled. "Jenny, how kind of you to come after me." He reached out and hugged her with one arm, leading her toward the door and the outside world.

When the door closed, she looked up at him. The light drizzle had turned to sleet.

"Are you all right? Did they treat you okay?"

"I'm fine, Jenny. They were very considerate and didn't lock me in a cell when I told them I was claustrophobic. I was in a large, open room and somebody went out and got me a hamburger and a cup of coffee. When they questioned me, I told them I was willing to take a polygraph so they sent for the technician. Then Michael Shaye came in and said you gave me an alibi for last night. I don't think I needed an alibi but I will never be able to tell you how grateful I am. We have only just met and yet you lied for me."

"Did Shaye treat you okay?"

"Oh, my dear, Michael Shaye is Michael Shaye. That's the way he is and he is not going to change. I'm sure he carries around a lot of burdens and it may be those burdens that make him cross and suspicious. As a matter of fact, he was the one who sent out for the food and coffee." His eyes narrowed. "I get the impression you and he got off on the wrong foot."

Hank reached up and pulled Ned's collar up. "You might say that and I don't think it will ever change. I must remind him of someone he hates."

"Or loves," Ned said as he quickly scanned the street for skidding cars. "Most of the men on the streets today are there because of or in spite of a woman or women, or alcohol and women, or drugs and women, or embezzlement and women. You saw what happened in the park yesterday. Duke attempted to rape that young girl. Rape is not an act of passion but an act of anger."

"Duke is an animal."

"Perhaps." He stopped and turned her to face him. "I find I sleep better at night if I don't judge others."

"Ned...Detective Andrews was interested in the fact that you're known as *the poet*. Do you know what that's about?"

"I haven't the foggiest notion. They asked me a lot of questions too. I quoted several literary pieces all the way through. Probably, it has something to do with the murders but I can't imagine what. Do you know, Jenny?"

"No, but I'm sure it's important. The newspapers reported that notes were found on the bodies of the first two victims, we don't know about the third victim yet. Do you think those notes could have been verses of some kind?"

"You mean like murder in rhyme?" He shrugged. "It's possible, I guess. I did learn the identity of the third man. It was Harry Timmins. He was knows as Harry the Greek on the streets. I haven't been able to understand why anyone would want to kill Harry, or Marty or Ken for that matter. All three were harmless men. I'm sure it must be as difficult to understand the criminal mind as to comprehend the plight of a woman scorned."

"They've even got you believing that the killer could be a woman. I think they're off base."

"Not if you use their logic. Who better to get close to a man than a woman without arousing his suspicions? I think there could be some validity to their theory. However, I do not know of any woman on the streets with that kind of obsession and I do not believe the murderer to be one of us. Once you are part of the street scene you realize the base conditions under which Streeters live." Ned shook his head. "We punish ourselves, we do not need outside help."

"Ned, I think you're burying your head in the sand. We have Streeters who have been confined in mental institutions for years and years, and then suddenly word came down from the government to discharge all but the criminally insane. The majority of those patients had no idea of who or where their families were. How many of those patients were on uppers or downers to control their behavior? If those patients ended up on the streets because they had nowhere else to go, who is to say we don't have a pathological killer among us? What do we know of the reasons why they were hospitalized in the first place?"

"We don't. Take Maxine for example, when she was..." His sentence trailed off, realizing he had compromised a confidence but he continued with a rush of words, "Not, mind you, that Maxine was ever in an institution but she has the same kind of vulnerability, the same kind of fear, the same timidity, the same defenselessness and instability. In her mind danger and peril are her constant companions. Think about her for a minute, would you say she is capable of committing such bizarre, wild crimes of passion?" Without waiting for an answer, he continued, "Her mind is incapable of harboring such thoughts. She's gentle, kind and considerate." Again his voice trailed off.

"We're not talking about Max," Hank said. "I don't know if she was a former mental patient and I don't care. All I am saying is, who knows if there are violent people among us?"

She watched Ned's facial expression. "Look at Duke, by your own admission, his attack on Bridget was an act of anger. What about these hidden angers? At least when these people were institutionalized, they were kept on tranquilizing drugs for their own protection and for the protection of others. What happens when they are deprived of that medication and they are subjected to stress? Duke threatened you."

Ned thought for a while. "Yes, he did, didn't he?" He shook his head. "Ridiculous. He was angry, yes, but I don't think he would.... Do you think he would?"

Hank thought for a moment. "I don't know. I didn't like the way he looked at her and said he would see her around. What did he mean when he said I looked different. Different from what? I never set eyes on him until the incident in the park. If I was on the police force, he would be my number one suspect."

It was evident that Ned was uneasy. "Perhaps I should keep a closer check on Bridget and the child."

When they arrived at the shelter, he smiled, "You have a good mind, Jenny. If I didn't say so before, thank you for what you did for me today."

Hank smiled back. "A valentine...from me to you."

Max and Molly were waiting inside the shelter. Max threw her arms around Ned's neck, laughing and crying at the same time.

"I'm so glad you're back."

Ned patted her on the back. "You didn't think a mere lockup could contain this spirit, did you?" He winked at Hank.

Molly slapped him on the back. "They're almost ready to stop dishin' out supper. We better hurry if we wanna eat."

It was the first opportunity Hank had to observe Max without her knowledge. Ned was right, she was frightened and shy and it was obvious she recognized in him a protectiveness she had not found anywhere else. She smiled. "The church up the street has opened up the hall to the homeless for tonight. There are no beds but at least we will be out of the miserable weather and we do have our own blankets."

The hall reeked with the odor of unwashed bodies. This was not the place to come immediately after eating. The group scattered to pick whatever spots were left. Ned found Bridget and the baby and parked his bones next to them. Molly and Maxine found a spot near the rear exit and saved a place for Hank.

Hank's experience at the police station took its toll and her eyes refused to stay open. She awakened briefly, probably because she was cold. She saw Max and Molly nearby and closed her eyes and drifted off to sleep again. Her body felt drugged and heavy, it was too much of an effort to cover herself with the blanket but before long she was warm again.

CHAPTER 4

The supports at the base of the Benjamin Franklin Bridge offered ample protection against the sleet. The lone figure of a man huddled against the steel and concrete buttress in a pocket of air, free from the cutting wind. He wrapped himself in a blanket he had stolen from another Streeter then opened a brown paper bag that contained a pint of whiskey and raised it to his lips. A noise drew his attention away from the liquor and he hid the bottle under the blanket. "Who's there?" His voice was deep and carried on the night air.

"Who were you expecting, baby?"

"That you, Suzie?"

The deep sensual tones warmed him more than the whiskey. "I told you I'd see you soon. Disappointed?" She moved closer so that she was standing in front of him.

"Disappointed? Hell no. I didn't think you'd come. Damn, you're a sexy broad." He reached under her coat and ran his hand up her leg. "How come you didn't let on you knew me when I saw you in the park yesterday with the poet and the old hag? The old bitch belted me good." He raised his hand to his mouth. "Even loosened a tooth."

"I wasn't in the park."

"You could have fooled me. You look like her. Molly said her name was Hank."

Suzie's throaty laugh echoed under the bridge. "Take a good look. Do you really think she's like me?" She leaned closer so that he could feel her breath on his face. She lifted one end of the blanket and slid in beside him. She unbuttoned her coat and rolled on top of him. Under the coat, she wore nothing. His hands began to explore the smooth contours of her breasts. "Do you really think you can compare her to me?" She kissed his mouth. He withdrew and touched the painful bruise between his nose and upper lip. "It must have been Molly who belted you, Hank wouldn't have the guts." She unbuckled his pants, pulled down his zipper and straddled him. She did some exploring of her own. Her body slithered over him and his moans of pleasure were interspersed with gasps of sheer ecstasy.

"Marty said you were the best. He was right." His hips began to gyrate. "Oh, baby, he was so right." Duke's lechery reached a fever pitch.

"Hang on, Duke, I'm taking you on the wildest ride of your life."

His undulations kept pace with his rapid breathing. His hands attacked her breasts with brutal passion and the unimpeded thrust of his hips demanded satisfaction for his unbridled lust. "Now," he gasped, "Now," and gave a final thrust. His hands released their hold on her breasts as he collapsed in an exhausted heap beside her. "Baby, I couldn't move now if you told me there was a million bucks ten feet away from me."

"I'm going to give you the best massage you've ever had. That's how I always end my nights of passion. Roll over, Duke."

"Baby, if I died tonight, I'd die happy."

"I know, Duke."

* * *

Somebody turned on all the overhead lights. It was time to clear out of the church hall. It was six o'clock. When they reached the street it had stopped sleeting. The sidewalks glistened with icy treachery. Hank was glad she still had her boots. The tread on the sole would give her a little traction and maybe she could stay upright. Her boots were still a little wet from the puddle they formed when she took them off. Max's shoes were also wet. Molly's galoshes were dry because she never took them off.

They headed toward the soup kitchen under gray skies that continued to drip misery. As they stood outside the shelter, Max leaned against the building and promptly went to sleep again. Molly roused her when the line began to move. They ate in silence.

As they were leaving, Storm Andrews appeared at the door. He pulled Hank aside and backed her into a corner.

"Where were you last night, Hank?"

"We all spent the night in the church hall up the street. Why?"

"Was Ned with you?"

"Yes. It was Ned, Maxine, Molly, Bridget and her baby and me."

He looked as though he had not slept.

Her eyes searched his face. "Was there another murder last night?"

He nodded.

"When is it going to stop? Have you any idea who is doing this?"

"We have a couple of theories. But a dozen theories and seventy-five cents will get you a cup of coffee. You're sure he was at the hall?"

"Don't take my word for it, ask anybody who was there. There must have been over a hundred people. Do you know who the victim was?"

"We have his name but that's all. Daniel Collins. Name mean anything to you?"

"No. I don't think I knew him."

"I understand he was known as *Duke*."

It was impossible for Hank to hide her shock. "Duke?"

"Then you did know him."

"I knew somebody named Duke but the name Daniel Collins means nothing. A big guy?"

"Yes, I would say so, probably six-one or six-two, broad shoulders."

"It sounds like the same Duke. Where was he found?"

"Under the Ben Franklin Bridge."

CHAPTER 5

Hank walked back into the world of hunger, ridicule and abuse. It was still early and she decided to go through Rittenhouse Square, the small park used by residents of nearby Society Hill apartments. She heard a faint moan coming from behind a park bench and slowly moved into the area, looking in all directions. Then she saw her. A woman propped against the trunk of a spindly maple. Her cheeks were sunken as were her eyes, which kept closing. Hank put the canvas bag down beside her and waited until the woman could focus on her. She judged the woman's weight to be around seventy pounds and her skin was pulled tightly over bone. The woman tried to raise her hand but the effort was too much for her. Hank held her hand. "I'll get an ambulance."

"No," she whispered. "Won't do any good." The effort to talk sapped what little strength she had left.

"Is there anything I can do?"

She nodded. "When it's over. Ask police to notify my daughter. Her name…." Her eyes closed, she was slipping away. Hank shook her gently. "Yes? Her name?"

"Catherine Hall. Her phone number on my wrist. So tired. Want to sleep now." She looked at Hank with unseeing eyes and her hand lost its feeble grip and fell lifeless in her lap. There were some numbers tattooed on the inside of her left wrist. At first Hank thought she must have been a prisoner in one of the German camps during the Second World War. There was no space between the ten digits, so she assumed it was an area code plus a seven-digit phone number. She stood up just as a well-dressed woman, walking a French poodle spotted them and began screaming for the police. Her screams attracted the attention of the doorman across the street and he ran to her assistance. Hank tried to move out of the way but the man signaled to someone else, then said to Hank, "If you so much as move a muscle I'll kick your teeth in."

"I was only going to call the police."

His sneer showed his disdain. "I'll just bet you were." To the woman whose screams would have awakened the dead, he said, "I'm real sorry you had to see this, Mrs. George. We've tried to get the mayor to do something about this element in the city but you know how slowly bureaucrats work." A second man came over and he gasped when he saw the dead woman propped against the tree.

"Robert, call the police."

"Hey, now just a minute. I didn't kill this woman."

He pushed Hank to the ground. "Save it, Sister. You can tell it to the police when they get here."

"You lousy sonofabitch." Hank got up and ran headfirst into his fat belly and he screamed louder than Mrs. George. A crowd had begun to form, which was what Hank did not want. Soon the police van arrived followed by two men in plain clothes. She recognized one of them as Mike Shaye.

"What's going on..." He stopped when he saw the body propped against the tree. He looked at Hank. "What do you know about this, Hank?" He turned to one of the uniformed officers. "Clear the area. Get these people the hell out of here, this ain't no circus." He looked back at Hank. "Well?"

She told him about her conversation with the woman and what she wanted to tell the police and showed him the numbers tattooed on her wrist. "I don't even know who she is, Shaye."

"Her name is Kate." He shook his head.

"You knew her?"

"Yeah. We knew her."

The doorman limped over to them. "I want this...this bum arrested."

Shaye was kneeling on the ground, writing down the numbers that were on the dead woman's wrist. He looked up. "On what charge?"

"Assault and battery. She ran into me with her head ."

Shaye looked at Hank. "Where did you get your training?"

"I didn't do that until he pushed me to the ground. Look." She turned her face to the side and Mike Shaye saw an angry-looking fresh abrasion.

"She was trying to get away." He smiled at Shaye. "I had no choice but to detain her."

"Trying to get away from what?"

"Obviously she killed this poor unfortunate woman."

Shaye stood up and spoke quietly to the man. "She didn't kill this woman. Cancer killed her. She died on the streets away from her family and friends because she wouldn't let them sell everything they owned to pay for her treatments. Kate would never let that happen." He looked at the number he had written down. "Now we know who her family is." He looked at the man again, "There was no criminal act here, do you still want to press charges? I should warn you, if you do, she can counter with charges of her own. She acted in the capacity of a good Samaritan. It's up to you." He turned to the uniformed officer. "Have the body taken to the morgue. Notify the medical examiner." He turned back to the doorman. "Well?"

The man mumbled something unintelligible and walked across the street.

Shaye looked at Hank and crossed his arms. "You seem to have a talent for being in the wrong place at the wrong time. If we ever run low on cases to investigate, we'll just put a tail on you. You turn up all sorts of goodies."

She looked at this man with interest. The sarcasm and contempt were gone from his voice. He actually treated her like she was a human being with rights.

"Am I free to go?"

"Sure." She took a few steps when he called to her. "Hank?"

She turned, expecting he had changed his mind about letting her go. "Yes?"

"Thanks. It's a shame you didn't get to know Kate. She was some lady."

Hank nodded. For the first time in weeks she felt she wasn't alone. Somebody else cared. That the 'somebody else' was Mike Shaye almost blew her mind.

A light drizzle began settling on the sidewalks and soon turned to sleet. It didn't seem to matter to the shoppers pushing their way through the crowds to get to the next department store. Hank walked through the revolving doors of the Gallery, a multi-storied mall with many specialty shops and places to eat. She walked slowly, looking in the shop windows. As long as she didn't enter the shops, nobody could say anything to her and at least it was dry inside. She felt as out of place there as a zircon set in a ring of diamonds. She wondered why the Streeters didn't go to the Gallery. She got her answer. It wasn't anything she saw but rather a feeling of being watched, maybe more than that. The feeling of uneasiness was surrounding her. She looked for the down escalator and headed for it. She was about to step onto it when she felt somebody push her from behind. She was propelled forward. Instinct, second sense, adrenalin, anything you want to call it, rushed through the synapses of her brain forcing her to react. She reached for the rubber handrail to break the fall and held tight. Within seconds she was on her feet again looking back to see who had pushed her. There was nothing unusual, just shoppers getting on and off escalators. Nobody seemed particularly interested that she fell and she knew she had to get out of there. When she reached the ground floor she hurried to the nearest exit to the street. Outside she watched through the large glass panes but there was nothing to see. Now she knew why street people didn't go into the mall. The sleet was coming down harder and she headed for one of the soup kitchens. She turned up the collar of her coat waiting for the soup line to move forward.

"Hello, Hank."

She turned. "Hey, Max. How do you like this weather? We get one good day and pay for it with five lousy days."

"I heard you were with Kate when she died today."

"Did you know her?"

"I guess everybody knew Kate. She's been dying for the last year. When she got real bad the cops would take her to an emergency room. They would keep her for a couple of days but had to let her go as soon as they could because nobody was paying for her to stay there. At first, one of the medical school hospitals was interested in her case but when the medicines they gave her didn't work, they stopped being interested. The cops would find her unconscious and bring her back but it never lasted for long. Well, at least she's out of it now. She's the lucky one."

What a strange way to think about her death, Hank thought, *of course I didn't know Kate and maybe she was in a great deal of pain for a long time.* She looked at the faces of the Streeters sitting at the tables eating the hot, watery beef stew. Occasionally you found a piece of meat, but mostly it was potatoes and carrots and green beans. There wasn't one face among them that looked glad to be alive. The body odors were stronger than the smell of food and her stomach undulated like a wave getting ready to break. She sat looking at her food. Somebody nudged her.

"You going to finish that stew?"

She looked into the eyes of the man Max had called Benny.

"No, you can have it if you want."

He picked up the plate and emptied it into his own. He reminded her of a dog she had when she was growing up. She was intrigued by the way the dog bolted his food. Swallowing it whole. That was the way Benny ate his food. The fact that he had no teeth didn't stop him from gumming his food and swallowing it in lumps. It was then that Hank realized the terrible odor was coming from him. She turned to Max.

"I've got to get out of here before I vomit."

She laughed. "Benny can get pretty ripe at times. Maybe the sleet will give him the shower he refuses to take." They walked out together, Max carrying her worldly possessions in her shopping bag. It was times like this when Hank felt like a phoney. She was intruding into something more than private, more than personal, almost...sacrosanct. She felt like she was tearing away the last veil that protected Max's psyche from the prying eyes of a public that had no right to that secret vault. Hank watched the slim form walk ahead of her. Even though the streets had ravaged her body, her determination seemed to be intact. Probably no one would ever know what drove Max out on the streets but Hank would always wonder. What could have happened in her life to bring her to this low ebb? Hank was almost sure she came from a fine family. The carriage of her body confirmed that theory. The softness of her voice made you think of a mother singing lullabies to her children. She belonged in an estate house with servants and formal dinner parties, Garden teas and dances for charitable functions and save the children projects. Somewhere, somehow, her world came crashing down and she probably had no spirit left to rebuild. The easiest way out was really out, where nobody would ever think of looking for her. Even if Hank's theory was wrong, it was a terrific plot for a book.

CHAPTER 6

Storm Andrews sat in the outer office, paging through a current issue of *U.S. News*. He marveled that he never saw patients in the waiting room. They seemed to be scheduled so that only one patient sat in the waiting room at a time, and after therapy, they left by a second door, which led directly into the elevator corridor.

The muffled, steady *tap-tap* of the receptionist's computer had a tranquilizing effect on him and he didn't hear the door open from the inner office. Suddenly she was standing in front of him, smiling.

"Doc!" He stood up and smiled. "I'm sorry. How long have you been standing there?"

"Every bit of five seconds."

They shook hands. He looked into soft dark brown eyes. She didn't look like any doctor he had ever known. She was beautiful and definitely feminine. "We have a problem…a big problem."

She spoke to the petite redhead sitting at the computer, "Nicole, hold my calls." She pushed open the door to her office. "Come in, Storm. There's fresh coffee on the table in the corner."

He poured a cup for himself. "Would you like one?"

"Yes, please…black."

She sat in an easy chair facing him.

"We've got a serial killer on the loose." He pulled a large envelope from his breast pocket. "Among other things, it seems our killer is also a poet of sorts. These are the verses that were found beside each of the four victims. We need a profile on the killer. We have to know what we're dealing with."

As he talked, she made a chart of the evidence and what facts were available. When she finished writing, he said, "Not much to go on, is it?"

"There's more here than you think. I would like to have a copy of the autopsies and a transcript of interrogations. Obviously, the murderer is playing with the police. He or she feels you can't catch, let's say, him—for the sake of brevity. In fact, he is so sure he won't be captured he even gave you the date for the next killing. I assume the murders have taken place in different locations?"

"He's covering the downtown area from the Delaware River to the Schuylkill River. The killer isn't setting a pattern for when or where he strikes. So far, the hits seem to be random."

"A serial killer does nothing randomly. You may not see the pattern but it's there." She jotted down some hurried notes.

He nodded. "I could set up a map and chart for you but it might upset your patients."

"We can still do that. There's a closet behind those double doors, which I don't use. We could set up the profile there and I'll keep the door locked."

"There is one other problem I have to discuss with you. Mike Shaye."

She sat back and listened to Storm's account of the events, which culminated in stalking Hank Castle and the physical abuse. "In all fairness to him, I have to say she does nothing to pacify him. If anything, she antagonizes him more. I'm worried. He's going off the deep end. Anybody that reminds him of his ex-wife is in trouble. I'm afraid Hank has the misfortune to resemble her and just the sight of her sets him off."

"Who is Hank Castle?"

"She's a journalist, posing as one of the homeless to gather material for an article and possibly a book. She found our first victim, so officially she's one of our suspects. She thinks Mike Shaye is crazy. Mike thinks Hank could be the murderer. He's oil and she's water. There's no way they're going to mix. Unfortunately, the file on Mike's abuse of women in lockup is getting out of hand. He needs help."

She picked up the phone and dialed one-three. "Nicole, when is my first opening for patients?" She waited. "No, that's too long. Set up an appointment for me to see Michael Shaye at seven o'clock Friday morning. No, there's no need to set up a new file. I saw him about two, maybe two and a half years ago. He's with the police department. Good." She hung up. "Tell Mike to be here Friday morning at seven."

"Thanks, Doc. Looks like we'll be seeing a lot of each other until we get our man...or woman."

Mike Shaye was unrelenting in his pursuit of street people. They were brought in for questioning, then released. The press was pressuring the mayor and city council to induce the police to reveal the contents of the notes found with each of the murder victims. It worked.

Hank cut the verses out of the paper, hoping she and Ned could analyze any hidden meanings. As a writer, she could mentally organize the few known facts and try sorting out as many of the details as possible. The first victim, on January 10, was Martin Higgins, age forty, the verse left with the body was a quote from *Julius Caesar. When beggars die, there are no comets seen; the heavens themselves blaze forth the death of princes.* The second victim, on January 11, was Kenneth Wooster, age forty-one. The verse beside the body was a quote from John Bright's speech to the House of Commons; *The angel of death has been abroad throughout the land; you may almost hear the beating of his wings.* Strange messages, she thought. Was the killer pre-selecting the victims to fit the verses? The third victim, on February 13, was Harry Timmins, age forty-two. The verse, *Death was now armed with a new terror.* She wasn't familiar with that quote, and decided to look it up. What did it mean? Was the killer going to change his crime signature? Or did it mean there was going to be a new innovation to the already established pattern of killing?

The fourth victim, on February 14 was Daniel (Duke) Collins, age forty-one. The verse was from Joseph Addison's *The Spectator*; *Death only closes a man's reputation, and determines it as good or bad.* Then almost as an afterthought was a quote from *Julius Caesar*, *Beware the ides of March.* Was the slayer actually saying when the next murder would occur? Was the killer mocking the police? It was ironic that the man who raped young Bridget should be killed on Valentine's day. Poetic justice? Concern mounted in the working community and people who normally stayed later in the evening to work were taking the early trains back to the safety of the suburbs. Even the apathetic street people were traveling in small groups. There was no evidence that the police were doing anything to protect them from the madness of a psychopath who was reducing their numbers...one at a time.

March 15 was quickly approaching and the police were no closer to the identity of the killer than they were in January. The only bright spot was the possibility that winter was over. The days were warmer.

It was a month since Hank had seen Storm. If he was on the streets, his disguise was good enough so that she couldn't identify him. Since she'd undertaken this assignment, she had lost fifteen pounds and the Catalina swimsuit in the store window caught her fancy. She found herself thinking how well it would look on her new figure. That's when she saw him, or rather his reflection in the store window. He was behind her standing at the curb watching her. She knew better than to give him away so she avoided looking directly at him and began walking west on Chestnut Street. When the crowds thinned out he caught up with her, walking about two steps behind.

"Don't turn around, Hank, just listen. Can you get off the streets tonight?"

"I can't. I promised Max and Molly we would be together. They feel there's safety in numbers."

"I wish you would get off the street. We think our friend is going to strike again tonight."

"So do we. That thing about the Ides of March has everybody unhinged."

"Why do they think they need an alibi?"

"Idiot. It's not because they need an alibi. So far the killer has only attacked loners. There's not enough room for everybody in the shelters so the only protection we have is to stick together. Where will you be?"

"Covering as much territory as possible. I'll have Shaye keep an eye on you."

"No. Don't do that, Storm. He scares the shit out of me. Besides, if the Streeters see him around they'll freak out. I'll be fine. If it doesn't rain we'll probably be around the Azalea Gardens. We don't want anything to happen to us, either."

"Meet me at your place tomorrow night?"

In spite of herself she felt an excitement like the first time she was asked out on a date.

She nodded. "Can you make it for seven o'clock? I'll throw a couple of steaks on the broiler."

"See you then."

He was like a phantom. When she looked around he was gone. She retraced her steps and met Max and Molly at the shelter. They had sandwiches and a watered-down chicken soup. She should never have mentioned steaks. Nothing was going to satisfy her until she ate a steak. At least it was something to look forward to. There was little enough of that since she came to the streets. Ned sat next to her at the table. He smiled, "How are you, Jenny?"

He had a gift for putting people at ease. "Fine, Ned. Have the police been leaving you alone?"

"For the time being. They followed me today so they must be expecting something to go down tonight."

"Have you seen the verses in the newspapers?"

"Yes. Interesting, don't you think?"

"When Harry Timmins was killed, the verse was, *Death was now armed with a new terror.* I can't identify that verse, can you?"

"I went to the library to look it up. It was a quotation from Henry Peter, also known as Lord Brougham." He stared at her. "You've lost weight, Jenny, are you all right?"

"Fine. Really, Ned, I'm fine. When the warmer weather is here to stay I won't have to walk so much. Right now it's the only way to stay warm. I guess I'm using more calories than I'm taking in. How are Bridget and the baby?"

"I haven't seen them for several days. I, too, hope the warm weather comes soon, otherwise that baby isn't going to make it. There seems to be something wrong with its legs. I suggested she take the baby to the Shriners Hospital and get her examined. I hope she did. If they can help the baby she doesn't have to worry about paying."

"That would be a blessing."

"Are you going to be with Molly and Maxine tonight? Maxine has been very edgy since the last murder."

"We'll be at the Azalea Gardens. What about you?"

"If I can find Kappy we'll probably go down to the waterfront." He smiled. "Friday night, you know. There should be a good crowd coming into town for dinner. Maybe we can pick up some change. If we get back early enough we might see you at the Gardens."

Molly was scavenging in department store trash and found several large pieces of strong, clear plastic that mattresses were stored in. She gave Max and Hank one each and kept one for herself. They used the plastic as ground covers to put their blankets on. Molly wore the wool gloves Hank had given her. She took them off only when she ate, and then she pinned them to her coat sleeves.

Max was unusually quiet. Hank brought out the bottle of brandy, which was two-thirds full and offered it first to Max. She shook her head. Molly took the bottle out of her hand and sat beside Max, with her arm around the younger woman.

"Take some, Maxie, it'll do ya good. It'll stop the shakin' inside."

Max's hand shook as she accepted the bottle and raised it to her lips. She took one swallow and handed it back to Molly, who took a good gulp before giving it back to Hank.

Hank held it out to Max again. "Drink some more, Max. Believe me, after about four or five swallows you won't worry about anything."

Max smiled and took another sip, then another and another before she passed it along to Molly. They repeated this ceremony until Max was almost passed out. She giggled her way to sleep. It was the first time she allowed her inhibitions to sink into the past. At about eleven o'clock Molly pulled the other half of Max's blanket over the sleeping form. "She's really an uptight lady." Molly moved to her own blanket on the other side of the footpath.

"If you hear or see anybody, wake me, Hank."

Hank promised before sliding into unconsciousness. She could hear the steady drone of Molly's snoring. She remembered looking at the stars and thinking how close they seemed. She thought she heard a noise. All of her senses were alerted and she turned her head slowly, to see if the sound was repeated. She tried to quiet her breathing, convinced that it could be heard from fifty feet away. She lay on her back, her eyes searching the velvety darkness. There was nothing. The cognac had taken the edge off her nerves too. She pulled the other half of the blanket around her and snuggled into her own body heat, thinking about tomorrow night and, on that note, fell asleep.

CHAPTER 7

Hank always kept a key hidden under the light globe on the wall sconce just outside of her apartment. The long-legged figure in the long black cloak and hood retrieved the key and entered the apartment.

Suzie sniffed the air and quietly closed the door. She turned on the lamp near the sofa and walked to the spare bedroom that Hank used as an office. She turned on the tape recorder and listened to Hank's notes to herself on what information was available on the serial killings. When the notes had ended, she turned off the recorder and laughed at the paucity of factual information Hank had gathered. "Shit, you're not even a good investigative reporter." She laid her fingers on the record-play keys of the machine and then changed her mind. She opened the middle drawer of Hank's desk and took out a mahogany framed picture of Hank and Julian Grant. "You know, Henrietta, you're a gutless twat. Julian should never have married you. He needed somebody like me. Somebody who had drives equal to his own. He needed somebody whose cravings were never completely satisfied.

"You offered him a sterile, pristine existence with no compensations. It's no wonder he took so many lovers. He could have gotten a piece of ass anywhere, if that was what he wanted, but that was never enough for him. He never pretended to be anything but what he was...a man of excesses."

She opened the closet door and eyed Hank's clothes. She chose a navy-blue miniskirt and cream-colored blouse with a deep V neckline that Hank had bought the year before. They still had price tags on them. She put them on and studied her reflection in the mirror. "That's better," turning to admire her image from every angle. She applied a splash of orange lipstick to her sensuous mouth and smiled at herself in the mirror. "Soon, Henrietta, I'll have everything you've worked for and you'll have nothing. Before I'm finished, I'll even have Storm Andrews." She opened the window, laughed and tossed out the picture of Hank and Julian. She walked to the door, touching the furniture as she went. "Mine, all of it will be mine." She locked the apartment door and replaced the key before leaving by the fire tower stairs.

Just before dawn, Hank awoke suddenly with a stifling sense of foreboding. Something was wrong. Her senses were alerted but she was afraid to open her eyes. Slowly her eyes became acclimated to the murky charcoal gray that seemed to envelop the area. She moved her head slowly taking in her surroundings. Everything appeared as it had when she went to sleep…quiet. Molly seemed to be a little more restless than usual, moaning and thrashing about before settling down again into a deep slumber. It looked as though Max had not altered her position since Molly covered her with the blanket. Satisfied that nothing was amiss, she closed her eyes again and didn't stir until Molly shook her.

"Is anything wrong?"

"No. Just thought you and Max might be interested in gettin' something to eat."

"Did you wake Max?"

Molly winked. "I think she's got a hangover."

Hank suppressed a smile. Max was on her knees trying to fold the plastic drop cloth. She handed it to Molly.

"Keep it, Max. You'll need it to keep the dampness off your bones."

At the shelter, Max sat beside Ned.

Hank asked, "Did you make any money last night?"

Ned smiled. "I probably made twice as much as I would have, because Kappy never showed up." He dug into his pocket and pulled out a handful of coins. "Five dollars and sixty-five cents. There are still people who like to hear poetry. I'm going back tonight, maybe I can earn more." He put the coins in his pocket. "Max looks like she got some sleep last night."

"She did, in spite of herself." She took out a couple of aspirins and handed them to Max, who swallowed them without liquid.

"Hangover?"

Hank grinned. "You might say that. It was the only way to get her to unwind. She slept like a baby all night."

Ned chuckled and patted Hank's hand before he left for wherever he went during the day. Molly headed for the shopping areas and Max headed for anywhere that was going to be quiet so she could nurse her pounding head. Hank was the last to leave the shelter and walked into the arms of Mike Shaye.

"Where're you going, Hank?"

"No place in particular. What do you want, Shaye?"

"Want to know where you spent the night."

She held her breath. "Another one?"

He sneered, "Didn't you know?"

She thought, *There's something about this oaf that brings out the worst in me.*

"No. What is it I'm supposed to know?"

"I don't give a shit who you are, Hank, as far as I'm concerned you're just as much a suspect as any other bum on the street. Now where were you?"

"We spent the night on the River Drive in the Azalea Gardens."

"We?"

She tried to read what was behind those cold blue eyes, and what was in that black heart. "Yes, we, Molly, Maxine and me. We were together the whole night."

"How convenient. How cozy," he sneered.

"Look, you bastard, stop hassling me."

His eyes never left her face. "What you need is a good screwing and that can still happen, some dark night. What do you think of that?"

"I wouldn't try it, if I were you. Unless you don't mind having your balls served to you on a plate for breakfast." She pushed past him and headed for the park. She felt his eyes following her and did her best not to hurry, or to show any signs that he had frightened her.

At four o'clock there was no reason not to go to her apartment, take the steaks out of the freezer and maybe get a short nap before Storm came at seven. When she let herself in, she froze in her tracks. The light in the living room was on. "I could have sworn I turned that light off before I left the apartment," she said aloud. She shrugged and followed her usual ritual. She stripped, threw her clothes in the washer, poured a drink and took a shower, then lay across the bed and luxuriated in the comfort of a bed without lumps or dirt or the odor of stale urine.

She was awakened by the sound of someone knocking on the door. She slipped into a clean pair of jeans, a loose-fitting shirt and hurried to the door.

"Storm?"

"Who else were you expecting?"

She slid the bolt and opened the door. As he passed, she almost choked with the malodorous trail he left behind.

"I would say you were ripe."

"You didn't exactly smell like a bouquet of flowers when I was following you yesterday."

"Give me your clothes and I'll toss them in the washer. You'll have to wrap yourself in a towel until your things are dry."

To her amazement, he stripped in front of her. His eyes never left her face. He was daring her to look at his naked body. He dropped the dirty clothes on the floor at his feet. She knelt to pick them up, studying the contours and angles of him as she stood up.

"Well?"

The word jogged her out of her trance. "Well, what?"

"Where's the bathroom?"

Hank got a look at the two of them in the hall mirror and began laughing. She pointed toward the bedroom.

"Through the bedroom and to the left."

"You can afford to laugh. You washed the stench off." He turned into the bedroom. She held his clothes away from her until she dropped them in the washer. She took frozen broccoli out of the freezer and a box of fettucini out of the cupboard. When she turned around Storm was standing in the doorway with a towel wrapped around his middle. He took the steaks from the counter, where they had defrosted.

"You take care of everything else, I'll do the steaks. How do you like yours?"

"Medium rare."

He smiled and for the first time, those steel-gray eyes sparkled. "I feel like I haven't eaten in weeks."

"Where have you been eating? You've lost a lot of weight."

"Whatever shelter I was closest to is where I ate. A couple of times I sat across from you. You've really studied your street people. I wouldn't have been able to tell the difference. You have all their mannerisms down pat. You never looked up. In fact, the times I did see you, you never spoke to anyone. I have to admire you. I didn't think you could stick it out but you have." He fixed himself a scotch and water before he turned the steaks. She watched him out of the corner of her eye. He was Greek all the way. Damn, he had a body like Adonis. He looked up from the broiler and caught her watching him.

"Your fettucini is boiling over."

That was enough to bring her out of her world of secret admiration. First things first.

He wolfed down all of his steak and half of hers before he sat back in his chair with a smile of contentment.

"Thank you. I feel human again. A shower, a great meal, good booze, and a pretty woman for company. What more could I possibly want?"

"If that's all you want out of life you're an extremely simple person.

Somehow the pieces don't fit. You're much more complex than you're letting on. Why do I get the feeling you're toying with me?"

He adopted a look of surprise. "Moi?"

She stood up, poured some cognac and held the bottle up. He shook his head and picked up what was left of his scotch and drained the glass. She took his glass, refilled it and walked into the living room carrying both glasses. He sat across from her in the lounge chair.

"So," she tried to sound casual, "who was the man that got killed last night?"

He put his glass down, studying her like she was something under a microscope. "Who said there was a murder last night?"

Hank didn't try to hide her exasperation and told him about her meeting with Shaye. "You know this guy started in on me the first time he saw me. Why?"

"Why? He thinks you're a likely suspect."

Hank looked away. "And you? Do you think I'm the killer?"

"I don't usually answer a question with a question, but do you think I would be here with you, alone, if I thought you were the killer? Did you see a gun in the dirty clothes you washed? You know damn well I couldn't hide one when I was buck-ass naked. I've got to have a talk with Mike. What else did he tell you?"

"Nothing. Does he know I'm a reporter?"

"I told him. I thought maybe it would keep him off your back."

"Obviously, it didn't work. He climbs all over me whenever he gets the chance. What the hell did I ever do to him?"

Storm chewed on his bottom lip before answering. "The only thing I can think of is that you resemble his ex-wife. She whored around on him. It tore him apart. The divorce was ugly."

"Yeah, well, I had a dirty divorce too but I'm not taking it out on the rest of the world."

"Aren't you?" Storm stood up and stretched, then walked into the alcove on the other side of the kitchen that served as a laundry area and pulled his clothes out of the dryer. "Is your taste in men as good as your taste in booze?"

"I don't know. I haven't tasted a man in quite a while." When she looked up, his gray eyes were soft and he studied her face, or more specifically, her mouth.

"It's a shame we don't have time to explore that situation. I'll be doing a lot of thinking about it."

It was difficult to see if he was smiling under all that facial hair but there was a touch of amusement in his voice.

"How did you get into the building? You need a key to get into the lobby."

"I used one of my many talents on the door to the fire tower."

She opened a drawer where she kept her flatware and handed him a key. "Use this. It's a new invention...called a key. I'll get my street clothes and head out too."

He walked to the door, turned and walked back, stopping only when her breasts were pressed against his chest. Slowly, deliberately, he lowered his mouth so that their lips barely touched. He pulled back slightly. She slid her arms around his neck and pulled his head down so that their lips met again. His arms tightened around her, pulling her body to him. His heart was pumping as rapidly as her own. Within seconds he stripped both of them and she could feel the coolness of the floor tiles against her back. Angrily, his mouth closed over hers and his hands slid under her, arching her back so that his penetration was deep and slow. His nostrils flared slightly as his breathing became more labored and the rhythmic push-pull of his body stepped up the pace. Both bodies were soaked with perspiration. Hank no longer felt the coolness of the floor tiles. Everything was steamy. He no longer needed to pull her hips up to meet his. Her back arched on its own, answering a need that both of them felt. He kept watching the expression on her face. It was only when he was sure of her satisfaction that he allowed his control to falter. His eyes rolled back as his body responded to an intermittent spasm. He shook his head from side to side and whispered, "This wasn't supposed to happen. Damn...it wasn't supposed to...happen." Still short of breath, he knelt in an upright position. His eyes scanned her body. "Damn you, Henrietta," his voice was low, controlled, "that was not supposed to happen."

It was only then, she realized he was more than angry, he was red-hot mad.

She was totally confused by his anger, so she countered, "Damn you, Storm, you're no different from Shaye. But you have to admit it was assuring to know you weren't going to end up with a knife in your back. You had your respite...now get the hell out of here and go back to your damn job."

She pushed him away and stood up. She switched on the light in the bathroom, slammed the door and turned on the shower. When she came out again, he was gone.

"Okay, Hank," she said aloud, "you wondered if he was married. There's your answer. Damn, damn, damn." Slowly she dressed for the streets, refilled the brandy bottle, turned off the lights and left by the tower stairs.

In spite of herself the tingling sensation she felt with him continued and she had to admit she enjoyed him. This one night with Storm was better than all the nights of sex with Julian Grant. Somehow, sex after marriage had become uninteresting and mechanical. Julian had to fantasize in order to have an orgasm, thus his interest in young boys and girls. Sex had to be kinky for him. She wasn't into that.

Sex with Storm was exciting, challenging. On this note she went to sleep under the protection of the bushes and trees in the Azalea Gardens.

The next afternoon she found a newspaper in the trash and fished it out. The front page gave ample space to the sensational headline, *Poet-Killer Strikes Fifth Victim.* The verse found beside the body was a quote from *Julius Caesar. Caesar said to the soothsayer, 'The ides of March are come'; who answered him calmly, 'Yes they are come, but they are not past.'* The victim was Jonah A. (Kappy) Kaplan, age forty, a derelict residing on the streets of Philadelphia. Kaplan, like the four previous victims, was stabbed in the back eight times. The body was discovered by city employees, clearing debris in Fairmount Park.

When the name Kappy finally registered, she hurried to find Ned. No one had seen him. She couldn't find Molly or Max. She thought maybe she didn't have the good sense to get away from the danger that apparently frightened her friends. She smiled to herself. Three months ago she wouldn't have classified the Streeters as people, let alone as friends, but they had become friends whether or not her subconscious approved.

Two days passed before she saw Maxine and Molly in the park.

"I've been looking for you two. Is everything okay?"

Max merely shook her head and sat down. Hank looked at Molly for an explanation.

"Ned's in the hospital. Intensive Care. The nurses got tired of us hangin' round and kicked us out."

Hank looked puzzled. "What happened?"

"What happened?" Molly paced, kicking at the dried grass. "Mike Shaye is what happened, that's what." He's been doggin' Ned ever since they first picked him up. We saw Ned at the hospital. That was before Shaye got the security guard to kick us out. The way Ned looked, somebody worked him over. He had a heart attack while he was in lockup."

"How bad is it, Molly?"

Molly patted Max's hand. "One of the night nurses came out and told us he was respondin' to the medicine and it looked like he was gonna make it, so we came back here. We looked for you to see if you could get him outta jail again but we couldn't find ya. Where were ya?"

"Molly, I can't remember where I was three hours ago. You think I remember where I was several nights ago? It was two days before I found out about Kappy. That's when I started looking for the three of you. Why did they take Ned? He had already passed the lie detector test. Did they book him?"

"The police feel they don't owe us nothin', so they don't tell us nothin'."

Maxine watched as a police van cruised by. "Somebody has to stop Shaye. Why don't the police do something about him? I can't believe nobody knew that Ned was beaten. Aren't doctors supposed to report things like that?" Her shoulders slumped forward and although there was no sound, the silent sobbing told its own story. When she raised her head, the tears had washed a clean ridge down her cheeks. "They can do whatever they want with us. Who's to stop them? Us? We're insignificant. We're nonentities. If you don't exist how can anyone care what happens to you?"

Hank was scared. This fragile creature was teetering on the edge of sanity. She put her arms around Max. *Tears can be a good catharsis,* she thought.

Hank wondered if Ned knew that Max was in love with him. She wondered if Max knew. It was evident by looking at Molly that she had guessed as much but now was not the time for discussion. Fortunately the days were warmer but nights were still cool, not really cold, but almost. They took their usual places in the Azalea Gardens and Hank brought out the replenished bottle of brandy, which delighted Molly. They teased Max into drinking with them and after a while she was going gulp for gulp with them. Once again they helped Max onto her own blanket, covered her and prepared their own sleeping spots for the night.

Once again Hank was haunted by the specter of her dreams, chasing her into a heart-pumping wakefulness. She turned over. Max was gone. After what seemed an eternity, she heard someone approaching. She closed her eyes pretending to be asleep. Through her dark long lashes she saw Max carrying an almost empty roll of toilet tissue back to her blanket. She put the tissue back in the plastic bag, covered herself and went off to sleep again. Hank followed suit. It was getting light and Molly shook her.

"Hank. Wake up."

Bleary eyed she propped herself up on one elbow. "What's up?"

"We gotta get Max outta here. Look down the River Drive."

Hank turned, following her gaze. What she saw were the flashing red and blue lights on top of police cars. She scampered to her feet and stuffed her belongings into her canvas bag while Molly tried to arouse Max. Max sat up, a confused look on her face. Molly was saying, "Hurry, Maxie, we gotta get outta here."

"Why?"

"Squad cars down the Drive. They're advertising."

Max spun around, looking for the flashes of light.

"Now, what? Oh, God, I hate mornings."

Hank picked up Max's bag and Molly helped her to her feet.

"Let's hate mornings up on Market Street, it's safer than hating them here."

"It's too far," Molly said. "We gotta chance it on Spring Garden Street. Let's head for that Doctors Society. It's easy to remember and it's away from here."

Max was bent over. "You go, I'll catch up."

Hank spun around, "No way. What's wrong?"

"Diarrhea. I've had it most of the night."

"Hurry, we'll wait for you."

She fished out the toilet tissue from her bag and disappeared. They waited for what seemed hours, actually it was only about five minutes, then they crossed over to Spring Garden Street and walked as close to the buildings as possible. They came to Twenty-First Street and settled down against the County Medical Society building.

Max began to shake. "What do you think happened?"

"Another murder, I hope," said Hank.

Both women stared at her in disbelief. It was only then she realized how it sounded. She shrugged her shoulders. "It's bad for the guy that got killed, if there was a murder but it would surely clear Ned, wouldn't it?"

Max brushed her hand across her forehead. "Guess I didn't think about it that way. You're right. It would clear him, wouldn't it?"

"When he's hooked up to all those monitors in the Intensive Care Unit, he has the best alibi in the world. He's not even going to fart without somebody being aware of it. I don't know, maybe we're getting excited about nothing. It could have been an accident down at the bridge on the drive. We're just assuming it's another murder. We'll find out soon enough. Max? How's your gut?"

"Giving me fits. I have to find some place to go again."

"Walk over to Eighteenth Street, to Community College. It should be open by now. At least you can go in comfort and you won't have to use your own toilet paper."

"Good idea. Molly suggested we meet behind the Rodin Museum tonight."

"Too close. If there was a murder, the cops will be combing that area for the next few nights. Let's meet at Thirtieth Street Station."

Hank walked to the park and claimed a bench for the rest of the morning. It began to drizzle and she dug into her canvas bag and took out the piece of clear plastic Molly had given her and tented it over herself, rather than find a sheltered place. She curled her legs under her to keep dry, and sipped some coffee from the thermos, wishing there was toast to go with it.

She was absorbed in fitting the bits and pieces of the murder puzzle into a mental picture but the information she had was too sketchy and nothing seemed to fit.

She was aware of shuffling sounds along the concrete path but paid no attention. Her senses were alerted when the shuffling stopped. She looked through rain-streaked plastic at the approaching figure of a man in dirty denims with a frayed hole just below the left knee. His jacket was missing all of its buttons and his crumpled brown felt hat was pulled down to his eyebrows. Her heart raced at the sight of him. "Storm? You look terrible." She saw a flash of white teeth through the matted facial hair.

The deep tones of his voice were almost a caress. "And I always speak so well of you."

She held out her thermos. "Coffee?"

He shook his head. "Do you happen to have brandy in that bottle you carry around?"

She pulled out the bottle and handed it to him. He unscrewed the cap and tilted the bottle, swallowing several times before handing it back.

"Share your tent?"

She moved over, put some newspapers on the wet bench and centered the plastic to cover both of them.

"Were you in the Azalea Gardens last night?"

"No," she lied. "We were over at the County Med. Why?"

"Then you don't know what happened?"

"Why do I get the feeling you're going to tell me there was another murder?"

He hesitated, studying the expression on her face. "Hank, I want you off the streets. In view of what's happened, I'm not convinced you can take care of yourself."

"I've covered almost every kind of crime from a kidnapping to a drug bust. It can't be any more dangerous than that." She saw concern registered in his eyes, concern that wasn't there before. "What's happened to make you think I can't handle it?"

He reached over and touched her cheek with his fingers. "There was a double murder last night."

She sucked in her breath and held it before allowing it to escape in a steady stream of silent air.

"My God."

"Yeah. Mine too," he said.

"Street people?"

"A guy named O'Neill, Terrence O'Neill. Know him?"

"I don't think so. The name doesn't mean anything. Who was the other guy?"

"The other guy…was a woman."

CHAPTER 8

Pam McGowan wrote the latest information on the profile chart hanging on the closet door and turned to face Storm Andrews.

"It seems the killer has a way of gleaning information about his victims prior to their deaths. The verses seem to be apropos, to the point of having been matched with something meaningful in the life of the victim, or at least what the killer thinks is meaningful. Could he have anticipated that the girl you call Gail Praxon would be with O'Neill on the night of the murder?"

"I doubt it." Storm studied the manner in which Doctor McGowan categorized the information he gave her. "Why?"

"The killer knew a lot about the Praxon girl. About the man too. He knew she was addicted to drugs. If he didn't know she would be there, he knew enough about her to quote Dickens' *A Tale of Two Cities* and he had to do it in a hurry. The handwriting on this copy you brought was scrawled hurriedly. Look at the difference when you compare it with the one left with O'Neill's body. This quote isn't judgmental like the others. It's almost apologetic. It was like he was saying Gail Praxon had nowhere to turn . That her only release was death and he provided her with that."

Storm studied the handwriting and the verse on the chart. *It's a far, far better thing that I do than I have ever done; it is a far, far better rest that I go to than I have ever known.* "You're right, Doc. It does sound apologetic. Especially if you compare it to the one left with O'Neill. *Cowards die many times before their deaths. The Valiant never taste of death but once. Of all the wonders that I yet have heard, it seems to me most strange that men should fear, seeing that death, a necessary end, will come when it will come.*"

The telephone intercom buzzed. Doctor McGowan picked it up. "Yes, Nicole?"

She turned to Storm. "It's for you. Police lab."

"Yeah, Andrews here." He listened and nodded. "Send a copy of the report to my office. Thanks, appreciate it." He turned back to Doc. "We just got some data on O'Neill. We sent a copy of his fingerprints over the police wire. He was a fugitive, wanted for questioning in a string of hotel fires in Chicago." Storm picked up his battered felt hat. "What do you think, Doc?"

"I think we're dealing with unbridled anger in a deep-seated, disturbed personality. He, or she, isn't going to stop until perceived wrongs, real or imagined, have been righted."

"I'd better get back on the streets. Incidentally, how is Mike Shaye doing?"

"He resents me. Not because I'm a psychiatrist but because I'm a woman. At least he's keeping his appointments this time around."

The rain continued for three days. Storm wandered through the park looking for Hank. Instinctively, he headed for the bench they had shared a few days earlier. She was sitting in almost the same position as the last time they were together.

Hank was preoccupied writing some illegible scrawls on a piece of paper. Storm looked over her shoulder and frowned at the markings. "Are you still here from the last time I saw you?"

She gasped and spun around to face him. "You scared the hell out of me." She moved over and held the plastic cover up for him to sit next to her. "I think we've all been fine-tuned since the Praxon woman got killed."

"I can see that. You're as jumpy as a thoroughbred in a storm…no pun intended." Storm Andrews wasn't sure he liked the way this woman affected him. He realized he had difficulty dealing with the antagonistic pull of his feelings when she was near. "What's all that chicken scratching on the paper?"

Her eyes followed his gaze to the piece of paper in her hand. She smiled. "It's called shorthand. With the advent of dictating equipment, not many people use this old-fashioned method anymore, but it comes in handy when you want to write notes to yourself without others knowing what you've said."

He put his arm around the back of the bench. "It would be much simpler if you went back to your apartment."

"We've been through this before."

"But women weren't getting bumped off before. The situation has changed."

"Couldn't it have been a copycat murder?"

"I don't think so, our killer has a flare for poetry and verse, remember? Why do you think it could be a copycat crime?"

"Well, it happened so far away from all the others. The news media has been sensationalizing the serial killings, maybe some nut wants to cash in on the fear that's being generated."

"It's our killer all right. I think the Praxon woman got it because O'Neill was making out with her when he got it."

"What makes you say that?"

"His pants were down around his ankles when we found him. He was probably on top, which gave the killer a perfect target. Gail Praxon had to have seen the murderer. In addition to her own blood, she was spattered with O'Neill's blood. The killer couldn't leave a witness to identify him…or her. They found Praxon's body about a hundred yards away."

"If she could run away, why couldn't he?"

"A broad with her skirt up can run a lot faster than a guy with his pants down. From the marks on the grass, she must have fallen several times before the killer caught up with her."

Hank shook her head in disbelief. "Was she stabbed in the back too?"

"No, her stab wounds were in the chest and face. Apparently she turned to fight off her attacker."

"What about blood? The attacker must have been covered with it. Somebody must have seen him." Hank was making mental entries to the notes in her hand.

"Could have gone to the river and washed off the blood. We're talking about a diabolically clever criminal mind that leaves nothing to chance."

"You're probably right, otherwise there wouldn't have been a verse left with the girl's body."

"That was probably a spur of the moment quotation. Hurried, but appropriate."

Hank laughed. "You're getting better at identifying the verses."

"I'm not as proficient as you but then I'm not a writer. I remembered that verse because whenever I hear it, I think of Ronald Coleman as an unshaven, heroic Sydney Carton, waiting for his turn to embrace Madam la Guillotine."

Hank shivered involuntarily and Storm looked around before he put his arm around her.

"I need to see you again," he said.

She felt her heart trying to thump its way out of her chest. She knew she should say no but she couldn't. She wanted him.

"Tomorrow is Sunday. There's never much happening on Sundays. My apartment, early afternoon? Maybe we can stay all night?"

Again, the flash of white teeth in the midst of facial hair. "I'll try to get there around two o'clock." He reached down and pinched her backside, then he was gone.

For a few moments she was lost in the memory of their last encounter. When she looked up, Molly was standing beside her. *Damn,* she thought, *we got caught.*

"Hi, Molly." Hank lifted the other half of the plastic cover. "Sit. Share my tent. Better you than the asshole that just left."

"Who was he?"

"Damned if I know. Asked me to share my shelter with him and I moved over and gave him half of my tent. I'm being altruistic, so he propositioned me. I told him to get lost, he rewarded my generosity by pinching my ass. Bastard."

Molly laughed and sat beside her.

"Maybe the shelters should put saltpeter in the food. Women on the streets have been screwed enough by life, we shouldn't have to worry about getting screwed by men too. Hank…"

Without answering she reached into her bag and pulled out the bottle and handed it to her. Molly took a swig and handed it back.

"Thanks. It's not cold but these old bones sure don't like damp days."

"Did you hear anything about what happened on the drive that night?"

"I was talkin' to Benny and he said there was two murders that night. He wasn't sure but he thought he heard somebody say one of 'em was a woman."

Hank feigned surprise. "A woman?"

"That's what Benny said. They was killed while they was screwin'."

Hank was developing a healthy respect for the Streeters' communication system and Benny seemed to be the pivot of that system.

"Did the killer leave another note?"

"Yeah, but Benny can't read or write so even if he saw the note he couldn't tell what it said. Benny said the same thing you said. It proves Ned didn't commit no murders."

"How's Ned doing?"

"Max went over to the hospital this morning. She was going to look for that nurse who was so nice to us. Maybe they'll let her in to see him for a couple of minutes. I hope so, she's been frettin' about him and nothin' will satisfy her until she can see for herself that he's gonna be okay."

The rain continued into Sunday but was tolerable because Hank knew she would spend the day in her own apartment. Closing the door meant shutting out the poverty, the tension, the uncertainty of the streets and the constant threat of death. It was coming alive again, sleeping without concern about whether or not she would survive until morning.

A shower went a long way toward making her feel human again and Storm's arms would go a long way toward making her... feel again. Suddenly she realized she had not felt much of anything for some time. It was like living in a vacuum. She slipped into a robe and began drying her hair when she heard him at the door. He was pocketing the key when she entered the living room. He carried a large paper bag.

"What's that?"

"Food and booze. It's easier for me to ask one of the guys at headquarters to get this stuff for me than it is for you to try to go shopping without being seen by one of the Streeters. I think Molly saw us at the park yesterday."

"She did. I told her after I was good to you I got propositioned for my efforts, as well as a pinched ass."

"Did she buy it?"

"I think so. She also knew about the two murders."

"How the hell do they find out these things so fast?"

"Well, you know the fastest communication in the world, telephone, television, telegraph and tell a woman."

"They know things as quickly as the police."

"Quicker. Benny knew about the murders and that one of the victims was a woman."

"Benny, huh? Maybe Benny's information is firsthand."

"He's not your man. Benny can't read or write. Are the verses typed?"

"No, handwritten."

"Then it should be simple enough to get handwriting samples from your suspects."

"What suspects? The only suspect we had was cleared by the latest murders. Besides, he wasn't a south paw."

"The murderer is left handed? How do you know that? Hell, that should eliminate quite a few of the street people."

"Your friend, Max, is a south paw."

"You can't possibly suspect Max. She cries if somebody swats a fly. She could never take a human life."

"That's what they said about Lizzie Borden."

"Seriously, Storm, I know she can't commit murder."

"How much do you know about her, Hank? For instance, did you know she was in a mental institution?"

Hank held her breath. "What's that got to do with anything? There are quite a few mental patients on the streets, there are people who were on some kind of medication to control their anxieties. They were released because some goody-two-shoes said to confine them to mental institutions was depriving them of their civil liberties. It didn't make any difference that those patients had no way to look after themselves."

"You're evading the issue. I asked if you knew Max had been in a mental institution?"

"Yes, I knew," she whispered. "Ned let it slip. Why was she institutionalized?"

"Probably so that her husband could run with his playmates; it looks like somebody gave her hallucinogenic drugs and she tried to fly from the roof of her house in Long Island. Authorities think her husband gave her the drugs but there was no way to prove it. Anyway, he kept her in a mental hospital for three years. Long after the doctors said she was okay. When he divorced her he stopped making payments to the sanitarium and they discharged her. She had no family and no place to go. She ended up on the streets. That was seven years ago. It may be that all men are a threat to her and the only way to eliminate the threat is to eliminate the men. She's well educated. According to hospital records, she would sit and read poetry for hours. The potential is there. Hank, she fits the profile."

"That's ridiculous. You're forgetting one very important point."

"What's that?"

"She was with Molly and me when most of the murders happened. So, according to your logic, I fit that profile as much as Max does."

"We're aware of that." He started emptying the bag. Fresh broccoli, potatoes for baking, a frozen cherry pie, a pair of cornish game hens, a bottle of Cordon Bleu and a bottle of Haig and Haig.

"You said I wasn't a suspect anymore."

"I said I didn't believe you committed the murders. That was my personal opinion, not an official statement."

He turned her around so that he was facing her.

"Why the hell do you think I was so uptight the last time I was here? You don't go around screwing suspects, it's called compromising your situation." He looked away.

"Is that why you were so angry that night?"

He held her face between his hands, his eyes caressed her for a small eternity. "I'm not supposed to ache for someone who is considered to be a suspect. I'm not supposed to remember how you looked, naked and full of desire for me. I'm not supposed to be here now. I'm not supposed to—"

His mouth sought hers hungrily. His hands untied her robe and explored her responsive body. The rest was like a dream sequence. He carried her to the bedroom and placed her on the bed. Then began a mutual exploration with hands, lips, bodies and souls.

Afterward she lay in his arms, not feeling used as she had before but feeling loved and loving in return. They showered together, made love again, prepared dinner, made love again and for the first time since her divorce, in the morning, she awoke in the arms of a man. He pulled her on top of him, kissing her eyes, her cheeks, her mouth. "Please get off the streets, Hank."

She pulled back a little so she could study the expression on his face. He was sincere. He really wanted her off the streets.

"I can't, Storm. I'm a writer and this is the only way I can gather the information I need, to write my book."

"I can supply you with the information."

"It's not the same, Storm. I have to write the book from my point of view, not yours. Look, maybe the killer's appetite has been appeased, maybe he'll stop now."

"Serial killers don't just stop. They may take a breather to let things cool down but you can bet our killer is still out there and soon his compulsion will make him restless. Whatever is driving him hasn't gone away and it will surface again. You can make book on it. His anger hasn't even begun to peter out. The bad part is we have so little to go on. Either that or we don't know how to interpret what we have. One thing we have now we didn't have before is his or her approximate height."

Hank was intrigued. Not only was this material for her book, it gave her insight into this orderly, complex, controlled, sensitive man who seemed possessed with a melancholia that made her want to hold him, comfort him.

"How could you possibly arrive at such a conclusion?"

"We couldn't do this until the Praxon woman was killed. When she turned to fight off her predator, the stab wounds entered the body in an almost parallel line to the ground, which means the assailant was the approximate height of the victim. Probably around five foot six to five eight. Which gives more credence to the possibility that it's a woman." He shifted his position. "Somehow, the number eight and the age of the victims are part of this overall puzzle."

"What about the fact that all these people are homeless? Doesn't that fit into the puzzle?"

"I don't think so. I think it's just convenient because they rarely travel in groups, or even in pairs for that matter. It's important that the victim be alone and dead when the killer leaves. Being a loner means no witnesses. Many Streeters have chosen to be assimilated into that lost society where there are no vestiges of a former life." He stopped talking when he saw the hint of a smile on her lips. "What's so funny?"

Her smile broadened into a grin. "You don't look like the type to think things out in such detail. At first I thought of you as being disorganized. Now that I'm getting to know you, I realize there is a definite order to your thinking."

The gray eyes seemed to penetrate into her thought processes. "Natura non facit saltum." He laughed at the puzzled expression on her face. "It means, order is heaven's first law."

She blushed. "You're also a lot smarter than I gave you credit for. What about the weapon?"

"The weapon has a double edge. Both edges are razor sharp."

"You mean like a letter opener?"

"What would make you think of a letter opener?"

"I saw one the other day while I was walking. It was in the display window of a shop on Chestnut Street that sells leather goods. It had a long double-edged blade and the handle was covered in leather. The only knives I'm familiar with are the kind you use in the kitchen. I don't know if a letter opener would be sharp enough to penetrate flesh and bone."

"It could be if it was properly sharpened. We were thinking along the lines of a stiletto...but a heavy letter opener would also serve the purpose."

Hank watched him as he put on his freshly laundered rags.

"Hank, do you have a sister?"

"Not unless my mother lied to me. To the best of my knowledge I was the first and only child. Why?"

"The night before last, down on the waterfront, I saw a woman who looked a lot like you. I think she was a prostitute. She goes by the name of Suzie. She seemed to be a little taller than you but then she wore with a miniskirt and spike heels. She was all over one of the Streeters. Then I realized she wasn't giving away free samples. If he wanted it badly enough he could steal the money. I'm sure most of the men know where to reach her. The resemblance was striking."

"I don't recall seeing anyone like that. Come to think of it, the day Duke raped the young girl, he pointed to me and said I looked different from the way I looked the night before. I thought he was high on booze or drugs. Now I'm curious."

Storm kissed her when he left the apartment. "Don't let anything happen to you. I think you're pretty special."

For days, she felt the warm glow of their lovemaking and his parting words echoed in her ears. She had something to look forward to, something to wish for, something to dream about.

She also had something to worry about.... Who was Suzie?"

CHAPTER 9

Storm Andrews staggered along Arch Street, carrying a pint bottle of caramel-colored liquid wrapped in newspaper. At Second Street, he turned north, then lifted the bottle to his parched lips and swallowed. The battered felt hat was pulled down to shade his face from the afternoon sun. Mumbling to himself, he swayed and held on to the side of the Betsy Ross House to keep himself in an upright position. Unsteadily, weaving a path the short distance to Elfreth's Alley, he turned east and zigzagged along the narrow cobblestone street and unceremoniously squatted on the steps of a restored colonial house. The newspaper covering fell away from the bottle and Storm picked it up just as a man's form stood between him and the sun.

"Hey, fella, how 'bout a nip outta that bottle, huh?"

Without looking up, Storm passed the bottle to the Streeter, who quickly guzzled two mouthfuls before forcefully spraying the next mouthful on the sidewalk.

"Shit," he said and wiped his mouth on the back of his hand. "What the hell is that stuff?"

Storm laughed and retrieved his bottle. "It's called iced tea without the ice, Mike, you should try it sometime."

Mike Shaye sat on the step beside him. "Got any of the real stuff?"

"You know I never drink on duty," Storm said.

"You could have fooled me. I watched you stagger all the way from Arch Street. I thought maybe the streets finally got to you."

Storm scanned the area. When he was satisfied no one was watching them, he asked, "What did the lab come up with on the Praxon case?"

Mike leaned over to tie his shoe. "There were some fibers in the wounds on her face that didn't come from anything she was wearing. Pieces of navy blue thread, a combination of cotton and polyester. It doesn't tell us very much. It could have come from a man's or a woman's lightweight clothes. But I'll bet it's a woman's clothes and they're probably spattered with blood."

"You're getting bogged down in your own hatred," Storm said as he studied Mike Shaye's face. "How are you getting along with Doctor McGowan?"

Mike's upper lip curled back in a snarl. "She's okay I guess…for a woman."

"She's working up a profile of the killer. She thinks there could be a strong possibility that the murderer is a woman."

"She said that?" Shaye asked. "She really thinks the killer is a woman?"

"I didn't say that, Mike, I said Doc thinks that possibility exists."

"Same thing."

Storm shook his head. "I'm looking for a woman called Suzie. Ever hear of her?"

"Yeah. Saw her a couple of times, why?"

"Curious," Storm said. "She was seen with one of the murdered men the night before he was killed."

"She's a whore."

"How do you know that, Mike?"

"She's been playing up to me. Told me she'd love to get her hands on my shlong." He patted the zipper of his pants. "Guess she knows talent when she sees it."

"What do you know about her?"

"What's to know? I told you, she's a whore." Her name's Suzanne Hoffman. I think she's a recent import from Chicago. That's all I got on her."

"Do you think she resembles Hank Castle?" Storm asked.

"You've got to be kidding. No way.… Well, maybe, when you first see Suzie, you might think they were related. They both have almond-shaped brown eyes but that's where the similarity ends."

"Okay, Mike. See if you can get me some background information on Suzie Hoffman. It may be just coincidence that she appears on the streets just when the serial killings start. It may be nothing but it's a place to start. I'll be in touch."

Mike Shaye straightened his back and looked down the street at nothing in particular. "Yeah, it's also the time that Hank hit the streets. When we questioned her she had only been on the streets three weeks when the first bum got knocked off."

There was no response from Storm Andrews. Mike shrugged and turned his back to his friend as he said, "See ya."

Three weeks after Ned's discharge from the hospital, the killings had stopped and Max began feeling secure again. She appeared wherever Ned was, to assure herself he wasn't going to drop dead on the streets. A bit of warm weather was all Molly needed to pull her neck up from between her shoulders.

Memorial Day brought people out in droves to picnic in the park. Hank chose the waterfront. The brandy was gone but the bottle came in handy for carrying water and although it wasn't cold, it was satisfying. She sat on the grass watching couples walk arm in arm along the Plaza of Penn's Landing. *One is a lonely number*, she thought. Solitude covered her like a shroud. Everybody had somebody. Everybody, except the street people. For them, there was no comfort. She wondered what drove them on. Theirs was a lonely lot, an unadaptable state. Whatever social intercourse there was could only be enjoyed vicariously from a distance.

Hank was brought out of her reverie by a soft droning sound. She looked for the source and about twenty feet away saw a newspaper-covered Streeter snoring contentedly.

A group of teenagers chose a spot several yards from where Hank sat, placed a portable stereo on the ground and turned up the volume. A pretty, dark-haired girl took several uncertain steps. Hank saw she was having trouble focusing and the odor of whiskey carried to where she sat. The girl swayed forward pointing to Hank. "You stink. Why don't you crawl back into the sewer. You're polluting our air."

Hank looked up without lifting her head. "Go home, brat, before I part your hair with a bottle." Hank reached into her canvas bag and pulled out the bottle of water and gripped it around the neck. One of the boys ran over and pulled the girl away.

"What's the matter with you, Jean, are you crazy? What if she's the nut who's been killing people down here?"

Hank was standing, the bottle still in her hand. The group hurriedly collected their belongings and moved upriver. Hank shook her head. "Ignorant bitch," she said. She watched them for several minutes, until her resentment was under control.

"Don't let them get to you, Hank," said a voice behind her.

"Max. I thought you were going to the park. Sit awhile."

"We shouldn't have to take that," Max said.

"I wanted to take that little bitch over my knee and smack her ass. Drunk as a sailor on liberty. Where the hell are her parents?" Hank unclenched her fist.

Max patted Hank's hand. "I see the fight hasn't quite gone out of you yet.

Give it a little more time. After a while the remarks bounce off like rain off a waxed car."

Hank bit her lower lip. "I'll never be able to accept ridicule."

"A great man once said, 'I have endured a great deal of ridicule without much malice; and have received a great deal of kindness, not quite free from ridicule. I am used to it.'" Maxine smiled. "He was very wise. Unfortunately, he wasn't appreciated in his time."

"I'm not familiar with that quote."

"Abraham Lincoln."

Hank saw an expression of wonder on Max's face and turned to see what she was looking at. Coming into view was a two-masted schooner. Amid the tears, the hint of a smile played around her lips. Max watched the stars and stripes waving at the rear of the ship. Max' face reflected unbridled pride, happiness, a sense of dignity and a joy of living that had been hidden and for a brief moment had unfurled for Hank to see, then quickly buried itself again. She stood up, shifting the bag to her other hand. "See you," Max said and walked up the riverbank.

Hank pulled the bottle out of the canvas bag and took a long drink. As she was replacing the cap she saw a shadow beside her and heard a graveled male voice.

"Give a guy a drink, will you, doll?"

She handed the bottle to him. He coughed and Hank felt a spray as he spat the water out in a fine mist. "Shit...it's water." The Streeter thrust the bottle back into her hand. "Lady, ever see what that damn stuff does to pipes?" He sounded angry. "Got anything stronger?"

Hank shook her head, tilted the bottle so that a small amount ran over her face.

"That stuff will rust yer outside as well as yer inside." He sat on the grass, looking at the ship. "Too bad this ain't two hundred years ago. I would have liked going to sea."

With the fetid odor that emanated from him, Hank would have thought water would have been his bitter enemy. She shielded her eyes from the sun, pretending to look downriver at the other boats entering the port. She wanted to see who this foul-smelling, non-water-drinking derelict was. One of his shoes was wrapped with a piece of rag to keep the sole from flapping. That was all she could see clearly. She got the impression he had a lot of facial hair. He moved around her so that the sun was behind her. She looked up into laughing gray eyes and gasped. "Storm!"

He looked over the river toward New Jersey. "Easy, girl."

She looked around to see how close they were to other people, especially Streeters. She looked for the snoring derelict under the newspaper but he was gone.

"That was me under the papers. You had me worried for a while this afternoon. I was convinced you were going to conk that kid over the head with your bottle."

Hank smiled and looked away. "Her head was never in danger. My aim would have been farther south."

He laughed. "At least you have the grace to blush."

She fanned her face with her hand and wrinkled her nose. "Would you at least have some consideration and sit down wind from me?"

"Pretty bad, isn't it? I slept in an alley last night. When I woke up this morning, some bastard had urinated on the ground uphill from me. I thought I had wet my pants until I saw the flow. The sun dried it. That's when the smell really got putrid."

"Meet me back at the apartment? I'll throw you and the clothes in the washer."

"I can't, but thanks. There are a lot of people in town today and I've got to keep moving, just in case. Be careful."

Hank enjoyed the rest of the afternoon on the waterfront undisturbed. She began putting a mental outline together for the book before she drifted off to sleep. Her stomach told her when it was time to wake up.

Molly and Maxine saved a place in line at the shelter. They agreed to go to the Azalea Gardens, which were now thick with rich leaves. The night was filled with sounds of laughter, loud radios, and traffic. Hank was sorry she slept in the afternoon because the swishing sounds as cars went by did little to promote sleep. She lay there listening to the night sounds and watched the stars twinkle whenever the breezes moved the leaves away from her line of vision. She found herself wondering if the stars she was seeing were still there or if they had fallen out of grace with whomever it was that kept the blinking cat's eyes up there, mocking the poor mortals who composed sonnets to those ethereal probing eyes. The bushes swayed as other Streeters shuffled their way along the paths looking for a place to sleep.

Somewhere between the shuffling, the snoring and star gazing she lapsed into a troubled sleep only to find herself running away from the black-robed, shadowy figure of her dreams. Finally, all sounds stopped and the eastern sky allowed a slight glow to caution the dawning of another day. In the twilight of waking Hank heard a lonely shuffling along the path just beside the bushes where she shared sleeping space with Molly and Max. She had an uncomfortable, somber, frightened feeling but could find no basis for it. She gave herself time to bring things into focus before sitting up. Hugging her knees, she waited for the uneasy feeling to pass. Her hands were trembling and she felt a chill in the warm pre-dawn air that cautioned her to stay where she was. She pulled some branches aside and saw the familiar form of Max, her back to Hank, obviously sleeping soundly.

Most Streeters had adapted to the nomadic life of the homeless. Max was different, vulnerable. All things considered she had fared well enough. At least to date, she had not been raped or mugged and she was still alive. The overhead lights on the drive went out and the city began to come alive again. Hank stretched and yawned and wished she could be anywhere but here.

She crossed to the other side of the footpath to wake Molly but she was up and gone. Max rolled over, opening one eye to confirm that it was indeed morning.

"I know, Max, you hate mornings."

She rubbed her eyes. "Anything that gets up this early should have wings. I think I must have died last night. The sound of traffic lulled me to sleep. Did you sleep okay?"

"Off and on. There was more than the usual number of people walking the path last night. I wonder if they found places to sleep."

Max was staring at her. "Hank, how did your hands get so dirty?"

Surprised, she looked and sure enough, her hands were dirty. "I have no idea. Hell, look at this blanket, it's practically rolled into a ball. That should say something about how restless I was last night." She brushed the dirt from her hands and poured water from the brandy bottle on them and dried them on her jeans.

Max looked across the path. "Is Molly awake?"

"She's gone. Unlike us, she's a morning person." Hank added, "She hides her wings well."

Max was looking under the bushes.

"What are you looking for?"

Max looked confused. "My blanket. It's gone."

"How could anybody swipe it, with you on top of it?"

"It probably happened when I got up to pee. I was groggy, I just collapsed when I got back. I guess I didn't notice the blanket was gone. No wonder I ache."

Hank folded her blanket and stuffed it into the canvas bag and they walked around behind the art museum. Max spotted her blanket under a tree. She could see only the corner of it but it was hers, a beat-up old patchwork quilt that looked like it had been in front of a firing squad.

"That's my blanket," she said indignantly. "It takes a lot of guts to steal a blanket and use it less than a hundred yards from where it was stolen."

She marched over to the low-hanging willow tree. Hank went with her. Two of them could fight off one person and for a few seconds Max stood there fuming. Finally she reached down, grabbed the end of the blanket and yanked it, revealing the feet of a man with holes in his shoes. She tugged at the quilt until it was freed. "Oh, God," Max gasped. Hank followed her gaze to the bloodstains on the quilt. Max pulled her hands away and the quilt fell in a heap at their feet.

Hank took Max by the arm. "Come on, we don't want to be anywhere near here when this body is found. We don't need any more grief from the police."

"But my blanket," Max wailed.

"You can't take it with you."

"But the police will find out it's mine."

"How? Is your name on it?"

"Of course not, but a lot of people know it's my blanket."

"You mean Streeters?"

Max nodded, still staring at the body on the ground.

Hank said, "I don't think you have to worry about them. They don't want to be involved with the cops any more than we do. Nobody will say anything about the blanket."

Max couldn't tear her gaze away from the bloody victim.

"Do you know him?" Hank asked as she pulled at the stunned Maxine.

Max shook her head. "I've seen him on the streets but never spoke to him. I think they called him Artie." She began to shiver in spite of the warm air.

Hank succeeded in pulling her away. "We have to put distance between the victim and us. We'll go out Twenty-Fifth Street to Fairmount Avenue and come back in on Nineteenth Street toward Logan Circle. Don't try to run. Just walk the way we did before we found him."

Max staggered to the hedge near the museum and vomited. Hank waited until she saw the muscles in Max's back relax. She assumed the retching was over for now. Hank took her hand and led her away toward Twenty-Fifth Street.

Max's cheeks were streaked with tears.

"It'll be all right," Hank assured her.

"Thank you, Hank. I don't know what I would have done if you weren't here. Just when you think everything is going to be all right your face gets shoved into the dirt again. How far do we have to go to get away?"

Hank hoped Max's mind wasn't as fragile as her body. They walked to the shelter for something hot to drink. Max's shivering intensified. She looked like she had D.T.'s. Everybody who knew her realized she was doing the best she could to get through another day.

Hank thought, *Could the shuffling noises she heard last night have anything to do with the murder?* She could still hear Storm's voice saying, *A serial killer doesn't just stop. His compulsion will make him restless. Whatever is driving him hasn't gone away and it will surface again. You can depend on it.* Was Storm's forecast correct?

Was human nature always so dependable, so predictable, so frightening?

Hank reasoned that the death of Gail Praxon was probably a fluke. She was in the wrong place at the wrong time. What if the killer was on the footpath last night? What is it that pushes someone over the edge?

Max rubbed her upper arms in spite of the warmth of the day. She shook her head in despair. "We're not alive, Hank, we're imprisoned in this man-made netherworld and there's no way out."

Hank carried two cups of tea to a table and gave both of them to Maxine.

Max's tortured expression would have evoked the sympathy of everybody in the room, had they not been struggling with their own internal problems, which deafened them to the silent screams of others.

Max's restlessness intensified. It was obvious she wanted to be alone. Hank left her at the shelter and walked to Penn's Landing. She sat along the bank of the river, questioning her inner self. Why didn't she hear the person who took Max's blanket? Why didn't she hear Max when she got up to relieve herself? Why didn't she hear Molly when she left? Where could Molly have gone? Is it possible to have a fitful sleep and yet not be aware of movement around you? Her thoughts were interrupted when a shadow passed between her and the sun. Shielding her eyes she looked up. The smell got to her first.

"Storm, I wish you would do something about those clothes."

"As you say, I'm ripe. Did you hear about the murder last night?"

"It was all over the shelter this morning," Hank lied.

"Where did you spend the night?"

Since she didn't have an alibi set up with Max and Molly, she told the truth.

"In the Azalea Garden."

"Did you hear anything? See anything?"

"There was a lot of shuffling. You know, Streeters walking up and down the footpath looking for a place to sleep. Max and Molly and I were all in the same area." She told him about the fear that engulfed her when she awoke.

"When you had that feeling, did you hear shuffling then?" he asked.

She thought for a moment and nodded. "Yes, I think so."

"Could you identify the shuffling if you heard it again?"

"You've got to be kidding. All Streeters shuffle. How am I supposed to tell one shuffle from another?"

"Stand on Market Street any day and listen to the shuffling, then look at the person that passes. Each person has his or her own rhythm in walking—or *shuffling*, as you put it; it's almost like a fingerprint, it's that individual. How do you suppose the blind learn to identify people? Unless they can touch, they have to depend on what they hear. For instance, did you know you developed a shuffle?

"Me? Shuffle? I do not."

"How could you hope to be aware of others when you're totally unaware of yourself? I don't think you're aware of the danger you put yourself in when you took on this project."

"When I took on this project, as you say, there were no murders. Obviously the killer is after men. You said yourself the Praxon woman was probably killed because she happened to be with Terry O'Neill, who was the real target."

Storm sat beside her on the grass.

"What if our killer exhausts his reasons for killing and starts to kill because he enjoys it? Do you think he'll be particular if his victims are male or female? They say the shark will attack anything that thrashes about in water. All you have to do is get this guy's attention and you may be his next victim."

"What about that psychological profile?"

"It takes time to build a profile but when it's completed, it'll be like having a photograph of the killer."

"Did the killer leave a verse?"

"Yes, but I don't remember all of it. It didn't make much sense. Something about charity beginning at home and every man being his own executioner."

"Did the note say where the quote comes from?"

"Now that you mention it, no, it didn't. That's unusual."

"I'll go to the library and look it up." Hank started to leave but Storm pulled her back down beside him. "Get away tonight? Meet you at the apartment?"

She could feel a current pass between their hands. There could be only one answer. Hank spent an hour in the library and found in Bartlett's Familiar Quotations, what she thought might be the verse, copied it then left for the apartment. When she climbed out of the shower she knew he was there.

"How long have you been here?" she called.

"How did you know I was here?"

"That awful odor announced your arrival when you were fifty feet from the apartment." She emerged wrapped in a towel. He stood there naked.

"I didn't think you would want me to stink up everything so I put them in the washer."

He held a small black kit in his hand.

"What's that?" Hank asked.

"I'm going to trim and thin out this beard and mustache. It's getting hot with all this extra hair on my face and neck. I thought I would never say this, but I'd love to get back to shaving every day. When I see my reflection, I'm always startled. I say to myself, who is that guy?"

"Did you pour a drink for yourself?"

"No," he said. "That's going to be the third thing I do."

She smiled, she didn't have to ask about the first two.

"Did you go to the library?"

Hank retreated into the bedroom and returned with the written verse.

"Good, read it to me while I'm showering, then let's try to figure out what it means." He left the shower door open so he could hear her.

"*But how shall we expect charity towards others, when we are uncharitable to ourselves? Charity begins at home, is the voice of the world; yet is every man his greatest enemy, and as it were, his own executioner.*"

Storm stepped out of the shower and picked up a towel. "Any ideas?"

Hank shrugged. "I'd have to know more about the victim before I ventured a guess about the verse."

He tugged at her towel and it dropped around her ankles. He was looking into her eyes, with just a hint of amusement.

"I wasn't talking about the verse. Let's get our priorities straight."

That was the first time anyone made love to her on a bathroom floor. She was beginning to think the only way they hadn't tried it was standing up in a canoe.

Later they sat in the living room, drinks in hand discussing the latest verse.
"How much do you know about the victim, Hank?"
"Nothing. He wasn't in the shelters much. He looked comfortably dissipated, like he was always high on something. If he was a user, I have no idea how he paid for the stuff. Once in a while, I saw him walking with the Praxon woman but I never had occasion to talk to either of them."
Storm sipped his drink. "Strange, nobody knew him. Only that his name was Artie. This one bothers me. I think our killer made his first mistake. This was the wrong victim. All of the other victims had no family. This one belongs to a wealthy family and they have a lot of clout. The commissioner and the mayor have been burning up the telephone lines to the police station. The victim's name was Arthur Webb Hamilton III." He was watching her expressions.
She shrugged. "So? Should that name mean something to me?"
"Depends. How much wine do you drink?"
"I've got a pretty good stash under the kitchen cabinet," she said. What's your point?"
"Hamilton Winery? Napa Valley?" He waited for a reaction.
"Oh, shit. You're not serious?"
"We're not sure yet but it's shaping up that way. In any event, we can't take credit for hitting on this possibility. A reporter from United Press asked the question. Apparently he got his start in journalism in Santa Rosa, California. The Hamilton name is pretty big out there."
"Is it a positive identification?"
Storm said, "He had an old California driver's license in his pocket. It's hard to say if the picture on the license is the same person. The victim could have lifted it from somebody else. He was so dissipated that any resemblance to the picture would be conjecture on our part. The family was contacted to see if Hamilton the third is missing. If so, somebody from the family will be here tomorrow to identify the body."

CHAPTER 10

Doctor McGowan took off her glasses and sat down. "Let's discuss the personalities of the suspects as you know them and add them to the chart. What about Molly?"

Storm opened his flip-top notebook and settled back in his chair. "Molly's full name is Mary Keller, sixty-eight years old but looks much older, partly due to the fact that she's almost toothless. She's very thin and I think very sick but I doubt if she would let the others know that. She's partially bent over and limps but she covers more territory in one day than most of the others cover in three. She's a survivor. According to other street people, what Molly says, goes."

Storm looked up from his notes and said, "I switched brandy bottles on Hank, without her knowledge, and the police lab lifted several sets of fingerprints. One of those sets belongs to Molly. We ran them through the usual channels to see if any of them had prior arrests. Molly spent fifteen years in prison for second-degree murder. She killed her husband after he had viciously beaten and raped her. Her prison record shows that one of the guards tried to rape her and she crushed his testicles in her hands. No formal charges were made because four other women also complained about that particular guard, over a period of six months. When she was released from prison, she came directly to Philadelphia from Chicago. She spent the last fourteen years on our streets."

Storm waited until Doc completed her notes before continuing, "Most nights, Molly sleeps at the Azalea Gardens, usually in the same area with Hank and Max. Nobody knows what time she leaves the Gardens, only that it's very early in the morning. She knows this city better than a veteran cab driver."

Storm turned the page to his next suspect before commenting, "No attachments, no ambition to get off the streets, makes Molly an excellent candidate as our serial killer."

Storm scanned his notes on the next suspect. "We thought we had the killer when Ned was arrested. He's a poet and does recitations down on the waterfront on weekends. Nobody knows where he goes nights. Unlike most street people, he rarely sleeps in the same place for two consecutive nights so he has the mobility the killer needs. He's probably in his early forties. We've come up with zilch on his identity. He has done a good job on destroying that. He has no priors and as far as we could determine, no motive. The first time he was brought in for questioning, I interrogated him. At that time he consented to a polygraph test. He was clean. Of course, there's always the possibility that he's smart enough to know how to beat the system. Even though the results of such a test are not admissible in court, it gives the police a handle on the personality of the subject. Ned's an intelligent, well-educated man with a slight accent...probably Bostonian."

Storm shifted uncomfortably in his chair. " According to police records, during interrogation, the second time he was picked up, he complained of chest pain. Eventually somebody was convinced that his pain was genuine when he passed out. He was taken to the nearest hospital. The diagnosis was acute coronary."

Doctor McGowan stopped writing and asked, "Who conducted the interrogation?"

Storm paused. "Mike Shaye." He watched for her reaction. There was none.

He continued, "While he was in the Intensive Care Unit, being monitored, the murders continued. That virtually eliminates him as a suspect unless the murderer has an accomplice. One of the victims was his street buddy, Jonah Kaplan. When he got the news about Kappy's death, he wasn't surprised and frankly it seemed as if he didn't care."

Storm paged to the next suspect. "Maxine, known as Max, is walking an emotional tightrope...blindfolded. She's probably in her early thirties, fair, short medium-blond hair, blue eyes, about five foot five; thin, frail-looking." Storm hesitated. "I think she could shatter like Humpty Dumpty...and all the king's men won't be able to put the pieces together again. Right now, she's our most likely suspect. She's left handed and was once a patient in a mental hospital. By her own admission, hates mornings and has trouble sleeping nights. She seems to know poetry fairly well, which was the initial attraction between her and Ned. Like Hank, she has a penchant for being in the vicinity where the murders take place. Max has been on the streets six or seven years and to the best of my knowledge was never in any kind of trouble. Everybody says she's an angel. Maybe she is...an avenging angel. She seems educated and probably came from a good family. She doesn't adapt well to stress."

Storm stopped and checked his notes. "When the latest victim was discovered, we found a crumpled blanket at his feet, like somebody had pulled it off him, then dropped it. According to the bloodstains on the patchwork pattern, it had to have been partially wrapped around the body. The blanket belonged to Max. She claims somebody stole it. I don't buy that. There are as many holes in her alibi as there are in the blanket. How could anybody steal it? She was sleeping on it."

Doctor McGowan interrupted again. "How do you know it was her blanket?"

"Mike Shaye's snitch told him."

"How does this...ah...snitch, know so much about street people?"

"Because the snitch is a Streeter."

Doctor McGowan's left eyebrow was raised in a quizzical expression. She shrugged. "Oh."

Storm continued, "Max has a habit of wringing her hands when she's upset or she rocks back and forth. If it's really bad, she does both. Hank seems to think Max is in love with Ned. Molly thinks so too. Hank said that Molly's sure the relationship will be catastrophic for Max. Hank is more optimistic, she thinks the relationship will rekindle a spark in Maxine. But I don't think she realizes such a spark could touch off a calamity...if it hasn't already."

Doctor McGowan stood up. "Let's take a break. Coffee?"

"Please," Storm said. "You live in center city, Doc?"

She carried two cups of coffee and handed one to him. "No. I live in Gwynedd. Sometimes when I'm sitting in the middle of a traffic jam on the Schuylkill Expressway, I wish I lived in the city. Driving the 'sure-kill expressway' can get pretty hairy."

Storm laughed at the nickname Philadelphians had given the dangerous expressway. He said, "Hank lived in Gwynedd for a time. Now she lives on the Parkway."

"What's Hank's last name?"

"Castle, as in citadel, or...propugnaculum."

Pam McGowan's laugh was musical and genuine. "I remember my professor in English 101 pulling that word on us. 'Look it up,' he said, 'let's talk about it tomorrow.' As it turned out, only two of us were able to find it. It was listed in the Thesaurus under Castle—defense. It was obsolete but it was there." She sipped her coffee. "I know a lot of people in Gwynedd, but the name Castle doesn't ring a bell."

"Her name, at the time, was Mrs. Julian Grant."

"Really? That's odd, I've known Julian Grant for about four or five years and didn't know he had ever been married." She shook her head. "Strange."

"They were divorced in 1988," Storm said, as he opened his note pad again, and continued. "Hank Castle is an investigative reporter who has penetrated the protective shell of the street people. She's gathering material for a book. She's about five foot six, give or take a half inch, weighs about a hundred twenty-five pounds. Her auburn hair has a way of curling around her face when it gets damp. Apparently, she's well respected in the field of journalism. The first time I saw her, she was a belligerent bitch." He laughed at the memory. "She was on the streets about three weeks when she reported the first murder. That alone proved she wasn't street smart."

Storm shook his head, remembering the first encounter between Hank and Shaye. "There was immediate hostility between Hank and Mike Shaye. I never saw him react to anyone the way he did to her. He abused and stalked her. That's when I had to step in. I talked to Mike about it and he thought she was a tightly wired deadly explosive and warned me not to be around when she blew up. Mike thinks I turned against him. Well, you know the rest of it. He's your patient. He also thinks I'm becoming too involved with her."

Pam McGowan studied Storm for a time before she spoke. "Are you? Becoming involved, with Hank?"

He scratched his beard, "No. Well, maybe...a little. I know, Doc, it's a bad move. Fortunately, I can walk away from it whenever I think it's necessary." Storm knew he was lying.

After an uncomfortable silence, he checked his notes. "I had Hank checked out. She has no criminal record but she was institutionalized for a nervous breakdown about a year and a half ago. The psychiatrist who took care of her was Doctor Jeremy Thornton. Do you know him?"

"Yes, I know Jere. We did our residencies together."

Storm said, "Hank is easily provoked. She doesn't flare, it's more like a slow simmer, unless it's Mike doing the provoking, then she loses it. She tries to keep her anger buried. When I first met her I wasn't sure if she hated all men or just cops. She seemed to carry that hard hate around like a precious bundle in a soft baby blanket."

Storm related the incident on the waterfront and confessed he was convinced that she would clobber the teenager with a bottle. "When Hank's with Max, Molly, or Ned, she's a different person. I think it's because each has a need that she fills. They think she can do anything and look up to her...almost like she was a savior."

"Are these all the suspects?"

"There's one more, but we can't get a line on her. She goes by the name of Suzie. Her name is Suzanne Hoffman but there's no way to verify it. In all probability she's a prostitute. She was seen with several of the victims before their bodies were found. I haven't seen her but they say she's very attractive, but hard. For all we know, she could be a scout for the killer. Those are my suspects. Not much to go on, is it?"

While he talked, she took notes. She put her pen down. "Obviously, the murderer could be male or female. We know he or she is between five foot six and five foot nine because of the angle of the stab wounds on the body of Gail Praxon. He or she is probably under a great deal of stress. However, I don't believe the stress is recent. I think it goes back a while. It probably started out as a hurt then turned into anger and was internalized. It is a slow-burning anger, which the killer feels could be assuaged only by spilling blood. This person pictures himself or herself as judge and jury and looks at the killings as justified executions."

Doctor McGowan clipped her notes to the victim board, behind the bifold doors of the closet. "The killer is educated," she said. "Not necessarily a formal education and could easily be self-taught, self-made, with an intense interest in literature and an overwhelming contempt for authority. Right now, this profile could fit any of your suspects. The number eight plays an important role in this person's life. The ages of the victims are significant and so is the fact that seven of the eight victims were males. I think the killer had no choice but to kill the woman but that killing wasn't in anger, it was simply to protect the killer's identity."

Doctor McGowan took each of the verses found with the victims and laid them in a horizontal line. She said, "Each of the verses is handwritten. The killer is either left-handed or ambidextrous. See how the stems of the *t*'s have their cross-bar slanted from left to right in a downward, arrow-like stroke, sharp, decisive. This denotes aggressiveness, sarcasm and a domineering personality. The writing is almost vertical, which shows the writer to be cold, lacking in warmth or emotional depth. Note the complete loops at the beginning of the circles in the words beginning with *o*, this person is a master at deception. The heavy pressure in the writing shows an individual who soaks up emotional experiences like a sponge, even after the incident is over and forgotten, the result of that experience becomes part of his or her personal nature. He has absorbed that feeling and will be prejudiced by it long after it has been forgotten."

She made a notation on the chart. "You're dealing with someone with a great deal of hate bottled up. The autopsies of the victims revealed some dirt, topsoil kind of dirt, in the stab wounds, which would indicate the killer buried the knife after each slaying. Indications are, you're dealing with a psychopath living on the streets, or there would be no need to bury the knife. There also exists the possibility you could be dealing with a dual, or a multiple personality."

"Those things really happen, Doc?"

"Absolutely."

"Would each personality know about the other personalities?"

"Not necessarily. Usually, there's one dominant personality, who would certainly be aware of the other personality. The one that comes out to protect or possibly to destroy the core personality, would be the dominant one. The danger of course is that the dominant personality, being in control, makes the decision when to materialize and if the personality is strong enough it could ultimately make the decision to bury the weaker personality forever."

Pandemonium erupted at city hall and the police department when the unchecked murders hit the headlines of every major newspaper in the country: *Victim Number Eight of Philadelphia Serial Killer Identified as Missing Son of California Wine Magnate.*

Hank was walking through the park, when she spied a newspaper that had been left on a bench. She read the account aloud, "*Arthur Webb Hamilton III, age forty-one, of Napa Valley, California, heir to the Hamilton wine fortune, was the eighth victim of a crazed serial killer. His body was found behind the Philadelphia Museum of Art. Mr. Hamilton and his secretary, Gail Praxon, were last seen boarding his private plane, bound for New York City, in August, 1999. At the time of his disappearance, Mr. Hamilton was being sought by California police for questioning in an alleged fraud attempt at the winery. The victim is survived by his father, Arthur Webb Hamilton II, prominent leader in California's Napa Valley; a wife, Leigh Farnsworth Hamilton; and two children, Arthur Webb Hamilton IV, and Germaine Devon Hamilton.*"

Hank folded the paper and put it in her canvas bag. She thought, *So, Gail Praxon was Webb's secretary.* Hank wondered what could have happened to split them apart. Obviously something had gone awry between them or she would have been with him instead of Terry O'Neill the night she was killed. She pulled out a pad and jotted down some notes. She looked around her and marveled that the peace and tranquility of the park by day belied the terror that stalked the city by night.

Hank saw the long, slender shadow floating in front of her before she saw the scuffed, badly scarred loafers on the tiny feet shuffling toward her. "Max?" She moved over and Maxine sat beside her. Max's lusterless eyes seemed to be staring inwardly. She looked so vulnerable. Hank was concerned. She recognized the symptoms of a prelude to a nervous breakdown.

Maxine closed her eyes. "Did you read about that poor man we found? He had two children. It's going to be hard on them, knowing their father was murdered. Poor, dear innocents." She was biting her bottom lip and didn't notice she had drawn blood.

"Do you think they'll be able to connect me to the blanket, Hank?"

"If they do, be honest about it and tell them it was stolen. It happens all the time." Hank reached out and held Max's hand. "Better let go of that bottom lip before you bite it off. Don't feel too badly about those poor children, at least they still have a mother. Besides, whoever committed the murder wasn't the one depriving those kids of a father. He did that himself when he walked out on them."

Max was wringing her hands and rocking back and forth to a rhythm only she could hear.

"You haven't been sleeping very well, have you?"

She merely shook her head and continued to rock. "I didn't do it, Hank, honest I didn't. I couldn't kill a another human being."

"I know that. Get hold of yourself." Hank dug into her canvas bag and produced a small cloth sack tied with string. She poured the contents out into the palm of her hand. "I think I have enough money for a pint of brandy. You stay right here. I'll be back as soon as I can."

When she returned, Max was sitting on the bench, still rocking. Hank pulled the bottle out of her canvas bag, broke the seal and put it in Maxine's hand.

Max looked blankly at the bottle. "I don't like to drink, it makes me feel drugged."

"You're going to drink now. It might help calm you down and tonight you'll drink more of it and I guarantee you'll sleep. I'll sleep near you, then we can always vouch for each other. See? It was a good thing we were sleeping next to each other when the murder happened. I know you didn't do it, and I can vouch for you."

The hint of a smile played at her lips. "If the police find out about the blanket, do you really believe they'll take the word of a street person?"

"Why not? We haven't broken any laws. My word or your word is just as good as the tax-paying public. Just because we don't have an address doesn't mean they can question our veracity." Hank's annoyance was echoed in her words.

Max put the bottle to her lips and allowed a small amount of the amber fluid to trickle into her mouth. She made a face before she swallowed, then coughed with a croup-like sound that sounded tubercular. She passed the back of her hand over her lips and shivered. "Oh God," she said, "this is terrible. How can you enjoy this stuff?"

"It's not the best brandy but it'll help take the edge off what you're feeling. You can drink some tonight and every night until you get some sleep. Here, put it in your shopping bag. I'll see you tonight at the Gardens. In the meantime, I'm going to the Salvation Army and some of the shelters to see if I can get you a blanket of some sort. Put my blanket in your bag so the people at the shelter think the blanket is for me." Hank felt her stomach tighten into a knot just looking at the anguish on Max's face. "Are you all right?"

"I...I think so."

When she was sure she was out of sight, Hank redirected her destination toward the apartment and entered as usual through the tower door. In the basement of the building, she pulled out her old footlocker and opened it.

There on top were the small figures of a bride and groom that had graced the top of her wedding cake. She stared at the figurines, then snapped the head off the groom figurine and hurled the cake topper across the open space in the basement. She heard it hit something solid, then thump to the cement floor. She found an old army blanket from her girl scout days. Moths had eaten a few small holes into the wool, but it would serve the purpose. She tore off the personal identification tag, put the blanket into her bag and returned to her apartment, opened a can of tomato soup and heated it. She poured the soup into the thermos she kept in the canvas bag. As she reached the door to the street she had the uneasy feeling that she was not alone. She turned and looked over her shoulder. The silence was undisturbed and there was no indication anyone was there. She caught a glimpse of a small figurine dressed in a bride's gown and veil on the floor of the basement next to a headless figurine of a groom. She hesitated, with her back against the tower door, her heart thumped a drum message to the rest of her body, *Get out of here. Now.* She ran for several blocks. She glanced over her shoulder. The street was empty except for a mail carrier rearranging the mail in his truck. She leaned against the fire hydrant near the corner until the shaking within stopped. For the rest of the day Hank felt like she was being stalked. She dreaded the dark that would follow the beautiful sunset. She shuffled along the footpath with other street people. Molly caught up with her. Without looking at Hank she talked in a whispered voice. "I don't know what you done but that detective Shaye was noseyin' round, askin 'bout you. Better keep low for a few days."

"What happened the other night, Molly? When I woke up you were gone."

Molly wiped her moist nose on her coat sleeve. "I don't know how you could sleep with all the traffic and the noise on the path. I picked meself up and slept in the park where it was quiet," she said as she shuffled off into the bushes.

Hank felt like someone had kicked her in the stomach. She thought, *What the hell does Shaye want with me?* "Damn it," she mumbled, "the last thing I need is Mike Shaye on my back. At this rate I'll never get off the streets. She turned to enter the bushes when she spotted Max coming toward her. Hank waved to be certain Max had seen her. Hank pulled the moth-eaten blanket from her bag and tossed it on the ground in the bushes about five feet from where she would sleep. Max smiled when she saw the blanket.

"How did you do it? It's wonderful."

"Well, you may not think it's so wonderful when you see moth holes in it but it should help keep the dampness off your bones." Max looked tired and beaten by life. "Did you get anything to eat today?"

"I wasn't very hungry," Max said.

Hank fished out the thermos. "I found this in the trash and rinsed it out and got some soup for you. At least it will be something warm."

Max accepted the container and unscrewed the cap. A little steam escaped and she gave a squeal of delight.

"How did you get it? I know they don't give takeout foods in the shelter."

"Well, I got to the north side shelter early and had my own meal there, then I went to the soup kitchen and got there in time for this. I just poured it into the thermos and stuck it in my bag. Sorry there weren't any sandwiches."

She smelled the soup. "This is marvelous. You're a dear friend, Hank."

"After you get that down, start sipping the brandy. You have to get some sleep. Don't worry, I'll be right here."

Max sipped the brandy. It seemed like such a waste to pour it into somebody who didn't like the stuff. She handed the bottle back and Hank was happy to see she had consumed a couple of shots. "Keep it in your bag, just in case."

An hour later, Hank checked on Max, who was lying on her side sound asleep. Hank settled back on her own blanket wondering what Mike Shaye wanted with her. She mumbled, "I'm not about to walk into the lion's den, if Shaye wants me, he'll have to find me." In spite of the mild temperatures, she snuggled deep into her blanket. She knew the chill she felt was fostered by fear but her exhaustion was greater than the fear. Opaque black curtains of sleep were falling in front of her closed eyes and she felt herself nestle into the embrace of Morpheus.

Unfortunately her dreams were not as blessed as the sleep that accompanied them. Wide circles invaded her dreams, whirling around her head. Inside the circles, she saw the sneering, menacing face of Mike Shaye and she ran…going nowhere. The faster she ran, the faster the ground moved under her. Her leaden legs refused to move any further. She fell and turned to confront her predator, fully expecting to see Mike Shaye but the face of her tormentor was obscured under a black hood. She sank deeper into the quicksand of an exhausted sleep.

The sound of sirens and the flashing blue and red lights went speeding by on the River Drive. Hank forced herself into consciousness. She was rubbing her eyes and someone was shaking her. She squinted into the misty gray light of dawn before she was able to focus on Maxine's face. "What's wrong?"

"It must have happened again. Look at all the police cars down the drive near Boat House Row."

Hank waved her hand in front of her face, trying to dispel the gathering mist. "We don't have anything to be concerned about, we still have our blankets and fortunately, we don't know anything about what happened down there." She pointed toward the flashing lights.

Maxine was pale and trembling. "I hope it stays that way."

Hank pulled Max's blanket closer to hers. "If anybody comes into this area, pretend you're asleep."

They lay there for at least another hour talking about inconsequential things, anything to keep Max's mind off the flashing lights. When daylight penetrated the bushes they folded their blankets and started walking in the opposite direction from the crime scene.

"Think you can eat something this morning?"

Max shrugged her shoulders. "We have at least two hours before the shelter opens."

"Let's go out Twenty-Second Street, at least it will get us out of this area. Want a sip of brandy before we go?"

She shook her head and made a face.

"It worked, though, didn't it?"

"It did that. I slept through the night."

"Do that for a few nights and you might be ready to face the world again. Sleep does marvelous things. Puts your feet in never-neverland."

Max lowered her eyes but not before Hank saw the hurt there. When they got to a shelter, they had a bowl of oatmeal, a cup of weak tea and a slice of day-old bread. Most of the others dunked the hard bread in the tea but Max broke off small pieces and put them into her mouth. She held her cup with both hands to prevent the precious liquid from spilling and to warm the trembling hands that seemed to be forever cold. When they were leaving Hank said, "Same place tonight?"

Max nodded and they went their separate ways. Hank started going uptown when she saw Storm Andrews. He staggered toward her, supporting himself on the walls of the buildings. Could he really be drunk? When she saw those granite eyes, she knew it was an act. He hung on her like he had stumbled. While he was trying to steady himself, he whispered, "Meet me at your place at noon." Then he continued staggering down the street. Hank didn't turn around but continued walking, brushing herself off as though he had contaminated her with lice. She smiled and said to herself, *At least this time he smells better. Not like lilacs, mind you, but at least not like a full bedpan, either.*

She reached the apartment around eleven o'clock, took off her clothes, tossed them into the washer and stepped into the shower. She checked the cupboard and picked up a can of tuna fish and took a loaf of sliced bread from the freezer. She made a tuna salad and defrosted enough bread for sandwiches. Exactly at noon she heard the key turning in the lock.

"There's tuna salad on the table and you know where the drinks are."

When there was no response she turned to look at him. He wore a strange expression, like a puppy that had been beaten and thrown out in the rain. The soft gray eyes had turned to granite and for the first time she felt he was shutting her out of his thoughts.

"Mike Shaye was looking for you."

"I got the word last night from Molly. Did you expect me to hike down to the precinct last night? You know where I am, if he wants something let him tell you. I've had it with 'Smilin Jack.' It's not enough he makes me feel like shit, you've got to come over here and rub my nose in it? What the hell do you want from me?"

He closed his eyes and leaned against the door. "Mike...bought it last night."

She felt the shiver start at the top of her head and bolt its way down to the bottom of her feet. She stared at him. His cheeks were wet and his eyes were closed. She bridged the distance between them and put her arms around him and felt him go limp.

"How?" Her voice sounded strange, even to her.

There was a catch in his voice. "He was victim number nine."

She was kissing Storm's closed eyes. "How could he let that happen?" Her arms held him protectively, comforting him.

He pulled away from her and poured himself four fingers of scotch. "That's the question I've been asking myself all morning."

"Same as the others?"

"Identical."

"Holy shit. If a detective who knows the score can be taken in, what chance do the rest of us have?"

"When did you get the message that Mike wanted to see you?"

"Last night, after dark. Molly said she didn't know what I had done but Detective Shaye was looking for me. She advised me to lay low for a while." She held his hand. "Do you know what he wanted?"

"He was told by a snitch about a woman named Max who has been very nervous lately, especially about a missing blanket."

"What? I don't believe this." Hank pulled away from him. "Damn right she was nervous, so have the rest of us been nervous. Besides, Max slept about five feet away from me last night, so I know she couldn't be involved. If she had left the area I would have known."

He poured himself a second four fingers of scotch. "You didn't know about Mike, did you?"

There was no avoiding his gaze. "Not until you dropped the bomb just now. I thought you wanted to talk about the Hamilton mess. I assumed you were getting pressure from above and wanted to ask me about possible feedback. I swear to you, Storm, I did not know about Mike until just now."

He finished the rest of his drink, put the glass on the table and looked out the window.

"Thanks for the drinks." He moved toward the door, before he turned. "You never asked where it happened." He was gone before she could stop him.

Hank walked through the park wondering what information Shaye thought she could give him. Could they really suspect Maxine? The police were looking for clues, questioning joggers, cyclists, city street cleaners, street people and anybody else they thought could shed light on the crime. Hank watched the investigative pace pick up and thought, *Now they're serious about finding the killer, one of their own is a victim.*

Hank was glad she and Max stayed away from the crime scene. She sat on a park bench watching the now common activity of police cars and vans. The heat of the late-afternoon sun made her drowsy and she dozed off.

She awakened to the poking of a billy stick. "Move along," the officer was saying to her. Hank gathered her canvas bag under her arm and started walking. There was no way out for the Streeters. She wondered if anyone had been charged with Shaye's death. It must be at least twelve hours since Shaye was killed.

The shelters were almost deserted that night. The soup kitchens had food left over. Word was out. "Lay low, cops are out in force." Maxine was in line just ahead of Hank. She whispered Max's name and told her not to turn around. "There is a snitch among the Streeters and he gave your name to the police. I told the detective you were with me the night before and I would swear to it."

Maxine's hands shook. "Who was it, Hank? Who was killed this time?"

Hank was surprised that she didn't know. "Mike Shaye."

Max dropped her tray. "The detective?"

Hank picked up the tray and handed it to her. "The same. Don't talk anymore. We'll meet at the Gardens tonight and I'll fill you in on what happened. Will you be okay until then?"

"I think so. Who could have told the detective about me? Why would anybody do that?"

Hank could see Max's defenses crumbling. "Hang in there. We'll talk about it later. Don't give the bastards the satisfaction of knowing you're scared. Eat your dinner. And for God's sake, stop wringing your hands."

Max looked at the delicate hands. "I wasn't aware I was doing that. Force of habit, I guess." She bit her lower lip. "Hank, I'm scared. What if they start questioning me? What if…" She stopped.

Hank countered with an optimism she didn't feel. "What if? What if a frog had longer legs? Do you think he would still hit his ass when he jumped on a rock? 'What if' doesn't count. The only thing that matters is that you know you're innocent."

"But I heard they can make you say things that aren't true, they can beat it out of you…like they did to Ned, and we know what happened to him."

"You still have some rights even if you don't have an address. You can demand to make a phone call."

She turned her face away. "There's no one to call."

"You can call the public defender's office and request an attorney to protect your civil rights. If anybody ever lays a hand on you, you make damn sure you tell that to the attorney…and to the newspapers. Listen to me, I'm talking like all attorneys are honest and that simply is not true. Once in a while you may meet an attorney with integrity who will represent you for the sake of justice and not because of the almighty buck. I doubt that the police would even consider you a threat."

"I couldn't stand it if they put me into a cell. I think I would go out of my mind. If they start asking me questions, I'm not sure I'll be able to answer. I forget things. If I forget, they may think I don't want to answer and they'll make me go back."

Hank thought Max looked so pathetically helpless. This hank of hair, skin and bone with eyes the size of saucers couldn't allow herself to go back. Wherever *back* was. For whatever reason, she was on the streets, for keeps. Whatever was in her past frightened her more than the killings, which terrified everyone else.

Hank realized these simple Streeters were the most complex beings she had ever encountered. She said, "The important thing right now is to survive this hour, this day. We'll worry about tomorrow when it gets here." Ned had told Hank that Streeters were the capsized victims of an ill-fated mission to sail into the mainstream of a society that was either too swift or too uncaring. And in their efforts to escape, they became the main contributors and perpetuators of the very perdition they faced. Hank looked at the empty shell beside her, for that's what Max had become, completely drained of emotion and energy.

Hank floundered in a sea of doubt, wondering, what horror could be worse than life on the streets? Would she ever be able to pick up the strands of her life, that she left so willingly to get a story?

Max and Hank walked toward the Gardens. As the stars began to appear, Max pointed to them, and said, "They're the eyes of the inquisition to come. I want to run but where can I go when there is no place to hide? It doesn't matter that eight street people were brutally murdered, at least it didn't matter until the ninth victim was a cop. It doesn't matter that he was a bad cop. He was a cop."

At the Azalea Gardens, police were systematically combing the bushes for clues. Hank said, "It's too hot to be here anyway. Let's go to Penn's Landing. It should be cooler along the Delaware."

They walked the twenty-two blocks to the riverfront in silence and spread their blankets under the stars. Max sat on her blanket hugging her knees to her chest.

"Do you have any brandy left?" Hank asked.

Max reached into her shopping bag and pulled out the wrinkled brown paper bag containing the small bottle of brandy and handed it to her.

"Not for me, for you."

Max shook her head.

Hank unscrewed the cap and handed it to her. "Drink some, Max. It might help."

"I don't want any, Hank. The next day I have a hard time remembering things."

"Great! All the more reason for you to take a swig. You don't need to do any remembering. You need to do some forgetting and this might help." Hank held the bottle out to her.

She took the bottle and sipped some of the liquid. "I don't know why you bother with me, Hank." Her voice was almost a whisper. "There is nothing here to salvage."

"I don't agree. You're probably the most salvageable Streeter I've met. Take another swig and you'll be amazed how much better things will look tomorrow."

She took another swallow and handed the bottle back. Within minutes she was asleep. Hank lay back on her blanket, watching the stars blink their secret messages to each other, wondering if she would ever get her story. It had all seemed so simple in the beginning. A matter of a couple of months, she had told her friend and former editor, Wally Stockheim. She was no closer to that exclusive story than she had been then. She had dialed his number at the newspaper. She remembered with a smile how he sounded on the other end of the line. "Stockheim, here." She had replied, "There are three things in this life that are eternal, death, taxes and Wally Stockheim."

"Hank." Stockheim had laughed. "How've you been, sweetheart? Are you okay?"

"I handle stress much better these days. I'm not sure how I do it, but it's like an inner self comes out of hiding and takes over like a protective shield and I find myself coping. Trust me, I can handle it."

As Hank rolled onto her side she could hear the echo of his voice, *big-time stress.* Then she felt the sweet serenity that precedes sleep. Just as her eyes were closing she thought she saw Storm Andrews but her eyelids were too heavy to open them again, so she supposed she would never know if he was really there or if it was only wishful thinking.

In the early hours of morning, Hank heard moaning and sobbing coming from the area where Max was sleeping. Cautiously she turned so she was facing in Max's direction. The only person she saw was Max, who seemed to be doing battle with a nightmare. "Please don't leave me here. Edward, come back." Her face was contorted in desperation. She sobbed, "Don't...leave..."

When Hank looked up the stars had disappeared and the sky was heavy with dark gray clouds. She felt a drop of rain, then another and another. She shook Max into consciousness.

"We have to find shelter. It looks like a bad storm coming." Quickly Hank folded her blanket and stuffed it in the canvas bag. Max wasn't responding very well so Hank helped her with her blanket and took her arm and they began running toward the Comfort Inn on Delaware Avenue. They stood under the overhangs for whatever protection they afforded. The rain on her face brought Max back to the present and out of her mental prison.

"I'm sorry I had to wake you like that, Max but if these blankets got wet we would be very uncomfortable tonight."

For the first time since the body of Arthur Hamilton was discovered, Max smiled.

"I don't mind the rain. I like the way it feels on my face. It reminds me how good it feels to be free."

Hank studied the woman who had become her friend and thought, *Who is this strange creature who loves freedom so much that the bondage of poverty is a welcome relief from the subjugation of whoever controlled her life or whatever experiences forced her to seek anonymity on the streets of Philadelphia?* Was Edward the one who had her confined to a mental institution? If so, why? Where was the place she once called home? Somehow, her life had bifurcated. She traveled one branch wherever it led but she was still tethered to the other branch by memories and troubled dreams. The rain had begun to puddle in the low areas of the concrete walkway. Someone was sloshing through the puddles toward the sheltered area where they stood.

"Is there room for one more?" came a voice out of the downpour.

As the figure approached, Hank could tell by the shuffle it was Molly. *Damn,* she thought, *Storm was right, if you listen you can identify sounds without seeing the source.*

Molly came into the arc of lights surrounding the Inn, carrying her umbrella with its four broken ribs and two holes in the nylon dome. She closed the umbrella carefully, fastening it with the tab snap attached to one of the broken ribs. She slipped out of her canvas shoes, turning them upside down to dump the water back into the street.

"There is always room for you, Molly," answered Max, taking Molly's bag and umbrella, putting them on dry ground.

Molly shook herself like a wet dog. "I guess I should be thankin' the good Lord it's not cold," but the few teeth she had chattered anyway.

Max felt inside her shopping bag and pulled out the bottle of brandy. "Try some of this. Guaranteed to stop your teeth from chattering."

Molly's hands shook as she reached to accept the bottle. She took a couple of swallows and handed it back. Molly shook her head and the dirty gray hair clung in matted clumps about her face. "Thanks, Maxie. I'm gettin' too old for this shit. Somethin' told me to look for a bed in a shelter last night but the stars were out. There wasn't a cloud in the sky. When I passed the bar on Sansom Street, I heard the weatherman on TV say it would be clear for the rest of the week. I shoulda knowed better than to believe him. Weather guys can predict the weather for every place except Philadelphia. Why is that? Betcha if he was takin' his kids campin' he woulda paid more tention to the forecast. What the hell does he care, he's in a dry bed, right?"

Max laughed. "It's not his fault because it rained, Molly. Look at it this way, now we don't have to go to a shelter to take a shower and our clothes get washed at the same time."

Molly patted Max's face. "You'd make excuses for the devil. You're a good girl, Maxie."

Molly was right, Hank thought, Max was a born pacifist.

Molly dug into her bag and came up with three blemished peaches and smiled her pumpkin grin. "I was down to the Italian Market today. This is the fruit they tossed, but I looked it over and it's still good. A couple a soft spots maybe but it don't affect the taste. They're juicy and sweet." She grinned again. "And free."

Max blinked hard. "You walked all the way to South Philly and back?"

"I had somethin' better to do?"

Hank watched Molly and marveled at how Molly covered so much territory. Where had Molly been for the past few days, Hank wondered.

CHAPTER 11

The week following Mike Shaye's murder was strangely, uncomfortably quiet and Hank noticed a change in the behavior of Streeters. They snapped and growled at pedestrians and each other. However, the new pressure forced them to travel in groups for protection. Some left Philadelphia and headed for Atlanta and points south.

Storm Andrews sat on the curb on Delaware Avenue, chewing on a toothpick. The sun was low in the sky, casting fiery shadows on the river. *Another day*, he thought, *and we're no closer to catching the killer than we were months ago. Damn, am I standing too close or back too far?*

He neither saw nor heard the approach of the stranger. "Hi," said a breathy, sensuous voice. "Mind if I share your throne?" Without waiting for a reply, she sat next to him.

Storm turned so that he could take in everything from her size-eight spike-heeled shoes to her blond head. "What do you want?" he grumbled.

She smiled, her glossed lips made more alluring by the moist shine and she traced a zigzag pattern with her index finger from his throat to the belt on his pants. "You. I want you."

He turned down the brim of his misshapen felt hat and stood up. "Beat it."

"You wouldn't like it if I blew your cover...would you, Detective Andrews?" she taunted, her voice barely audible.

Slowly he turned and faced her again, his eyes narrowed. "Who are you?"

"Suzie." Her voice was low. She stood and walked a few paces from him.

"Suzie? Suzie who?" he asked.

"Just...Suzie."

"Okay, just Suzie, what the hell do you want?" His mind raced, chasing his memory, trying to attach a time, a place, an incident, to this painted marionette.

She walked toward him, slowly. She stopped only when her body was pressed against his. "I've already told you what I want."

Storm put his hands on her hips and pushed her away so that she staggered back several steps. "You can't have me," he said.

"I always get what I want, Detective. Try me. I'm much better than that phoney, Hank, that you've been screwing."

Something in the shadows of his mind set off an alert signal. "What do you know about Hank?"

"Enough." She paused. "For example, I know why she's on the streets. I also know where she lives. I know more about her than you do. I've been watching her for quite a while. I make it a point to know my adversary."

"Hank knows you?"

"I didn't say that. I said I know more *about* her than you do."

Storm bridged the space between them in a single step, taking one of her arms, he twisted it behind her back. "Stay away from Hank."

"You're hurting me." With her free hand she dug her nails into his arm and aimed her knee at his groin in her struggle to free her arm.

He avoided her knee and pushed her backward, releasing her. "Remember what I said."

Suzie rubbed her wrist. Unbridled hate encapsulated her words. "Bastard. Nobody tells me what to do." She looked him over from top to bottom. "Least of all a second-rate cop." She spat out her venom like a king cobra with its fangs hooked into a struggling prey. "Remember, in the end it's me you'll have to deal with." She turned and walked up Delaware Avenue toward the Benjamin Franklin Bridge.

Hank wondered why she hadn't seen Max or Molly for two days. She reasoned that Max was spending more time on the waterfront listening to Ned's recitations, while the nomadic Molly was constantly on the move.

Hank was leaving the subway at the City Hall Station, when she collided with Molly.

Molly held on to Hank's sleeve. "How come you snubbed me yesterday?"

Hank looked into Molly's confused face. "How could I snub you when I haven't seen you for a couple of days?"

"You saw me on the waterfront," Molly insisted. "I was standin' ten feet away and I said 'Hi,' and you turned your back on me. Then I saw you again last night when I came out of the police station and you ignored me again. We coulda used your help, Hank, that's not like you."

"I don't know how you could have seen me on the waterfront because I wasn't anywhere near there," Hank said, "and I certainly wasn't at the police station." Hank shook her head in confusion, "What were you doing at the police station?"

"Me and Max got brung in."

"What for?"

"The police found out about Max's blanket and they're holding her for questioning. Poor Maxie, she was so scared, all she could do was vomit."

Hank looked around. "Now we know for sure one of the Streeters is a snitch. The question is, which one? How could the police have known about the blanket? There were only three people who knew about it, Max, you and me. I know you wouldn't tell and I know I didn't tell and it's a cinch Max didn't say anything."

Molly gasped, then looked away from Hank.

"Molly?" Hank shook her, "What's the matter?"

Molly's eyes narrowed and her lips formed a tight straight line. "There's four of us that knows. I guess that tells me who the snitch is."

"Who?"

"Benny." Molly shook her head. "That bastard! I wouldn'ta believed he would snitch on Maxie. Well...we know how to deal with snitches on the streets. He probably told the cops about Ned too."

"Molly, we don't know what the cops put Benny through. Remember, a cop was murdered."

"Yeah. A cop who hated street people and the Streeters hated him right back. I don't care what kinda pressure they put on Benny, he's got no call to squeal on Max. She never done nothin' to hurt nobody. He's got no call to finger her."

Hank tried to reason with Molly. "Maybe it was the only way to get himself off the hook. Is Max still at the station?"

"Yeah. They better not lay a hand on her."

"Molly, when Ned was arrested, it was because a Streeter was killed. They're holding Max because four days after they found Artie's body with Max's blanket over him, a cop was killed, there's a big difference. I'll try, but I might not be able to do anything. Did the cops question you about where you were when Shaye was killed?"

"Sure, same as they questioned everybody else."

"What did you tell them?"

"I told them I was with you and Max the whole night. I figured it was better not to tell them I went to the park...you know, because of the noise on the drive. I figured if they thought the three of us was together all the time they'd have to let Max go."

"Okay, as long as I know what you told them. I'll go down to ask about Max and if they question me I'll say the same thing."

"You're okay in my book, Hank. Bring Maxie Back." Molly flashed her best semi-toothless smile. "I knowed you wouldn't let Max down."

Hank patted Molly's shoulder. "Don't get your hopes up. I'll do what I can."

It took an hour to walk to the station and a light rain began to fall. Hank's hair was soaked when she pushed open the door to the police station. She recognized the uniformed officer at the desk as the one who brought sandwiches to Storm's office the night he took her in for questioning. The nametag on the officer's chest read *Lafferty*.

"Officer Lafferty, I understand you're holding a friend of mine in jail, a Streeter, her name is Maxine."

Officer Lafferty stared at her for a few moments before he recognized her. "Your name is...Hank? Right?"

"Yes, sir, it is."

"Detective Andrews is in his office. Would you like to talk to him? He said you would probably be in to ask about Maxine."

She nodded. She became aware of a beating drum somewhere in her chest keeping time with her heartbeat.

Officer Lafferty picked up the phone and punched in some numbers.

"Lieutenant Andrews? Hank is out here. She's asking to see Maxine." There was a pause before Lafferty answered, "All right." Then to Hank, he said, "Go on in."

She pushed open the door to Storm's office.

He looked up when she came in. She hadn't seen him since he told her about Mike Shaye's murder. He looked tired.

"Lieutenant, huh? Congratulations. What did they do, throw you into a tank of disinfectant before you were allowed to sit at your desk again?"

There was a flash of white teeth as he locked his hands behind his head and leaned back in the swivel chair.

"I told them to keep the tank warm that you would probably be in smelling every bit as bad as I did." The smile faded. "You asked to see Max?"

"You knew I would come as soon as I heard she was here. She didn't commit any crimes, Storm, she's so beaten by life she doesn't even have the potential toward anger anymore."

"I would say that's a pretty fair assessment. Maxine said she was with you and Molly the night Arthur Hamilton was killed and that she was with you the night Shaye was killed. Is that correct?"

"Yes. Max wouldn't lie. Where is she?"

"Doctor McGowan's with her now."

"What happened?" Hank's voice took on an edge.

"I don't know. She may have gone over the edge. You were right, she is extremely fragile." He studied Hank for a time before he continued. "Even fragile people reach a point where they have to make a stand. That could have happened with her."

"What are you saying?"

"There's a good possibility she's our murderer." Storm held up his hand, "No, hear me out, Hank. Max has complete lapses of memory which appear to be very convenient."

"Recent memory, or past memory?"

"Past memory...that part of her life which would establish a motive for what's happening now."

"You were the one who told me she had been in a mental institution before she came to the streets. Did she have any electroshock therapy?"

Storm's eyes narrowed. "What are you getting at?"

"Shock therapy could be responsible for destroying whole blocks of memory. Did any of you jackasses ever take that into account? I'm telling you Max can't be your killer. It's impossible to be in two places at the same time. I'm a light sleeper and I would have heard her if she left the area."

Hank's anger was mounting. Hank knew she was losing control but she couldn't stop. The words kept tumbling out like concrete mix down a chute. "You fucking cops are all alike. You don't give a shit if you have the guilty person or not. All you want is a warm body that won't or can't fight back, so you can get the commissioner off your back and hope it happens before the news media finds out how incompetent you really are."

Hank studied the suspect chart on the wall, then turned and faced Storm. "You know what I think? I think your Mike Shaye got exactly what he deserved and you want to know something else? I'm glad he's dead. If your killer didn't get him, I would have. He was a sadistic, immoral, corrupt, mad, iniquitous...asshole. You and every other bastard in this precinct were protecting him, not because he was a great cop, or even a good cop...just because he was a cop. Get back on the streets and listen to the ones who were his victims."

Tears rolled unchecked down her cheeks. Hank pointed to the window. "The people out there had his number even if you were too blind to see him for what he really was. You're condemning Max because she was unfortunate enough to have been in a mental institution. Even at the time when mental institutions flourished, there were more nuts on the outside than there ever were on the inside. Shaye needed to be institutionalized. Instead…the police department gave him a gun, a badge, and a license to commit crimes in the name of the law. He was a psychopath and you," she thumped his chest with her finger, "you son-of-a-bitch, protected him."

Hank pulled a dirty, wrinkled rag from her pocket and blew her nose. "I'm putting you on notice. If anything happens to Max to push her over the edge, I'll do an exposé on Shaye that will tear into this department for the next twenty years."

The soft gray of Storm's eyes turned to granite as he studied Hank's tear-streaked face. His expression was probing, accusing, even hating. When he spoke his voice was a controlled whisper. "Where's all this bitterness coming from, Hank? You sound just like the verse that was left beside his body." He backed away from her. "You never asked about the verse left with Shaye's body. Aren't you curious?"

"It must have been Handel's Hallelujah Chorus."

Storm unfolded a piece of paper and laid it on the edge of the desk and directed the light from a gooseneck lamp onto the paper. It was a quote from *Alice's Adventures in Wonderland, I'll be judge, I'll be jury," said cunning old Fury, "I'll try the whole cause and condemn you to death."*

Hank tossed the note back at him. "I'm developing a little respect for our killer. If he could read Shaye that well, he's smarter than you think."

"Why do you keep saying, he?"

"Why do you keep thinking, she? No woman could have killed Mike Shaye. He hated women. The only woman who could have gotten close to him would have to be under him…impaled. I can't think of anything more disgusting than to be a sex partner to that pig."

Storm walked to the door, opened it, turned to her and in that same whisper said, "Get out of here before I forget you're supposed to be a lady."

"What about Maxine?"

"She stays until the doctor is finished with her psychiatric evaluation. That could take another week. Now get the hell out of here before I deck you."

She looked him in the eye. "You and what army?"

He slammed the door behind her and Hank could feel the flush on her cheeks as Officer Lafferty watched her leave the station.

Oblivious to the rain beating against her face, she took long strides down the street. Gone was the Streeter's shuffle. Her stride kept pace with her anger. After a few blocks, she heard what she thought was a muffled laugh.

Her heart pounded out a warning. *Oh God,* she thought, *the killer is after me.* She broke into a run, looking over her shoulder for signs of her pursuer. Hank turned the corner, gasping for air, she leaned against the building and waited. She waited for several minutes but there was no sign that anyone was following.

Her anger was spent and her clothes were soaked through. Exhausted, she said, "There's no reason to go to the Azalea Gardens tonight. I could do with a good night's sleep." She turned off of Twenty-Second Street onto the Parkway.

She stood in the doorway of the laundry room, peeled off the sopping clothes and left them on the floor. She poured two fingers of cognac and lay naked across the bed. Anger spent, she fell into a restless sleep, a troubled sleep with her dream tormentor in hot pursuit. Hank tried desperately to see the face of her phantom but all she saw was the bony, eyeless skull with that horrible, perpetual grin.

She awoke as the first light of dawn filtered its gauzy gray light through the opaque curtains on the windows. The feeling of impending doom was as pronounced as it had been when she left the police station.

She was lying face down on the bed, the brandy snifter had slipped out of her hand and was lying on the floor. Every nerve in her body was aware that someone was in her apartment. She could hear nothing above the pounding of her heart. Her eyes searched the darkened room for an object...any object with which to defend herself. There was nothing.

Too late! A shadow appeared in the doorway of the bedroom. *This can't be happening,* she thought, *it's like my nightmares.* Her heart thumped loudly and she was convinced whoever was standing there could hear it. Hank saw a shadow beside the bed and was paralyzed with fear. She opened her eyes to fine slits and in the dim light that filtered through the curtains, she watched helplessly as a hand reach down and picked up the brandy snifter that had fallen to the floor. Her throat was like sand paper. She couldn't swallow. She couldn't scream. She couldn't move. She could only stare at the spot where the brandy snifter had been. Was she already dead? She couldn't even be sure she was breathing. Everything stopped. She heard breathing but it wasn't hers. She had a mental picture of a knife poised above her naked back. Would she feel the knife when it went in? Somewhere, she had heard if the knife is sharp enough you don't even feel it until it's over. Then, the most insane thought of all...*What about my book?*

Feigning sleep, Hank moaned and turned onto her back so she could see her attacker. She saw a silhouette outlined against the window but the form didn't appear to be menacing, it was just observing her. The silhouette turned and she saw the broad shoulders and untrimmed beard. The hammering inside of her chest continued, only the reason had changed.

She opened her eyes and held out her arms. Within seconds Storm had stripped down to bare skin and two sets of arms and legs were intertwined. The terrible anger, the hurtful words were part of the past. All that mattered now was the meshing of two bodies, the seeking and finding, the probing, the tasting, the feeling, the response of one need to another…the love.

Later, with his arms still around her, Storm kissed her throat, her cheeks, her lips. "When you walked out of the precinct last night, I don't think I ever came so close to hating anyone in my life. After a couple of hours, I don't think I ever loved anyone as much as I loved you. I thought you might come here and I knew I had to set the record straight. This love-hate relationship is like hanging off the edge of a cliff by your fingernails."

The back of his hand caressed the contour of her face. "In your anger, I heard what you said and I know why you want to protect Max. When I know you better I might even understand why there is so much anger inside you. I'm obsessed by you. That makes me uncomfortable because I can't be objective. I'm like a junkie, I need a fix. I need to have you. You're an addiction, Hank. You tear out my guts and I come back for more." He took a deep breath and let it out slowly. "I just hope there's a cure."

Hank kissed his mouth and looked into his eyes. "I hope there isn't. I like being your obsession."

The clock beside the bed registered six fifty.

"When I got home last night I just peeled off my clothes off in the laundry room and left them on the floor. Want me to throw your clothes in the wash with mine?"

"Why don't you do that, then we can shower together."

The idea was appealing to Hank and she hurried, picking up his clothes from the bedroom floor. Her own clothes were still sopping from the rain. She set the machine and went into the bathroom. Storm had printed a sign and taped it on the shower door. "Conserve water. Shower with your lover."

His hair and beard were white with lather but he left the rest of his body for her.

"You put our clothes in the dryer and I'll get breakfast." She loved the way his hair curled over his forehead when it was wet. She enjoyed watching his naked body, the way he moved, the way he reacted when he looked at her naked body. They ate pancakes and drank black coffee.

It was early afternoon before they returned to the streets. The rain had stopped and the sun made a brief appearance but the clouds hovered ominously over the city.

Molly began talking to herself as she walked the streets. That worried Hank. Word traveled quickly that Molly and Benny were feuding. Hank was the only other person who knew what the feud was about. She also knew that Molly was fond of Benny and the feisty old veteran of the streets didn't relish the fight she was having with him, so she talked to herself.

On Saturday morning Storm stood behind Hank in line at the shelter. He stumbled and grabbed her hand. When he did he palmed a note into it. She couldn't read it until she was alone, walking toward the subway.

Max will be released at noon. You can pick her up at the psychiatric ward of the hospital near the station. I love you.

Hank got to the hospital at eleven thirty and was told to wait, Maxine was accompanied to the lobby, by a nurse. When she stepped off the elevator, she looked like a different Max. Hank expected to see the shadow of the woman she had been. She was pleasantly surprised.

Max opened her arms and embraced Hank. "It's so good to see you. Somehow I knew you would be here when they discharged me."

"How do you feel?" Hank asked.

Maxine thought for a minute. "Better. I think."

They laughed. Max carried her plastic shopping bag in one hand and a small paper bag in the other.

"What's in the paper bag?"

Max smiled, "Lunch. I was too excited about getting out of here to eat, so the nurse put my food in a paper bag and told me to take it with me."

"That was nice. How did they treat you?"

"The staff was wonderful. I don't remember very much about what happened at police headquarters. I remember an Officer Lafferty. He was very kind and gentle. All of them were. I got scared when they sent for a psychiatrist, but Doctor McGowan was so good to me. I guess I went to pieces. I couldn't stop vomiting and I couldn't remember very much about anything. The police kept asking questions about my blanket. I did what you said. I told the truth. Do you know who told the police about me?"

"Benny."

"Benny? Are you sure? He has always been...kind to me. Why would he do such a thing? How did you find out about Benny?"

"Molly told me. Apparently she told him about the blanket and he told Mike Shaye. I think Molly is going through a rough time. She's really fond of Benny. I guess that's all over now. The Streeters know there's a war between them but that's all they know."

"Has Molly been talking to herself?"

"How did you know that?"

"It happens whenever she's upset about something. She has to talk it over with somebody and the only one she trusts is herself, so she mumbles as she walks along. Sometimes she gets into some heated arguments with herself but in the end she resolves the problem. This must be a tough one for her," Max said.

"I would have been in to visit you but they said you weren't allowed visitors."

"I know. But I had a visitor anyway. He sneaked in after hours, Monday night and last night.

"Ned?"

Max blushed. "He's making quite a hit down on the waterfront. He misses Kappy."

"I'm sure he does but I'm sure he misses you more." They reached the corner of Broad and Arch Streets. Hank asked, "Where would you like to go?"

Max spread her arms to encompass the world. "It's such a beautiful day. I would like to walk in the park. Do you mind?"

"The park it is."

Max didn't speak again until they were seated on a bench. "Have… Were there any more murders?"

"No. Shaye was the last one."

"I know it's a terrible thing to say, but I was hoping there would be another one while I was in the hospital, then they would know for sure I didn't kill anybody."

"I think they know that now," Hank said

"Before I left the hospital they gave me enough medicine for two weeks. Then I'm supposed to go back to the mental health clinic and they'll check my blood and give me more medicine. It really works. It keeps me calm. I haven't been wringing my hands and I don't feel like I'm going to throw up all the time. I've even developed an appetite."

"Great. Now we've got to keep you that way. Maybe you should sleep in a shelter, where you won't be exposed to all the shit that's going on in the streets."

"I don't like the shelters. They remind me of...." Max turned away.

She had no way of knowing Hank was aware she had been in a mental institution.

"I enjoy having the stars for a ceiling too, rather than the peeling paint in a shelter. I guess that means you want to go to the Gardens tonight?"

"Believe it or not I missed the sounds along the drive."

Molly joined them when they reached the Azalea Gardens. They marked off sleeping areas, then sat and talked. The conversation centered around Ned and his sudden popularity on the waterfront as poet and philosopher. Molly missed supper at the shelter and was beginning to feel the pangs of hunger. Max dug into her shopping bag and handed her the brown bag containing the sandwich she brought from the hospital. Molly was about to take the bag but thought better of it.

"Naw. It's okay. I'll wait till mornin'."

"Nonsense," Max said, "Hank and I ate at the shelter and the cheese in the sandwich will probably go bad before morning." She smiled. "Besides, we don't want to stay awake all night listening to your rumbling stomach."

Molly accepted the bag. "Thanks, Maxie, you're a good girl." She took a big bite of sandwich, which left the peculiar pattern where the bread passed through the areas of missing teeth. She seemed to be swallowing the food whole, she wasn't making much effort at chewing. She wiped her mouth on the back of her hand, burped and settled back with a contented expression on her face.

At eleven o'clock they settled down for the night. For a while Hank lay awake listening to the night sounds. The flutter of bat wings above the trees, the gentle stirring of leaves as breezes hopscotched through the crowded area of trees and bushes, the swish of tires along the East River Drive and the ever present sound of snoring among the Streeters hidden in nearby areas. She heard Molly join the chorus of snorers and she checked Max to be sure she was all right. Apparently, the medication was doing what it was supposed to do because she lay motionless, her right arm under her head, her breathing slow and regular. It took four yawns before Hank's brain got the message it was time to sleep.

She dreamed she was back in the apartment trying on clothes that were definitely not hers and laughing at her own selection of miniskirts in loud colors and see-through blouses. It was as though she was having an out-of-body experience. She kept trying to tap the other Hank on the shoulder but she was being ignored. She struck out at the other Hank but her hand passed through the other woman's face as it would through mist. The image sneered at Hank and walked away. Hank tried to run after her but as happens in dreams, all of her actions were reduced to slow motion and when she opened the door and looked into the hall, it was empty except for a hooded black cloak that lay at her feet. Without realizing it, she stepped on the cloak, only to be pushed aside by unseen hands.

When she looked up again, her dream tormentor was wearing the black hooded cloak and the eyeless sockets reflected the horror on Hank's face. She began running. All she could see was her own shadow running in front of her. Suddenly, her shadow had a pursuer and the action of running was again converted into slow motion. When she turned to face her tormentor it was gone but its shadow continued to menace Hank's fleeing shadow. The undulating black fog-like substance swooped down on her shadow, gathering it under the black cloak, then the shadow evaporated. Hank woke in a cold sweat. She was sitting bold upright on top of her blanket. Molly was beside her, holding her hand. Hank looked at Molly wondering why she was there.

Molly whispered, "You had a bad dream." Her face wore a worried expression. "You okay now, Hank?"

Hank nodded, obviously upset. "Was I talking in my sleep?"

"Naw. You was just walkin' round in circles, like you was lookin' for somethin'."

Hank shook her head, trying to clear it. "I dreamed somebody stole my shadow. I had to find it.... Maybe the shadow is symbolic of the soul. Maybe he didn't take my shadow...maybe he took my soul."

CHAPTER 12

The day shelter was crowded and the line moved slower than usual. Ned's eyes met Max's across the room and he elbowed his way toward her. He saw Hank and Molly but his focus was on Max, his words for her. "What light from yonder window breaks? It is the East, and Juliet is the sun."

Molly shook her head, leaned close to Hank and said, "I don't believe this guy is real. How come he talks so funny?"

Hank laughed. "He was quoting Shakespeare; the balcony scene from Romeo and Juliet. In a way, he and Max are like that. Star-crossed lovers. Destined not to find happiness in this life but they're given small glimpses of what might have been."

Molly lifted a contemptuous upper lip. "Well, that Shakespeare guy sure had a funny way of talkin'. Why couldn't he just say she looked good, instead of sayin' a window was breakin'?"

Max overheard the last part of the comment. "Who broke a window, Molly?"

"I don't think Molly appreciates Shakespeare," Ned said, taking Max's hand and smiling into her eyes. "Feeling better now?" he asked.

"Yes, much."

Hank nudged Ned. "She looks great, doesn't she?"

Ned nodded and put his arm around Hank's shoulder and said, "Ah, Jenny, you're like a fresh breath of spring."

"There," Molly said. "See what I mean? Your name's Hank. Why the hell does he keep callin' you Jenny?" She muttered to herself, "Must be a full moon."

Breakfast consisted of a bowl of cereal with milk and a slice of bread with margarine." Max lifted the slice of bread to her lips and said to Ned, "When your heart is light, bread and butter can be as satisfying as eggs Benedict."

Hank caught sight of Storm as they were leaving the shelter. He motioned for her to meet him outside. He was standing beside the building, waiting. Hank stooped, pretending to tie her shoelace. She was looking up at Storm's back.

"Our killer struck again last night," he said.

"Oh, God, not again. Where?"

"Uber Street. Behind the library," Storm said.

"Do you know yet, who it was?"

"A Streeter named Benny." He hesitated. "He was Mike Shaye's snitch."

Hank gasped, and Storm looked around at her. "Know him?"

"Of course, every Streeter knows Benny." She paused. "But he doesn't fit the pattern. He's at least sixty-five years old."

"Same M.O. Eight stab wounds in the back and a verse left beside the body."

"Has the news been released yet?" Hank asked.

"It was on TV and radio. Why?"

"Molly." Hank looked around to see if anyone was watching. "She was very fond of Benny. I'm sure she doesn't know about this. The three of us were together at the Azalea Gardens last night, so she had no way of knowing." Hank bit her lower lip. "I think I should be the one to tell her. She's not going to take it well."

Storm's voice was soft and tender, he said, "I thought street people didn't get involved?"

"They try not to show their feelings because it makes them vulnerable. When someone finds your Achilles heel, you're an open target." Hank looked around to see if Molly had come out yet. "How did the broadcaster identify him?" she asked.

"As a derelict. Known on the streets only as Benny."

Hank wanted to reach out and touch Storm but she resisted. "I'd better move along," she said, "See you Sunday?"

"If I can wait that long," he said.

Hank felt a pleasant flush color her cheeks. She moved closer to the door waiting for Max and Molly to come out. Ned was with them.

"Let's go to the park," Hank said, "okay?"

"Grand idea, Jenny," Ned said. "A day like this should be spent in the park communing with nature. And who could be more fortunate than I, to be in the company of three such beautiful women."

Molly watched him out of the corner of her eye. "Pick up your feet, gals, the shit is almost ankle-deep." Maxine laughed and put her arm around Molly's shoulder as they walked toward Fairmount Park. Ned walked beside Hank and she tried to keep her voice low while she told him about Benny. "I wish there was an easy way to tell Molly."

Ned stared at Molly's back. "That's not the kind of news she needs to hear right now."

"It's not the kind of news any of us needs to hear but it's better if she hears it from a friend rather than from a radio as I did."

Ned shook his head. "She's not going to take it well, especially since she and Benny were feuding. Everybody gave Molly a lot of latitude when she started talking to herself that told us the rift went pretty deep. I always thought she had a soft spot in her heart for Benny. What could have happened to cause such a problem? Then Molly stopped talking to herself, which meant she was probably ready to call off the feud and forgive him. Now she can't. What was the problem, do you know?"

"No," Hank lied. "Whatever happened was between Benny and Molly."

Ned took her arm. "Let's catch up with them. I don't envy you. I know I couldn't do it, I don't have the stomach for this sort of thing."

Molly and Hank sat on a park bench, Ned and Max walked to a shaded area. Hank put her arm behind Molly and rested it on the bench. "Molly, I don't think there's an easy way to say this but you'll hear it sooner or later. Better you hear it from me." She waited until Molly looked at her before she continued. She took a deep breath. "Benny was murdered last night."

Molly avoided looking directly at Hank and stared blankly at an invisible spot somewhere over Hank's shoulder. In a soft voice, she said, "You sure?"

"I'm afraid so. I'm sorry, Molly, I know you were friends."

Molly's manner showed a hint of anger and agitation. The anger seemed to be directed back at herself. Finally, she asked, "How did you know about Benny?"

"I heard it on a car radio when a pimp stopped to talk to one of his girls." Molly seemed preoccupied with her shoes then Hank saw a tear escape from under her lowered eyelids.

Ned told Max about Benny's death. She was visibly shaken when they joined Hank and Molly. Ned took Molly's hand and walked with her over the patches of bare earth interspersed with tufts of wild grass.

Hank studied Max's expression and realized the news had upset her as much as it had Molly. *Damn!* Hank thought. *Max was doing so well.* She sat beside Max and put an arm around her. "Did you take your medicine this morning?"

Max shook her head. "I was feeling so good. It's easy to forget about medicine when you feel good." Max reached into her bag and took out the brown cylinder with the hospital pharmacy label and took out a lithium tablet. Hank handed her the bottle of water.

Max swallowed just enough to get the pill down. When she looked at Hank, there were tears on her cheeks. "Why is the killer doing this? We've done nothing to him. Why are we being punished?"

Hank satisfied herself that Ned and Molly were out of hearing range. "I'm sure Benny snitched on quite a few of the Streeters. Sooner or later somebody was going to resent it."

"Then you do think the murderer is one of the street people?"

"I didn't say that," Hank said. "It could be a pimp or one of his girls. For all we know it could be a cop who hates Streeters."

Max said, "I don't think that's true and neither do you. Most of the police are compassionate people. Mike Shaye was the exception. I imagine he was difficult to know and even more difficult to understand. People like him have feelings and fears too. I can't believe he did anything so terrible that he deserved to die for it."

Hank smiled, she remembered Molly had said, *Max would make excuses for the devil.* "I'm afraid I don't agree with you about Shaye. He was one bad hombre and he hurt a lot of people. Hell, even his wife couldn't live with him."

Max looked at Hank a long time before she commented, "How do you know that? About Shaye and his wife, I mean?"

Hank knew if she was to convince Max the knowledge was only hearsay, it would have to ring true. "When I was at police headquarters, he tried to rough me up. Another detective stopped him. So I asked the other detective why Shaye was so angry with me. He said he thought it was because I resembled his wife who had bedded down with half of their neighbors. It was a nasty divorce." Hank shrugged. "My opinion was that he hated all women."

Max said, "He was the one who gave you the black eye last winter, wasn't he?"

Hank stared at Max. "How did you remember about the black eye?"

"It's easy to remember violence. It's the nice things we forget."

"You're incurable, Max. Have you always turned the other cheek?" Hank regretted the words as soon as they were spoken. She knew better than to pry into Max's past. To cover the faux pas, Hank laughed, "You and Pollyanna."

Max watched Molly and Ned. "I think I should be with Molly, don't you?"

"I think Molly needs Ned right now," Hank said.

"You're probably right. He has that special way of making you feel important; of making everything seem right again." She looked at Hank. "You have that talent too. You and Ned are leaders. The rest of us are sheep. We simply follow. I guess we would follow you into hell if you led the way."

Hank asked herself, *Who is this wounded dove? What could have happened to cause the total destruction of her self-esteem?* To Hank, Max was an impossible combination of paradoxes and dilemmas, the unsolvable equation. She was a leftover of bygone days, a disposable commodity of no significance in the current marketplace.

Hank watched the back of Ned's head as he tried to console Molly and thought, *How strange that Max and Ned should meet. Both seem to belong to that same bygone era. Two misfits, struggling to form a symbiotic relationship that was doomed by the mere passage of time.*

Following behind the unusually warm spring, the hot, sultry days of summer were early. Families picnicked along the banks of the river and joggers shared space with bicycles on the path beside the river drive. Home and apartment dwellers turned out en masse for the broad spectrum of activities planned for the Independence Day weekend.

The main activity at Penn's Landing on the Great Plaza on the Delaware was a restaurant festival with a variety of eateries bringing their specialties to the waterfront area. There was a regular schedule of musical entertainment, extending from soft rock to swing, from jazz to rhythm and blues, with a little classical thrown in.

Automobiles were not allowed on most downtown streets, so the people poured out of the subways like ants leaving their colonies in search of food. Streeters were busy checking the curbsides for loose change the crowds might have dropped in their eagerness to push their way to the front for the best view of the passing parade. Molly watched from the back row of people standing along Broad Street. Some of the Streeters were working the crowds, begging. Others exerted hidden talents by picking pockets.

Hank decided to check out the waterfront. She saw Max sitting on the ground with a small group of non-Streeters, listening to Ned's recitations. His eyes traveled over the group around him but mainly his eyes wandered back to Max. It was evident to Hank that the poetry was for Max.

Someone from the crowd called out, "'The Definition of Love.'"

Without hesitation, Ned launched into the opening stanza:

"My love is of a birth as rare
As 'tis for object, strange and high:
It was begotten by despair
Upon impossibility.

Magnanimous despair alone
Could Show me so divine a thing,
Where feeble hope could ne'er have flown
But vainly flapped its tinsel wing.

And yet I quickly might arrive
Where my extended soul is fixed
But Fate does iron wedges drive
And always crowds itself betwixt."

Ned continued with the second and third stanzas as though he was reading it from a book. The crowd was captivated by the poetry and the distant stare of the poet. Hank studied the group, a varied mix of economic stability, but all were completely engrossed in the storytelling talent of a Streeter named Ned. Maxine sat motionless, watching him with tear-drenched eyes and a sad smile that said, *What might have been...* Then Hank saw Storm sitting on the fringe of the crowd, listening to the gentle vagrant, who not only recited but felt and lived each line and carried each person along on the journey.

"For Fate with jealous eye does see
Two perfect loves; nor lets them close
Their union would here ruin be,
And her tyrannic power depose.

And therefore her decrees of steel
As the different poles have placed.
(Through love's whole world on us doth wheel)
Not by themselves to be embraced."

Hank's gaze compelled Storm to look up and his eyes searched the crowd. When his gaze met hers, she felt she was drowning in the softness of a gray cloud. He made his way around the periphery until he was beside her, and settled down on the grass. The silence of the crowd was such that a whisper would have sounded like a clash of thunder. Storm touched Hank's hand as he settled in beside her. Ned's voice continued telling the tale.

"Unless the giddy heaven fall,
And earth some new convulsion tear;

And, us to join, the world should all
Be cramped into a planisphere.

As lines, so love's oblique may well
Themselves in every angle greet;
But ours, so truly parallel,
Though infinite, can never meet.

Therefore, the love which us doth bind,
But Fate so enviously debars,
Is the conjunction of the mind,.
And opposition of the stars."

Hank and Storm sat on the outer fringes but had the best view of Ned and Max. Ned's eyes held Max in an invisible quiet embrace. The naked passion he felt was mirrored there. Max's eyes responded with a yearning that reached out, answering his embrace.

Hank thought, *Two souls, wandering hand in hand, in the abyss between heaven and hell.*

The more sensitive listeners in the audience were dabbing at their eyes to prevent the tears from spilling over. Max's smile never wavered in spite of the tears that now streaked her cheeks. For Max and Ned the crowd had disappeared. They were completely alone, lost in each other's pain.

The audience stared at the poet of the waterfront, not really knowing what to do. To applaud somehow seemed sacrilegious because his recitation was almost a prayer. There was something so profound in his recitation that had it not been for his age, one might expect he had written the verse rather than Andrew Marvell.

Ned automatically went into Richard Crashaw's *An Epitaph Upon Husband and Wife, Which Died, and Were Buried Together.*

"To these, whom death again did wed,
This grave's the second marriage-bed.
For though the hand of fate could force
'Twixt soul and body a divorce,
It could not sunder man and wife,
Because they both lived but one life,
Peace, good reader. Do not weep

Peace, the lovers are asleep.
They sweet turtles, folded lie
In the last knot love could tie.
And though they lie as they were dead,
Their pillow stone, their sheets of lead
(pillow hard, and sheets not warm)
Love made the bed; they'll take no harm.
Let them sleep: let them sleep on,
Till this stormy night be gone.
Till the eternal morrow dawn.
Then the curtains will be drawn
And they wake into a light
Whose day shall never die in night."

Finally, one of the listening audience removed a bill from his wallet and placed it on the grass in front of Ned. Others revived and showed their appreciation by following his example.

When Hank turned to talk with Storm, he was gone. There were only the three of them sitting on the grass. Hank too, started to leave, but her movement jolted Ned from his reverie. In a valiant effort, he tore his gaze from Max and motioned for Hank to join them. The money still lay on the grass, unnoticed. Ned's blue eyes were slightly darker than the sky and the soft white clouds above were mirrored there.

"Jenny," Ned said, "we were hoping to see you before the day was over."

Hank looked down at the pile of money on the ground. "It looks like you made quite a hit today. I'll bet there's more money in that pile than you've seen for a long time."

When Ned looked down, he was confused. For him, the crowd disappeared once he started the poem. Even though the request came from the audience, his performance was for Maxine alone.

He picked up the money and smiled. "You're right, Jenny, there's twenty-three dollars here. How about a hamburger and fries for each of us? You've both shared in my problems; it's only fair that you share in my good fortune as well." He stood up holding out an arm for each of them. "Ladies, may I have the honor of escorting you to the bistro?"

He bought sandwiches and fries and a fresh peach for each of them, from a street vender who insisted on having his money before he handed over the food. They found a spot by the river, where they enjoyed their picnic lunch. Hank saved her peach.

Max sat looking at the river, her arms around both knees, hugging them to her as Ned watched. Hank wondered if Ned realized Max was in love with him. She knew Max was unaware of her own feelings for him.

Ned sat beside Max and put his arm around her.

Hank gathered her canvas bag and water bottle. "See you later," she said.

"Where are you going?" There was a hint of alarm in Max's voice.

"Got to get the kinks out. My body isn't used to sitting so long."

Max asked anxiously, "Where will you be later, Hank?"

"If you've got something that works for you, don't change it. I'll be at the Azalea Gardens."

"Save me a place?" Anxiety was reflected in Max's voice.

"Sure. See you later." Hank knew only too well what anxieties and doubts Max was experiencing, especially if Max admitted to herself that she was in love with Ned. Her psyche would have to find safe ground. She wasn't ready to handle this sudden realization of her feelings. Hank remembered the uncertainty, the skepticism she felt when she thought she was in love with Julian Grant. Fear was her first reaction. She refused to trust her emotions but in the end, emotion won out over reason.

"Ned, thank you for the best holiday I've had in a long time. I mean that sincerely. I spent it with two very caring people."

The litter in the streets made it appear like a ticker-tape parade had passed through the city. The trash barrels were overloaded and spilled onto the sidewalks. An eerie quiet crept over the city spreading a misty mantel over the concrete jungle. Most of the people headed for the riverfront for the customary display of fireworks that would begin after dark.

Night hovered over the city like a soaring eagle, waiting for his prey to move before making the final swoop to conquer. There were still some traces of sunset's magenta-streaked clouds that were giving up possession of the day in favor of the coolness of the breezes of night. Hank found a spot where three people could bed down comfortably, when she heard a familiar shuffle approach from the road. Without turning around, she said, "Andros?"

Storm laughed, "How did you know it was me?"

"I recognized your shuffle."

"I told you it could be done." She was rewarded with a flash of white teeth. "I fully expected Max would be with you."

"She'll be here later. She and Ned are staying for the fireworks."

Storm shook his head. "Ned is impressive, isn't he? He has that rare ability to extract all the meaning from a piece of poetry and lay it at your feet. It's no wonder he had a large audience." Storm's eyes twinkled and Hank knew he was smiling under all the facial hair. "Does Ned know he's in love with Max?"

"I doubt it," Hank said. "I think Max just found out she's in love with him and it scares the shit out of her. I'm afraid she doesn't associate happy memories with being in love."

He looked around to be sure they were not seen, then he kissed her.

"Are you staying the night?" Hank asked.

He shook his head. "Can't. I can't be this close to you and not have you." He watched the traffic on the River Drive. "Besides, the last time a couple did that along this drive, he ended up with a bloody back and she with a bloody front. I have better plans for us than that. See you at the apartment Friday?"

She didn't trust her voice, so she nodded. He looked around quickly and pushed her to the ground and covered her body with his.

They heard shuffling on the path and he rolled off onto the ground. About fifty feet away Hank saw the faint outline of Molly wending her way toward them. Hank stood up, pushing him away. "You stinking bastard, I shared a piece of fruit with you but I'll be damned if I'm giving you a piece of ass too. Before I'm finished, you won't have anything left to screw with." She raised her knee and went through the motions of kicking him in the groin. Before he stood up, he reached up and pinched her backside. He held both hands to his groin as though she had actually kneed him and he backed away. "Don't get uptight, bitch, I'd have been doing you a favor. You look like you need a good twelve inches." He winked as he backed away.

"The only twelve inches you ever got was from three separate erections of four inches each."

In the dimming light she could see his eyes sparkle as he whispered, "You sure know how to hurt a guy." Then he was gone, just seconds before Molly came up behind her. Hank pretended she didn't know Molly was there. Aloud she said, "Damn men. They all think with their loins." She took a bite out of the peach Ned had bought her. "Bastard!" she shouted to the gathering twilight.

"I sure hope the rest of your day was better than the part I just seen."

Feigning surprise, Hank spun around, an angry expression on her face. "I hate a guy who thinks your body is open territory for his hands and any other part of his body that gets a craving."

Molly laughed. "Be happy you're still attractive enough for them to want to screw around. Look at me. Nobody's made a pass at me for at least the last fifteen years." Her tone hushed. "'Cept maybe for Benny." Then in an effort to dismiss the thought, she smiled her semi-toothless grin and asked, "See Maxie today?"

"I left her a little while ago at the landing. She and Ned are going to watch the fireworks. I promised to save a spot for her."

Molly looked concerned. "I never seen two Streeters fall in love before but I guess it's possible." She looked off in the direction of the Delaware River and in a low soft voice said, "He'd better not hurt Maxie."

Hank felt a chill course its way up her spine.

Molly turned and caught Hank watching her. "Nobody's ever going to hurt that girl again. Not while I'm around. Why don't he just leave her alone?"

"Ned wouldn't do anything to hurt Max. He's as protective of her as you are."

"They're spendin' too much time together and Maxie's too trustin'."

Hank thought it best to change the subject. "Molly, is it my imagination or are there more families on the streets than there were a couple of months ago?"

"It ain't your imagination. In the last couple of years, there are a lot more families livin' outta shoppin' bags. Them poor little babies never done nothin' to deserve this kind of life. I'm tellin' you, Hank, this country's going down the tubes. It's bad enough when you're on the streets because you ain't got a family but when you got parents or sisters and brothers or grown children and you still have to hit the streets because you can't afford to live in a house, then I think we got a really sick society. I ain't never seen so much child abuse in all my sixty-eight years as I seen in the last three to five years. Seems like men just don't know what else to do with a hard-on. Maybe somebody oughta start doing cockectomies on these guys who molest kids. I tell you, Hank, it's disgustin'."

Hank smoothed out her blanket and sat facing Molly, who had just revived a painful memory from Hank's past. Pictures flashed through her memory of Julian Grant in bed with a thirteen-year-old girl. Back then, Hank would have enjoyed seeing him get a cockectomy, as Molly aptly put it. She shook her head as though the mere motion could erase the lewd pictures stored in her memory. Hank cocked her head at the sound of shuffling coming from the drive. "Max is here," she said, without looking up.

Molly watched the footpath until Max came into view. "How'd you do that?" The concern that furrowed Molly's brow disappeared at the sight of Maxine.

Hank said, "It's no big thing." She waited until Max sat down. "I thought you were going to stay for the fireworks?"

"I was, but I began to feel like the boats in the harbor.... My anchor was dragging, so I decided to turn in early. It was a wonderful day though, wasn't it?"

"It was better for some than others," Molly said as she rolled onto her side and closed her eyes.

Max spread out her plastic ground cover and blanket and used her shopping bag as a pillow. "I'm going to enjoy sleeping tonight. I'm exhausted."

Hank made several unsuccessful attempts to stifle a yawn and finally yielded to the urge to close her eyes. She dreamed about Storm but Mike Shaye kept invading her slumber and she could feel him poking and shoving her from side to side. Hank tried to reach for Storm but the way was blocked to her and she could hear him calling her name again and again. Reality took hold and Hank realized somebody was actually calling her. When she opened her eyes, Molly was shaking her and calling to Max. Hank sat up, rubbing her eyes. "What is it, Molly? What's wrong?"

"What's wrong? Do you have to drown before you know it's rainin'?"

Max sat up but couldn't keep her eyes open and slumped across her blanket again.

Molly bent over Max. "Help me with her, Hank. Get the plastic ground covers out from under our blankets and we can use them as a tent."

She had moved her blanket close to Max's and put her plastic cloth over top of the bushes, shielding the ground under the azalea leaves from the falling rain. Hank followed her direction and they moved Max around until they got her plastic cover and overlapped it with theirs, then they butted their blankets together. Hank looked at her watch, turning her wrist to catch some of the light shining on the river drive. It was four forty-five.

Molly said, "I went to take a pee about twenty minutes ago and it was spittin' a little then. By the time I got back it was coming down fast and hard. I swear, you and Maxie could float downriver and not wake up till you was in New Jersey. You guys can sleep through an earthquake. When I left, you must have been tucked under the bushes, then when I got back, I saw your foot stickin' out on this side. Probably in your sleep you felt the rain and tried to get under some shelter. Those pills the doctor gave Maxie must be pretty strong. She sleeps like she was dead."

"Yeah, the sleep of the innocents," Hank said, "maybe I should try to get some of her pills, I could certainly use some sleep without dreams."

"With all the murders going on you should want to sleep light so you don't wake up dead." Molly looked at Hank in the dim light from the drive. "Come to think of it, you look like hell. Like you ain't been sleepin' at all."

"Gee thanks, Molly, that sure did a lot for my ego. Maybe if I can get back to sleep, I won't look so bad in daylight." Hank turned her back to Molly and closed her eyes. She thought, *If I look like I feel, I could believe I look like hell. The tiredness is imbedded in my bones.* She had the floating sensation that comes in the twilight of sleep. Within seconds, Molly, Max and the rain were forgotten as she cuddled up against her canvas bag into the arms of Morpheus, oblivious of the thunderstorm raging in scattered areas around them.

When Hank awakened again, Molly was gone and Max was still sleeping peacefully. It was eight thirty and her stomach was letting her know she should be in line for some food. Hank shook Max until she responded with more than a grunt. Max knelt and started gathering her blanket. "What happened to my ground cover? Hank, somebody stole my ground cover. How could they do that when I was sleeping on it?"

Hank pointed over her head and said, "It rained during the night, so Molly and I moved you around to get to the plastic cover. We butted the three covers together and made a tent over the bushes to keep out the rain. Molly must have left early and took her cover with her. Aren't you hungry? I'm starved."

Max looked up at the few patches of bright white imbedded in a variegated gray sky. "Thank God it's cool. I can't remember a summer where the humidity and ninety-degree temperatures started this early. Really makes you appreciate overcast days like today. Hank, are we in a global warming, like the environmentalists say?"

"The evidence seems to point in that direction, doesn't it? I guess I don't really want to believe them because prophets of doom scare the hell out of me."

"Maybe that's the idea," Max said.

"As long as I'm on the streets, I am not against global warming. Cold, dreary, damp, dank days of winter are not my idea of comfort. Nobody really cares. We can be freezing our butts off and nobody really does anything about it. If we manage to find a sheltered place to warm up, that's a plus; if not, it's just another bum taking up space under the ground instead of on top of it."

"You sound depressed, Hank, what's wrong?"

"It's probably the weather. Gray skies do nothing to lift my spirits."

They walked southeast on Benjamin Franklin Parkway and turned south on Twenty-Second Street and crossed the Vine Street Expressway on the overpass.

"Lots of people heading for the Jersey shore," Max said, looking wistfully at the traffic below. "Wish we could go to the shore. I'll bet New Jersey has some of the most beautiful beaches in the country." She sighed, "Well, maybe…someday."

Flashing blue and red lights coupled with the mournful wail of sirens drew their frightened attention.

"They seem to be turning into Race Street," Max said biting her lower lip.

"It looks more like the area around the Board of Education building. I can't tell if that's an ambulance or a police van."

"Let's take another route," Max said, backing up. "What if it's another murder?" Max's hands trembled and she blinked quickly, repeatedly, to keep the tears from flooding her blue eyes. "The murderer kills all around us, Hank, it's like he's trying to tell us something. Death follows us like a shadow…a deadly shadow."

CHAPTER 13

"Why does this bother you so much?" Doctor McGowan asked.

Storm Andrews paced off the twenty feet between Dr. McGowan's desk and the door leading to the waiting room. He turned and faced her. "I don't know. I've turned this problem over, under and inside out. Maybe Mike Shaye was right, Maybe I'm getting too involved."

"How involved are you?" The tone of her voice was impersonal.

"More than I should be. More than I ever wanted to be." He sank into the chair on the opposite side of the desk.

"You're not happy with that situation?" Doctor McGowan asked.

"How can I be?" Storm looked away from the doctor's questioning. "Technically, she's still a suspect in the serial killings."

"Do you think Hank is capable of murder?"

"No." The word exploded like a shot from a cannon. He sucked in some air and let it hiss through his teeth, then shook his head. "I thought so in the beginning but I don't think so now."

"What made you change your mind?"

Storm ran his fingers through his thick black hair, randomly streaked with gray. A lock of hair curled over his left eye and he brushed it away impatiently. He looked across the desk, "Because I'm in love with her."

"That's not a reason, it's an excuse."

"I know, Doc, I know. I've got to work it out for myself." Storm pulled a piece of paper from his pocket. It contained two names, Stockheim and Thornton. He put it on the desk. "I talked with Wally Stockheim, he was her editor before she went the independent route. Hank is doing a piece on the homeless for the *Journal*. He's concerned about the stress she's under. It seems she spent some time in a private sanitarium after having a breakdown. The doctor who took care of her was Jeremy Thornton. Hank calls Stockheim every couple of weeks or so and keeps him up to date on what's happening on the streets. She tells him she's not under stress."

"What do you think?"

"She has to be under stress. Being on the streets without a serial killer on the prowl is bad enough...but when you add that dimension..."

"You've been on the police force for some time. How would you rate the stress on a scale of one to ten?" Doctor McGowan asked.

"I guess I would rate it differently for men and women." Storm said, "Since men appear to be the primary targets, I would give it a nine or a ten. So far only one woman has been killed but that can change at any time. I'd give it a seven or an eight on the stress scale."

Max and Hank avoided the Board of Education Building by cutting through Chinatown. At the oriental fruit and produce stand, Max stumbled into the arms of the proprietor. He held her until she regained her footing, then he released her and bowed. Max returned the bow and spoke to him in his native tongue. He smiled and a brief conversation followed. Max introduced Hank to Kai Wha Yu. As Hank and Max turned to leave, Kai Wha Yu picked up two of his biggest oranges and gave one to each of them. Max lowered her eyes and bowed slightly, thanking him for the unexpected gift and they continued through Chinatown to Franklin Square. They found an empty bench and sat down to enjoy their breakfast of fresh oranges.

"Where did you learn to speak Chinese?"

"I was born in Taiwan. We didn't come back to the States until I was ten years old." That was all the information she offered and Hank didn't pursue the subject. Max picked at the orange skin until she had broken off minute pieces, then she fed them to the pigeons.

"It's no wonder Philadelphia has such a problem with pigeons, when people like you keep feeding them."

Max smiled as she fed the birds. "Everything and everyone has a reason for being. We may not know what that reason is but if pigeons didn't fit into the overall plan of things, God wouldn't have wasted His time on them."

Hank was fascinated by one particular bird that stood on the periphery of the scavengers vying for the scraps. The crown of his head looked like an untended lawn. Its tiny pin-feathers surrounded some bald spots, giving him an air of intoxication. On uncertain, spindley legs, the pigeon made his way to Max and took some of the orange crumbs from her hand.

Hank laughed, "I'll be damned, you and Francis of Assisi. If I did that, the dumb bird would take my finger off."

A laugh started in Max's eyes and spread to her mouth with a child's delight, something unexpected and wonderful.

"Believe me, Hank, there is nothing sainted about me. In fact, there aren't many people who are more flawed than I... but thank you, it was a lovely thing to say."

Unfamiliar shuffling steps approached and Hank turned to see who it was. Hank had seen the Streeter before but didn't know his name. He acknowledged her presence with a nod but spoke directly to Max.

"Maxie, Ned's trying to find you. He said to stay away from the area around the Board of Education. Looks like another one down. Why don't you stay here until late afternoon? We're going to have to look after each other, at least until the cops catch the killer. I'll tell Ned where I found you."

"Thank you for the warning." Max looked from him to Hank, realizing Hank didn't know him. "Franz, say hello to Hank. She's been trying to keep me out of trouble too."

Franz grunted something that Hank felt was probably an acknowledgment of the introduction. It was then Hank recalled where she had seen him before. He was the one who knocked her on her butt, on Chestnut Street in the snow. She remembered how angry Molly had been. Hank concluded that his manners had not improved over the spring and summer. They watched as he walked away, his left shoulder held higher than the right, and he dragged his left leg.

"That's a pretty bad gait," Hank said. "It's a wonder he gets around at all."

"Franz wasn't always like that," Max said. "A couple of years ago he was hit by a truck and dragged for quite a distance. He's lucky to be alive."

"You call that lucky? He seems to be in pain. Maybe it would have been more merciful if they had let him die." Hank didn't miss the sad expression on Max's face.

"I know," Hank said. "Everything has a season and a reason."

By two o'clock Hank could no longer control her restlessness. She had to make some excuse to get to the apartment to meet Storm. "Why don't we walk to the park?"

"I think we should wait for Ned," Max said as she continued to feed the pigeons.

That was the opening Hank needed. "I can't sit anymore. My bones are protesting. You wait for Ned and I'll see you later at the Azalea Gardens. Will you be okay?"

"You're beginning to sound like Ned. Of course I'm going to be all right. I'll see you later."

Hank took a circuitous route to her apartment, being cautious that she wasn't followed. She entered the building by the tower stairs and was assaulted by the invisible presence of a now familiar emotion…fear. A fear that she was alone and a greater fear that she wasn't alone. She hurried up the stairs and let herself in to the apartment. A mouth-watering aroma of spaghetti sauce greeted her as she shut the door and a pair of arms spun her around so that she was pressed between the door and Storm's body.

"Now, what was that comment you made a few days ago, about three erections of four inches each?"

"That really got to you, huh?"

His mouth was searching for hers. "I brought a ruler along just to prove a point." His mouth found hers, as she pulled down the zipper on his trousers and felt for his probing passion.

"I won't quibble over a couple of inches."

Later as they sat eating spaghetti and meatballs she told him about the feeling somebody was in the tower stair when she arrived. He frowned. "Why didn't you say so when you came in?"

"Let's get our priorities straight, Detective Andrews."

"I wonder." He shook his head. "Naw, it can't be."

"Can't be what?"

"Remember the gal I told you I thought was you?" He didn't wait for an answer. "I saw her again last night. She must be a hooker. She tried to proposition me."

"Do you still think she looks like me?"

"She does…until she opens her mouth. She's as hard as nails."

"Where did you see her?"

"I had a feeling the killer was ready to strike again, so I kept moving trying to cover as much of the waterfront as I could when this dame comes rubbing up against me. I think she wanted to play house."

"Just like that?"

"Well, not exactly. When I said no, she told me she does a lot of other things, said I would have a good time. I told her to get lost. Her name is Suzie, said she does her best work late at night. Now I wonder…" He omitted the conversation about Hank. "Apparently Mike Shaye knew her. He told me her name was Suzanne Hoffman."

"That name sounds familiar." Hank looked pensive. "I have the feeling that I know her, or know of her. My mother's maiden name was Hoffman." Hank raised one eyebrow. "Be careful, I think I'm jealous."

"You don't have to be jealous of anybody like her." Storm put another helping of spaghetti on his plate. "There was another murder last night."

"In the same area where you saw her?"

"No, but that doesn't mean anything."

"Who was the victim?"

"Don't know. He's a Streeter for sure but I didn't recognize him."

"Where?"

"Spring Street, behind the Board of Education Building."

"Was it..." Hank couldn't finish the sentence.

"Yes, the same as the others. The victim was probably in his early forties. There's something about these murders that we're missing. It's probably so obvious that we're overlooking it because it's right there in front of us. Why are there always eight stab wounds? What the hell does the number eight mean?" He picked up the plates from the table, rinsed them off and put them in the dishwasher. "Much as I would like to stay the night, I had better get back on the streets."

She nodded. She had an ominous feeling that sent shivers up her spine. "Let me go out first, Storm. In that way you can see if anyone follows me."

"Okay. Where will you be tonight?"

"The usual place."

"Be careful." He held her in his arms and she could see the worried look in his eyes.

Hank was the first to arrive at the Azalea Gardens and the ominous feeling was still very much with her. She shivered in spite of the warmth of the night. She imagined danger behind every tree, every bush. The thought that some bimbo named Suzie was after Storm didn't help matters either. Hank propped herself against a tree and listened to the night sounds, waiting for the familiar shuffle of Max or Molly's steps. Uncomfortably, Hank realized she was afraid, no, terrified to be alone. She heard the excited voices of Molly and Max. Hank stood up so they could see where she was.

"Hank," said Max, "remember the police cars this morning?" She didn't wait for confirmation. "Lester was killed. Whoever is doing this is wiping us out one by one and nobody's doing anything about it."

Hank said, "The killer's bound to make a mistake. When that happens, the police will get him."

"But there might be another dozen of us dead by then." Max was wringing her hands.

Molly put her arm around Max's shoulder. "You got to stop worryin', Maxie, before you know it, you'll be back in the hospital. You don't want that to happen, now do you?"

Max shook her head and laid down her ground cloth, carefully spreading out her blanket on top of it. She looked up at Hank. "Ned told me old Gil saw the murder."

Hank knew Gil Harvey had been on the Philadelphia streets for at least three decades, possibly more. She said, "Didn't he go to the police?"

Molly put her blanket across from Maxine's on the other side of the footpath and sat on her blanket, shaking her head at Hank's question. "Gil's gonna stay as far away from the cops as he can get."

"But," Hank tried to reason, "wouldn't he be better off in protective custody than out on the streets where the killer can get to him? He should know his age is no protection. It didn't help Benny and I doubt it will protect Gil either."

"He don't look at it that way," Molly said. "Gil's afraid they won't believe him and lock him up him for the murders."

"Gil thinks he's safe because he's over sixty years old and the killer is only interested in killing younger men," Max said as she wrung her handkerchief into a twisted ball.

"Dumb jerk," Molly mumbled to herself. "Did he forget about Benny already? Hell, Benny was his age."

"But Benny was Shaye's snitch," Hank said. "I guess he got killed for that fact alone."

Molly put her shopping bag down for a pillow. "Yeah, and if the killer knows Gil saw the killin', he's not goin' to be any safer than Benny was."

Max was shivering now, in spite of the warmth of the night. She stuttered, "Ned said Gil didn't see the killer's face but he did see the murder. But I'll bet the killer won't take any chances. Oh, God, Hank, we already know who the next victim is."

"We don't know anything of the kind. We don't even know if the killer knows that Gil saw the crime."

"If he's one of us, he knows." Max began biting her fingernails.

Molly interrupted her mumbling to comment, "Stupid jackass. We should put on his tombstone, *He was too old to get killed.*" She looked off in the distance and said in a barely audible voice, "You're never too old to get killed." When Molly looked at Hank and Max again, she was completely drained of emotion.

Max crossed the footpath and put her hand on Molly's shoulder. "You all right, Molly?"

Molly nodded. At that moment, Hank thought Molly looked ancient.

The papers gave a detailed account the death of Lester Philander. Streeters couldn't understand how the police were able to get information about them. No one on the streets knew Lester's last name. How did the police find out? The killer's selected verse was a quote from Socrates. *Either death is a state of nothingness and utter unconsciousness, or, as men say, there is a change and migration of the soul from this world to another.*

The Streeters seemed to hug the buildings as they walked, in what came to be described in the newspapers as the death march. No place was safe and despite the threat of death, very few Streeters slept in the shelters at night.

Four days passed since the latest killing and the panic within Hank mounted. She determined Storm had to be told that Gil had witnessed the murder.

Maxine's eyes were dark ringed with the fatigue of sleeplessness. Ned's eyes mirrored everyone's concern. Max was withdrawing from all of them. Hank knew she shouldn't interfere but she couldn't stand by and watch what was left of that fragile ego crumble into ashes, never again to be pieced together.

"Max, Did you take your medication today?"

Max looked up her eyes reflected terror and confusion. "I don't have any more."

"How long have you been out of medicine?"

"I don't remember. It doesn't matter."

"I don't want to hear that shit from you. Do you understand?" Hank wanted to shake her, to wake her up, to bring her back to reality. She also realized that reality might put her into a catatonic state with the possibility of...no return. Hank recognized the symptoms of Max's reaching the overload mode in her emotional scale. Max's psyche had to find a haven, a protected safe zone, even at the expense of her life. Hank talked Max into going to the waterfront. She was looking for Ned. He had to be told how close Max was to disaster.

They found him in a small gathering of tourists listening intently to his verses. Hank signaled him to break away. Once he saw Max, the signal wasn't necessary.

Slowly he closed the gap between them, his gaze riveted on Max. There was a hint of a smile in his blue eyes, but his lips never got the message.

"Hello, Jenny." Shock registered in his eyes. " Max?" he closed his eyes. "Oh, my dear girl." He held out his arms and Max looked questioningly at this man who was becoming a stranger.

Max cocked her head to one side, studying his face and extended arms. He moved a step closer but she backed away. Her vacant stare sent a shiver up his spine. He stopped, dropped his arms to his sides and looked questioningly at Hank.

Hank broke the silence. "Max is out of medication…probably has been for several days. She doesn't remember how long."

Ned's eyes held Max's gaze. "We're going back to the hospital pharmacy to get your prescription. Do you still have the card they gave you at the hospital?"

"Card?" Max asked, bewildered.

Hank took the shopping bag from her arm and rummaged through it looking for the hospital clinic card. At the bottom of the bag she found the card but she also found a knife. One with a double edge…a stiletto.

Hank pulled both out of the bag, handed the card to Ned and held the knife in her hand so he could see it. Sadly, he shook his head and bit his bottom lip.

"Max, where did you get this beautiful knife? It looks like it came from Spain."

Max stared at the dull metal object in Hank's hand, slowly shaking her head, trying to remember. Finally, she said, "It's a pity that men and women forget that they have been children. Parents are apt to be foreigners to their children." She paused, looking not at them but inwardly, at herself. "Maturity is the gate of Paradise which shuts behind us; and our memories are gradually weaned from the glories in which our nativity was cradled."

Ned shrugged his shoulders. "I don't recognize that verse, Max. Can you tell me what it's from?"

Hank said, "It's from George William Curtis' *Prue and I.*

Max blinked several times and smiled at him. "Ned. How nice to see you."

Ned returned the smile. "It's good to see you too, Maxine. Did you know you were out of medication? Walk with me to the hospital pharmacy. I have your card and the empty container, we can get it refilled.

Max took the hand he extended to her.

Hank put the knife back where she found it and handed the shopping bag to Ned and watched as they walked toward busy center city, Ned with a protective arm around Maxine, who walked trance-like beside him. Her body was there but her mind had found a temporary shelter where no one else could be admitted.

Questions raced around in Hank's mind, like cars at Indy 500. Where did Max get the knife? How long had she had it? Obviously, she didn't have it on her when she was taken into custody by the police or Storm would have said something about it. Could someone have planted it on her? For what possible reason? What was the fear Max harbored, that was so painful that it was forcing her into a world that excluded everyone else?

Hank's thoughts halted when she felt a hand slide over her derriere. She spun around, fist raised. Laughing gray eyes met hers. How long had he been standing there? Did he see her take the knife out of Max's bag? Or put it back?

"I just passed Max and Ned," Storm said. "She looks like she did at headquarters, like she's hanging by a thread."

"She's dangling over that chasm of nothingness and you're right, she is hanging by a thread, one that's spider-web thin. Her medicine ran out and she never told us. Then Lester's death. All this heaped on top of a low self-esteem makes her a likely candidate for being institutionalized...or worse. Ned is taking her to the hospital to get her prescription refilled." Hank reached for his hand, then pulled back. "Let's walk. There's something I have to tell you."

Storm studied Hank for a brief time. "Sounds serious. You okay?"

"Do you know a Streeter, named Gil?"

He thought for a moment and nodded. "Little guy, maybe five foot four or five, bald. Walks like his head is buried in his shoulders, early to middle sixties. Is that the guy?"

"Good description. It certainly sounds like Gil." She wasn't sure she should tell him. Then she thought about Max again.

"Gil was there when Lester was killed. We think he saw the murderer." There was only silence between them.

"Why...didn't he...go to the police?"

"Remember Mike Shaye? He's the reason Gil won't go to the police. Shaye put the fear of the police into a lot of street people. Gil fears the police more than he fears the killer. A lot of Streeters feel that way. He has some mistaken notion the killer will leave him alone because he doesn't fit into the age group. He saw the crime but not the killer's face. No one has seen Gil since Lester was killed four days ago."

"Did he forget Benny? He was also in his sixties. Doesn't Gil realize we're dealing with a psychotic? There's no place for him to hide. If, as we suspect, the killer is also a street person, then the killer knows all the hiding places as well as Gil does. If he tries to leave the area the killer will be on his heels. The killer can't afford to have anyone around who can identify him." Storm scanned the dock area. "Does Gil know if the killer saw the him?"

"I don't know. Ned said if we know Gil saw the crime then surely the murderer knows too. The street news-network is quite thorough."

"Then I had better find him first."

"You'll blow your cover."

"I'll try not to. Once I know where he is, if there's time, I'll call the precinct to have him picked up. If there isn't, I'll have to blow my cover. A lead is a lead, no matter how small. If Gil can help us at all, we'll be ahead of the game. Right now, all we have is a psychological profile, which could fit either a man or a woman. I probably won't see you on Sunday unless I can find Gil before the killer does. He's a street veteran, I need to know where somebody like him would go to hide. Any ideas?"

Hank spread her hands in a helpless gesture and said, "Subway tunnels, train stations, the park, underground garages, or he could go to north Philly and hang out there until he thinks it's safe to come back. If he's smart, he'll head south to the warm weather states. I guess if I was going to make a career out of being a Streeter, I would go south. But then, I don't know Gil except by sight, so I can't predict how he'll react. He may make tracks out of here for good, or he may do nothing."

"I'm interested in what Max is going to do," Storm said as he turned away.

"Surely you don't still suspect her?"

"I suspect everyone."

"Even me?"

"Especially you."

Hank could feel her heart beating in her throat, until she looked into his laughing eyes.

Storm said, "Why do you think I'm always doing complete body searches on you? You think I'm having fun?"

She laughed. "I keep hoping. I know I enjoy your searches. You...you're so...thorough."

"It's nice to know you appreciate good police work."

"Tell me," she said, "what was *that* particular course of study called?"

"Search and seize her." Storm turned and walked away. Hank looked at his departing back and felt a slight emptiness in her chest and realized she was more involved than she wanted to be.

Hank headed back to the Azalea Gardens. There wasn't a lot of activity on the River Drive so she put the drop cloth down and covered it with a blanket and closed her eyes when she heard Ned's familiar shuffle. He was supporting an almost unconscious Max. Hank hurried toward them and took the shopping bag from his arm and helped him lower Max onto her blanket. She curled into the fetal position as soon as she felt the security of the blanket under her.

"She'll be all right," Ned said, "The doctor gave her a shot and let her sleep it off for a couple of hours but they couldn't let her take up a stretcher that was needed for somebody else, so he gave me enough pills for a month, then he wants me to bring her back to the clinic. He'll examine her then and renew the prescription. They pulled her records, the doctor estimated she had been without medication for over a week."

Ned mopped his brow with a torn handkerchief. "We can't take any more chances with her. I was scared. I was certain she was retreating from reality. Will you watch her, Hank? I'm going down to the waterfront to try to earn some money. I don't think you have to worry about today or tonight. She'll sleep. If I can bring food to her, she won't have to go to the shelters and she'll be removed from the pressure of what's happening to her world."

"Of course I'll stay with her. Thanks for taking her to the hospital. Where are her pills and when do I start giving them to her?

"I put them in her bag. You can start giving them to her tomorrow." He wiped his mouth with the back of his hand and looked down at the sleeping Max. "Where did that knife come from?"

"I don't know. I've never seen her with it before and I've been through her bag to get her blanket. It wasn't there before." Hank shook her head and looked at the sleeping Maxine. "She's so vulnerable. Maybe somebody put it there?"

"Anything's possible," Ned said as he stooped over and kissed Max on the cheek. "But who would do such a thing? Why would anyone do that to Max? If she knows it's in there and we take it out, she'll think we don't trust her with it. If she doesn't know it's there and she finds it by accident, it's going to upset her and she'll agonize over how it got there. We have a no-win situation. I'll be back in the morning with breakfast. Business on the waterfront has been quite good." He took off his left shoe and sock and took out a fifty-dollar bill and put it into his pants pocket. "There should be enough money to buy food for you and Max for a week or so. I'll stop at a grocery store and get a loaf of bread and maybe cheese for sandwiches. Each day I'll bring some lunchmeat or cheese and unless the police hustle you out of here, she should be comfortable. At least until the medication starts to work and she's ready to face the world again."

"You've really been good to her, Ned." Hank almost added, *No wonder she's in love with you.* Hank was afraid those words would scare him away for good.

He smiled down at the sleeping Maxine, and said, "She's almost childlike in her trust. She lives in a dream world where no one ever hurts anyone. That snug, safe little haven that she can retreat into when bad things happen." Ned shook his head and said, "She just found out there is no such place. She needs to be protected, against herself more than anything else. No one could ever be as harsh in judgment of her as she is in judging herself. Poor Max. She was born five centuries too late." He patted Hank's shoulder. "I'll be back in the morning, Jenny."

The night breeze wafting through the bushes brought a pleasant coolness. It was almost dark when Molly lumbered onto the scene. She leaned down and ran her fingers over Max's hair, smoothing it behind her ears. "She's a pretty little thing, ain't she?"

"Yes, she is," Hank agreed.

"She'll never survive out here."

"She survived out here for six or seven years, Molly. She's a lot stronger than she looks. As long as she takes her medication, I think she can handle it."

"Sooner or later they're gonna stop givin' her the medicine she needs. What happens when she has to pay for it? And it's got to happen that way. It always does. Them research doctors gets us street people into a study they're doin' and they take good care of us. Then the research money runs out and it's over and these poor saps are no better off than they were before. The doctors use them to get the results that they can show on one of those fancy charts, go to some meetin' with other fancy doctors who pat them on the back for the fancy charts and everybody forgets about the Streeters who was the guinea pigs. And that's what's gonna to happen to Max. It's easy to use Max. She trusts everybody. You tell her to shit, and she squats."

"Her friends have to help her," Hank said.

"Help her how? We can't even help ourselves. Where's that fancy Ned? Why ain't he helpin' her?"

"He is, Molly, he is. He took her to the hospital and brought her back. I should say carried her back. Ned cares about her. He cares about all of us. The picture isn't as bleak as you paint it."

"No?" Molly's eyes narrowed into slits. "Try tellin' me that in five more years, when your teeth rot out of your mouth. Tell me that, when they cut off some of your toes because of frostbite. Tell me that when you get raped and the bastard breaks your back and leaves you out in the street to die. Tell me that when you go into a church to get warm and they push you out because you stink. Tell me that when you mess yourself because they closed the city restrooms so we don't use them as places to sleep. After you go through all that...then...tell me how bleak the picture looks."

Hank stared at her. Had all these things actually happened to her? "I...I'm sorry, Molly, I didn't know."

"Yeah, well, sorry don't cut it on the streets, Hank, and in the end, if it's you or me, I'm gonna look out for me. That's what this life's all about. How long you survive tells how tough you are. The good guys don't make it so don't go lookin' for white hats down here."

Hank lay awake long into the early morning hours, hashing and rehashing what Molly said. It was evident that Molly cared for Max, but if it came down to her or Max, would she sacrifice Max?

It was a little after nine o'clock when Max opened her eyes, blinked at the morning sun and tried to sit up. She almost made it. She lay back down and rubbed her eyes. "I feel so dopey, like I'm walking in my sleep."

"No wonder. It's been a long time since you got a good night's sleep." Hank saw Ned coming toward them. "We have company. It's a man with a paper bag, or is it a paper bag with a man?"

Ned smiled. "Good morning. Still sleepy, Max?"

"Can't keep my eyes open."

Ned opened the paper bag and produced three cups of steaming black coffee, three scrambled egg sandwiches on English muffins, and three jelly-filled donuts. He sat next to Max, propping her up against his knees, and laid the coffee and food on the blanket in front of her. "Now, if you are both good girls and make happy plates, I have a surprise for you."

The old twinkle in Max's eyes struggled valiantly to come back. They ate in silence. Max pulled a small brown envelope from his shirt pocket. "Now for the surprise." He opened the envelope with great exaggeration and produced four tickets the way a magician produces playing cards from his sleeve.

Max frowned. "What are they?"

"Her vision is still a little blurred, I think. You tell her what they are, Jenny," he said putting the tickets into her hand.

She looked at them carefully, and roared with delight. "How did you get these, Ned?"

"Will somebody please tell me what you're getting so excited about?"

Hank sat in front of Max and Ned. "Somehow, Ned got four tickets to the Philadelphia Orchestra concert at the Mann Center." A hint of excitement flushed her cheeks.

"You mean...real seats and everything? Like real people?"

Ned smiled. "Just like real people, Max."

Max's interest was aroused. "When, Ned, when?"

"The tickets are for July twenty-sixth. They're certainly not orchestra seats and we'll have to sit on the grass out under the stars, but we'll get to hear some of the most beautiful music ever composed."

"How did you get the tickets, Ned?"

"Maxine always brings me luck. When I went back to the waterfront yesterday afternoon, I took up my usual position and recited verses on request, as I usually do. One of the men in the group handed me this small brown envelope and he said, 'Anyone who can love poetry as you do would enjoy hearing poetry set to music.' At first I thought he had put a couple of dollars into an envelope, then I pulled out the tickets. I almost kissed his feet."

They laughed at the mental picture of Ned paying homage to this patron of the arts.

"Of course, I want you to come with Max and me. We owe you so much. It's a good feeling when I can do something for you, Jenny, to show you how much you are appreciated."

Secretly, Hank felt like a heel. Her motivation for being on the streets was less than altruistic. Hank was touched and humbled by Ned's sincerity and caring.

"I'll have to think about inviting a fourth person since I have four tickets."

"Oh, Ned, please invite Molly," Max pleaded.

Ned's eyebrows knitted together. It was apparent to Hank he didn't feel Molly was a viable choice but he would do anything for Max and if Max wanted Molly to go along, that was fine with him. "Of course, Max, why don't you ask her?"

For the first time in weeks Maxine smiled. "Isn't it wonderful, Hank? It's like being a child again and feeling all the excitement of being invited to a birthday party. I was never quite sure if it was the party that caused the excitement or the anticipation."

Hank found herself wishing Storm could go with them to the concert. Thinking about him always brought on its own special kind of excitement, the anticipation of being with him, loving him. On Sunday afternoons she knew she could close the door on poverty, desperation and death, which loomed like a specter over the streets of Philadelphia. Hank knew what she needed most was freedom from the nightmares that plagued her sleeping hours.

Sunday came and she knew Storm had not found Gil, which meant he would not be going to the apartment. An empty apartment was no way to boost her spirits, so she stayed with Max. The day dragged and the only bright spot was that after five days of medication, Max was almost her old self. They spent most of the day sitting on the banks of the Schuylkill River along the East River Drive. Molly joined them, which she had not done for several days. Max told her about the tickets and said Ned had one for her too. Her reaction was a complete surprise to Hank, but apparently, not to Max. At first, she was silent, then two tears washed a clean track down her cheeks and her hands trembled.

"Are you sure, Maxie? Are you sure you want me to come along? Ned won't mind?"

"Absolutely. All three of us want you to come with us. We wouldn't have it any other way."

Molly nodded and wiped her nose on the back of her hand.

Ned brought a container of hot soup and cheese sandwiches with lettuce and mayonnaise. "Last meal being served, Max. Tomorrow you start back to eating at the shelters."

Max smiled. "Do you know how wonderful that sounds?

"Wait for me to pick you up in the morning and I'll walk with you to breakfast."

Hank said, "Ned, why don't you just stay here in the Gardens tonight?"

"I can't, Jenny. I'll be on the waterfront until people go home, then it's too late to walk all this distance. I'll spend the night down there and see you tomorrow."

Hank pretended nature was calling, so Max and Ned could have a few minutes alone. When she returned, Max was lying on her blanket, staring up at the stars. "Ned leave?" Hank asked.

"He got me settled for the night then left. I don't know what I would have done without the two of you. It's like having a family again."

"Did you take your medicine today?"

"Yes." She sat up. "Somebody's coming."

Hank listened and recognized the shuffle. "It's Molly."

"You're amazing, Hank. How do you do that?"

"Listen. You hear that slide and slight thump? Remember how Molly limps? Her shuffle is different from what I call the street shuffle. She really drags her heels."

"You're right. I had forgotten. She had a couple of toes amputated because of frostbite, which accounts for the limp, and she hasn't walked right since her back was broken."

Hank knew better than to ask questions but she remembered what Molly said about there being no good guys on the streets. She never thought of the Streeters as being good or bad, just unfortunate, until the incident with Duke Collins, when he tried to rape Bridget. Remembering that day prompted her question. "Whatever happened to Bridget? I never see her anymore."

"She took her baby to the Shriners Hospital. They examined her and determined they could help her. So they admitted her right away. I think they knew Bridget had no place to go, so they offered her a job in the kitchen and she's living at the hospital."

"That was a lucky break. I'm happy for her."

"So am I. You know, Hank, good things seem to happen when you're around. Before I met you, it was so much harder on the streets."

Hank couldn't imagine how it could possibly be any harder than it was for Max right now.

Molly spread her blanket on the ground on the other side of the path that had become known as *her spot.* "Did you take your pills, Maxie?"

Max smiled. "Yes I did."

"You'd better go do your business before you go to sleep. You been sleepin' so sound you might wet your pants if you don't go now."

"Good idea, Molly." Max stood on wobbly legs and wandered off into the thicker bushes. Hank laid her blanket out and when she looked around, Molly was straightening Max's blanket and smoothing out the shopping bag, which doubled as a pillow.

The dream specter invaded Hank's nightmare again. After a long chase down the highways and byways of hell, it caught up with her, capturing her shadow and swooping it up, under his cape. She couldn't see the face under the black hood but she heard the laugh, the sound of a deep, throaty laugh, whose volume and pitch increased until it became maniacal. There was something strange about the high pitch, the derision that made her shudder in fear. Hank tried desperately to escape. Just as the specter claimed her shadow, she was sure it would also claim her body. When she opened her eyes the sun was shining. Max was still deep in slumber but Molly was gone, obviously following her morning routine of getting up at the crack of dawn and starting on her daily rounds. Hank sat on her blanket, not wanting to disturb Max until it was necessary. It was eight forty-five when she heard a familiar shuffle. She was delighted and frightened. Storm never came to the Gardens when he knew anyone else was there with her. Hank stood up and he motioned for her to come to him. She checked Max again to be sure she was sleeping and hurried to Storm.

"What's wrong?"

"We found Gil last night."

Hank didn't like the tone in his voice. "Where?"

"Along the banks of the Delaware, near Penn's Landing."

"Was he…dead?"

"Yes."

"When did it happen?"

"Last night probably, or early this morning." He anticipated the next question. "Same as the others, stabbed in the back. The verse was strange, it started out, *Madame La Guillotine celebrates Bastille Day*. Then a quote from Euripides. *Old men's prayers for death are lying prayers, in which they abuse old age and long extent of life. But when death draws near, not one is willing to die, and age no longer is a burden to them*."

CHAPTER 14

The news of Gil's murder had upset Hank more than she wanted to admit. She knew the news would chip away at Max's ability to stay calm, in spite of the medication.

Hank heard Ned's familiar shuffle on the footpath. She looked up as he got closer. He carried a brown paper bag. "Good morning, Jenny. How's our patient?"

"So far, so good. Wish I could say the same about you. You look upset."

"I brought breakfast for both of you. I think it's wise to stay here a while longer."

"Why?"

"The police found Gil's body this morning, near the river." His hand shook as he handed her the paper bag. "Now I'm sorry I didn't come back here last night. We can't tell Max what happened."

"She's going to wonder why you brought breakfast when she told you we were going to the shelter this morning."

"I'll tell her I waited for her and when they closed the kitchen, I decided to bring breakfast for the sleeping beauty."

Hank nodded. "You might get away with that. I wouldn't but you might. If you told her you were taking her to the moon, she'd start packing."

"We had better wake her or the coffee will be cold," Ned said, putting his hand on Max's arm. Her eyes fluttered open.

"Ned. What are you doing here?"

"Couldn't wait for you to wake up or your coffee would be cold."

"But Hank and I are going to the shelter."

"I don't think so. The kitchen closed when I left, so I stopped and got you coffee and a scrambled egg sandwich." He paused. "For Jenny, too."

Max ran her fingers through her hair. "What time is it?"

"Nine forty-five," Hank said.

"Why did you let me sleep so long?"

"I thought you needed the sleep more than you needed breakfast, so I let you snooze away," Hank said, matter-of-factly.

"You're probably right, as usual," Max said. "I woke up during the night, feeling anxious and it was a while before I could go back to sleep."

Hank handed her coffee and sandwich to Ned. "Why don't you take these and Max and go sit along the river. The scullers are out today. I'll fold our blankets and be along in just a minute."

"Great idea, Jenny. There's nothing as romantic as breakfast along the river. Max can carry the two sandwiches and I'll carry the two coffees. Hurry before your coffee gets cold."

"I'll be along in a minute."

Hank began folding her blanket and made sure they were well on their way before she opened Max's bag. The knife was gone. Nausea washed over Hank like a cold wave. She checked the area to be sure it had not fallen out of the bag. She gathered their things and headed for the river. Max smiled and handed Hank one of the sandwiches and Ned handed her a cup of coffee. Ned could see Hank was disturbed but kept talking to Maxine. Max took one of her pills and swallowed it with a sip of hot coffee.

Hank tried to organize her thoughts to form a clear mental picture. Yesterday, Ned straightened Max's blanket and had access to her shopping bag. Molly did the same thing last night after she got Max to go and relieve herself. Was the knife in Max's bag then? It was possible Max found it there and, not knowing how it got there, tossed it away. Hank knew deep down that wasn't true. If Max found the knife she would have asked if anybody lost it. There was no way to be certain she had even seen the knife. Hank couldn't remember if she had ever seen Max dig down into the bottom of her shopping bag. It could have been at the bottom of her bag for months without Max knowing it was there. Hank knew she couldn't discuss it with Storm and now she couldn't talk about it to either Ned or Molly.

Ned couldn't possibly have done it, hadn't the police given him a polygraph test? *But the polygraph isn't accurate if the subject is a pathological liar. But,* she reasoned, *Ned was in the intensive care unit when one of the murders was committed and that had nothing to do with the polygraph. It was physically impossible for him to leave the hospital...So why was he so curious about Max's shopping bag?* Hank agonized over the dilemma. Ned knew Max had the knife because Hank showed it to him. Could he have disposed of it? Was he afraid, as Hank was, that the stiletto was the murder weapon? How far would he go to protect Max? Looking at them together, Hank thought she knew the answer.

What about Molly? She didn't know Max had the knife in her possession. Or did she? Ridiculous, she thought, Molly was a self-acclaimed protector of

Max. Or was she? Her conversation with Molly came back to haunt Hank. Molly had said, *It's easy to use Max. She trusts everybody.* She could still hear Molly's words, *In the end, if it's you or me, I'm going to look out for me.* Hank shivered in spite of the ninety-degree temperature. What did anybody know about Molly? Yet she seemed to know about everybody else. She was always complaining about the ache in her bones but she covered more territory in a day than Max and Hank combined. It was only Molly, Max and Hank who knew about Benny being a snitch for Shaye.

Didn't Max say Molly had a habit of talking to herself when she had a problem, and when she stopped talking to herself, that was an indication she had resolved the problem? Damn, why couldn't she remember when Molly stopped talking to herself? Was it before or after Benny was killed? Other than Storm and Ned, Molly was the only other person who knew Max preferred sleeping in the Azalea Gardens. Hank's thoughts raced. *I can only presume Molly gets up at dawn and leaves for parts unknown. What about the number of times when she woke me out of a sound sleep either because I was dreaming or because it was raining, or because she saw blue and red lights flashing on the river drive. Where did she go when she left us?* Hank remembered when Storm took her to police headquarters after the first murder, Molly was there, watching as the car left the area. When the murder happened on Sansom Street in the snow storm, it was Molly who awakened her and warned her to get out of the area.

Molly was always complaining about the noise on the river drive. Why did she stay? Was it because of her feeling for Max? Or was it because Hank and Max were the perfect alibi in case she got picked up by the police?

When Hank looked up, Ned was watching her. The cup of coffee was still in her hand and the sandwich lay in its wrapper on the grass.

"Is something wrong, Jenny?" he asked.

"No, why?"

"You haven't touched your sandwich."

Surprised, Hank looked at the small package beside her. "My stomach is a little upset." She handed it to him. "Why don't you eat it?"

Max leaned in front of Ned to look at Hank. "You didn't tell me you weren't feeling well, Hank. Is there anything I can do?"

"It's no big deal. The warm coffee is just the ticket. I'll be feeling better in a little while."

Max stood up. "I feel like walking. It's a beautiful day. Let's go to the park."

"Why don't you and Ned go ahead. I'll sit here for a while."

"Good idea," said Ned.

Hank watched them until they were out of sight then waited an additional ten minutes before starting for the Parkway and her apartment. As she started up the tower stairs, she heard the door to the street open and close. It was important that she not be seen, so she hurried to the apartment. She stood inside the apartment, leaning against the door, trying to catch her breath when she heard the key in the lock. Startled, she moved away and watched as the doorknob turned. For a moment, all movement stopped then slowly the door opened. Storm stood in front of her.

"Anything wrong?" he said.

Relief flooded over her and she almost collapsed into his arms. "How did you get here? I kept checking behind me all the way home. No one was following me but here you are, not ten seconds behind me."

"You kept looking behind you but you never looked across the street. I've been following you since you left the River Drive. I hoped you were coming here." Then as an afterthought, "Why did you?"

"I guess I got tired of playing chaperone to Ned and Max. She needs to be alone with him. I needed to be alone. This is just one of those days when the world seemed to be closing in. I had to get off the streets, to my safe haven." She pulled herself closer to him. "When is it all going to end? Why haven't the police found the murderer?"

"We're getting closer. We may have a substantial lead."

Hank pulled away so she could read his expressions. "No kidding? Somebody can identify the murderer?"

"I didn't say that. Do you remember the hooker I told you about?"

Hank nodded. "Suzie Hoffman, we call her Bimbo."

"I have witnesses who can put her near the scene of the crime around the time the murders were committed."

"You think she did it?"

"I didn't say that, either."

"What are you saying, Storm?"

"If somebody was following her around and didn't like the way she was throwing herself at men, she could become the catalyst that brings on the murder reaction."

"You said yourself, she's a hooker. That's what hookers do. They sell their favors for cash."

"What if she's shielding someone?"

"You're reaching, Storm. Why would a hooker waste her time on street bums?"

"Ah, but we're finding out they may not all be street bums. What about victim number eight? Arthur Hamilton III may have been on the streets but he was not a bum."

"Of course he was a bum," Hank said. "The fact that his family had money didn't make him any less a bum. He left his family to be with another woman. In my opinion, that qualifies him as a bum. After the Praxon woman got what she wanted from him, she went looking for new thrills. That's probably how she ended up with Terry O'Neill. She went looking for trouble and she found it."

"You're not following my line of reasoning. You're going off on a tangent. Forget about the victims. Concentrate on the hooker. She is seen making out with a Streeter. The next morning we find a dead body."

Hank thought about all the coincidences of Molly, Max and her, also being in close proximity to the murder scenes. "Do you honestly believe somebody is going to kill a man because a hooker tries to 'make out,' as you put it? Besides, you have no proof the victims were making out. It could be a coincidence."

"You may be right," Storm said, "but I can't shake the feeling that somehow she's involved in the murders. Nobody seems to know where she goes or where she hangs out during the day. The only thing we know about her is her name. I doubt if she has a pimp. She's a loner."

"Why would a guy care about whether or not a hooker is hitting on some other john in the streets? You're not being logical."

"What if it's not a guy?" Storm took both her hands in his. "What if it's a woman?"

"Oh, shit. Are you back to that again? The woman who is going to make all men pay? Pay for what? You're going to give me this bit about 'Heaven has no rage like love to hatred turned, Nor hell a fury like a woman scorned?' Well, I don't buy it and I don't think you do either."

"Don't be so quick to discount it, Hank, it's possible."

She studied his expression and decided he was really serious. "Anything is possible, but I think the probability is almost zero."

"Okay. You tell me why a hooker would waste her time on street bums. They don't have enough money for a cup of coffee, let alone a piece of ass, and I doubt if she gives credit. So why is she hanging around these guys?"

"Maybe she was a Streeter before she went into business for herself. Maybe she feels she owes some of the guys. Maybe the only way she knows to say thanks is to share the only thing she has, her body. There could be hundreds of reasons. I think you enjoy telling me the murderer could be a woman because you know it upsets me."

He smiled, "I have to admit I enjoy seeing those sparks shoot from your eyes when you get angry but the truth is, the murderer could just as easily be a woman as a man. My mind has to be open to that possibility. Think about it. If our friend Suzie teases these guys and then finally one day tells them she's going to deliver. Don't you think they would be anxious to collect? What better way to get them to trust her?"

"Would you trust somebody like that?" Hank asked. "Would you turn your back, not knowing if you were going to end up with a knife in it? I think men are smarter than that, even if you don't."

"To quote you, Hank, *a stiff cock has no conscience*."

"You're exasperating."

"You're sexy when you're exasperated," he said as he pulled her into the circle of his arms. His eyes, that could be so cold and granite-like, were warm and gentle. As he lowered his head to kiss her she could feel herself being pulled into the depths of the gray whirlpool, sinking, spinning, being raised up only to be pulled down deeper into the infinity of his love.

Hank opened her eyes, surprised to find the day had ended and they were in the shadow of evening. She nestled closer into the crook of Storm's arm, happy and contented. His fingertips passed lightly over her back.

"I'm not sure if you needed the loving or the sleep more," he said.

"Sleep I can always get."

"You can get the loving too. Whenever you say."

She held her breath. "Is that a proposal?"

"Whoa ... don't put words in my mouth. Let's take this one step at a time. What I meant was, if you come off the streets, we would be able to see each other more often. Then, who knows?"

Hank felt a hot flush creeping over her neck and face. She thought, *Damn, why did I say that? Now he was going to feel I was cornering him.* "That was a joke, son. I screwed up in the marriage game and I'm not anxious to try it again."

"You never talk about him. What happened?"

Hank wasn't sure she wanted to talk about it but before she could make a conscious decision, she found herself telling him about Julian Grant.

"When I first met Julian Grant, I didn't like him. I should have stuck with my first impression. Usually first impressions are accurate. Nobody else seemed to like him either. I think I felt sorry for him. If there is a loser in the crowd, you can bet he's going to migrate to me. I guess I've got this thing about underdogs. They need somebody to fight for them. That's where I come in. I'm a born fighter. Anyway, he gave me this bullshit about his first wife being a psycho and how his life was so unhappy. Of course I fell for it and never thought to question why he didn't have any friends. The only friends he had were my friends and later I found out they only tolerated him because of me. When we got married, I resigned from the *Journal* and did freelance writing. I would go out of town for a couple of weeks at a time on an assignment, sometimes longer. He called me every night, always telling me how much he missed me and when was I coming back home? At the time, I didn't suspect that he just wanted to know so that he wouldn't get caught with his pants down.

"Julian always ended our telephone conversations by saying, 'I love you, precious one.' That in itself should have been a clue. When a guy calls you precious one, or sweetheart or darling all the time, it's because he's afraid of getting his names mixed up. To make a long story short, I came home a day earlier than I anticipated, and walked into our bedroom. There he was with a girl, a child, for Chrissakes. She couldn't have been any more than fourteen. Later he told me she was a whore. I guess that was supposed to make me feel better. He was a real prick. Believe me, that's defiling the male sex organ."

"How did you feel?"

"Used. Dirty. But when it was finally over, I couldn't understand the feeling of relief I experienced. No more pretending, no more having to go to the mat for him, no more putting up with his stink."

"When were you divorced?"

"1988."

"What did you do between nineteen eighty-eight and now? Before you started to gather information on street people?

"I spent some time in Israel and Palestine with a media photographer. I was commissioned to write a series of articles about the Israeli-Palestinian hotbed. Before that, I had an interview with Castro and that was also an assignment. Then there were trips I took on my own looking for an interesting twist on what was happening in the world. Then I realized the biggest story of all was in my own backyard. So I studied the actions and dress of Streeters and became one of them. From that point on, you know as much about me as I do."

"I would feel a lot better knowing you were safe in your own apartment.

I hate the idea of you being out there, unprotected, with a psychotic killer on the loose. Reconsider, Hank, please."

"I can't. Writing about things like this is what I do for a living. It's what I am. I don't like the idea that you're out there either, especially since it seems to be the men the killer is after...but I understand you have to be out there. You're a detective. It's what you do for a living."

"I have a gun. If necessary, I can use it. You have no protection."

"I have the protection of other street people. I don't need any more than that."

"I'm sure all the victims thought the same thing."

"You're trying to frighten me," she said, "and it's not going to work. With one exception, those victims were alone. Besides, it's good to have a snitch telling you things. Don't you agree?"

"I never considered you as an informer and I hope nobody else does. I'm not forgetting that our killer got to Benny when he found out Benny was Mike Shaye's snitch. I don't want you to end up like that. I want you around for a long time."

* * *

The next week was difficult for Hank, seeing Molly every night, wondering why she was so interested in the contents of Max's bag. Molly's attitude toward Max had not changed, she was still the clucking hen around her chick. Twice Hank awakened before six o'clock and both times Molly had already gathered her things and left the area. To follow Molly would have been impossible. She seemed to have a-built-in radar that told her when things weren't right. Hank had seen it work, so she knew.

The weather got steamier as July progressed and Hank sat along the river's edge watching the boats and hoping for a cool breeze. She saw a shadow approach from behind, and studying the shadow, she knew it was Molly, her footsteps muffled on the grass. Without looking up, she said, "Really hot today, huh, Molly?"

"There ain't nothin' movin' out there 'cept air-conditioned cars. Howd ja know it was me?"

"I watched your shadow as you came near."

"I'll be damned. Never thought about a shadow givin' a person away. I'll have to try it sometime." She settled down beside Hank. "I saw that gal that looks like you."

"Did you talk to her?"

"Yeah. But I got the impression she wasn't much interested in talkin' to women. She would rather talk to the men."

"Where was she? Who is she?"

"She was talkin' to Speaks and I heard him call her Suzie."

"I've got to see this woman that looks like me."

"She looks like you from a distance but not when you get up close. She's hard lookin' and talks like a drunken sailor. I've heard a lot of bad language but that one invents sex words I never heard." Molly mopped at her brow with the back of her hand then continued, "Speaks had his hand up her dress and she was talkin' dirty to him. When Speaks saw me he tried to slide his hand away but she just took his hand and shoved it under her dress again and told me to take a walk."

"She was doing this in broad daylight?"

"Naw. It was early, maybe five o'clock this morning. It was still dark. There wasn't much to her dress, she was wearing one of them miniskirts and I bet she wasn't wearin' no pants. Anyway, Speaks seemed to be havin' a good time."

Hank shielded her eyes against the sun. "Who is Speaks?"

"I guess you don't know him. He's an ornery son-of-a-bitch. If you met him, you'd remember him. He talks sex all the time. Until this mornin' I woulda sworn it was all talk, now I'm not so sure. I'll never understand how a woman, any woman, would want to be mauled by him."

"That doesn't say much for Suzie, does it? If she's a hooker, she must know he can't pay."

"If he's half as good as he says he is, maybe he don't have to pay."

Hank remembered Storm telling her that the hooker was all over him too. Hank wondered if his theory had any merit. What if she was the killer? What better way to worm into a guy's confidence, than through his sexual fantasies?

"Where's Maxie?" Molly asked.

"Ned told a bunch of students from Penn that he would be at the waterfront today and recite whatever poetry they wanted. Max went along with him."

"Does she know about Gil yet?"

"I don't think so. Ned kept her pretty busy until the papers reported on something else."

Molly nodded. "It don't take much for people to forget about Streeters being killed. It would be different if it was one of them. They would be houndin' the police night and day to find the killer. Who the hell cares about forgotten people, huh? Nobody."

Max and Molly took showers at one of the shelters.

"We're going to see and hear the Philadelphia Orchestra tonight, isn't that exciting? Max tried to smooth out the wrinkles in her slacks. "Molly, aren't you thrilled?"

Molly smiled and shook her head. "I guess I'm thrilled because a ray of sunshine came into your life. Maybe you should give my ticket to somebody else. I never been to no concert before. I might embarrass you."

Max concentrated her gaze on the woman who had been her friend for seven years. The pronounced limp, the semi-toothless grin, the thinning hair brought tears to her eyes and she put her arms around Molly. "If you couldn't go, I wouldn't go either. You could never embarrass me. Everything you've ever done has been to protect me. I love you, Molly."

Molly turned away but not before Max saw the tears escape from her tightly closed eyes.

"Yeah, well, you'll probably have to tell me when to clap tonight." She wiped her eyes and blew her nose on a large tan handkerchief.

The concert was scheduled to begin at eight o'clock. At five o'clock, a deluge of rain blanketed the area. Their seats were out in the open on the now saturated grass. They put one of the plastic covers on the grass and used the other two to cover their heads. The rain stopped just before the overture.

Max was completely under the spell of the magic baton of the conductor and Ned's eyes shone as he watched her.

Hank nudged Ned and motioned him to look at Molly. There was an elusive softness that could be seen only when she thought no one was watching. She had closed her eyes and given herself up to the mystic beat of Rimsky-Korsakov's "Scheherazade." It seemed to Hank that Molly was remembering when music, laughter, family and love were paramount in her life. At least for the time being, the streets of Philadelphia were carpeted with roses. Molly was totally oblivious to the tears that ran in a steady stream down her cheeks and collected in the wrinkles in her chin and neck. For a while, no one existed for her. She was carried away into another world, a world that others could never share with her.

When the concert was over, the orchestra received a standing ovation and two of the most devoted fans were Molly and Maxine. Hank squeezed Ned's hand and thanked him for all of them.

"No thanks necessary, Jenny. I received the best reward just watching the pleasure on your faces. I don't know who my benefactor was but I'll have to say a special prayer for him for making all this possible." He and Max walked behind Molly and Hank and they ended up at a diner and each had a cup of steaming coffee. The perfect ending for a perfect night.

The dog days of July passed, unchanged, into August. Max, Molly and Hank spent most of their time on the waterfront, where breezes weren't hampered by multistoried buildings.

Molly was beginning to accept the fact of Maxine and Ned, even though they seemed to be unaware that love was blooming and they were the blossoms. The three women sat on the outer fringes of the crowds that inevitably formed around Ned on the waterfront. He always looked directly at Maxine. "The Definition of Love" was a favorite of the crowds and whenever he recited the poetry, he and Max walked into a world where no one could follow and only they knew of the ecstasies there.

The crowds along the waterfront made Molly uncomfortable. She left telling Hank she would meet them back at the Azalea Gardens. She had to go where humanity was less oppressive than the heat. When Max and Hank returned to the Gardens, Molly had saved their usual spaces. Hank got the impression something was wrong.

"You okay, Molly?"

She looked startled, then smiled without parting her lips, "I'm fine, Hank, just a little restless."

Hank dug into her canvas bag and came out with a bottle of brandy. "Maybe this will help take the edge off."

Molly's face lit up, "God bless you, child. It may not take the whole edge off but it will certainly blunt it." She took several swallows, closed her eyes, took a deep breath and handed the bottle back, reluctantly. "Thanks, Hank, that really helped."

"Have a couple more swigs before I put it back."

Molly didn't argue. By the time she stopped, she had consumed a quarter of the bottle. Hank smiled as she put it away. Molly plumped up her plastic bag as though it was a feather pillow, put her head down and mumbled herself into sleep.

Maxine didn't need anything to help her sleep, she closed her eyes and that was that.

Hank lay awake for a time, thinking about Storm, wondering where he was and what he was doing. When sleep came, it was clothed in her constant nightmare. She turned and twisted, trying to wake up to stop the frightening dream. She heard shuffling footsteps but they seemed to be coming from the footpath...they seemed to stop adjacent to where the three women were sleeping. Someone touched her arm and she pulled it away but it was impossible to open her eyes. It was impossible to know if this was part of the dream or if it was actually happening.

When Hank awakened, it had started raining. She took the plastic ground cloth out from under her and covered the area over Max and her. She looked over to where Molly was and to Hank's surprise, she was still sleeping soundly. Hank looked at her watch, it was six forty-five. The rain clouds seemed to pull an invisible curtain over the city and the dark prevailed. Hank slid Molly's ground cover out from under her and put it over top of the azalea bushes to shield her from the rain. Her snores continued undisturbed and the unmistakable smell of brandy wafted up into Hank's face. She lay back down and watched the rain make snowflake patterns on the dirty plastic ground cover. She was exhausted after being chased by a nightmare through a maze of dreams. She closed her eyes and drifted off to sleep again, a peaceful sleep. It was almost eight thirty when she heard a moan from the other side of the footpath. Molly was grimacing and holding her head.

Hank propped herself up on one elbow. "Hangover?"

"Would you believe this? That musta been a real cheap brandy, Hank."

"I'm afraid you're right but who can afford the good stuff?" Hank wasn't about to tell her it was the good stuff. "I'll wake Max and then we can get to the shelter and get something in your stomach. That will probably make you feel better."

"I could sure do with a cup of coffee."

"How about some of the hair of the dog that bit you?" Hank held up the bottle.

Molly smiled. "Now that just might do the trick." She tilted the bottle until a good slug went down her throat. Her eyes opened wide and she smiled. "That did it." The sound of their laughter woke Max and she looked at them in confusion.

Molly laughed. "God's in His heaven and all's right with the world. Come on, Maxie, time to get somethin' to eat."

Max smiled. "A good night's sleep is worth a million dollars," and as an afterthought, she said, "and fifty cents."

Amen, Hank thought, *but why is it so illusive?* She watched Molly help Max gather her things. Hank thought it was strange that Molly slept until eight thirty. Usually she had at least three hours of cruising under her belt by this time. By the same token, Hank had never seen her with a hangover before and Hank knew she could put away a lot of booze. She dismissed it, chalking it up to the aging process, and packed her blanket into the canvas bag. They walked to the shelter slowly, to give Max a chance to wake up.

They took their coffee and watery scrambled eggs to the table where Ned was waiting for them. Hank could tell by the expression on his face something had happened and they weren't going to like the news. He smiled a loving smile at Max and nodded to Molly. "Jenny, my girl, it happened again."

Hank could hear Max's sudden intake of air. "Where are your pills, Max?"

She reached into her plastic bag, feeling for her medication. When she handed them to Hank she had a faraway look on her face. Hank took one out and handed it to her, watching as she put it on top of her tongue and downed it with lukewarm coffee. Finally she looked directly at Ned. "Who was it?"

"From what I could gather, it was Speaks."

Max frowned. "I didn't know him very well. Poor man. He's probably better off than the rest of us. At least his waiting is over." She buried her face in her hands.

Ned put his arm around her shoulders. "I wish I could protect you from this."

For the first time since she hit the streets, Hank saw anger in his eyes. "It's all so futile," Ned said. "We're utterly at the mercy of a madman and no one is doing anything to protect us."

"I don't think that's true." Once the words were out, Hank realized they were the wrong words. Ned's anger flared and he brought his fist down on the table with such force that coffee spilled out of the cups into the already watery eggs.

Hank continued cautiously. "I think the police are just as baffled as we are. You know how the police are about one of their own being killed. If they do it for no other reason, they'll hunt the killer down for Shaye's murder. It's just that the clues have been so sparse. It seems all they have right now is that the killer is adept at verse and we both know that could be any number of people in this city." Hank touched Ned's arm. "Was it like the others?"

"It certainly had all the earmarks...right down to the verse," Ned said.

"Do you know what the verse was?" Hank asked.

"No. Gimpy was there right after the police found his body on the waterfront. I don't know how well you know Gimpy but he can't even remember 'Mary had a little lamb.' He did say the police picked up one of the Streeters. Doesn't know his name. He thinks the Streeter is a transplant from New York. He came on the scene last February as close as we could determine. Gimpy thinks they might finally have their killer. He said he got a look at the man's eyes, and they were icy cold like a slab of gray granite in the cemetery in winter. The man calls himself Andros."

Hank choked on her coffee, spraying the two men who sat across from them, and Molly kept hitting her on the back. "Easy, Molly, I break easily." Hank kept thinking it couldn't be Storm. Why would the police pick up one of their own men...unless they needed to get him off the streets. Hank knew she had to do something to get in touch with him. What if the cops really suspected him? No! They couldn't do that to Storm. Hank was acutely aware that Ned was watching her. "If he wasn't on the Philadelphia streets until February, he can't be the killer. The murders started back in January, didn't they?"

Ned thought for a moment, "I think you're right, Jenny. Besides, what motive could he have? I hope they're not going to pick up people indiscriminately...again."

Ned's voice droned on but Hank's thoughts were elsewhere. Could Storm have been right about the hooker? Molly had seen the prostitute with Speaks. But why? What possible motive could she have? *This is nonsense.* But what if...there was a pattern emerging? What if Suzie had been with each of the victims prior to their murders? Didn't Storm say she was rubbing her body against him? Did that mean Storm would be the next victim? Idiotic. What if...she only went after those men who responded to her teasing? Didn't Molly say Speaks had his hand up Suzie's dress? Obviously he was fondling her and possibly setting the stage for his own murder. Her thoughts kept going back to her original question. Why would they arrest Storm?

Hank felt the tide of apprehension knocking her down and rolling her over. Why? Why would they do this to one of their own? There were four days left before Storm and she would meet at the apartment. There was only one answer. She had to get to the apartment and hope he would come to her. Storm was no killer. Why didn't the cops know this? When she looked at Ned and the others, they seemed to be eating in slow motion. She could hear the rage inside of her screaming for them to hurry up so she could go to the apartment.

She closed the door to the apartment and began shaking with the violence of a tornado. When she turned around, she walked into the arms of Storm Andrews.

CHAPTER 15

Storm paced off the length of the office for the tenth time. There was no indication he was about to stop.

"Maybe if you give verbal expression to your thoughts, the puzzle will begin to fall into place."

He stopped pacing and studied the attractive dark-haired psychiatrist. "Think so?"

"It happens."

"It's been months and we're no closer to finding our killer than we were after the first murder. We've elevated a suspect from possible to probable. I still think our victimizer is female. I told you about Suzie. I have no hard evidence to back up my suspicion but I think Suzie is the one we're after."

Doctor McGowan eyed the prepared chart. "She's the prostitute?"

"That's what we think. Nobody knows for sure because we can't find anybody who knows her. Mike Shaye knew her and maybe he paid for knowing her. As things stand now, we can pinpoint her to be at or near the scene of the crime within a few hours of the murders. I get an uneasy feeling when I think about whether it's coincidence or clever planning. We have nothing on her. No information, no fingerprints and nobody who claims to know her."

Storm wrote the word "print" in his notebook before he continued. "Right now, she's a woman without a past. It's rare that she's seen in daylight hours but she's quite visible between midnight and six in the morning. But then again, prostitutes sleep during the day and take care of business after dark. Molly said she talks like a longshoreman in a street brawl. I think she probably does this for the shock effect."

"Isn't Molly another one of your suspects? Has she now been eliminated as a possible suspect?"

"Hell, no, that broad's right up there on top of the list with Suzie. She roams around in the dark and according to Hank, she knows the city better than anyone. She's at the Azalea Gardens when Max and Hank are ready for sleep. She sleeps on the opposite side of the footpath from them and it doesn't seem to matter what time they wake up, Molly is always gone."

"Have you had her followed?" Doctor McGowan asked.

"Sure. Somehow she always manages to shake the tail. She waits until she gets into an area where there are alleys or parking garages and that's when she disappears. She's well known to a lot of the other Streeters and they trust her. She could get behind any of them without arousing suspicion and plunge the knife in before they have a chance to react."

"Didn't you tell me you thought she was sick? Did you mean physically sick?"

"I think she is but then again, I'm not a doctor. She has that gray pallor, like cancer victims get. If she's our killer, she has nothing to lose."

Storm walked to the chart hanging in the closet and pointed to Maxine's name. "This one is an enigma. She's as frail as a woman can get but she has made it on the streets for seven years. So how fragile can she be?"

"Very fragile," Doctor McGowan said. We have her on lithium and it seems to be helping. I looked at her clinic chart at the hospital and she forgets to take her medication, which could get her in trouble."

"Could she be violent?"

Doctor McGowan shifted in her chair. "Everyone has that potential. If she has a tendency toward violence, it certainly didn't manifest itself while she was under observation."

"Could she be pushed into it?"

"Create enough stress and anyone will react, either by fight or flight. She also demonstrated a love of poetry."

Storm hesitated before asking the next question. "Does Hank have the same potential toward violence?"

"From what you've told me about her, I think...yes. It takes a very strong-willed person to withstand the rigors of the streets, especially since she went there voluntarily. The others had no choice. She harbors resentment because of an abused childhood and a rotten marriage that terminated in a dirty divorce. She felt violated." Doctor McGowan studied Storm's body language and realized he was uneasy with the present discussion. She continued, "The question is how deeply rooted is the resentment? She also has more than a passing acquaintance with poetry and literature."

Storm nodded, studying the chart of possible suspects. He slammed his fist on the desk. "I'm convinced the killer is a woman." He turned and looked at the psychiatrist. "I hate the way she's making the police look like jackasses."

Doctor McGowan closed the doors of the closet that hid the chart of suspects, and said, "It certainly appears like the killer is toying with the police. She's probably enjoying the excitement of pitting herself against the entire police department."

Storm walked to the door and turned around. "She's probably keeping score," he said. "Twelve to zip…in her favor."

* * *

No one claimed the body of Noah Speaks and there was a brief graveside service in the city's "potter's field" with only a few Streeters attending, among them was Storm Andrews. He listened intently to what other Streeters said about Speaks. Some felt his death was imminent, if not by murder then by alcohol. One man said, "Speaks swilled *white lightning* for years. At one point, he drank *sterno*, and ended up in the hospital, when most other men would have ended up on a slab in the morgue."

As miserable and depressing as their lives were, Storm realized there wasn't one person at the gravesite who would have traded places with Speaks. Hunger, though real and painful, was still preferred over death.

Storm thought that death was the ultimate insult. The victims were found lying in their own urine and feces; the final indignation to a life spent digging out of the fecal matter, both real and verbal. He knew it was the dimension no one wanted to explore. It was frighteningly…final.

Max, Molly and Hank sat on a bench in Franklin Square, a small park that seemed to be labeled for the homeless. Police rarely ventured through and city dwellers avoided the forbidding square. There was a playground of sorts, used half-heartedly by the homeless children. It was a place for them to explore the excitement that more fortunate children took for granted. It was a welcome relief from the squalor that seemed to be the legacy of homeless children.

Max was solemn as she watched the children. She said, "It's not fair, Hank. Everybody should have somebody to mourn them when they leave this life. There's only one thing worse than death…. Dying without anyone knowing you were ever here in the first place. Do you think God has a special place in heaven for Streeters? Do you think we'll be segregated up there too?" she asked, looking up at the sky. "Do you think there's another Franklin Square beyond this life? Is that what happens to us when we die? Will those children be able to play with children who lived in homes, or will there be a separate, ill-equipped playground like this one?" She smiled at a toddler who brought her a shiny button. "Who's there to mourn for the children when they die from hunger or cold? Who will be there to mourn for me? There will be no one to mourn my passing...or even take note of it." She bit her bottom lip.

Molly listened to Max's words. "I don't want to hear you talk like that. Do you hear me, Maxie? It's bad enough livin' like this, we don't have to talk about it too. If there is a God up there, He gave up on me a long time ago. But you're different. You see beauty where there ain't none. You see the good when all I see is the bad. I don't expect that there'll be anybody to miss me after I'm gone but it's a different story with you. It's people like you that's goin' to pull the poor bastards like me outta this hell. If we ain't got people like you pulling people like me out of the filth, what hope is there for any of us poor bastards?"

Max stared at Molly, touched by the deep affection of the older woman. "I'm sorry, Molly. I guess I was just feeling sorry for myself." She reached over and squeezed Molly's hand. "I'll behave myself. I promise."

Molly raised her hand to shield her eyes from the sun's rays, "Here comes Sir Galahad. Wonder where he left his horse." The derision in her voice was unmistakable. Max's brows came together in a frown. Molly's jealousy was apparent even to the ever-forgiving Maxine but she said nothing. The frown disappeared and obvious happiness took its place as she looked into the smiling eyes of the poet of the streets. Ned grinned in reply.

Hank never considered Ned as having an age. He was one of those ageless people that seem to belong to every age but today, he was definitely forty, going on sixteen. He touched Max's cheek. "You look a little pale, everything all right?"

She smiled and he knew everything was all right.

Ned sat beside Hank. "Jenny, I brought yesterday's paper for you, thought you might be interested," he said as he handed her the newspaper. It had been two days since Noah Speaks' death and an hour since his burial and he was no longer news enough for the front page. The verses which had been found with the body were printed on page three; one from Benjamin Disraeli—*Experience is the child of thought, and Thought is the child of Action, We cannot learn men from books*—and the other was a quote from Socrates—*Must not all things at the last be swallowed up in death?*

Hank handed the paper back to Ned. "What do you think?"

"I don't know what to think. I'm sure there must be some symbolism but it escapes me."

"This is a long shot, Ned, but what if...what if the serial killer is a woman? A hooker...the symbolism would be obvious, wouldn't it?"

He took a while before answering. "By God, Jenny, you may have something there. It would seem our killer is getting brave."

"Or cocky?"

"Why would you think it was a hooker?"

"Before the murder, Molly saw Speaks with a hooker. Why would a hooker fool around with a derelict? He couldn't possibly pay her. But what if...?"

"You think she might have been setting him up?"

"I don't know. What do you think?"

"The first thing I would have to ask myself is, why? Remember, Jenny, if your theory is correct, this woman, this hooker, would have to be strong enough to take on Mike Shaye. In my opinion that eliminates any woman."

"Not necessarily. I think most women are strong enough to plunge a knife into someone's back. I would think a couple of quick plunges with a knife would take the starch out of anybody. I see this individual as being extremely angry, particularly where Mike Shaye was concerned. Remember the verse?"

Ned nodded, "Yes, from *Alice in Wonderland, 'I'll be judge, I'll be jury', said cunning old Fury, 'I'll try the whole cause and condemn you to death.'*" Ned thought for a moment, "In the case of Mike Shaye you could be right, he bullied people, particularly hookers. He was seen on more than one occasion degrading women by forcing them to their knees to satisfy his peculiar need for oral sex."

"Bastard." Hank spat the word out. "I'm glad he's dead."

"Jenny, you don't mean that."

"Don't bet on it."

"I'm sorry, I forgot. He treated you rather shabbily, didn't he?"

"That's not important," Hank said. "He was a pig and he deserved to die. The pity is that he had already done irreparable damage to the homeless. No one should ever have to look into the eyes of such contempt. He got exactly what he deserved. It just didn't come soon enough."

Ned was silent, Hank's anger took him by surprise.

Hank dismissed the subject of Mike Shaye with a wave of her hand then continued with her theory. "The one thing we know for sure is that Speaks was with a hooker within a few days of the time his body was found. Now that may be just coincidence but if we can find a similar liaison with the other victims, I think we'll have our answer."

"That won't happen."

"I keep thinking if they're scared enough, they'll do whatever it takes to stop the killings."

"I think you're wrong, Hank," Max said, "We're more afraid of the society that put us on the streets than we are of the killer. There are many ways of dying. The murderer kills quickly and with finality. That society out there first kills the idealist within then it cuts the pride out of you, just as expertly as that killer uses his knife. That society smashes your dignity and grinds it underfoot then it gets you on your knees, begging for warm clothes in winter…for food, for drink. We even have to beg for a place in the sun. That society out there, Hank, is killing us more efficiently and completely than the serial killer, who is merely taking our lives. Am I afraid? Of course I'm afraid but I'm more frightened of having everything peeled away before I face the finality of death." There were tears pooling in her eyes, making them a deeper blue. "I'm more afraid of the day-to-day dying, of becoming less than human, of reacting to the way we're treated by that faceless society. I would prefer that they stone us outside of the city than to ignore us the way they do. They never look at us, they look through us, as though we aren't there."

Hank thought Max the pacifist finally spoke her mind.

"Right on, Maxie." Molly slapped her gently on the back. "If you get your feelin's out in the open more often, you won't ever have to go back to that shrink. Give 'em hell, girl."

A crimson blush started at the base of Max's throat and slowly traveled over her cheeks, seeming to electrify the roots of her short blond hair. "I…I'm…sorry. I should keep my opinions to myself."

Ned took her hand and kissed it. "No indeed, my love. Molly is right. You should speak your mind more frequently. It's much better than keeping it bottled up inside. It's nice to see there's fight left in you. I promise, no one will ever make you feel invisible as long as I'm around."

Ned's statement seemed to startled him. However, his smile said he accepted what he suspected all along…that he was in love with Max.

Happiness registered on Max's face, which Ned confirmed with words, his actions of the last few months.

Ned smiled at Hank. "We really should have had this conversation much sooner, Jenny…it would have prevented many sleepless nights." He quoted,

"All thoughts, all passions, all delights,
Whatever stirs this mortal frame,
All are but ministers of Love,

And feed this sacred flame." He winked at Hank.

"I know," Hank winked back at him, "Samuel Coleridge."

"Are you gonna start that crazy talk again? Do you know what he's talkin' about, Hank?" It was obvious Molly was confused and perhaps a bit jealous. She wasn't sure if she should entrust the frail Maxine into his care, real or imagined.

Hank thought mother hen was clucking and Ned got the message.

"I would never do anything to hurt Max, believe me, Molly, the crazy talk you're so concerned about is nothing more than poetry, just a different way poets had of expressing their feelings."

Molly's eyes spoke volumes but her voice gave her feelings no expression. "Then why don't they just say so in everyday language?" she muttered under her breath.

It was clear to Hank that Molly didn't like what she saw happening between Max and Ned. That she wanted only good things for Max was obvious but she was convinced Ned was not the one to make them happen. Hank also suspected Molly knew something about Ned the rest of them did not know. It bothered her...perhaps even frightened her a little.

Molly gathered her shopping bag and grunted her way into a standing position.

"Where are you going, Molly? The question was innocent enough, particularly coming from Max.

"Down to the Landing."

"Wait for us. We'll go together, all right, Ned?"

"Sure," he said. Hank thought the word came from his lips, not his mind.

Hank was certain there was an antagonism between Molly and Ned that wasn't there before. She had begun to notice it when Max wanted Molly to go to the concert. It was obvious Ned would have preferred having someone else use the ticket, someone he felt could better appreciate the music.

Molly spoke directly to Ned. "You gonna be spittin' out them weird words down there?"

"Yes, I'll be reciting poetry, if that's what you mean. It's my first love."

Molly's eyes narrowed into thin slits and it was difficult to tell if her eyes were open. "That's what I thought," she said.

Hank felt tension mounting like an oppressive heat. She said, "You and Max walk up front, Molly and I will follow."

Max smiled but she didn't miss the sarcasm in Molly's voice.

When Max and Ned were out of hearing range, she asked, "What's wrong, Molly?"

"There ain't nothin' wrong."

"Are you upset because Max and Ned are getting involved?"

"They ain't involved, they're tangled up. He's bendin' her like a pretzel. Did ya hear what he said? He said them silly words was his first love, then after that first love comes his second love...him...then him...then him again. Where the hell does Maxie fit in? You mark my words, Hank, he's gonna hurt her, just as sure as he's breathin'."

"Why do you say that?"

"Never mind. Just remember what I'm sayin'...'cause he's gonna pull back and when he does, that girl's gonna get hurt. She trusts him. She forgot rule number one. On the streets, you trust nobody...sometimes it's not even safe to trust yourself. Nobody betrays us more than we betray ourselves. *For truth is precious and divine, Too rich a pearl for carnal swine.*"

Hank stared at her. "I didn't know you could recite poetry."

"Yeah, well I ain't completely stupid." She stared back at Hank. "And I wasn't always old."

"I never thought you were stupid, Molly, far from it. If it hadn't been for you I couldn't have made it on the streets. Do you remember where the verse came from?"

"Some guy by the name of Samuel Butler. See, even I know some of them weird words."

Suddenly, Hank realized Molly understood much more than she let on...to anyone. "I think Ned will be good for Max," Hank said. "Obviously, he cares for her. When she stopped taking her medicine, you and I could do nothing for her but he was able to take over and get her back to the hospital to be seen. He protected her from further pressure by making sure she had food and didn't have to go to the shelters and be stressed out again. He's there for her when she needs him. I don't think there's any question about Max's feelings. I could see this relationship was happening months ago. I guess it was reinforced when he had the coronary and she was almost a basket case. You remember what she was like then. You were upset too."

"Sure I was," Molly said, "so was everybody else who knew her. Maxie is a lady, a fragile lady. She needs to be protected. She needs to be respected and...respect is something you don't find on the streets. You could sooner find a thousand-dollar bill. I don't know how necessary love is but I think Max can live without it. She can't live without respect. That's why bein' on the streets is tearin' her heart out. To most people we're a fungus feedin' off of society. I know a lot of Streeters from all over and I don't know any who really want to be on the streets. Most of us don't believe there's a God up there but we say prayers and sing hymns in some of the shelters because we know if we do, we're gonna get fed. We hear the workers at the shelters say, 'God loves you,' and we answer, 'Amen.' But most of us don't believe that for one minute but if we say we agree, we're gonna get food. An empty belly will get a body to say anything you want it to say, as long as the reward is there. Take the reward away and you got nobody to warm up them chairs. I never did get much respect, even before, so I can't miss somethin I never had. It's different with Maxie. Respect is one of the conditions of life with her and if she don't get it, she's cashin' in her chips. Respect ain't a bargaining chip. The rest of us do what it takes to get food or booze. Not Max. That's why I'm worried. If he loses respect for her, she'll never recover. If they're together a lot, he's gonna start seein' glimpses of a life he ran away from. What do you think will happen then?"

It was obvious to Hank that Molly had thought this through and was upset.

Molly continued, "If it gets uncomfortable he can take off for another city and start all over with his poet talk. Why do you think he knows that poem about the 'The Definition of Love' so well? He's a rover and he ain't gonna change, not for nobody."

"People change," Hank said, "if they're properly motivated."

Molly made a guttural sound that seemed to come from deep inside. "What if he has a wife already? I ain't sayin' he has, I'm just sayin' what if?"

"You think he's using Max?"

"I didn't say that." Molly held up her hand, "All I'm sayin', is...he's a rover, a wanderer, a rambler. They used to be called hobos or bums, now we call them vagabonds. Anyway, Max sees a cottage with a white fence and nobody's gonna sell him on that idea. You're gonna tell me he loves Maxie. Well, hell, who wouldn't love her. She's kind and considerate and she has a way of makin' you feel like a tower overlookin' the ocean, even though you're low enough that you can crawl under the belly of a worm." Molly had a faraway look. When she spoke again, her voice was barely audible, "Seven years ago, I got raped and the bastard that did it broke my back. He left me in an alley. It was cold and my clothes was all tore up. He stole everythin' I had, includin' a nice canvas bag, somethin' like yours. Everything I had in this world was in that bag. Stuff that couldn't have mattered to nobody else, 'cept me. I must have laid there for a couple of hours or so. There was nobody to help me.

"Then, out of the dark comes this skinny figure of a woman, shiverin' and pale as a ghost. She sees me and comes over to help. She didn't try to move me, I think Max was afraid somethin' was broke. As it turned out, she was right. So she takes out her blanket and covers me with it but I couldn't stop shakin', so she takes off her coat and puts that on top of the blanket. There she is with nothin' on but a thin blouse and a pair of slacks. She tells me to lie still, that she's gonna get help. She must have been gone an hour. An hour in the winter time without a coat can be pretty cold. Finally she came back, her hands and lips was blue with cold and her teeth chattered so loud I could hardly understand what she was sayin'. She told me she finally got a police car to stop and told them about me and they was callin' in for the police van to pick me up. That took another half hour. I wanted her to put her coat back on, but she said she would be fine until the cops got there. Then it started to snow. She made a tent out of newspapers to cover my head and face. When the cops came, I swear I could hear her bones rattlin' in her skin. They put me on a board, strapped me down and took me to the nearest hospital. I was in the hospital for a long time and every couple of days Maxie would come to see me. She looked sick and there wasn't no fat at all on her bones. That night she helped me took its toll. She was walkin' around with pneumonia. It was a long time before she got any color in her cheeks. Somehow, she managed to get me some warm clothes and a coat and woolen cap. She even got me this plastic bag I carry around. She went with me everywhere to make sure nobody bothered me. When spring came I was feelin' better and able to do things for myself. I'll never forget what she done for me. I owe Maxie...big time. There's probably some people who thinks I'm a dyke and that's why I'm protective. You know different, Hank, and I know you never thought nothin' like that. Sure I'm worried about her. I don't want to see her get hurt. She had to pick up enough dirty pieces from a broken life and it ain't goin' to happen again if I can stop it."

"I think she already made up her mind. What do you think you can do to change it?"

Very quietly, Molly answered, "I can give him a warnin'. If she gets hurt, he's gonna answer to me. This world ain't big enough for him to run away. I'll follow him to his death. I'll cut his heart out if he ain't good to her. He's like one of them lizards that changes color...you know what I mean?"

"Like a chameleon?"

"That's it. He wears one color when he's spurtin' his poetry and everybody thinks he's the twentieth-century Shakespeare but his color changes and he ain't quite so wonderful when he comes back down to earth, when he remembers he's only one more homeless man, no more, no less."

"Everything will work out, give it a chance. I think Ned knows you don't approve of the relationship but I believe he loves Max and wants to do the right thing."

"I hope you're right, Hank," she shook her head, "I hope you're right."

* * *

Hank hurried along the Benjamin Franklin Parkway to her safe haven and Storm. She hadn't seen him for two weeks. She assumed he would meet her at the apartment and the now familiar excitement started somewhere in her chest. When she turned the key in the lock he was standing there waiting with a dozen red roses.

"How lovely," Hank said as she took them from him.

"I had them delivered and told the florist to leave them outside your door. I hoped you would get here first. I beat you by fifteen minutes." He took her into his arms. It was then Hank knew how much she really missed him. Making love was maddeningly slow, deliciously deliberate, intoxicating and indescribably filled with sensations, recalled and new.

Later they lay wrapped in each other's embrace, the streets of Philadelphia and their problems were worlds away. The only thing real was the here and the now. They drifted off into an exhausted sleep. Evening was making an appearance, bathing the room in shadows. Storm tilted her chin so that his eyes were looking directly into hers.

"I'm in love with you, Hank."

"Ditto." It sounded stupid to her ears. *Ditto?* she thought. *Who the hell says ditto when a guy says he's in love with you?*

"I hope we can wind up this case so we can be seen together. I feel like a kid playing hooky from school and hiding out at a friend's house."

Hank ran her fingers over his hairy chest. "Any new developments?"

"Not really."

"I've been wanting to talk to you. Molly saw the hooker with Noah Speaks a few days before he was killed. Your theory may be correct." Hank slipped out of bed and into a robe. "Let's go to the kitchen, I'll get dinner together and we can talk." She gathered up their dirty clothes and threw them into the washer. Storm took a clean pair of shorts out of the bureau drawer and slipped them on.

"What made you change your mind?" he asked.

"You mean about the possibility of it being a woman?"

Storm nodded. "I didn't think you would ever consider the possibility, let alone admit that it was a possibility."

"When Molly told me about seeing them and how Suzie was taunting him, I thought about what you said. There was no hope of getting paid so she must have been doing it for another reason. It seems far-fetched until you analyze it. Who would be in a better position to set these men up? Have you seen her anymore?"

"Not since the time she tried to sit in my lap when I was standing up."

Hank studied his face, she said, "What if she's not a hooker? What if Suzie's a nymphomaniac?" She saw a flash of white through his facial hair.

Storm said, "If you were a nymphomaniac, would you pick on some worn-out Streeters with their myriad of stinks or would you go to a sure thing like virile, passionate young college students, who are much more interesting and available? She doesn't seem to be interested in gang-bangs but is very selective in her choice of a partner. I can't say for certain but my guess is that her choices end up dead at some point in the relationship."

Hank said, "Maybe I'm dense but how does she make contact with these men?"

"The street men will notice any female who is not wearing oversized shoes and baggy clothes." Storm smiled at her. "Street men may be worn out but they're not dead. Oddly enough, she always shows up between midnight and six a.m. A more interesting question is where does she go the rest of the time?"

"You think there's a possibility she could have something to do with the killings?"

"The fact that she likes sex doesn't mean she would kill for it. Right now, it's a coincidence that she happened to be seen with several of the men, at some point, prior to their deaths. But there's no law that says she can't talk to those men or have sex with them. Those same victims were seen talking to any number of street women day and night prior to the murders. We can't accuse our hooker, or our nympho, whichever the case may be, because she was seen with them. There are no witnesses that came forward to say she was with any of the victims on the night of their murders. By your own admission, Molly saw her with Speaks days before he was killed. A lot could have happened in that time. I think the theory has merit. Certainly worth looking into but we have nothing that will tie her in with the crimes. If she is, in fact, a hooker, that would be the time of night she would be trolling with her bait."

"I wish it would end," Hank said. "I'm so tired."

"I know. There's a lot of pressure out there. Molly must leave very early in the morning to be a witness to these things. Doesn't she ever sleep?"

Hank told him about Molly's reaction to Ned's attraction to Max.

"Does she usually make threats like that?"

"Oh, I don't think it was a threat. That's just the way Molly talks. She's the lioness watching out for her cub."

"Didn't she get upset once before when Benny fingered Maxine when we found her blanket over one of the victims? And didn't he end up dead?"

Hank gasped. "You don't suspect Molly, do you?"

"I told you, the police department suspects everybody. She's an older broad but she gets around better than the rest of you and she covers more territory. Now, if Molly is properly motivated? Sure, she could be a suspect. You can make a case against almost anybody, the only thing lacking is motive."

"What possible motive could anyone have to commit these senseless crimes?"

Storm ticked off on his fingers, "Love…hate…jealousy…revenge."

"Against one person, all right, but against all of the victims?"

Storm poured each of them a glass of Châteauneuf-du-Pape before he answered. "For the sake of argument, let's assume the killer is a woman. She could have had a relationship with a man and let's say he conned her out of her life savings, a considerable sum. Maybe she can't get to him because he took off, so she gets her revenge by punishing all men for what one man did to her. Or say our woman is in love with a man and he throws her over for her best friend. She now has all this hurt bottled up inside and she doesn't know what to do with it. So every man she meets is a reminder of how he made her feel. All those feelings of ecstacy and passion, all the pleasure and gratification, now turns into bitterness and pain, misery and rejection. The strong feeling of love turns into a stronger feeling of hate. Now she projects this hate onto every man who reminds her of her lost lover."

"But all of the men were derelicts. Does that mean her lover was also a derelict?"

"I would say it's symbolic. Physically the lover was probably not a derelict, but in her eyes, he had become morally bankrupt, so he was a derelict of another kind. Anyway, if any man fits the preconceived mold, he becomes the lover who rejected her, the one who made her feel used, dirty, unwanted."

"You know, Andrews, you've got quite a head on your shoulders. I'm impressed."

Again the flash of white teeth. "Coming from you that's a real compliment. Thank you, Castle…as in propugnaculum."

Hank had developed a new respect for his reasoning ability, which did not fit into her concept of how a law enforcement officer thought.

He smiled, "You must be impressed…you're letting our dinner burn."

She spun around only to be greeted by black smoke coming from the pan where she had put four pork chops. Her look of dismay made him laugh. "Here, better let me take over before we don't have anything at all to eat. You put our clothes in the dryer. If you burn those, we're going to make quite a spectacle on the streets."

As she passed him she allowed her hands to wander over his body, firing up her own passion for him.

He hardened at her touch. "You're really not hungry, are you?" He turned off the burner under the chops.

"Oh yes I am…" she put her arms around his neck, "but not for food."

She felt the hunger in him, the urgency of him, almost as though they had not made love just a short time before. That was then and this was now. Their bodies meshed in a slow motion of lovemaking. Each touch, an exquisite rapture; each kiss, a journey into paradise; each word, a litany of endearments never before uttered; each look, a caress; each sigh, a discovery of heights never before scaled. To Hank, this was as close as anyone could ever come to perfection. And so this haven became the reality and Hank's life on the streets became the fantasy of lurking, hooded shadows with grinning skeletal faces.

* * *

When Hank had spread her ground cover and blanket under the azalea bushes, she heard Molly's familiar shuffle. She said, "I saved you and Max your usual spots. It's a beautiful night."

Molly readied her sleeping space without comment but her agitation wasn't any less than it had been that morning. Hank was glad she remembered to refill the brandy bottle before leaving the apartment. Molly looked over at Hank's canvas bag, occupying the space held for Max.

"I don't think Maxie's gonna be sleeping here anymore," Molly mumbled.

"Oh?"

"She's probably gonna sleep down on the waterfront with Mr. Words Almighty."

"What makes you think that?"

"Well, she ain't here, is she?"

"That doesn't mean she won't be here. It's only ten o'clock. There's still plenty of time."

Molly continued to mumble to herself as she dug into her shopping bag. "Damn it!" she cried as she pulled her hand back and the tips of her fingers were dripping blood.

"Molly, what did you do?" Hank dug into her own canvas bag and came up with an old handkerchief what was torn, but clean. "Here, put this on it to stop the bleeding."

"I shoulda throwed that old glass away before it got me."

"Give it to me and I'll throw it in the trash bin."

"Don't bother. I'll do it tomorrow." She sucked on the tips of her fingers drawing the blood out. "That's what I get for not payin' attention to what I'm doin'."

Hank took out the bottle of brandy and held it out to her. "Maybe this will help dull the pain."

Molly looked at the bottle and smiled. "That's mighty good of you, Hank." She reached for it. Hank noticed that Molly winced in pain.

Hank said, "What's wrong, Molly?"

"Nothin', it's just a little gas." Molly blinked hard several times, then smiled again, unscrewed the cap and tipped the bottle up. A thin trickle ran out the side of her mouth down her chin. She lowered the bottle and wiped her chin with the back of her hand. Then she filled her mouth with brandy, held her head back and put the cut fingers into the brandy in her mouth before she swallowed it. "Not the best disinfectant in the world, but it works. The nice part is you don't waste any of it."

Molly looked very tired, very sad, very old. She was concerned about Max and nothing would change that. Not even brandy.

"She shouldn't trust him. Men takes what they wants then leaves you with the problems."

The more brandy she downed the more she muttered to herself. Hank knew that Molly was having one of her famous confrontations with herself and the rest of the world was excluded. Hank heard Max approach but said nothing until she was in sight.

"See, Molly, Max isn't staying at the waterfront. Look, here she comes."

Molly squinted, trying to see through the fog that was beginning to form. "You sure that's her?"

"I'll bet my life on it."

Molly's eyes clouded over with tears as she capped the brandy bottle and handed it back. "Thanks, Hank."

Max picked up Hank's canvas bag and handed it to her. "Looks like I'm the last one here. Wasn't it a beautiful day?"

Molly took Max's bag, removed the ground cloth and blanket and spread them out in the usual spot and put the shopping bag down to be used as a pillow. "You okay, Maxie?"

"Couldn't be better." She smiled warmly at her protector. Then she turned to Hank. "I didn't see you all day. Did you have a good day?"

Before she could answer, Molly said, "Didn't you notice, Hank disappears every Sunday. I think she's got a fella."

Hank could feel a flush of color heating her cheeks and was grateful for the darkness and the fog.

"Sunday is my day for me. I can go anywhere. I can go to the Wagner Free Institute of Science and lose myself in a world of my own creation. I can examine the fossil remains of extinct and endangered species and imagine I lived way back then. Sometimes I'll go to the Thomas Jefferson University, Eakins Gallery, and pretend I'm an important part of founding one of the oldest medical colleges in the United States. On a nice day like today, I might just walk around Elfreth's Alley and think about what it was like in colonial times. Other times I'll walk up on Seventh Street to the Edgar Allen Poe National Historic Site and in my mind I can recreate the ghoul-haunted mansions and imagine what it was like to be a part of the House of Usher. Sometimes I could almost hear the beating of the wings of the raven. Other times I'll sit on the steps of the Academy of Music and pretend I'm the first lady of the theater and I have to think of what I'll say to the reporters outside the stage door after my performance. Still other times I'll go to the Art Museum before one o'clock, when I can get in free. There are so many things you can do, places to go, and without the usual crowds, I can go to these places without feeling like I brought the plague with me. Sundays are the best times, even for people like us. Don't you ever read the propaganda the convention and visitors bureau puts out? *Touch the Liberty Bell, sit in Madison's seat at Congress Hall and carry a cry of freedom from Franklin's print shop at Independence National Historical Park.* Hell, you don't have to be a tourist to enjoy some of the things around town, and some of them are free."

Molly's mouth dropped open. "You really go to those places? Nobody kicks you out? I guess it's because you look intelligent. Me, I look dumb and nobody believes I can be interested in history or science. They just assume I'm there to pick pockets and smell up the joint, so they kick me out and make me feel like a bum. I guess they don't do that to you, do they, Hank?"

"They'd better never try it. That's when they'd have a tiger by the tail."

"Here all the time I thought you had a guy you was sneaking out to see."

"I do, Molly, quite a few guys, but they're all dead. Guys like Billy Penn, and Ben Franklin, Georgie Washington and Tommy Jefferson. But I assure you I'm perfectly safe with them. Why don't you come with me next Sunday?"

"You nuts? If I want to see somethin' old, I'll look in a mirror. If I want to see somethin' dead, I'll go to a cemetery. But maybe Max would like to go with you."

"No thank you," Max said, "I do enough walking all week, just to keep the cops off my back, I don't intend to do it on Sundays, when the cops are still filling out papers on the people they arrested during the fracases of the Friday and Saturday night knife and gun club encounters. I enjoy sitting along the riverfront and listening to Ned's poetry." She looked at Molly. "He's quite good, you know."

Hank saw the stiffening of Molly's shoulders and tried to halt a confrontation between Max and Molly, and said, "I'm sure Molly can appreciate poetry. She even recited some for me." Hank smiled at Molly. "She's quite good too. I think we have more poets among our Streeters than they have in the theaters. Good ones too."

Molly looked pleased and Hank was able to relax knowing there would not be a problem that night.

The fog rolled in and engulfed the river area and soon even the halo of light above the East River Drive was obscured and the area took on an eerie, soupy appearance. Even the shuffle of the Streeters was hushed by the denseness of the shroud that cloaked the city. Hank settled down on the blanket and the tiredness washed over her like a comforting warm bath. Hank had no idea how long she slept. In the quiet whiteness of the fog she thought she saw the specter of her dreams with the hooded cloak, standing above her. Not threateningly…just watching her. The specter leaned closer and Hank was terrified that she was going to see the perpetual grin on the skeletal face as she had seen in other dreams.

It was different this time. As the form leaned closer, she could see the outline of a face, a hard and sneering face, full of disdain…but familiar. The face was hers. She reached out to touch the form but the specter pulled away, laughing, a deep-throated chuckle, daring her to follow. "Come," she said, "watch me while I make love to your lover. You can't have him, Henrietta. He's going to be mine. I'll never let you have him." As she backed away, the black cloak, like the darkness of the night in contrast to the white fog, enveloped her in a swirling mist and all that remained was the deep-throated chuckle that she had heard in the basement of her apartment building. Hank reached out to stop the apparition from disappearing but all she did was disturb the fog and beyond that, more darkness. She struggled for what seemed an eternity, trying to free herself from the bonds that tied her to the ground. Hank pleaded for her tormentor to stop, to come back. At last the form broke through the fog and came at Hank from out of nowhere, grabbing her shoulders and shaking her. Hank tried to pry her hands away, but she continued to shake Hank.

"Hank, Hank, wake up." It was Max's voice she heard and her face came into focus. Max could tell by the expression on Hank's face she was frightened. She put her arms around the shivering Hank. "It's all right, Hank, it was only a dream. It was only a dream."

When Hank's heart stopped pounding its way through her chest wall, she was able to slow her breathing and take a deep breath. "Did you see her?" Hank asked.

"There was no one here, Hank, you were dreaming."

Hank rubbed her eyes. Max said she was dreaming but it was so real. She was here. She was menacing. She was…Hank.

Molly made her way through the fog, across the footpath, and sat next to Hank. She took the brandy out of Hank's bag and handed it to her.

"Here, drink some of this. It'll help." Hank took a swallow of the burning liquid and coughed.

"I could have sworn she was here. I saw her."

Molly walked around the area looking under bushes, then came back after a few minutes. "I think somebody was here, Hank. With all this fog I couldn't see nobody. Hell, I can't even see my hand in front of my face. But I heard somebody talkin' to you, and I heard a laugh, then I heard you yell for her to come back. I heard a kinda crazy laugh. I started to come over to you but Maxie reached you first."

"Didn't you see anything, Molly?"

"No, hon, I sure didn't. Here, have another swig of brandy."

Hank pushed the bottle away, and rather than have it go to waste, Molly took a swig before she put the cap back on. Molly said, "Who was it, Hank? Did ya know her?"

Hank felt the perspiration beading on her forehead and throat. She shook her head, trying to clear it. "She looked like me."

"But she was hard looking, right?

"How do you know that, Molly?"

"It must be the same dame I saw talking to Speaks. The hooker. I told you about her. I thought she looked like you until I got close to her, then I saw she didn't look like you at all. She was hard as nails and twice as sharp. She must have followed you back from wherever you were. You must have a guy that she wants."

Hank recovered enough to protect her cover. "That's stupid. I haven't got a guy. Not her guy or anybody else's. What the hell could she want with me?"

"There could be a guy interested in you and you don't even know it, or maybe he told her he was your guy just to get her off his back and maybe she don't like that."

"This is ludicrous." Hank shifted uneasily. "Obviously she has me mixed up with somebody else. Damn, and I was having such a nice sleep, too."

Max was still holding Hank's arm with her finger pressing on the pulse. "You're pretty upset. Your pulse rate is a hundred and twenty."

"Well, no wonder," Hank cried, "she scared the shit out of me. Hell, I didn't know if I was going to end up with a bullet in my head or a knife in my chest." She shivered. "I don't think I want to have a repeat performance. She was a damned creep is what she was." Hank saw the worried expressions on Molly's and Max's faces. "I'm fine. Go back to sleep. I'm sorry I woke you up."

"Are you going to be able to go to sleep again?"

"Sure, Max. I'm sure it was a case of mistaken identity."

Hank lay back on the blanket and thought back to the number of times she came out of her apartment building with the feeling she was being followed. *She must have been outside of my apartment tonight and followed me here. Storm made jokes about her trying to sit in his lap when he was standing up but if she is the murderer, it's entirely possible that Storm is slated to be one of her victims, but obviously not until he has succumbed to her deadly charm.* Hank muttered, "As soon as this fog lifts, I've got to find Storm. I've got to find him before she does."

Hank rolled over on her blanket. Sleep eluded her but fear didn't. Fear was no longer in her dreams, it came out into the open with its ugly fangs and terrorizing paralysis.

CHAPTER 16

Hank searched the waterfront, the subway stations, Rittenhouse Square, Penn Center and the Thirtieth Street Station looking for Storm Andrews but to no avail.

The mist turned liquid, a warm late-summer rain that left the streets steamy with its oppressive heat. Aloud, Hank said, "I've got to get out of this sweltering garbage before I pass out." Her throat felt parched and it was difficult to keep her eyes open.

When she reached the apartment building she felt faint. She staggered to the tower entrance and pulled open the door. Before the door closed, she saw a shadowy figure enter behind her. She gasped and lost her footing as she spun around.

Storm Andrews caught her and planted her firmly on her feet. Her arms felt clammy to his touch and her face was drained of color. Hank? What's wrong?"

A feeling of relief flooded her body and she clung to him. "I...feel so light-headed...dizzy. I looked all over for you then I began to feel funny, so I decided to come back here."

Storm supported her as they went up the stairs. "Looks like heat prostration to me," he said. "A cool bath and some decent food will go a long way toward making you feel human again."

Storm filled a bowl with water and ice cubes and wrung out washcloths and put them on her forehead and the back of her neck. When her breathing and color returned to normal he gave her sips of cool water.

"That never happened to me before. I felt like I was going to pass out."

Storm kissed her lightly on the lips. "You almost did. Now why were you running around on a day like this looking for me?"

She told him about her night visitor and the threat. She said, "At first I thought it was a dream, but Molly heard her too."

"Did Molly see her?"

"No," Hank said, "the fog was so thick you couldn't see more than a foot in front of you but Molly said she heard her laugh and heard her warn me to stay away from…you." A tear ran down her cheek. "She was so full of hate. If she can't have you, I'm afraid she'll try to kill you."

"Don't worry about me. I carry a gun."

"So did Mike Shaye."

Storm brushed away a stubborn lock of Hank's hair that insisted on falling over her forehead. He said, "I think any man is safe around her as long as he doesn't play her game. Once he's enticed, he makes himself eligible to be air conditioned with a knife." He kept his arms around her but was lost in thought. "How did she find you in the fog?"

"I wondered about that too. When I left the apartment last night I had the feeling I was being followed. Remember, I told you I had this feeling before but never saw anyone behind me. Obviously, she followed me and waited until Molly and Max were asleep before she made her move. If it wasn't for Molly I would have sworn it was a dream because it followed a dream pattern I've had ever since I came to the streets."

"What dream pattern?"

Hank told him briefly about the recurrent dream, then shook her head. "It doesn't matter. The important thing is for you to be aware that you could be in danger."

"She really frightened you, didn't she? I hate to add to your misery but our killer struck again last night."

Hank rubbed her temples. "Who?"

"All I have is a name. George Franklin. Know him?" Storm waited for her to reply.

"I don't think so. Depends on what name he used on the streets."

Storm walked to the window. "Looks like the fog is rolling in again, in a little while it'll be like pea soup. Do you want to stay with me on the waterfront tonight?"

"I can't. If I don't show up at the Azalea Gardens tonight Max and Molly will be convinced Suzie Bimbo made confetti out of me."

"Later tonight I'll make rounds that will include the Azalea Gardens," Storm said, as he kissed her. His eyes told her what she wanted to hear. Storm loved her.

Hank felt suddenly secure, her fears dissipated, there was no danger, no streets, no hunger, there was only the promise in his eyes, the yearning of her body for his, the warmth and passion of his kiss.

The fog gave eerie shapes to common forms and muted familiar street sounds. Hank had difficulty finding her way. The shelter was crowded and Hank's eyes scanned the room for Max and Molly. She saw Ned first and waved to him. After she got her food, she made her way to the table and Ned moved over to make room for her between him and Molly. Max sat across from him.

"Not a good day to be walking, Jenny," Ned said.

"Tell me about it," Hank said. "You take your life in your hands trying to cross a street in this fog. I heard the cars but I couldn't see them. If I can't see them, I know they don't see me but it doesn't slow them down, they come barreling through like the city was bathed in sunshine. There'll probably be a few accidents tonight. Let's try not to become a statistic."

Molly leaned close to Hank and whispered, "The fog can also be your friend. It keeps people in their houses and keeps the cops away. To me that means a hassle-free night. Did ya ever watch somebody comin' toward you in the fog? It looks like they is walkin' on clouds. Makes everythin' mysterious." She looked toward Ned and added, "Even a little sinister." She studied Hank's face, "See, if you was a writer, you could make up lots of stories about what can happen on a foggy night."

Hank tried to determine if Molly knew something about her true identity or if the remark about being a writer was happenstance. She said, "Don't you have difficulty getting around in this murk?"

"Naw. I know this city like the back of my hand. I don't have to see to know where I'm goin'."

"Good. You can get us back to the Azalea Gardens."

"No problem," Molly grinned, "but it's gonna cost you."

Hank laughed. "You're incorrigible."

"If you say so, Hank." Suddenly, Molly's head snapped around in answer to some silent signal that only she could hear. "Wait for me outside," she said.

As they neared the door, Hank was aware of a low buzzing sound. She looked at Ned. "What's that?"

He watched Molly's progress. "That, dear Jenny, is the Streeter's communication network. Molly'll find out what's happening. She's unbelievable. I think she has built-in radar. She always knows when to leave an area before the police get there. You may fool her once but never a second time."

Molly motioned for the group to keep moving. When they turned the corner she stopped them. "George Franklin got hisself killed last night."

Ned's face took on a worried expression. "George was on the waterfront with me last night." He spoke directly to Hank, "When he left, he said he had an appointment to keep. I thought he was kidding. I guess he wasn't." Ned left the women, his walk slower, his shoulders bent, his head lowered.

Molly guided them back to the Azalea Gardens without a problem. Her course was as direct as a homing pigeon.

True to her word, Hank produced the brandy. Everything was a murky blackness until Hank looked toward the overhead lights along the River Drive, there it was milky white with night particles circling through in a clockwise direction. Traffic sounds all but disappeared in the soupy atmosphere. Hank thought that even the familiar shuffling of Streeters took on a new sound...like a broom sweeping a rough paved surface.

Hank lay on her blanket listening to Max's slow, even breathing and the steady drone of Molly's snore across the footpath. Hank realized it was the drone of Molly's monotonous snoring that lulled her to sleep each night but also gave her a feeling of security, knowing she and Max were nearby if needed. Hank gave in to the overwhelming urge to study the insides of her closed eyelids.

The interminable dream returned and the face of the skeletal nightmare with the perpetual bony grin stared back at her, taunting, daring her to follow where it led. But in the dream, Hank refused to go. The black-hooded specter took hold of Hank's shadow, leading it through a labyrinth of indistinct shapes and forms. Terror seized the mesmerized Hank and she ran after her shadow to save it from destruction. Her arms reached out to her captive shadow but it was just out of reach. In desperation she plunged after the elusive form and managed to get a stronghold on her shadow and held tight. When she looked up, it seemed the moon was laughing at her just before it pulled a cloud in front of its face. Hank wasn't sure she was awake until she heard Molly mumbling under her breath.

"Molly? Everything okay?" Hank couldn't see her because of the fog but she could hear her. "Do you need help?"

There was no reply, so Hank got up and felt her way across the footpath. There was Molly trying to straighten out her blanket.

"Molly?"

Molly looked up and it was plain to see she wasn't very happy.

"What?" she barked.

"Can I help? You seem to be having a bad time."

"I'm sorry, Hank. Didn't mean to bite your head off. I went to take a pee and when I got back, everythin' was a mess. Kinda like an animal was sniffing around looking for something to eat. Everything in my bag was dumped out on the ground. My blanket was almost rolled into a ball. Damn, that makes me mad." She stopped trying to make order out of chaos and studied Hank. "Whatcha doin' up so early? Can't be but five o'clock."

"I heard you mumbling, and after what happened to me last night, I decided to check it out just in case."

"No sense in looking for anythin' now. When it gets light I can rearrange my bag to make sure I have everythin'. Thanks anyway, Hank."

"Sure. Yell if you need me." She felt her way back across the footpath. She gave in to her exhaustion, closed her eyes and drifted into oblivion. Three hours later she stirred again. Some of the fog had dissipated and the morning was a little cooler than it had been. Max was sitting up rubbing her eyes and massaging her stiff neck. "Good morning, Hank."

"You sound happy this morning."

"I had a good night for a change. I didn't have to get up once to go to the toilet."

Hank looked across the path to where Molly had been. "Looks like Molly left early, as usual. I wonder if she was missing anything. I think if she could have found the animal that rummaged through her things, she would have eaten him raw."

Plainly, Max didn't have the slightest idea what she was talking about, so Hank explained how she heard Molly mumbling to herself and how angry she was.

"Poor Molly. It looks like somebody or something is always after her things. She doesn't have anything of value but she's always getting ripped off. I've come to the conclusion that being homeless and getting ripped off are synonymous."

"But we're doing it to ourselves."

"Yes, I know we are, Hank, but that doesn't make it any more palatable. If the street people could be more cohesive there's no telling what we could accomplish."

"Do you think that'll ever happen?" Hank watched for Max's reaction.

"No, I know it will never happen. The reasons for being on the streets are too diverse, too personal...too painful." Max had a faraway look, "I wonder how many normal people out there appreciate what they have. How many people out there realize what a luxury it is to sleep on a mattress or to have heat in winter and air-conditioning in the sweltering summer? We take so much for granted. If we had a choice and we could see what we would become later in life, I wonder how many of us would choose to be born."

"All of this because Molly got ripped off?"

Max's laugh was contagious. "In another life I must have been an orator." She finished stuffing things into her shopping bag. "Finished. Now I'm ready for some hot tea or coffee."

The shelter was almost empty by the time they got there and there was very little food left, so they had a slice of bread and a cup of coffee. Max was always happy on Fridays because it meant lots of people on the waterfront to listen to the poet of the streets. Hank was looking at a much stronger Max. She thought either Max was better able to take things in stride and deal with problems as they arose, rather than allowing them to multiply so that they were overpowering, or the medication was stronger than any of them imagined. Hank preferred to think Max was stronger. That she was happier was evident. Her step was lighter, her smile brighter. She seemed to be at peace with herself. They walked to Franklin Square, where Max fed the pigeons half of the slice of bread she had gotten at the shelter.

At noon Max suggested they go to the waterfront to hear Ned.

Hank said, "It's hard to believe we're starting the Labor Day weekend. It has always been a sad time for me, it meant the fun of summer was over and the long, dreary days of winter were beginning. I'm not looking forward to another winter. As Molly would say, 'Br-r-r-r.'"

Ned saw them coming and went to meet them. "Hello, Jenny, I'm glad you were able to come. It looks like it's going to be a great weekend. Look the crowds are gathering already. Hopefully it will be like this for the whole weekend."

The audience was captivated by Ned's recitations. He recited verses from Ovid to Spenser; from Poe to Shakespeare; and from Keats and Shelley to Jefferson and Lincoln. The audience clamored for more. It was during his recitation of Hamlet's soliloquy that Hank's eyes scanned the crowd. She saw a familiar face in the crowd. One she had hoped never to see again.

Julian Grant.

The years melted away and she was once again standing in the doorway to their bedroom, listening to his animal grunts as he impaled a teenage girl on their bed. Hank had walked inside the room and slammed the door. The girl tried to cover her nakedness with the pillow that had been under her hips. The expression on Julian's face was one of rage. Hank remembered lunging at the girl, slapping her bare bottom. Julian grabbed both of Hank's hands and threw her to the floor, pummelling her face with his fist. Hank tried to ward off the attack by crossing her arms in front of her face. There was an empty beer bottle on the floor near the bed. In desperation, Hank picked it up and struck back at Julian. Once, twice, three times she struck at his head with the bottle, until he lay motionless on the floor, blood oozing from an open wound over his temple. She heard a scream and realized she was standing over him. Hank couldn't remember what happened to the girl.

Hank heard Ned's recitation of Shelley's "Queen Mab," but his voice seemed to be a long way off. The flashback evaporated and Hank looked at the girl with Julian Grant and although it was not the same girl, this one was also very young. Hank wondered if Julian was a latent pedophile and actually preferred them younger than this girl, who seemed to be in her late teens. Before he could notice her, Hank inched her way backward. As she reached the fringes of the crowd, she felt someone pinch her on the bottom. She spun around and saw a flash of white teeth. His eyes scanned the crowd, content that they had not attracted attention, he whispered, "That's the best-looking ass I've seen since last Sunday. What's your hurry?"

Hank pulled him away from the crowd. "See the man with the young girl?"

His eyes followed hers to the spot where Julian Grant was standing. "You mean the balding man who is trying to cover his baldness by combing his hair over from one ear to the other?"

"Yes. That's Julian Grant. I've got to get out of here before he sees me or there goes my cover."

Storm took another long look, studying Julian with the expert eyes of a people watcher. Finally, he nodded and led her away. They walked to Fairmount Park in silence. When they were seated on a bench, he said, "What the hell did you ever see in him? He looks like Digger O'Dell. What a creep. How come he has to rob the cradle? Can't he get a woman interested in him? What the hell makes these perverts go after the kids?"

"Probably because it's the only way he can feel superior to anyone and he can be reasonably assured that the child isn't smarter than he is."

"He must have money. I can't believe a woman would be interested in him for himself."

Hank kissed his cheek. "Thanks, pal, I needed that."

"You know, you wouldn't have to worry about your cover if you get off the streets. You must have enough information for that book by now."

Hank said, "I should have enough information in another couple of months. Then we can live like normal people."

He smiled and took her chin between his thumb and index finger. "The first thing we should do is take a vacation." He stopped at the expression on her face. "What's the matter?"

Hank shook her head. "I can't help thinking about Max and Molly. They can't take a vacation. Hell, they can't even get off the streets for a little while. I guess I feel guilty. I feel like I'm betraying them."

Storm shook his head. "They're not on the streets because of you. They were here long before you came on the scene. With Molly, the streets are a way of life. Maybe Max will be a little luckier. Do you think she would think twice if she had the opportunity to get off the streets? What do you think she would do if Ned asked her to go away with him? Even if he asked her to go to another city, not to get her off the streets but just to move to another city. Do you think she would give you a second thought?"

"Yes. Yes, I do," Hank said.

"Then you haven't learned anything about the streets or the street people. Ten minutes after she left, you wouldn't even be a memory. Didn't Molly say when it comes down to Max or her, she would have to think about Molly first? Survival. That's the first law of nature…and the streets. You're thinking with your emotions, not with your brain. Let's set a definite date for you to leave the streets. How about Thanksgiving Day?"

"That would really be something to be thankful for, wouldn't it? You're right. I'm going to have to make the break sooner or later. I just hope they never find out that Henrietta Castle is the Hank they knew on the streets. I don't think I could face that. I wouldn't want to look in their eyes if they found out I was using them."

"I don't think they were on the short end of the stick. You befriended them, you didn't use them."

"Of course I did. How else could I get the material for my book? They had to be my friends. They had to trust me."

"You're the one who said street people trust no one." Storm could see she was upset. "Why are you punishing yourself?"

"Guilty conscience, I guess."

"You can't take on the responsibility for anyone but yourself and you can only do that for today, because tomorrow brings its own responsibilities. There are no guarantees in this life. I love you. Here and now, I love you."

Hank could feel what little energy she had left being drained from within. She was tired. She thought seriously about abandoning the streets now but something inside said the job wasn't done and she had to stay and see it through.

Now there was another consideration...Storm. There was no doubt in Hank's mind that she wanted him to love her as she loved him...but somehow the knowledge that he did now filled her with terror. What if he became a victim of this mad killer? Why was she trembling inside? Why was this feeling of foreboding constantly with her? Why was she allowing the threat of a hooker to depress her? She knew for certain if anyone could take care of themselves it was Storm. Yet the feeling was there, just under the surface, that he would be taken from her. Her fear was that there was no future for them. When she thought about tomorrow she drew a blank.... There were no more tomorrows. She had used them all. The feeling wasn't one of impending death, but the feeling that her future was being determined by forces beyond her control.

Evening shadows were claiming the waterfront. Molly signaled Hank from the other side of the crowd gathered around Ned, and Hank wended her way through the fringes of the crowd. Her eyes scanned the people gathered to be sure Julian Grant had left. When she reached Molly, Hank could see she was upset.

"I talked to Maxie and she's going to stay on the waterfront tonight." The sadness in Molly's voice was unmistakable.

"She's probably tired and it is a long walk back to the Gardens. Max will be back with us before you know it."

Molly watched Max and Ned together. "Not this time. I knowed she was battlin' with herself about what to do. He won." She took a deep breath and let it hiss slowly through her lips. "He better take good care of her."

They walked in silence. She wasn't certain but Hank thought she saw tears on Molly's cheeks. Hank thought that Molly had just lost her drive to go on. Max had become her child and now that child was leaving the nest and Molly was totally unprepared, totally devastated. They were stretching out their ground cloths when just before drifting off to sleep, Hank caught a glimpse of Storm Andrews and felt safe again. The next morning, her blanket was rolled into a ball and she had dirt on her clothes.

Molly was nowhere to be seen.

A light mist was falling and it had turned cool. Hank reached into her canvas bag, pulled out a wrinkled sweater and put it on before she left for the shelter and some hot coffee. She could only imagine how Molly felt on these damp days and Hank regretted she had not given her the bottle of brandy. There were only a few familiar faces at the shelter, which was unusual. She wondered where Max and Ned were. She knew Molly wouldn't be there and she would do whatever it took to avoid seeing them together.

Hank was warming her hands around the cup of coffee she held, not paying attention to the man sitting next to her, until he whispered into his cup.

"There was trouble on the waterfront last night."

Hank knew that voice belonged to only one person, Storm.

"Another killing?" Hank asked.

"Afraid so. Max is being held at headquarters."

"Oh, God, it wasn't Ned?"

"No, but I don't think Max knew that. The guy looked enough like Ned to be his twin."

"You don't think Max could have done it, do you?"

"She's being held as a material witness. We think she might have seen the murder, if not the murderer. The victim was only about ten feet from where she and Ned were bedded down."

"Why aren't you holding Ned instead of Max?"

"The killer made a try for Ned too."

"Is he…?"

"No, he rolled away in time, all he got was a superficial laceration. Max screamed when she saw the blood and that probably scared the assailant away." Storm paused. "Then she lost it, retreated…withdrew into herself. Ned thinks she didn't actually see the person. The police think she not only saw the assailant but knew the killer."

Hank said, "She loves Ned. If she knew the killer she would tell."

"Maybe she also knows and loves the person who tried to kill him."

Hank stared into space. "Who do you think it was?"

"What time did Molly leave the Gardens last night?"

"To the best of my knowledge she didn't. Well, hell, you were there and saw the two of us."

"That was eleven o'clock. Where was she between three and six o'clock?"

"I don't know, but I would assume she was asleep."

"I don't think so. I stayed around until two o'clock, and she still wasn't asleep at that time. I would say she was a little upset last night. She did a lot of pacing and if she had the money to buy cigarettes, she would have smoked a couple of packs. Why was she so upset?"

"Because Max told her she was spending the night on the waterfront with Ned. Molly's afraid he's going to hurt Max." Hank studied Storm's face and realized he wasn't telling her everything. She asked, "How is Max? Has anyone let her see Ned so she knows he is still alive?"

"Max is in no condition to see or talk to anyone right now. The attempt on Ned's life sent her into a tailspin."

"Where is she?"

"In the hospital. The doctor says she is unresponsive to painful stimuli. She retreated into that safe world. The one she built in her mind. The only place where no one can hurt her...but it's also the place where no one can reach her."

Ned...Ned can help her. I know he can reach her. Let him try, Please, Storm, let him try."

"We can't do anything without the psychiatrist's approval. Right now they're using music and passive stimuli, hoping she'll come out of it. Doctor McGowan's afraid anything more at this time may push her beyond anyone's reach. We have to be guided by her advice."

"What if she did see the killer and the killer knows she saw him...or her, don't you think an attempt will be made on Max's life?"

"The danger isn't now. It's later...if she recovers, when she's capable of identifying the murderer, that's when she'll be in danger. The murderer is probably banking on the fact that she'll be in this catatonic state for good."

"I don't believe Molly could do this to Max. She loves Max like a daughter. Molly would never hurt Max. She would rather cut off her arm than see anything happen to her. You've never seen how Molly hovers over that girl."

"How upset was Molly when Max told her she was spending the night with Ned? I don't understand how Molly could have found her way in the fog last night."

Hank turned away so that Storm wouldn't see the horrified look on her face. She remembered how well Molly guided them back to the Azalea Gardens in the fog. Hank closed her eyes to block out the image and sound of Molly's words. She turned back to Storm. "When you find her, what will you do to her?"

"There's nothing we can do to her. We've no proof that she committed a crime, unless Ned makes a positive identification. But I doubt if he saw the assailant. If anyone saw, or knows who the killer is, that person is Maxine. Unfortunately, she's incapable of identifying anyone in her present condition." Storm took Hank in his arms. "I want you to go to your apartment. I want you off the streets."

"What about Suzie Bimbo? Is that theory dead now? Because a nice old lady found a soft place in her heart for another human being, does it mean

Suzie Bimbo is no longer a suspect? What happened to your suspicions about her? No, Storm. I'm not going to the apartment or anywhere else. I'm going to find Molly. I don't believe Molly could or would do such a thing. If I'm wrong, we'll find out soon enough. If I'm right, at least one person will believe in her. One person who didn't give up on her."

"That's not loyalty, Hank. It's stupidity. If Molly is guilty, we'll find out. If Molly is not guilty, we will find that out too."

"In the meantime, Molly dies a slow death. You said you have nothing concrete against her. Well, until you have something on which to base your suspicions, I'm going to be with her. She needs somebody to believe in her."

"How can I protect you if you deliberately put yourself in the line of fire?"

"That's what I'm trying to tell you. I don't need protection from Molly. I need protection from Suzie Bimbo, but you don't seem to think that's important. I'm worried that you will be her next victim and all you can think about is that Molly is this wild killer, going off half crazed and trying to kill the only person who could make Max happy. You just don't know or understand Molly. She would do anything to put a smile on Max's face. If it meant Ned was going to take her away, then so be it. As long as it was what Max wanted. What makes Max happy makes Molly happy. Why can't you understand that?"

"A modern-day good witch of the North, huh."

"Storm, I've been with Molly for eight months now and there has never been a time when I felt threatened or afraid. Quite the contrary, I always felt safe when Molly was near. The one visit I had from the Bimbo scared the shit out of me. She found me in the fog, which means she knows this area pretty well. Why the hell aren't you out looking for her? You know she was seen with some of the victims prior to their deaths, yet you do nothing about finding her. Why?"

"Because she's not like the street people. She's rarely seen during the day. She's a night person and nobody knows if or when she is going to show up. I never said she isn't a suspect. She's very much a suspect. We think she may be leading a double life. It's probably the reason why her appearances are so erratic. She probably has to account to somebody for her time or we would probably see more of her. However, that doesn't mean Molly is off the hook. She has to account for her time…and I don't think she can do that."

"If you left at two o'clock and Molly was still with me, you have no way of knowing if she left the area. Besides, with the way Molly limps, it would take quite some time for her to hobble down to the waterfront. Then you think after all that, she would still have the stamina to kill one man, make an attempt on another man's life and still hightail it out of there while Max was screaming her head off and gimp her way out of there without being seen? I would say Molly is a very old sixty-seven. Maybe older. I can tell you for a fact, Molly cannot run. She would fall flat on her face. If, and that's a very big IF, Molly is guilty, I'll know it. And if she is, I'll turn her over to you myself."

"You're that convinced she isn't the one?"

"Yes."

Storm jammed his hands into his pockets, "All right, Hank, if you're that sure, but I'll be keeping an eye on her. I don't like the idea that you're putting yourself in danger." He raised both hands in surrender. "I know, you've got to write this thing your own way. I don't pretend to know what motivates a writer or how important a story is, the only thing I'm sure of is that I love you and it would destroy me if anything happened to you."

All the fight went out of Hank when she saw the distress in those granite eyes turned to soft gray clouds.

"Nothing will happen to me, my love, I have too much to live for. A wonderful future lies ahead of us when this is over. Then we can concentrate on us."

He caressed her with his eyes. "Be careful, Castle, as in propugnaculum."

Hank began a systematic search of the areas Molly frequented but no one had seen her. Exhausted, she ended her tour at the Azalea Gardens. She listened for the familiar shuffle of Molly's steps but all sounds were strangely absent and finally Hank surrendered to a deep sleep.

CHAPTER 17

The persistent rapping on the door brought Suzie out of the spare room to look through the peephole at the ruddy-faced man. She was about to turn away, when a thought struck her and she opened the door and smiled at Wally Stockheim.

"You promised to stay in touch with me. What is it? You get your kicks from keeping me worried?" He stared at the miniskirt and silk blouse tied with a knot at the bottom so that her midriff was exposed.

"Whoa, Pops, don't go jumping the gun until you know what side you're on." Suzie opened the door wider to allow him to enter. She looked at her watch. "It's almost the witching hour, seems to me it's past your bed time." She passed her tongue over her lips and smiled.

Stockheim leaned against the doorjamb and studied her face. He said, "I saw your light from the street. You're not Hank, what are you doing in her apartment?"

Suzie struck a seductive pose, her eyes took him in, from his scuffed brown loafers to his hazel eyes and gray-fringed baldhead. "Right on, Pops. I'm Hank's cousin, Suzie Hoffman...from the side of the family she prefers to forget." She reached over his shoulder and rested her hand on the wall. With the spike-heeled shoes she wore, she was two inches taller than he. "You want to leave a message? I'm not sure I'll still be here when she decides to come off the streets, but I can always leave her a note."

Wally Stockheim slid against the jamb until he was outside the door. "No," he said, "No message. I'll talk to her later." He turned and hurried to the elevator.

Suzie watched until he disappeared at the turn of the hall. She chuckled and kicked the door shut with a shapely foot, attached to a shapely leg, attached to a shapely body. She picked up her shoulder bag, left all the lights on, locked the door, walked slowly to the elevator and pushed the down button.

Storm Andrews looked up at the light in Hank's apartment, and smiled. He went to the fire-tower door and let himself in and walked up to Hank's apartment. He heard the hum of the elevator as it reached the fifth floor. The doors opened and closed, then there was silence. He knocked softly on the door and waited. When there was no response, he unlocked the door with his key and entered. He looked around the apartment, satisfied that Hank wasn't there and turned off all the lights and took the tower stairs back to the streets.

* * *

Morning sounds were muffled by a fine mist. Even the swishing of passing cars somehow sounded muted and far away. Hank looked around cautiously before sitting up. She checked the area Molly normally used but there was no indication that the ground had been disturbed. She gathered her things and began walking toward the waterfront. The mist was slowly turning into fog and the density increased as she neared Delaware Avenue. Finding Ned would be difficult, she thought.

Activity on the piers seemed to be in slow motion with containerized cargo being transferred to and from ships. Longshoremen grunted and cursed at the slippery conditions created by the fog. When Hank reached the mooring of the USS *Olympia*, Commodore Dewey's flagship during the Spanish-American war, she saw Ned standing nearby looking out over the river. She approached slowly, noticing the usually straight, proud posture of the man was now bent in despair.

"Ned?"

Slowly he raised his eyes. He shook his head and said, "All the world is cloaked in fog this day, Jenny. Forgive me if I seem out of reach."

Hank stood in front of him and took him in her arms. She felt the emaciated frame quiver as he put his arms around her. The silent tears were punctuated by sporadic intakes of air. "I'm afraid our Max has gone away.... She'll never come back again."

"She will, Ned, she will. She has so much to live for now. She has you."

He peered into the fog digging holes into the mist with his eyes, in which he buried all hopes of a brighter future. "No," he said, "I took that away from her just before the killer took away her sanity."

Hank pulled away from him sightly, studying his face, hoping he didn't say what she thought she heard. "What do you mean?"

"I'm wretched, Jenny. The trouble with words is that once they're spoken, you can never retrieve them. They stand out in the open for all the world to see."

Hank took his hand and they began walking toward the Parkway. "Talk to me, Ned."

"We made love...Max and I..." He spoke as though he was remembering something that happened years before. "When it was over, she became as all the others...in my life...in the past...just another conquest. I think she saw the contempt in my eyes. I tried to hide it, God knows I tried...at least I think I did. But she knew. She knew my feelings had changed. Just as I knew hers had changed. She bared her soul to me during our lovemaking and it scared me. I couldn't go through it again, I just couldn't do it. I told her she could only get hurt because I was incapable of a sustained affair. That our...relationship...could never be any more than that...an affair."

Hank was horrified. "You couldn't have done a cruel thing like that. You knew how fragile her ego was. She adored you. I've seen you together. You were in love with her too. What happened?"

"I don't know. What always happens, I guess. When victory is in my grasp, I begin to look for other lands to conquer. The thrill is not in the victory but in the strategies of the battle." He winced with pain.

Hank remembered he had been wounded. "Is it very painful?" she asked.

He looked at her as though she had just materialized on the scene. "Is what painful?"

"The stab wound."

He rubbed his right shoulder, then looked away. "Not very." His hand went into his pocket and he pulled out some change. "It's very damp, come, I'll treat you to a cup of hot coffee."

They found a small coffee shop and sat at the counter. A waitress served them then went about her chores getting things ready for the lunch crowd. Hank looked around to be sure no one was near. She watched the poet as he sipped the hot liquid. She hesitated, then said, "You can tell me to mind my own business and you would be absolutely right in thinking I'm prying into your private life. But I need answers, not just for Max but for myself...and for you, if you're going to stay alive. Did you see your assailant?"

"No, I didn't. My back was to the murderer. An absolutely perfect target."

"Then how did you know someone was behind you?

"I saw a shadow and a look of horror on Maxine's face. For a split second, I thought the look was because of what I said, that's when I became aware of the shadow. I guess I shouted and tried to roll out of the way. I felt a hot searing pain, then a kind of numbness. At first I thought he had gotten Max because there was blood on her face and hands. Apparently the blood was mine. Max screamed and stared at the blood on her hands and that's when it happened. Like somebody turned off the audio. Her mouth moved but there was no sound, then no movement at all. Her eyes died in their sockets. All her sensory systems stopped functioning and she stared straight ahead." He blinked, "That was it." He snapped his fingers. "Exit Maxine."

Hank felt her anger rise to the surface but she needed answers and the only way to get them was to talk to Ned. Cautiously, she spoke in whispered tones. "There has been a hooker seen among the Streeters, you remember, we talked about her. Her name is Suzie. Do you know her?"

"Finished your coffee, Jenny? Let's get out of here." Ned paid for the two coffees and held the door for Hank. It was apparent he didn't want to answer the question.

"It's important, Ned. You may have been the intended target. I understand the man who was killed looked very much like you in coloring and build. It could have been a fluke that he got it instead of you."

Ned looked uncomfortable. "Yes, he said, "I know the hooker."

"How well do you know her?"

"Intimately." Ned couldn't look into Hank's face. He continued, "She has thrilled these weary bones beyond verbal description. Suzie's like a well-oiled machine, programmed to please men. She could make a man beg for more even after he's sated. When the body refuses to respond anymore, the imagination conjures up pictures that would stress the devil himself."

"Is that why you treated Max the way you did?"

Ned looked guilty. "Probably," he answered.

"How many encounters have you had with the hooker?"

"One...only one."

"How long ago?"

"Two, maybe three nights ago. Why, Hank? What's your interest in all this?"

"I'm afraid she's going to hunt you down. I think Suzie's the serial killer. She's the common denominator. There's a link between each of the victims and Suzie. You're the only one who can identify her. You're the only one of her victims still alive."

"That's nonsense, Jenny. She could have finished me off at any time during that night but she didn't. She's definitely a nymphomaniac. She can't get enough. She can probably take on men all night long and never be satisfied. I think you're barking up the wrong tree."

Hank said, "Molly saw Suzie when she was with Speaks, just before the police found his body. Molly said Suzie resembled me. Is that true?"

Ned studied Hank's face and figure. "Facial features, maybe. But your features are softer, more delicate. I'd say she could be related to you. Figure wise, I would have to say no. Of course, the clothes you wear hide a lot. Her clothes hid nothing. She is the most exciting woman I have ever known. To sum it up, Jenny, she is nothing like you. I don't mean that unkindly and I'm in no position to make...comparisons. You might be just as exciting as she was, sexually, but you asked me about similarities in appearance. The first time I saw her I thought you were playing a joke but once I talked to her, I realized the similarities were only at a distance."

"I've just one more question," Hank said. "Have you seen Molly?"

"Molly? No. Why?"

"You know how she is about Maxine. I've been looking for her to tell her before she hears it from anybody else."

"I know Molly and I'm sure she knows already and is camped at the hospital, just in case Maxine comes back to reality."

"Thanks. That's the only place I didn't think of looking for her. Before I go, where did you and Suzie Bimbo have this night of ecstacy?"

"Boathouse Row."

Hank nodded. "See you." She eyed him from head to toe then turned away.

Hank walked along at a good clip, her mind racing in all directions. *Damn,* she thought, *Molly was right. Ned was using Max and when he was finished he tossed her aside like an unwanted, broken toy. Damn, damn, damn. I've got to find Molly.* Hank looked around and realized she was lost. The fog continued to roll in. The city was wrapped in a gray-white gauzey haze. In the distance she heard foghorns and realized she was moving away from the river. She slowed her pace. The streets were marked by a glare of lights from the steady stream of cars. There were occasional patches where the fog hung about ten feet above the ground and Hank could then get her bearings and alter her course.

Trying to find her way to the various center city hospitals would be especially difficult. Hank didn't know where they had taken Max. There were only two places she could go, to the apartment or to the Azalea Gardens. She opted for the Gardens and set up her ground cloth on top of the bushes to keep the moisture down to a minimum. She reached into her bag and took out a sweater and slipped into it, then lay on top of the blanket. She heard the faint sounds of a Streeter's shuffle. Her heart hammered in her chest. She sat up and listened. Her mouth and throat felt dry. She tried to moisten her lips with the tip of her tongue. She was on her knees ready to bolt when her mind took control of her emotions and she was able to recognize Molly's shuffle. Within seconds the lumbering figure cut through the dense fog.

Molly nodded to Hank and dropped her bag on the ground.

"Molly, I've been looking all over for you. I even went to Thirtieth Street Station. Where were you?"

"At the hospital. They wouldn't let me see Maxie and I wouldn't leave the hospital, so they called the cops."

"It's not just you, Molly. They're not going to allow anyone to see Max until they have a sufficient amount of medication in her and hopefully, she'll be able to respond to them." Hank put her arms around the older woman. "I'm sorry, I wish there was something I could say."

Molly wiped her nose on the back of her hand. "Hank, do you think they're gonna give Max them shock treatments?"

Hank held her breath, watching Molly's hands twitch. "I don't think they do much of that anymore."

"Oh yes they do," Molly protested, "but they don't tell nobody. They did it to me. Whole blocks of memory…gone. I don't want them to do that to Maxie. My poor Max." Molly took out a dirty piece of cloth, blew her nose and buried it somewhere inside her shirt.

Hank dug the bottle of brandy out of her bag and offered it to the older woman. Molly reached for it and took a long swallow, replaced the cap and set in on the ground between them.

"I can't even get anybody to tell me what the hell happened. What set her off? Do you know, Hank?"

"I've been trying to find out myself. The only thing I know for sure is that a man was murdered on the waterfront. I think the murdered man wasn't the real target but resembled the intended victim. When the killer discovered the mistake, he set out looking for the original target. I think Max saw the murderer and screamed. Ned suffered a glancing blow that ended up by being a superficial laceration on the back of his shoulder. The blood from the wound got on Max's hands and face and it sent her into shock. They haven't been able to get her out of shock yet. They may never be able to bring her back. She's catatonic."

Molly shook her head, "The hell ye say. She'll come out of it. She's got to. What about Ned? How come Mr. Wonderful ain't there with her? When he was in the hospital Maxie wouldn't go away until she knew he was going to be all right. Why ain't he at the hospital?"

Hank bit her lower lip, and said, "Remember, he was stabbed. Then he had to answer a lot of questions from the police."

"Is he at the hospital now?

"They wouldn't let you stay. Do you think they would allow him to stay?"

"Did he try?" Molly studied Hank's face. "Well, did he?"

"No."

"I knew that son-of-a-bitch would let her down when it counted most. I knew he wouldn't be there when she needed him. Didn't I tell you that, huh, didn't I?"

Hank countered, "The thing now is whether or not the doctors can reach her. Ned isn't important."

"What do you mean, not important? She wouldn't be in that hospital right now if it wasn't for that no-good, poetry-spouting phoney. Well, he got what he wanted but he ain't gonna gloat over it. I'll see to that meself."

"Don't talk like that. You're angry now. You'll feel better later."

"It ain't gonna change," Molly said. "We can't be in the same city at the same time. There ain't no place that big. Maybe he got his oar in the water, but I'm gonna make sure his boat ain't goin' nowhere. If he gives me any problems the Streeters will find out what kind of worm he really is."

Hank unscrewed the cap from the brandy and lifted the bottle to her lips. Molly watched and she moistened her lips. Hank smiled and handed the bottle to her.

"Help yourself," Hank said, "and I'll lay your blanket out for you."

Molly laughed. "You ain't kiddin' me, Hank, I know you're tryin' to settle me down. Don't think I don't appreciate what you're tryin' to do. You're a good girl." She took another swig from the bottle, handed it back to Hank, crossed over the footpath and settled down on the blanket. "I'm glad it's foggy tonight. It'll keep a lot of Streeters out of the Garden. Good night."

"Good night, Molly." Hank settled down, feeling secure and at ease, and fell into a sound sleep. At four o'clock she awoke with the feeling that she was being watched. She sat up, trying to penetrate the chocolate-milky haze. There were no sounds, no movements, yet her fear began to mount. She knew something was out there. Watching. Waiting. She was helpless. Then she heard a deep-throated laugh. The sound came from every direction, as though it was bouncing off the invisible walls of fog. She thrashed about, flailing her arms, fighting the invisible threat. Hank stopped and listened. Just as she was beginning to believe it had all been her overactive imagination, she heard the voice, deep, sultry. Hank felt drugged. The voice sounded close to her ear, taunting her.

"It won't be long now. He'll be mine and you'll be gone...forever. Thought you were smart, didn't you? Thought you had it all figured out? But Ned didn't believe anything you said. Although I have to admit, it was pretty good logic. But don't worry, baby, if they ever catch up with me, you won't be around to see it. When the chips are down, men will always prefer me to you. Every man has his fantasy to have a whore of his own. Detective Andrews is no exception. Do you want to know what men think about when they're socking it to you? That you're a flesh and blood sex machine, programmed for their ultimate pleasure, and that your pleasure is derived from their sexual satisfaction. That's your reward...they think. Look at you, so virtuous. There's nothing interesting or seductive about virtue. Virtue makes men uncomfortable. It doesn't go with a man's macho image of himself. I've been watching you. You're a lousy piece of ass. You're not even a good survivor. You just don't have what it takes. Look at you. You're dirty. You stink. You even look dissipated, like the rest of these bums. You expect him to see you in a different light just because you screw him on Sundays? Oh...you thought I didn't know about that. I know your every move. That's my advantage. By the time you find out about me, I'll have everything I want...your book...your man...your life." The voice laughed and drifted away back into the fog.

For a long time Hank sat, paralyzed with fear. When her panic subsided, she gathered her blanket and bag and crawled across the path to be with Molly. *There's safety in numbers,* she thought. Suzie Bimbo wouldn't make any moves on her life as long as she was around Molly. Hank felt along the ground looking for Molly's blanket. There was none. She stood up, peering into the grounded nebula.

"Molly?" She took several steps. "Molly?" Then reality struck a familiar chord. Molly was gone. She was alone in the soupy pre-dawn mist. Hank put her hand to her throat trying to stop the passage of the scream that exploded in her stomach. From a distance, she heard the laugh of her nemesis, deep, threatening. She closed her eyes and the scream she heard was strange to her ears. Hank had never screamed before. "M-o -l -l -y." The sound reverberated off the wall of fog and fell silent.

CHAPTER 18

"What have you got for me, Doc?" Storm Andrews sat wearily in a chair and accepted a cup of coffee from Doctor McGowan.

"I think we have about eighty percent of the profile you wanted. It looks more and more like the hooker you told me about; however, I don't think she is in this alone. She has an accomplice. It's the accomplice we know nothing about."

"Is the accomplice male or female?"

"Female, I think."

"Great. Now I've got two wacky dames."

"Let's analyze the verses found with the victims. Martin Higgins, victim number one, age forty. *When beggars die, there are no comets seen, the heavens themselves blaze forth the death of princes.* It looks like our slayer is saying the death of this man is unimportant and no one will take note of his passing. Prophetic, wasn't it? It's sad, there was no one to claim the body. No one to grieve his passing.

"Victim number two was Kenneth Wooster, age forty-one. *The angel of death has been abroad throughout the land; You may almost hear the beating of his wings.* Here, I believe the killer established herself as the avenging angel. She would be the one to call the shots and there would be no one to stop her. Obviously she found out about her intended victims before she wrote the verses.

"Victim number three. Harry Timmins, age forty-two. *Death was now armed with a new terror.* This one is a puzzle. What new terror? The killer's M.O. didn't change, so what's the new terror?"

"Doc, you're thinking the new terror in part is the way the victims meet death. There are many kinds of terror. I think the new terror is being alone. Street people are notoriously loners, now comes a fear of being alone. It's a choice between being alone and possibly getting killed or being with others and possibly revealing secrets that are best left hidden."

Doctor McGowan studied the lines of fatigue around his eyes and said, "It's good you know so much about street people. I wouldn't have thought about that aspect. Okay. Victim number four is Daniel Collins, a.k.a. Duke, age forty-one. *Death only closes a man's reputation, and determines it as good or bad.* Okay, that's from Joseph Addison's *The Spectator* but in addition to that quote, the killer leaves a second quote from *Julius Caesar, Beware the ides of March.* This is the man who raped the young girl in the park, is that correct?"

Storm Andrews nodded. "Yes. Hank verified that."

"Good quote," said Pam McGowan, "because death, being the final entry of life, can do no more than confirm if the individual was good or bad. This next part is really bold thinking. Now the killer is broadcasting when the next murder will take place and saying, in essence, that even though you know when the next killing will take place, the police department is powerless to stop it. This is where the killer is beginning to enjoy the game.

"Victim number five was Jonah A Kaplan, a.k.a. Kappy, age forty. True to her word, the next murder occurred on March 15. Fulfilling the Ides of March. *Caesar said to the Soothsayer, 'the Ides of March are come'. Who answered him calmly, 'Yes they are come, but they are not past.'* also from *Julius Caesar*. The message seems to be that the promise of the next killing was fulfilled but there were more murders to come."

Doctor McGowan picked up the coffee pot and refilled their cups. She continued, "Victims number six and seven were Terrence O'Neill, age thirty-eight, and Gail Praxon, age thirty-three, killed together. The verse left with O'Neill's body was also a quote from *Julius Caesar*. *Cowards die many times before their deaths. The valiant never taste of death but once. Of all the wonders that I yet have heard, it seems to me most strange that men should fear, seeing that death, a necessary end, will come when it will come.*" Doctor McGowan pursed her lips together and said, "It seems strange that so many of the quotes are from *Julius Caesar*, when Julius Caesar himself was murdered by stabbing. Now with Gail Praxon, the quote from Dickens' *A Tale of Two Cities*, was more gentle, almost regretful. *It is a far, far better thing that I do than I have ever done; it is a far, far better rest that I go to than I have ever known.* I think the killer honestly believed she was doing Gail Praxon a good turn by releasing her from this mortal coil.

"Victim number eight was Arthur Webb Hamilton III, age forty-one. *But how shall we expect charity towards others, when we are uncharitable to ourselves? Charity begins at home, is the voice of the world; yet is every man his greatest enemy, and as it were, his own executioner.* That's from Sir Thomas Browne's *Religio Medici*. Besides Mike Shaye, Mr. Hamilton was the only other victim who did not fit the pattern of homeless males. But I would think the killer knew in advance that Hamilton was a member of a wealthy family. It would appear the killer knew about Hamilton's wife and family and the fact that he left to pursue a drug habit with another woman. Again, the punishing angel, the avenging angel." Doctor McGowan sipped her coffee, and continued.

"Victim number nine. Michael Shaye, age thirty-nine...member of the police department. The verse was concise and to the point. *I'll be judge, I'll be jury, said cunning old fury, I'll try the whole cause and condemn you to death.* I'm sure you recognize that as the quote from Lewis Carroll's *Alice's Adventures in Wonderland*, again, the form of the avenging angel, freeing the street people from a pestilence. The question is, how could anyone have gotten close enough to Mike Shaye to stab him in the back? If it was, as you suggested, the hooker, she would have been in the wrong position to stab him in the back. Apparently he enjoyed degrading women. If we are truly talking about a killer who is female that had to be a well-thought-out encounter.

"Victim number ten, Benjamin Lynch a.k.a. Benny, age sixty-eight. *Like misers, our usurious memories bring their coins each day of greedy reckoning—Grieved if they miss one as they count their store, or find one brass, long loved as gold before.* Of course the age doesn't fit the pattern but I think Benny was not one of the planned victims, but was taken out because he was an informer and was probably paid for his information, thus the quote from Lloyd McKim Garrison

"Victim number eleven, Lester Philander—age forty-three. Apparently, our killer is also acquainted with Socrates; *Either death is a state of nothingness and utter unconsciousness, or as men say, there is a change and migration of the soul from this world to another.* I think the change and migration the killer referred to was a sexual encounter, in which the victim was transported into ecstasy, thus the migration into another world. She probably feels her prowess as a temptress and seductress are unequaled. Apparently, her tactics work.

"Victim number twelve, Gilbert Harvey—age sixty-five. *Madame La Guillotine celebrates Bastille Day,* then a quote from Euripides. *Old men's prayers for death are lying prayers, in which they abuse old age and long extent of life. But when death draws near, not one is willing to die, and age no longer is a burden to them.*" Pam McGowan said, "To me the killer is saying that old men insist they pray for death to get them out of this mired world but they lie, and life is never as precious or as worth holding on to until they are actually faced with death."

Storm took both cups and refilled them, handing one to her and sipping on the other one himself.

"Victim number thirteen is Noah Speaks, age forty-three," Doctor McGowan continued. "There are two quotes, the first taken from Benjamin Disraeli, *Experience is the child of thought, and Thought is the child of Action, We cannot learn men from books.* Then there is a quote, again from Socrates, *Must not all things at the last be swallowed up in death?* I believe the killer was talking about herself here, 'We cannot learn men from books.' She ends it by saying at the end we all end by being swallowed up in death."

Storm nodded. "The more you break it down, the more I'm convinced it's a woman. A very angry, exploited woman."

Doctor McGowan glanced at the last page of her notes, and said, "The latest killing was yesterday's victim, George Franklin, age forty-two. This next quote from Swinburne tells us even more about the killer. *We are not sure of sorrow and joy was never sure, today will die tomorrow, time stoops to no man's lure; and love grown faint and fretful, with lips but half regretful, weeps that no loves endure.* No one was really safe, there is no such thing as true love because man is incapable of such love and even when they profess love, it's only for now. It's not a thing that could endure." Doctor McGowan put her hands at the back of her neck and leaned her head against the chair. Storm stood behind her chair and massaged her neck.

"Detective Andrews, I'll give you just ten hours to stop that." She laughed. "I'm sorry, that just slipped out. My husband gives a marvelous massage and I'm so used to saying that to him. It was an involuntary reaction. It feels wonderful, thank you."

"You're welcome," Storm said. "What's the final analysis?"

"Your killer is extremely and dangerously unbalanced. She's guided by the worst of emotions—hate. When I said she had an accomplice, that accomplice could be an unknowing and unwilling participant. If we're dealing with a multiple personality, the most dominant personality will want to take over and when that happens, our killer could go on a homicidal rampage and nobody knows what could trigger that rage. If the accomplice is innocent of involvement, there would have to be some signs, the undue stress would cause unexplained restlessness, extreme fatigue, and probably even sleeplessness and nightmares."

Storm stopped massaging her neck and went to look out of the window. His mouth felt dry. He tried desperately to remember what Hank said about having a bad dream but she had dismissed it as unimportant. He decided to say nothing to Doctor McGowan.

Pam McGowan turned and watched the back of Storm's shoulders constrict into spasm, then release, then constrict again. She said, "I'm sure the number eight has a definite significance and the ages of the men are also significant. Probably the age of the man who caused all the anxiety, which is now manifesting itself by killing. That doesn't necessarily mean the present age of the man, it could have been how old he was at the time of the trauma, which could conceivably have been twenty or thirty years ago, or as recent as a year ago. There's no way to tell."

"What would happen to her once she's caught, if she has this multiple personality problem?" Storm asked. "Would she be tried as the murderous personality or the docile personality? Would all the personalities be punished, Doctor?"

"That would depend on many factors. In all probability, she would be confined to a mental institution for the criminally insane because it would be impossible to tell when the criminal personality would emerge again."

"What if the killer turns out to be terminally ill?"

"That would depend on a judge and jury but I would venture to guess the patient would still be confined to a mental institution, where she could get the medical attention necessary. You're thinking of Molly, aren't you?"

"She certainly has to be considered."

Storm saw the doctor watching him and he could almost read her thoughts. What if it turned out to be Hank? He couldn't even contemplate that possibility. He had to find Suzie Hoffman and bring her in for questioning. She was the pivotal point in all the cases.

It was ten o'clock before the fog burned off and Hank went in search of Storm Andrews. By mid-afternoon she gave up the search and headed for the apartment. *Everything's falling apart,* she thought, *Max is in never-never land, Ned is a turncoat, Molly is getting really weird and Storm is never around when I need him.* Aloud, she said, "Maybe a couple of days away from it all will give me a new perspective." She kicked off her shoes as soon as she entered the apartment, switched on the television to the news station, peeled off her clothes, sniffed them and quickly turned her head aside. She thought, *The Bimbo was right, I do stink.* Her clothes smelled of cat urine. Her face flushed at the memory of a whore telling her she was dirty. She stood in front of the mirror studying her reflection. She had lost over twenty pounds and had what she thought was a nice figure but what the Bimbo thought was dissipation. She stepped into the shower and allowed the steady spray of water to relax the tension in her shoulders and back. When she was waterlogged she dried off, slipped into a light robe, poured herself a drink and sat in front of the television. The news anchorman was talking about the most recent murder. Victim number fifteen was Nicholas Carroll, an import from New York. Hank vaguely remembered seeing him at the shelter, as she would remember a face in a crowd. The newsman was reading a copy of the verse left with the body. He identified it as a quote from *Othello. An honourable murderer, if you will; For naught I did in hate, but all in honour.*

Hank downed her drink and went for a refill. When she lifted the glass to her lips her hand shook. "Stop it," she said aloud, "stop it." She heard the door to the apartment close. She held her breath and waited.

Storm's face wore a tired, worried expression until he saw her. "Thank God. When I couldn't find you I began to panic. I hoped you would be here."

Relief flooded her face and her body shook with the built up tension. He bridged the distance between them in three long strides and took her in his arms. The trembling continued.

"You're shaking like leaf in a wind storm. What's wrong?"

Hank found herself stumbling over words trying to tell him about the night visit from the mysterious Suzie.

"Whoa! Slow down, baby, your thoughts are running ahead of your words. Now, let's take it from the beginning. She came to the azalea gardens. What time?"

"I don't know. It was still very dark. Obviously she had no problem finding me in the fog."

"Were you there alone?"

"I don't know."

"What do you mean you don't know? Either you were alone or you weren't."

"Well, when I went to sleep, Molly was across the foot path. After the Bimbo left, I was really scared and I felt my way across the path. Molly was gone. I guess I panicked. As soon as the fog cleared I started looking for you. Then I came here."

"All right, let's go over it all again. You said you were asleep. How did you know she was there?"

"It was a feeling. Like the feeling you get when you know someone is watching you. Eventually the feeling turns you in the direction of the observer. That's how it was. I couldn't see her at any time. But her voice seemed to be coming from every direction."

Storm nodded. "She was making the most of the tricks of the fog. Go on." He realized she needed his strength and he took her in his arms and listened while she recounted Suzie's monologue.

"Did she actually say she would kill you?"

Hank thought for a moment. "No. She never used the words kill, or murder. She just said, 'It won't be long now and he'll be all mine and you'll be gone forever.' And she said if they ever catch up with her, I won't be around to see it. She didn't say murder or kill, but how else am I to interpret it? What do you think she meant?"

"I think she meant to scare you. Obviously, she succeeded."

"She knows things that only you and I know."

"Like what?"

"Like the fact that we meet here on Sundays and make love. She knows I'm gathering material for a book. How does she know that? You and I are the only two people in the world who know that."

Storm looked pensive. "There were four people who knew about the book. You, me, Stockheim and Shaye. Since Shaye was killed, I guess it could be possible that she was able to get that information out of him before he died." He walked to the kitchen and got the bottle of Scotch and poured himself a four-finger measure. "The part about us making love on Sundays could have been conjecture on her part. She probably followed you here a few times and came to her own conclusion. Why you? Why is she after you? What about Julian Grant? She sounds like the type he would want to be around. Is it possible he's behind this?"

"You're giving him credit for more brains than the Lord gave him. He doesn't think with his brain. He thinks with his libido. Besides, he has no imagination. He would never be able to concoct a plot like this. His imagination is confined to the bedroom."

"You really hate him, don't you, Hank"

"I hated him when I first met him. I should have stuck with my first impression. Now he isn't worth hating. Actually, I think I feel sorry for him. He has no friends. When he stops spending money on the girls, they walk out on him. I guess that tells a story without any embellishment from me. When he reaches a point where he can't buy what he wants, he's going to be a miserable, lonely, pathetic excuse for a man."

"Like I said, you really hate him."

"We're not talking about him. I thought we were talking about Suzie Bimbo. You were so anxious to nail Molly, how come you're not interested in investigating Suzie baby?"

Storm sat in a corner of the sofa, studying Hank over the rim of his glass. He said, "There are lots of investigations going on at headquarters. All of them connected with the serial killer. I can assure you we're not overlooking Suzie Bimbo. Incidentally, how did you come to call her that?"

"Nobody seems to know who she is, other than that her first name is Suzie. Just from what I've been told about her from various sources, the only surname that fits her activities is Bimbo. I could have named her Suzie Floozie but it wouldn't be as descriptive. A floozie is someone who's not dealing with a full deck. That's not this Suzie. Not on these streets. She's intelligent and she's got lots of street smarts. She's cool, Storm. She's a cool, calculating bitch. She's not going to let anybody stand in her way. She's not going to let me stand in the way of getting to you." Hank raised her eyebrows and winked. "As far as she's concerned, your soul may belong to God, but your ass belongs to her."

Storm's face was expressionless. He said, "From all reports, she has been getting a lot of that. Especially if she has sex with all the men she seems to know. If she is the killer, it makes you wonder where she finds the time to commit the crimes."

"You think I'm wrong?"

"I didn't say that. However, if we hone in on Suzie Bimbo we could be letting someone else get away."

"Molly?"

"Molly.

"Why? Why do you think Molly is the one?" Hank's anger was showing.

"I'm not saying she is. I'm saying we have to cover all possibilities. She's the only one who knew all of the victims. By your own admission, she was really upset when she found Benny was Shaye's snitch because he fingered Maxine and put her under suspicion. You also said when Molly's upset she mumbles to herself and when she has determined what needs to be done, she's quiet again. She stopped talking to herself just before we found Benny's body."

"That was a coincidence," Hank shot back angrily. "She was genuinely fond of Benny. Besides, she had no reason to murder Shaye. There are too many holes in your theory. Molly was protective of Max, that's true, but I can't believe she would kill for her. All these street people are doing is trying to survive. I don't think Molly is doing too well in that department."

"You keep trying to paint a picture of a helpless old lady. She has succeeded where you never could. Do you think you could have survived the years she was on the streets? I doubt it. She's a survivor from way back. She survived fifteen years in prison."

Hank gasped. "How do you know that?"

"I lifted your brandy bottle and substituted a similar one. The lab analyzed the fingerprints. There were three separate sets of prints. Yours, Maxine's and Molly's. Molly's prints matched up with prints on file with the F.B.I.

"You lifted my brandy bottle? You used me to get to my friends? What else have you used me for?

"Aren't you going to ask me why she spent time in prison?" Storm waited for a response. When there was none, he continued. "She did time for second-degree murder. The man she killed was her husband. When Molly got out of prison she came here. She has probably been on the streets fourteen years, plus spending fifteen years in jail. I would say that qualifies her as a survivor. Unfortunately, it also qualifies her as a suspect. I'm sorry, Hank, I had to do what I could to protect you."

Hank felt herself go limp. Storm did this to protect her.

Storm continued, "Molly fits the mold the psychiatrist has formulated. It's very possible she has a split personality. I am not saying she's aware of the other personality. It's entirely possible the second personality developed to protect Molly from certain destruction. If Molly needs Maxine to function as a whole person, whenever Max is in danger, the other personality, the protective one, emerges, which gets Max out of trouble but, at the same time, fulfills a long-denied need within Molly."

"Do you mean it's possible that Molly could have committed these crimes and not been aware of it?"

"Yes. At least I think that's what I am saying. I don't pretend to understand the workings of the human mind and its various defense mechanisms. But I understand from the psychiatrist it's entirely possible for multiple personalities to develop in an individual person without the original personality being aware that any changes have taken place. If the original personality is weak, it's possible for the stronger of the other personalities to take over and call all the shots."

"Sounds good, but there's only one thing you're not taking into consideration."

"Molly's age?

"I assume each of the personalities will be the same age?"

"I would think that's a correct assumption."

"Then how can a sixty-seven-year-old shop-worn, partially crippled woman accomplish so much?"

"I don't know that answer, Hank. I don't like to think that Molly is even a remote possibility but she certainly fits the profile in everything except age. She may be a lot stronger than you or I, or anyone else, suspects." He pulled Hank onto the sofa beside him. "You don't think she could do it, do you?"

Hank's voice was barely audible. "What you told me about the time she spent in prison answers a lot of questions I had about Molly but I still don't see her as the serial killer. I admit she is protective of Max, perhaps even overly protective, and maybe the night Max and Ned spent together somehow was translated in Molly's mind as Ned replacing her. Because Molly is so single minded when it comes to Max, she wouldn't have stopped until she was certain she had eliminated the source of Maxine's pain. That wasn't the case. The killer delivered only a glancing wound with the knife to Ned, who, at the time, was apparently on top of Max. Why would she have left such an important job undone? You don't know Molly. If she was after Ned, she wouldn't have stopped until she carried out her vendetta. I think Suzie Bimbo is still your most viable suspect. She knows a lot of the street men, she's young and agile and has no pangs of conscience. Look, she made open threats to me and how many others? I think she's your killer."

"You could be right. Time will tell."

"Are the police doing anything about finding her?"

"It's not as easy as lifting your brandy bottle," Storm said. "The only way we'll get fingerprints from her is at police headquarters and I can't arrest her for no reason. We don't even have proof that she is soliciting on the streets. It's conjecture."

Hank shook her head impatiently. "What do you know about her? Where does she come from? Why don't you ask Ned about her? He knows her well enough to toss Max over for her. At least it's a start."

"I don't think that's a good idea," Storm said. "You tried to talk to him and got nowhere. What makes you think he'll open up to another man? If she's as deeply imbedded in his psyche as you think, he is going to protect her at all cost, which means he'll tip her off that she's a suspect. Maddening as it is, we'll have to take the roundabout route. We've been able to trace her appearance on the streets back to the end of December or the beginning of January. Opinions vary as to where she came from. Some say New York, some say California. Nobody really knows. Nobody ever sees her during the day."

"Maybe she's a vampire. She only comes out at night."

"Vampires don't use knives. That's why they have fangs. If she's guilty we'll get her."

"She frightens me, Storm. I've never been afraid of another human being in all my life. Suddenly I'm quaking at the idea she's after me. There's no doubt in my mind she means everything she said. She's going to get rid of me and there is nothing I can do about it. I'm scared, Storm, really, truly…scared. There was something about the way she talked, a…a determination. If the government announced we were going to be hit by a hydrogen bomb at midnight, Suzie would hunt me down and make good her threat before a bomb could ruin her plans."

Storm studied her face, stress was evident, she was serious. Hank was afraid. All of her exterior bravado had melted and her psyche lay exposed, naked, vulnerable. He gathered her in his arms. "As long as I'm alive you won't have to worry about Suzie Bimbo or anyone else. The only one I can't protect you from is you. Please, Hank, get off the streets."

"What good will that do? She knows where I live. She can get to me here much easier than she can out there on the streets. At least out there, I'll have other people around and it's not as convenient as it would be in the apartment. Here, she can pick the day and time. Out there she has to wait for the right opportunity. My chances are better on the streets."

"Great. All you have to do is pray we don't have any more fog. I can picture you standing in the middle of the Azalea Gardens, looking up at the sky and yelling, 'Hey, God, are You up there? The Bimbo's after me, can You please keep the fog away?'"

In spite of herself, Hank had to laugh.

Storm smoothed away a furrow that knitted her brows together. "Incidentally, sweetheart, you forgot to put out the lights in the apartment last night."

Hank looked at him, the furrow appeared again. "I wasn't here last night and the last time I left the apartment, I turned off the lights." She headed for the door and opened it. She reached up and retrieved the spare key from the wall sconce in the hall, breathed a sigh of relief and replaced the key. "I was afraid somebody found my hiding place for the spare key. When I look back, I came into the apartment one other time and the lights in the living room were on and I thought you had gotten to the apartment before me but you hadn't. I passed it off as being forgetful but I was extra cautious about turning off the lights after that."

Storm felt a wave of nausea wash over him. He refilled his glass, then hers and changed the subject. "I think we might have our first lead. I think for the first time, we know where the killer is going to strike next."

"Really? How could you know that?"

"I'm banking on the fact that Nicholas Carroll was the wrong victim. I think the intended victim was Ned. With Max out of the way, getting to him will be much easier, especially if Suzie is the killer. She's like a black widow spider. She mates then kills the male. I wish I had an inkling of the possible motive she would have. Damn it! Why is the number eight so important?"

"Why do you think the intended victim was Ned and not Nicholas Carroll?"

"Mainly because of the quote from *Othello. An honourable murderer, if you will; For naught I did in hate, but all in honour.* Just assume for a minute that the killer is Molly. The quote wouldn't suit the crime. However, if she thought she was saving Max from a fate worse than death, then in her eyes there would be honor in what she did. If, as it turns out, the wrong victim was felled, the quote doesn't make much sense. Therefore, to correct the error, she has to go back and kill the person she intended to get in the first place."

"What if Molly's not the killer? As far as I've been able to determine, all of the verses have been cryptic. Why do you think this particular one doesn't fit the pattern?"

"Gut feeling."

"If you didn't have Molly to blame, would you still have that gut feeling?"

He smiled and looked guilty. "I don't know."

"That's fair enough. At least you have the grace to blush."

Storm sobered. "Stay here, Hank. I'll see if I can get you some police protection. I can't even hope to protect you on the streets. There are too many variables."

"I love you, Storm."

His eyes softened in answer.

"And I'm scared," Hank admitted. "But if I run away now, Bimbo wins by default. I can't live the rest of my life being afraid of every shadow. Fear is a new experience for me. Give me time to get used to the idea and I'll be able to brazen it out. I think the main fear is that I'll lose you to her, not that she is going to end my life."

"Why do you think I'm protecting you?"

"Because you love me?"

"There. That wasn't so hard to figure out, now was it?"

"It wasn't hard to figure out but it is hard to understand why you love me."

"It's not hard for another man to figure out. You're everything a man could want; God knows you're attractive. You have a figure most women would kill for. You make love with complete abandon. So many men look for this in a woman and go a lifetime without finding it. You're intelligent, you're witty, you laugh easily and you have a way of making a man feel like a man without being threatened by your brains. I went through thirty-eight years of life without finding such a woman and then you came along. Now, I could never go back to the way things used to be. You've made big changes in my way of life...and I can't change back. I love you, Castle...as in propugnaculum."

She was in his arms, promising, kissing, loving, longing, wanting, giving, demanding, and the floor became a cloud for love.

Emerging from the apartment building, she was greeted by a cloudless, bright day. Something in her had changed. Returning to the streets was no longer a chore, she had something concrete to sustain her. It was difficult to maintain the slow Streeter shuffle when she felt there were wings on her heels. Strangely enough, even the book lost some of its importance. She realized her values had shifted and she was putting things in their proper perspective. She wasn't any less concerned about Maxine and Molly but she wasn't allowing their plight to depress her and dictate how she would act or react.

Labor Day was approaching, signaling the end of summer activities and the long fall preparation for the coming of winter. Gratefully, she would not be on the streets when winter came. She promised Storm she would be off the streets by Thanksgiving Day. Now it would be easier for her to honor that date. Now she had a purpose to her life. They hadn't talked about marriage but Hank knew it would follow the natural course of events and they would get married and share a life together. If he was against marriage, that was all right too, they could live together. She decided she would never be alone again. The thought of a whole gambit of emotions shared with Storm left her with a warm, satisfying feeling and her fears began to abate. Armed with the knowledge that Storm loved her, she could face anything.

Without realizing she had walked so far, Hank found herself on the waterfront, on the fringes of the crowd listening to Ned, once again reciting "The Definition of Love," but this time, the recitation lacked the emotional impact it once had. The audience listened, but he no longer commanded the quiet that once prevailed, no longer did he hold his listeners in the palm of his hand. Ned knew better than anyone that things had changed. The poet laureate had fallen from favor and the fickle audience that had once restored his pride, took it away again. They were no longer captivated. They had taken his wreath of laurel and hurled it into the flames of mediocrity, never again to rise out of the ashes. Hank caught his attention and saluted. Ned stopped in the middle of his recitation and looked directly at Hank.

"The king is dead," he said. "Long live the king." He picked up the coins that lay on the ground in front of him, bowed to his audience and walked away. Hank saw him reach up and touch the place where the imaginary crown once sat so proudly. She sympathized with him because she too had known the agony of having victory snatched from her hands when it seemed assured. She wondered if he would go back to Max. Then she thought about Suzie Bimbo and realized he couldn't go back. Even if Max would recover and take him back, there was no way he could erase the words that had already been implanted in her memory. He threw away his only chance at salvation. No one would ever worship at his shrine as Max had done. The question now was whether Molly was satisfied with his literary demise, or did she still want vengeance? Would it be enough that he had toppled or would she demand his soul in payment for the hell he created for Max?

It was late when Hank reached the Azalea Gardens. She found her favorite spot and laid out the ground cloth.

"I didn't think you was ever comin' back, Hank. Thought maybe I lost Maxie and you too."

Hank was genuinely happy to see Molly. She said, "I looked for you after the fog but couldn't find you. I was afraid that maybe you had left the city."

"Ah, Hank, you knowed better than that. I could never go away and leave Maxie alone in that empty world. If she decides to come back, somebody she knows oughta be here waitin' for her. The world she's in now is lonely enough. When she comes back, she don't need to be alone again. I'll be here when she comes back."

"She'll be back, Molly. When the wounds are healed and she can face the world again."

"Have you seen the asshole?"

"You mean Ned?"

"You know a better name for him?"

"Not really. Yes. I saw him early today on the riverfront. He didn't look very happy. I think he knows he screwed up the only good thing that ever happened to him. Well, he made his choice and he knows he can never go back. You were right, Molly. You said he would hurt her...and he did."

"It was clear to me he loved hisself more than he could ever love her. You know Maxie...she can't love a little bit—she has to love with everythin' she's got. She's never gonna be able to trust another man. That bastard saw to that. He couldn't tell her first. No, he had to screw her first...then tell her he wasn't interested in her anymore. It wasn't enough to hurt her, he had to shit on her first then rub her nose in it. For that, I'll never forgive him. This city's too small for both of us. When Max comes back, maybe I can talk her into leaving here and going south. At least we won't have to cope with cold weather. Maybe she can get over him. They tell me time heals everythin'...." The words just trailed off. Hank knew the tears were choking Molly. She reached into her bag and pulled out the brandy. "Here, Molly, I think we've both earned a couple of belts." Hank took a couple of swallows and handed the bottle to Molly.

"It's a shame we can't give some to Max. It might help to dull the pain."

"She's not feeling pain right now. Her mind has shut that out. She's just in a state of limbo until the healing takes over."

"You mean *if* she heals. My poor Maxie. Never had a chance in this lousy life. Why is it that there are certain people in this world that always end up on the dirty end of the stick? No matter what they do, or how good they are, they always end up with nothin'...with nobody and nothin'. Why is that?"

Molly didn't expect an answer. She was musing aloud. But Hank knew Molly was hurting.

It was time to change the subject. Molly took another swig from the bottle and handed it back. Hank decided to tell her about the visit from the Bimbo. When she finished telling her tale, Molly grabbed the bottle and took another mouthful of brandy, swished it around in her mouth before swallowing it. "What the hell does she want with you, Hank?"

Hank was silent for a long time. When she looked up, Molly was studying her closely.

"I think she wants my soul, Molly.... I think she wants my soul."

"Don't talk like that, Hank. It ain't good. In fact, it can only bring you bad luck. Next time that slut comes round, you holler for me and holler loud. I'll part her goddamn hair with a bottle."

Hank tried unsuccessfully to hide the smile that was playing around her mouth.

"It ain't funny, Hank. That bitch is makin' a career out of makin' our lives miserable. I had all I'm gonna take of her. If I see her, the cops'll have to pick up what's left of her with an ink blotter." She began mumbling to herself. Then she looked at Hank. "What do you say we go to the hospital tomorrow and see if they'll let us in to see Maxie?"

It was clear Molly needed to see Max, just to convince herself that Max was still alive. Hank agreed, even though she knew chances of seeing Max were slight to nonexistent.

Hank slept soundly, comforted by the thought that Molly was nearby. Hank thought life had dealt Molly a pretty lousy hand.

Storm walked softly through the park, staying away from the walkways. In spite of the danger, Streeters were creatures of habit and the groups that had been formed for protection had broken up and the Streeters were once again loners. Then he saw them, a man and a woman. He didn't know the man but he knew the woman. Suzie Hoffman. Her hand was buried inside the man's open fly. The man saw Storm's shadow as he approached and fled without warning.

"Hey, where the fuck are you going?" Then she saw Storm and laughed. "He must have thought you were the killer."

"How do you know I'm not?"

A hint of a smile played at the edges of her mouth. "Because you don't have what it takes to be a killer."

"And how do you know that?"

"I know everything about you, handsome. I made it a point to find out." She slid her hand down the front of his pants.

Storm grabbed her wrist and pushed her away. "I think you contaminate everything you touch. Who was loverboy?"

She turned to watch the retreating form. "You mean Roger? Don't sweat it, I can have him any time I want. I'll have you too, in time. I always get what I want because I know how to get it. I've wanted you since the first time I saw you. I could be a lot better for you than the wimp you're screwing. I could make you beg. I could satisfy you more than all the women you've ever had in your life. I could carry you to heights you've never dreamed of, and bring you down just long enough to prolong the ecstasy, then send you up again and again. You'll stay hard for so long that you'll begin to wonder if you have priapism." Her hand reached out again and tried to undo the large, shiny buckle of his belt. Her lips parted in a slight smile and her tongue slowly moistened the edges. He reached for her hand and slowly brought it up and twisted it behind her neck. He wasn't smiling. "Women like you make me puke."

The smile never left her face. "Just goes to show you how different two friends can be. Mike Shaye didn't mind it at all; in fact I had him begging for more. He said I gave the best head in town."

Storm's eyes matched his name. "Bitch!" He turned, heading in the direction of the waterfront. He could hear the soft, deep-throated laugh following him. He smiled to himself and headed for police headquarters. He removed the belt from his pants, using a handkerchief, so as not to disturb the perfect set of Suzie's fingerprints on his belt buckle.

CHAPTER 19

When Hank and Molly arrived at the hospital, an attendant called Doctor McGowan about their request to see Maxine. Pam McGowan met them in Max's room and spoke with them briefly.

Hank and Molly approached their friend with more than a little trepidation. Fear of upsetting Max's precarious mental balance manifested itself in their whispered reassurances and gentle pats on her hands. Max sat in a chair near the window, looking not outwardly but inwardly. Molly held Max's hand and crooned to her as she would to a child. They spent an hour with the non-communicative Max before they were told it was time to leave. Molly asked, "Can we come back to see her?" Molly looked imploringly at the attendant.

"I think it'll be all right. She probably needs somebody to keep her in touch with the world she once knew. Come back in a couple of days, around this same time. I'll be on duty and I'll make sure I have approval from her doctor. Did she give any sign that she knew you were here?"

Molly kissed Max on the cheek. "No, but she will. Once she knows we love her and want her to get well, she'll come back. Thank you, miss, we'll be back day after tomorrow…and we'll take a bath before we come. Let's go, Hank." At the door she turned and looked back at Max. "I loves ya, Maxie, and I'll take better care of you when you come back. I promise."

Molly didn't want to be alone so Hank and Molly went to the shelter for food and together they went to the Azalea Gardens and talked and drank long into the night. Molly set up her blanket where Max used to sleep and it gave Hank a feeling of security.

During the night Hank thought she heard the Bimbo laughing. The brandy and exhaustion won out over her attempt to open her eyes. She heard nothing more and drifted deeper into sleep. When she awoke, Molly had gone but she left the almost empty brandy bottle beside Hank's blanket, just another reminder of a throbbing headache and sick hangover. She reached into the bottom of her bag and pulled out a bottle of aspirin. *Well,* she thought, *wash them down with a hair of the dog that bit you.* She took a swallow of brandy and almost vomited. Aloud, she said, "God, there has to be an easier way."

"A little under the weather, are we?"

Hank opened one eye so as not to let too much light in to her pounding head, and saw the laughing face of her beloved.

"How come you always see me at my very worst?"

"Lucky, I guess. Don't you know it's bad to drink alone?"

"I wasn't drinking alone. Molly helped me kill this bottle. We went to the hospital to see Max yesterday. They let us in. I think Molly had to see Max, to assure herself that Max was still alive. We talked and drank and talked and drank then we drank and drank and finally passed out...I guess."

"I just wanted to check and make sure you were okay. The Department contacted me, they found a body floating in the river this morning."

Hank looked alarmed. "Not another..."

"I don't think so," he reassured her. "It looks like a simple drowning but they want me to check it out. They took the body to the morgue. I'm going there now. A drowning already, and the Labor Day weekend hasn't even started. Meet me back at the apartment this afternoon?"

"If I don't die first."

"There aren't too many people who die from a hangover. You just feel you would be better off if you died. If your stomach isn't settled by the time I reach the apartment, I'll make you one of my special concoctions, guaranteed to cure headaches and hangovers." He reached over and gave her a quick kiss on the mouth and whispered, "I'll see you later, Castle, as in propugnaculum."

Hank wasn't that far from the apartment and all she could think of was a warm shower, an ice pack for her head and that pink stuff for her upset stomach. She stood up and that was the most effort she was going to exert for the rest of the day. She staggered up the Parkway, somehow finding her way into the tower entrance, crawled up the steps, opened the door and promptly vomited all over the floor in the entry.

"Never again. Never again. I promise, God, never again."

Since she couldn't wrap up the apartment and toss it into the trash can, she decided she had to clean up the mess, thankful for paper towels and spray disinfectant.

An hour later she was standing under the shower, allowing the water to rain over her head, carrying her misery down the drain. When she started feeling she was once again among the living, she ventured out of the shower and wrapped her hair in a towel and her body in a terrycloth robe. A glass of orange juice was the strongest drink she was going to take. She stood at the window of her apartment overlooking the Parkway collecting her thoughts about the book. She opened the desk drawer and pulled out her notes and tapes and scanned the mountain of disorganized notes, trying to come up with a mental outline. She sat at the typewriter and allowed the last nine months of experiences to dictate the path her book would take. The ringing of the telephone did nothing to calm her jangled nerves. "Hello," she whispered, fearing that any more volume in her voice would blow the top of her head off.

"Hank? Is that you?"

She smiled to herself. "Yes, it's me, Wally. I'm just suffering from a hangover and vibration of my voice in my head makes it pound more. How's my favorite editor?"

"Fine…fine." He hesitated. "Are you alone?"

"Sure, Wally. What's up?"

"I just wanted to be sure you were okay. When I stopped by last week and your cousin answered the door, I got concerned."

The silence that followed was deafening. Finally Hank found her voice. "What cousin? I don't have any family, I thought you knew that. This person…was inside my apartment?"

"Yes. She invited me in, but I only went in as far as the threshold. Pardon me for saying so but she looked like trouble."

"Would that have been last Wednesday?"

Wally Stockheim thought a moment before answering, "Yeah, it was Wednesday."

"What did she look like?"

Stockheim gave a perfect description of Suzie. Hank felt waves of nausea sweeping over her again, a combination of hangover and fright. She tried to keep the terror out of her voice. "I guess one too many people saw me hide my spare key." She ended the conversation, promising to be off the streets in November.

Absorption in the new development canceled out all extraneous sounds and movements.

"I love you, Castle, as in propugnaculum."

Startled, she pulled away from the hands that had begun to encircle her waist, until she realized it was Storm. She entered the circle of his arms. "Welcome into my world of humanity."

"Hangover all gone?"

"Almost. Smell the disinfectant?"

"Is that what they call losing it?" He looked at the damp spot on the hardwood floor. "I guess we all use the same thing. It's still better than that pine stuff."

Hank wasn't sure she would tell Storm about the unwelcome visit from Suzie. Besides, he said he would assign somebody to keep an eye on her.

"How would you like to go to the Achaea for dinner tonight?"

She smiled her answer.

"Good. I'll give Uncle Nick a call."

"This time I'm going to dress appropriately. I don't want your uncle to think you only date vagrants."

"I have to let headquarters know where I'll be."

"Was the body in the river another Streeter?"

"I don't think so. At least the M.O. wasn't the same as the others. It looks like this guy just fell in the drink and drowned. The medical examiner will let me know if he gets an identification on the guy. While you're getting dressed, I'll take a shower." He kissed the tip of her nose.

This time he introduced her to Nick Andros as his future wife and invited Nick to join them for dinner. Uncle Nicky turned out to be a very wise man and Hank found herself wondering if this was true of all Greeks. After dinner, they sat at the table, sipping Metaxa and talking, when Storm was called to the phone.

Uncle Nick said, "It's good to see Storm happy. I think you're good for him. He looks better than he did a year ago. He's content, like he finally made peace with himself. Did you know Mike Shaye?"

Hank nodded. "Yes, but I didn't like him."

"You were smart. I told Storm, stay away from that guy, he was bad news, he enjoyed hurting people. But like always, Storm listens to nobody but himself. When Shaye got killed, I said a prayer of thanksgiving. I was afraid he was going to get Storm killed. A lot of people hated that man. He used his position as a detective to frighten people. He finally met up with somebody who would not be intimidated and it ended the only way it could. God have mercy on his soul...but I'm glad he's not hanging around Storm anymore."

"So am I, Uncle Nicky, so am I."

When Storm came back, the two men embraced and Nick kissed Hank on the cheek. "You take good care of her now, Storm and bring her back soon. Such a pretty woman, you should want to show her off."

"I will, Uncle Nick." He took Hank's arm and ushered her onto the street.

"The call was from the coroner's office. They identified the victim found in the Delaware."

"It couldn't have been a Streeter."

"How do you know that?"

"They won't get that close to water, unless it's in a glass."

He stopped and pulled her into a doorway, away from the people leaving the bar up the street and turned her face up to his. "He was identified as Julian Grant." He waited for a reaction. There was none. "Did you hear what I said?"

"You said the body was identified as that of Julian Grant."

"How do you feel about that?"

"After all this time, he's nothing more than a bad dream. How did you expect me to feel?"

He smiled. "I hoped you would feel this way but I couldn't be sure. Sometime when someone hurts you, the hurt goes on long after the relationship has ended."

"I wouldn't have wished him any bad luck but hearing that he drowned doesn't upset me in the least. I'm a firm believer that you have to harvest what you plant. I wouldn't want to have to answer for the life he led and the people he used." She took Storm's arm as they walked toward the Parkway. "It does seem strange that he died that way."

"Why do you think it's strange?"

Hank said, "He was terrified of deep water. So what was he doing so close to the river when he had a fear of water? Knowing him, he tried to walk on the water, absolutely convinced he could. Weren't there any witnesses?"

"Not that we know of. The only thing really strange about the drowning, especially in the light of his fear of water, is the time of death. The coroner estimates he drowned about two o'clock in the morning. What the hell was he doing on the waterfront at two o'clock?"

Hank shrugged. "In all probability, we'll never know. He wasn't laced too tight. He wanted people to think he was sophisticated but his thinking was too erratic for that. I think he needed psychiatric help. As long as I had known him and that dates back to nineteen seventy-eight, he was a pathological liar. Since he didn't know the difference between a lie and the truth, I wonder if he knew there was a difference between right and wrong. One thing I know for sure...he thought rules and laws were made for other people, never for him. It was probably fortunate he didn't have any kids. Particularly girls. He probably would have tried to screw them."

Storm said, "At least he never met up with Suzie Bimbo."

"It's too bad he didn't, she could have given him a run for his money and she's the type he would have preferred."

Storm opened the door to Hank's apartment with his key. He turned her around and kissed her, pressing her against the doorjamb with his body.

"I can't come in. The medical examiner wants to talk to me. I told him I would be there in an hour. Promise me you'll stay here tonight."

"I can't promise that. Molly and I have permission to see Max in the morning. Molly will be looking all over for me. She was even going to take a shower today so she would smell better when we get to the hospital tomorrow. I'll be in the Azalea Garden. You know where we usually sleep."

"Okay. I see it's useless to try to talk you out of going back. Be careful. The murderer is starting to get careless and desperate. A desperate killer doesn't pick and choose. Anyone who gets in the way is a potential victim."

"I'm not going to allow anything to happen to me. You told Uncle Nicky I was going to be your wife. I'm not going to allow anyone to screw that up for me. A dead wife makes a poor partner."

CHAPTER 20

"Where'd you go to get cleaned up, Hank?"

"Why, do I still stink?"

"No," Molly said, "I wondered if you went to the shelter to get a shower. I hate to say this, but it feels good to get down to clean skin again. That soap smelled so nice. Nobody at the hospital will have to hold their noses today."

"Is that what they did? Did somebody at the hospital say something to you?"

"Nobody said nothin'. But when we passed some of them attendants, they made faces and wrinkled up their noses. So I thought before they tell us we can't see Maxie no more, I'd tell them we was going to get washed. Clean really smells good, don't it?"

"I don't smell as good as you, Molly, but then I didn't have any soap and I sort of took a bath, rather than a shower."

"They didn't have no soap where you were?"

"Not so you could notice. I took my bath in the river. That way, my clothes got washed with me. I think my clothes smelled worse than I did. Pretty soon I have to check with the Salvation Army to see if they have any clothes to give me. These clothes are really shot. Look at the seat, you can almost see my butt through the threads." Hank felt at ease that Molly accepted her explanation.

"I wish we had somethin' to bring her," Molly fussed. "Flowers, or candy, you know, the things that people in hospitals get from friends. Poor Maxie, all she ever gets from people is misery."

"If she's the same as she was the other day, she won't even know we're there, let alone flowers."

"I think you're wrong, Hank. She would know. There weren't that many people in her life that did anything good for her or gave her things just because they liked her. It's people she loves and trusts that's going to get her out of that hell she's in. Not the doctors and nurses. People like us. People who love her and care what happens to her. Not like that phoney Ned. Always spoutin' words that don't mean nothin'. Playin' her for a chump so he can get in her pants. He knowed what would happen to her if he dropped her and he did it anyway. Well, I think the bastard left town. Nobody's seen him for a couple of days."

"Maybe he was afraid to face you. You were the only one who thought he might pull a stunt like this." Hank thought for a few moments. "How did you know?"

"A gut feelin'. I just knowed he was goin' to hurt our Maxie. He knowed she was in love with him. He knowed she trusted him. And all the time, pretendin' he cared about her. Hell, he never cared about nobody but hisself since he was born. And them stupid people throwin' money at him for spoutin' poems somebody else wrote. If he was really so good, why wasn't he teachin' in some school? Because they woulda been able to see right through him. They woulda knowed he wasn't much good. He could fool people like me because we don't know no better but he could never fool them professors in college. I guess them that can, teaches; and them that can't, scrounges around on the waterfront tryin' to impress people."

"I won't argue with you there, Molly. You were right from the beginning and we were wrong. I hope he does leave the city. If Max gets out of the hospital, it would be best for her not to be running into him every time she goes to a shelter. Maybe in time she can learn to trust again. If she doesn't see Ned, maybe she'll get over him. I hope so."

They walked into the hospital and took the elevator to the psychiatric floor. Max was sitting in a chair near the same window, staring out into the nothingness which had become her protected world. Molly put her arms around the painfully thin shoulders and kissed the pale cheek.

"Hiya, Maxie. It's me, Molly. Hank's here too. We come to see how you're doin'. We got a lot to tell you. All your friends on the street miss you and are askin' about you. I was talkin'…" Her monologue went on for forty minutes, all the time, Molly held Max's hand, gently stroking her hair, crooning in a tone Hank had never heard her use. Molly talked about everything except the serial murders and the poet. The attendant came in and told them they had another fifteen minutes to visit. Molly looked imploringly at Hank. Hank sat on the other side of Max and took her other hand and talked to her about the current news and what was happening in the world, avoiding mentioning anything about emotionally charged subjects. Hank watched her eyes for some sign of recognition. There was none.

Hank wasn't sure if anyone benefitted from the hospital visit. Molly was depressed all the way back to the waterfront. Max was as firmly ensconced in the vast silence of nothingness, a retreat, which was a living death. Hank thought briefly about the drowning of Julian Grant and wondered who or what could have lured him that close to the river. She was grateful Maxie had not been one of Julian Grant's victims. At least the separation from Ned was sudden and final with no bad memories. The situation would have been different if Julian had been that "important other" in her life. The bad feeling would have continued for a long time. She was sorry the Ned situation happened. She had liked Ned a lot. She liked the sparkle in his eyes when he was amused and the sound of his laughter when he was delighted. It was a shame he was such a rat. She watched Molly and realized the woman was hurting and she put her arm around the older woman's shoulders.

"She's going to make it, Molly. I'm sure of it. The healing takes time and she has a lot of time."

"Yeah, Hank, but I don't. I got the feeling my time is runnin' out. I want to be sure Maxie'll be all right."

Hank was startled. "Have you been feeling sick, Molly?"

"I feel all right. Sometimes, people know when the end is comin'. Without knowin' why, they start preparin' for the long journey; kinda straightenin' out what's left of their lives. I writ some letters and they're in my bag, addressed and everything, so when the cops find my body, they can send the letters out."

She smiled her semi-toothless grin. "Don't feel bad for me, Hank, anythin' has to be better than the way we have to live. We don't even go from day to day, we have to take it minute by minute. That's no way for human beings to live. Them people treat us like we had choices and we chose this wonderful life over some comfortable, serene, draggy kind of existence. Anybody who thinks he is master of his fate has never been down in the gutter where we are. I'd like to see some of them positive thinkers down and out, with nobody to help and nobody to turn to and the cops doggin' their tail every time they turn around. I'd like to see them tell people how to be positive when everything around them is negative and they get just enough food to keep them alive but not enough to give them energy to keep walking or to keep livin'. We continue to live because there's not much of an alternative and we know what to expect here. Nobody knows what happens after you die. Nobody ever came back to say don't do it, or do it now because you get treated better in the hereafter. So, the poor slobs like us do our best to stay alive because we don't know if there is anythin' else out there. Just once before I die, I'd like to hear somebody say, 'Molly, you done a good job with the little bit the Lord gave you.' But nobody can say that because the world is no better when I leave it than it was when I came into it. You know, Hank, that's how you measure success. If when you leave this world somebody is better for having known you, even one person, then you did somethin' really good."

"Then you were a success, Molly," Hank said. "I'm a better person for having known you and certainly Max is blessed because you're such a good friend. So, I guess when you get to those pearly gates, the gatekeeper will be looking these things up in his big book, where he keeps all accounts and he'll say, 'Molly, you've earned a place of comfort and warmth. Go in and join your friends who have come before you. Here there's no hunger, no cold, no pain…there's only love.' But being very selfish, I hope you'll be around for a long time yet."

A single tear escaped from under Molly's eyelid and she hurriedly wiped it away with the back of her hand. Hank turned her head to save her friend from further embarrassment.

"You shoulda been a preacher, Hank. You got a way of talkin' to people that makes them feel good about theirself. That's a gift so don't ever sell it short. It's a shame that since you came to the streets we've been plagued by that serial killer, but you're takin' it all in stride. Besides carryin' your own weight, you go to bat for everybody else. You did it for Ned, you did it for Max and for me. You're a good girl, Hank."

* * *

The police seemed to be gaining ground in their investigation of the serial killer. Storm attended a seminar on stress and related problems, which kept him off the streets for a week.

During that week, the killer struck again.

Molly found the victim on the periphery of the Azalea Gardens. She hurried back to the sleeping area and shook Hank into wakefulness.

"Wake up, Hank, wake up." She began gathering up Hank's belongings along with her own. She shook the sleepy Hank again. "Hank, you gotta get up. We gotta get out of here."

Hank sat up but her eyes refused to cooperate with the position of her body. Her lids dragged over sleep starved eyes. "What's wrong, Molly?"

Without looking at her, Molly began folding the plastic ground cloths. "Another murder."

Hank felt a cold shiver start at the back of her neck and electrify each vertebra on its way down to her heels. She focused on the scurrying Molly.

"Where?"

Molly nodded toward the beginning of the Gardens.

"Here? In the Azalea Gardens? How do you know?"

"Went to pee in the bushes at the far end and I saw a hand stickin' outta the bushes beside me. Right beside me, Hank. I parted the bushes and there was blood, a lot of blood...all over, and the guy was layin' on his face. I didn't stay no longer than that. I hightailed outta there as fast as these gimpy legs would carry me. What time is it, Hank?"

Hank manipulated the dial of her watch until it caught the light from the streetlamp. "It's four twenty. Where should we go?"

Molly had gathered everything in sight. "Best head for the park. The farther we get from this place the better."

Hank could see Molly was in pain, so, she picked up both bags. "Lean on me, Molly, but let's move slowly so we don't attract attention. Before we start, take a few swallows of the brandy, maybe the pain will ease."

Gratefully, Molly reached for the bottle and took several swallows before handing it back. She tried to smile. "That oughta do the trick. Thanks."

They made their way, slowly, painfully out of the area. It helped that there was no moon and black clouds had moved into the River Drive, shrouding everything in a damp, black mist. Hank had learned a lot from Molly. She had no problem finding her way. When she had time to think, Hank realized she was more frightened than usual. Was it because this time the killer was in her territory, or was it because Storm wasn't there to protect her? Her vulnerability was showing and here she was with a very sick woman, at four thirty in the morning looking for a safe place for them to go where they would be out of danger.

The pain on Molly's face said she couldn't go on much longer. They had reached the beginning of the park.

"Let's stop here, Molly. I'm exhausted," Hank lied.

Molly smiled and patted her cheek. "Let's go over to that cluster of trees, we can bed down there."

Hank laid out the ground cover and the blankets and watched as Molly pulled the blanket over her head and fell into a deep, exhausted sleep.

Hank thought Molly's pain must be getting worse or she gave up. Strange, how fast she went downhill after Max's unfortunate departure from reality. It was almost like Molly was saying if Max couldn't be here then she didn't want to be around either.

Hank's tears were very close to the surface. The friends she made were leaving her, one by one.

The day after the victim was found in the Azalea Garden, Storm returned to the streets and Hank had to find an excuse to go to the apartment but she didn't want to desert Molly when she needed someone.

"I'm going to the library for a while this afternoon, Molly, I'll save you space at the Garden tonight."

"I'm gettin' a bed at the shelter tonight. I need somethin' soft under these bones, but I'll meet you at the hospital in the mornin'."

Hank dug into her bag. "Here, take the bottle with you, it may help you to sleep, and if it doesn't, at least it'll make you feel better."

Hank watched as Molly walked away. She bit her lower lip. Molly had lost a great deal of weight within the last two months. Hank noticed how her clothes hung, how Molly wheezed when she breathed. Hank tried to put the thought out of her mind as she headed for the apartment.

When she turned the key in the lock, Storm was waiting for her. With a sigh of relief, he gathered her into his arms. He was like a clock with the main spring wound too tight. "Are you all right?" He stood back and studied her face.

"Now I am. I wasn't while you were gone. I was hurting. I've missed you. There was such an empty space, here." She put her hand over her heart.

"When I got word about where the latest killing took place, I freaked out."

"I knew you would come to the apartment," she said between kisses. "Molly found the body when she went to relieve herself and she hurried back to warn me. We got out of there, fast." Hank bit her lower lip. "I think Molly's dying. She thinks so too."

Storm nodded. "Did either of you know the victim?"

"Molly didn't see his face. Do you know who he is?"

"Does the name Roger Trator mean anything?"

Hank shook her head. "Not off hand. There are several Rogers on the street, describe him.

"About five foot ten, a hundred forty pounds, probably around thirty-nine or forty years old, sandy-colored hair, blue eyes, always wore a kerchief tied around his neck."

"I think I know who you mean. Always wearing a smirk?"

"Not anymore," Storm said. "What can you tell me about him?"

"Don Juan type, thought women were invented for his pleasure. He's a selfish, egotistical, asshole."

"He must be the one I saw with Suzie just before I went to that seminar."

"You saw them, together?"

"Yeah, as a matter of fact, it was in the park. It was night, of course, and she was doing a fine job of exploring his family jewels."

Hank laughed. "You mean she was exploring the wastelands."

Storm thought it prudent not to mention his own encounter with Suzie. He took a piece of paper from his pocket and read from it.

"*Is not short pain well borne, that brings long ease,*
And lays the soul to sleep in quiet grave?
Sleep after toil, port after stormy seas,
Ease after war, death after life does greatly please."

Storm folded the paper, "Incidentally, the author—"

"I know," Hank interrupted, "Edmund Spenser." She walked to the kitchen to start something for dinner. The last rays of the sun came through the living room window, casting long shadows as she and Storm went into the kitchen. Hank gasped, "Well, thank God, my shadow is back."

Storm smiled. "What did you do, misplace it?"

"It was stolen." She looked into his eyes and blushed. "Sounds stupid, doesn't it?"

"Well…it sounds intriguing, to say the least. How does one go about stealing a shadow?"

The blush deepened and Hank laughed and covered her face with her hands. "When I was a child, a bunch of us would sit in a circle and tell weird stories. Like if you wanted to know if someone was a vampire, you would stand him in front of a mirror, and if he didn't have a reflection, then he was a vampire. If somebody stole your shadow, you became a witch."

Storm laughed at her embarrassment. "Don't worry, sweetheart, the days of witch hunting— in Salem are over and I promise I'll keep your secret."

"You'd better, or I'll use my witch's power on you and turn you into a frog."

Storm reached out and pulled her to him, and kissed her. "Not fair. It only took one kiss from the princess to turn the frog back into a prince," Storm teased.

"That's because he was a dumb frog. He didn't know about prolonging the ecstasy."

Half of his clothes were strewn on the rug and her hands were quickly unfastening the other half.

Not to be outdone, he began unbuttoning her blouse, slowly, deliberately, allowing his fingers to investigate, manipulate, thrill and excite. Her laughter changed to sounds of pleasure and the playful kisses turned to passionate caresses. Their world took on a new dimension, where everything happened in slow motion. Each response became a tantalizing experience, their senses were fine-tuned. The pulsations and palpitations raced like earth tremors heaving their contorted bodies in unison, sprinkling magic dust, turning an otherwise ordinary room into a fairy tale castle. Holding on to the moment was like trying to catch the mist. Bodies dripping wet, they fell side by side, spent, exhausted, panting and totally euphoric.

Storm smiled at her. "You're sensational. It never fails, rockets, comets soaring across the sky, summer lightning. It's New Year's Eve, Christmas and the Fourth of July all at the same time. All of this wrapped up in a hundred and twenty pounds of pure dynamite."

Hank kissed his closed eyelids. "Sometimes, I think you wrote the book on the ultimate heights and satisfaction in loving."

"Only because you spur me on to those heights. It was never like this before you came into my life, Hank. With you, there are no inhibitions, only raw passion and complete delight." He picked her up and carried her into the bedroom.

Morning's rays filtered through the drawn curtains and danced on the mirror on the wall. Hank smiled, stretched, and tried to peer through the slits in her eyes. If she didn't open her eyes, maybe she could continue the marvelous dream she was having. A voice within said, *It doesn't work that way, Hank.* Once she realized the dream was gone, she ventured to open her eyes. The other side of the bed was empty. There was a note on the pillow. She sat up and reached for the note and slanted the paper so it would catch the light.

> *I could get used to waking up next to you. I would have kissed you before I left, but you looked so happy with your dream I didn't have the heart to disturb you. I found your shadow asleep on the floor beside the bed, so I tucked her in with you. I love you...Storm.*

Hank let the water run in the shower, picked up her clothes and put them in the washer before returning for a leisurely shower. She ate a good breakfast and left by the tower stairs.

Halfway down the tower stairs, she felt an icy shiver make its way internally. It was a cold the summer heat couldn't eliminate. She hurried to open the door, to let in more light. She saw nothing unusual. She stayed close to the building and headed toward the hospital, occasionally looking over her shoulder.

The psychiatric floor was a hive of activities. A variety of therapists were on hand, working with patients, reassuring them, teaching them to adjust to the outside world. Hank stopped at the desk and asked to see Maxine. The attendant studied a chart and nodded. "There is only one visitor in with her, so it will be all right. Do you know where she is?"

Hank nodded and walked down the corridor toward Maxine's room. The door was open. She heard Ned's voice, low, almost pleading. He knelt on the floor beside Max's chair, stroking her hand, calling her name.

"Hello, Ned." Hank didn't wait for a response. "How is she today?"

Ned's expression was answer enough.

"Molly is absolutely certain Max is going to pull out of this," Hank said. "When the attendant said someone was with her, I thought it was Molly." She couldn't contain her curiosity. "I heard you left the city, what made you come back?"

"Max. Max made me come back. I can't recite poetry anymore. I can't seem to remember any lines other than the lines for 'The Definition of Love,' and I can't get the words to that poem to pass my lips. I didn't realize how I came to rely on Max for my own...feeling of worth. I thought I could run away and resume my life. I can't do that. I'm trapped and held in the grip of this tiny hand." He kissed the tips of Max's fingers."

"What about Suzie?"

Ned's eyes looked blank, then his understanding registered. "Ah, yes, the creature of the flesh. It would seem she is not interested in me. Her only interest was in breaking up our quartet...and she succeeded in that, didn't she?"

"But in doing so, she almost destroyed us. Look at Max. What little she had gained is gone, perhaps forever. Molly is...dying. But before she goes, she has to know Max will be all right. Then there's you. Suzie tried to kill you."

"That's not fair, Hank. I have no idea who stabbed me. I couldn't see who it was. If it was Suzie, and if Suzie is the serial killer as you say, why didn't she kill me? Isn't it the first time she left anyone who could identify her?"

"No, you couldn't see who it was, but Max did and she's in no condition to identify the killer. She doesn't even have her own identity anymore." Hank was almost screaming at him.

"Dying? M-M-M-olly d-dying?"

Hank and Ned turned and stared at the woman in the chair.

Slowly, Max turned her head and looked at Ned. "Dying?"

Hank was on her knees beside Max. "No, no, Max. She's just giving up. I think she can't face not having you around. So she got dramatic and said she was getting ready to go to a better life. You know Molly. Tomorrow she'll be on top of the world and she'll have forgotten everything she said."

"Molly…dying?"

"Ned, go find Molly. Bring her back here. Max has to see her. Hurry.

"Max, it's all right. Ned's going to bring Molly here to see you. Talk to me, just keep talking to me."

"Molly…my Molly…dying?"

There was a noise at the door. Hank turned and saw Doctor McGowan. She entered the room and walked slowly toward Max.

"Maxine! Maxine, can you hear me? It's Doctor McGowan."

"Doctor?"

"Yes. I'm here to help you."

"Help? Yes. Yes, help Molly."

The doctor looked at Hank, questioningly.

Hank continued to hold Max's hand. "Molly is Max's friend. Probably the best friend she ever had. I was talking to another friend of Max's just before you came in, and I told him I thought Molly was dying. That's when Max came out of the limbo her mind was in. She asked if Molly was dying. I thought the best thing to do was send for Molly so that Max could see for herself that Molly is alive. Was I wrong?"

"Definitely not. If her concern for Molly transcended that safe haven Max retreated into, then it is vitally important that she know Molly is alive." The doctor turned her attention to Max. "Maxine, tell me about Molly."

"Molly? Molly's gone. Nothing left."

"That's not true, Max," Hank said, "Molly's alive. Ned went to get her so you can see for yourself."

"Ned? Ned's dead." Max looked at her hands, an expression of terror on her face. "See? His blood…all over my hands."

"No, Max," Hank said, "Ned isn't dead. He had a flesh wound but he's fine now. He was here a little while ago. He went to get Molly. They're both coming back. Look at me, Max. Do you know who I am? Do you recognize me?"

Maxine turned her head and raised her eyes to Hank's face. There was no recognition.

Hank reached for Dr. McGowan's hand. "Don't let her go back into that netherworld. Please, you've got to keep her here."

The doctor placed herself between Maxine and the window. "Maxine, tell me about Molly."

At first there was a puzzled expression on Max's face and she tried to ignore the doctor, but Doctor McGowan persisted. "Tell me about Molly. Was Molly your friend? Do you want to help Molly?"

Each time the doctor mentioned Molly's name, Max blinked hard, trying to remember...something.

"Maxine, was Molly the one who protected you?"

"Molly. Molly showed me."

"What did Molly show you?" Doctor McGowan's voice was soft and gentle.

Maxine shook her head, as though she was trying to stop the flood of memories gushing into her head. She raised her hands to her ears, trying to shut out the voices of her memory.

"What did Molly show you, Maxine?" Doctor McGowan's voice droned on.

Max looked down. There was a hint of a smile on her face. "She showed me how to live on the streets. I would have frozen to death...except for Molly. I would have starved to death...except for Molly. I would have been a victim, many times, except for Molly. I hurt Molly."

"How did you hurt Molly, Maxine?"

Max looked at the doctor and shook her head. "No."

"You don't want to talk about it?"

"No."

"All right, we don't have to talk about that. Was Molly like a mother to you?"

Maxine frowned. "Better. Much better. No one could hurt me when Molly was around. She wouldn't let them." Max looked away from the doctor and her eyes rested on Hank. "Hank. What are you doing here?"

Hank could feel the knot in her stomach relaxing. "I care about you too, Max."

Max looked at the doctor. "Hank and Molly were always worrying about me. Sometimes I wouldn't sleep for long periods. Hank always had her bottle of brandy ready. She and Molly teased me into drinking. They knew I couldn't drink but they got some brandy in me, to make me sleep. Most of the time it worked. Poor Hank, she had to provide the booze for Molly and me. Lots of times Molly couldn't sleep either. Molly's bones were always cold and that little bit of brandy warmed her and she could go through one more night. I guess you could say Hank took care of both of us during the last year." Max rubbed the outside of her arms as though she was feeling cold. "Hank got us off the hook with the police more than once. One night she even got a black eye from Detective Shaye. But that didn't stop her, she went right on fighting for us, like we had some rights...like we had...dignity. Through all the bad times, Hank made sure we stuck together."

Doctor McGowan stood behind Hank. "Everyone has rights and everyone has dignity. Unfortunately, some people go to great lengths to rob others of that dignity. If they succeed, they also succeed in robbing those people of a good self-image. Hank was right, when people stick together they are usually safe. The bad times you referred to, do you mean the hunger and cold?"

"Hunger and cold," Max said, as though the words were foreign. "At one time they would have been the bad times. No, the bad times I'm talking about were the killings. So many street people murdered. Someone was out there, determined to get rid of the Streeters. Every time we saw the flashing blue and red lights of the police cars we had to run so we wouldn't be accused of the crimes. Molly tried to protect me from Ned too. Poor Molly...she tried to warn me. I wouldn't listen. I told her she was wrong about him." Max smiled a sad, rueful smile. "But she knew him better than anybody else. Molly knows a lot about human nature, things that most of us will never understand. Isn't that true, Hank?"

"Amen to that, Max."

"Molly is dying. Do you know about that, Hank?" The words brought back the fear and Max began wringing her hands. Doctor McGowan left the room and returned in a short time with a hypodermic syringe.

"No...Don't put me out. I have to see Molly."

"I am not going to knock you out, Maxine. This is just to relax you. I promise. You won't be quite so anxious when your friend Molly gets here."

Maxine's shoulders sagged in resignation. "I don't want to sleep. I don't want to sleep," she repeated until the handwringing stopped and she appeared calmer. There was some commotion in the corridor outside her room and they could hear Molly's gravelly voice say, "Get your hands off me, Ned. I can walk by meself. I don't need any help from you." Molly stumbled into Max's room and froze in a tableau stance.

"Maxie?"

Max smiled, and held out her arms. She could see Molly's physical condition had deteriorated.

Molly's face lit up with her pumpkin grin and she was unashamed of the tears that gathered and spilled over onto her cheeks. "You okay, Maxie?" She leaned over the chair and gathered the younger woman in her arms. "They treatin' you okay? You ain't none the worse for wear," she said as she touched Max's cheek. "You're still the prettiest girl I ever seen. What do you mean by scarin' the life right outta your Molly?"

Max smoothed down Molly's tangled hair and held on to her. "You've lost so much weight, Molly. Have you been sick?"

"Naw. I just ain't been eatin' much. You know how bad some of the food is at the shelters. But I took a shower and I been tryin' to stay clean so they won't throw me out when I come to see you." She pulled Max's hands to her lips and kissed them. "I sure do miss you. It's good to have you back."

"You brought me back, Molly. It was only because I knew how much you cared. I could hear you, even when I was lost. You came here and talked to me and told me what was happening. I tried to come back before but I couldn't find my way. Then I heard somebody say you were sick, maybe dying. I knew I had to come back. I had to be with you. It's the first time you needed...me. Nothing else mattered. I had to be with you."

"I don't want you leavin' here until the doc says it's okay. I can wait."

Maxine looked to Doctor McGowan. "When will I be able to leave, Doctor?"

"Not for a while yet. Molly is the last person to want you to leave the hospital before you're well. We're going to see what you can do while you're here, maybe we can do something about finding you a job, something to allow you to manage your own life, something you can handle comfortably. Would you like that?"

"Would I be able to keep Molly with me?"

"I think that's a real possibility. In the meantime, we'll need your help in weeding out your problems and help keep you out of hospitals. Are you willing to work with us?"

"I'll do whatever you say. I want to be a whole person. I'll work hard."

"Good. I think you've had enough excitement for one day. Your friends can come to visit you tomorrow. You and I have a lot of territory to explore in the next few weeks."

Max smiled and squeezed Molly's hand.

"Me and Hank will be back to see you. You're gonna be just fine."

Ned waited for Hank and Molly at the shelter. He said, "We'll have to be very cautious with Max once she leaves the hospital. Poor child, her ego is so fragile."

Molly grabbed his arm and turned him to face her. "You listen to me, Ned, she wouldn't be in this mess if it wasn't for you. As far as Max is concerned, you're bad news. I don't know if she still loves you or how important you are to her. One thing I do know is that you're not gonna get another chance to use her again. Besides breakin' her heart, and puttin' her into that never-neverworld, you coulda got her killed. In this day of AIDS, I don't know how you coulda had sex with that whore and then had sex with Maxie. We better not find out that Maxie is HIV positive. I can't tell you to stay away from her because I don't know how Maxie feels about you anymore but I'll be watchin' you, and if you try hurtin' her again, I'll kill you meself, we won't have to wait for that serial killer. I'll kill you on the spot. Do you get my meanin'?"

"I think you've made your point abundantly clear, Molly. I know what I did to Maxine. I know it was unconscionable and like you, I don't know if she'll ever forgive me. Back at the hospital, she didn't look at me, only through me. But even if she won't have anything to do with me, I owe it to her to protect her. That's the least I can do. If I step out of line, I'll expect the full impact of your wrath. If the doctor manages to find some kind of work for her and gets her off the streets, I won't see her again, unless she wants to see me. I'm not so stupid that I don't realize what I've lost. Unfortunately, I never gave any consideration to the possibility of AIDS. But you are absolutely right, I have no idea where Suzie came from or how many men she was with. My impression is...there were many. Even if she's not the serial killer, she can still be a purveyor of death, in a different form...a more sinister form. I'm not going to try to justify my actions. They speak for themselves and they were indeed reprehensible. God knows I've had many regrets in my life but none as distressing as my transgression against the lovely Maxine. I promise I will not impose myself on her except by invitation and that, only with your prior approval. Is that all right?"

"I couldn't say this in front of Maxie, but I won't be around much longer. Maxie is young and she's pretty but that's not going to be enough to keep her off the streets. If she makes it back to that world where she can live a normal life, she should be able to find some man who'll have a job and come home to her at night and treat her like the lady she is. You're not that man. I don't think you want to be that man. Stop me if I'm wrong. I'd like to find out I misjudged you."

Ned lowered his head. "No. I think for the first time in my life somebody has me pegged just right. Once I lived the good life and I could have had it all. That life didn't elude me. I pushed it away with both hands. I'm a vagabond, a wanderer, a rogue, a scoundrel. I am all the things that are bad for Max. But I do love her. I didn't realize how much until she wasn't there to share things with me. If she doesn't want me in her life, so be it. I'll step aside and leave the city for good. Perhaps she has already made that decision. If so, she's wiser than I've given her credit for and I'll abide by whatever decision she makes. Is that fair enough?"

"I told Hank how good I thought you was with them fancy words. It was them fancy words and all that poetry stuff that Maxie fell in love with. Maybe if you just talk plain to her without all the lacy trim, she'll know if she loves the words or the man."

"I can't separate them, Molly, not even to please you. My words are a part of me just as poetry is part of me. It's all of those things and more that makes the entire man. I'll do my best to help Maxine. More than that, I can't promise."

Ned loosened Molly's fingers from his arm and walked in the opposite direction.

"Molly, that wasn't fair. Ned's not responsible for what happened to Max. Say it's life on these streets, say it's her past life that keeps returning to haunt her, say it's an inability to cope with society in general, but don't blame it all on Ned."

Hank's gaze followed Ned. "When we were trying to shield her from the horror on the streets, it was Ned who bought her meals and brought them to her at the Azalea Gardens so she wouldn't have to face all the death that was running rampant. He took us to see the Philadelphia Orchestra in concert. That was the highlight of Max's entire life. He made that possible, no one else...him. I know how much you love Max and I know that you want to protect her but laying all the blame at Ned's feet isn't the answer. Max is the only one who can make up her mind about Ned's importance in her life. I think Doctor McGowan will play an important role in whatever decisions Max makes. I think you'll agree that Doctor McGowan has absolutely nothing to gain if Max goes back to Ned or if she doesn't. We should be grateful Max is in a position to make any decisions at all.

CHAPTER 21

"Obviously, the last encounter you had with Suzie upset you. Why? Usually you're more detached."

Storm Andrews stood beside the chart in Doctor McGowan's office. "You mean apart from the fact that the guy I found her with is now dead? All I know, Doc, is that my gut feeling tells me this woman is unstable and lethal. I honestly believe she can be a killing machine. No remorse, no conscience, no emotion, she's programmed for sex, hate, and death…and in that order. I think she's like an old bottle of nitro, standing on a shelf, in an earthquake. You know it's going to explode but you don't know when. If you pick it up, it might explode in your face. If you don't pick it up it's going to explode anyway and there's no way of telling how many people she'll take down with her. If she's our killer and I think she is, she already has sixteen victims to her credit, and there's no sign it's going to end. It's ten months since the murders began and I still don't have a viable suspect."

He saw the concerned expression on her face. "I'm sorry, Doc, it's frustrating, I feel like I'm being manipulated and I don't like it."

"Why do you feel you're being manipulated? You're doing everything you can to apprehend the killer."

He hesitated, not really wanting to discuss Hank's encounter with the notorious Suzie. "Not too long ago, Suzie sought out Hank in the Azalea Gardens. It was during a heavy fog. She found Hank and threatened her."

Without changing expression, Pam McGowan asked, "In what way did she threaten Hank?"

"She never actually came out and said she was going to kill her, what she said was, 'It won't be long now and he will be all mine and you will be gone forever.' She said, 'Don't worry, if they ever catch up with me, you won't be around to see it.' There were other things but it's confused in my mind, something about Suzie being programmed for sexual satisfaction and that every man secretly wants a whore….Words to that effect. Hank was almost in a panic. I have to protect Hank but I also have an obligation to the

Department and if I'm with Hank, I can't be out there looking for the killer. I'm caught on the horns of a dilemma. To say that Hank was scared is putting it mildly and believe me, Doc, she doesn't scare easily. This thing has been giving her nightmares and I can understand why. I got her to agree to get off the streets by Thanksgiving. Now that Max and Molly aren't walking the streets anymore, Hank spends more nights in her apartment but Suzie followed her and knows where she lives, which doesn't make the situation any better."

"Are you saying that Hank and Molly are no longer suspects?" Doctor McGowan asked. "We already know the killer can't be Maxine. As you know, the Mental Health Center got her a civil service job and she has a small apartment and took Molly in to live with her. She seems to be happy. She hasn't talked about her night of terror. Eventually, she'll bring it out in the open, although I don't think she actually saw the assailant. Pushing her to recall that night could jeopardize her sanity."

Storm seemed uncomfortable. "Molly is still up there on the suspect list and technically, I guess you can say Hank is too. That's why it's so important for me to nail Suzie. I'm certain she's the killer but I don't have anything concrete that I can take to the D.A. for an indictment. We have to be very careful not to leave any loopholes for an attorney to get the killer off on a technicality. When we close the circle, our killer can't have any avenues of escape."

"Tell me what you know about Hank's nightmares."

"At first, she felt foolish talking about it. Then gradually, she would mention it in passing but we never really got into it. She started to open up when she saw her shadow and made the remark that she was glad her shadow had returned. In a dream, she was being chased by a specter in a black cape and hood. The dream is basically the same, with some variations. She's running from this figure in black and like a lot of dreams, she runs and gets nowhere, eventually the black-robed figure catches up with her and the dream ends, except one time, she saw the specter pick up her shadow and hide it under his cape and when she awakened, Molly saw her walking in circles around her blanket, looking for her shadow. Molly shook her and she was a little disoriented. But I should have prefaced this with the fact that Molly and Hank usually had a few nips of brandy at night. Anyway, Hank was convinced the apparition had taken her soul. That her shadow was a symbolic representation of her soul."

"This is a recurring dream?"

"That's what the lady said. She said when she was a child, she was raped by her stepfather. Her mother refused to believe her. She had recurring nightmares about that."

"She was sexually abused by her stepfather?"

"That's what she said."

"You mentioned that Hank was divorced from Julian Grant. How long ago was that?"

"I think she said they were divorced in 1988."

Doctor McGowan sat back in her chair. "Do you know why they got divorced?"

"She came home from an overseas assignment a day early and caught him in bed with a teenage girl. After that it was all downhill. We talked about it before. I told you when she came home to an orgy and called the police, he beat the shit out of her."

"And now Julian Grant is dead. But his death was an accident and not tied to the serial killings, is that correct?"

"I don't think there's a connection. But I'm not certain it was an accident either. He had a severe head laceration, which could mean he was knocked unconscious and thrown into the river."

"How did Hank take the news of his death?"

"I don't think it affected her one way or the other. In retrospect, she doesn't think she ever loved him. When I told her about his death, there was no reaction at all. It was as though I told her it was going to rain. I think she just didn't care. She did say she couldn't understand what he was doing on the waterfront, especially since he was afraid of deep water."

"I see. We'll explore Hank and Molly in more depth later, right now, let's talk about the last two murders and the verses."

"Okay, Doc. Victim number fifteen was Nicholas Carroll. The verse was from *Othello*: *An honourable murderer, if you will for naught I did in hate but all in honour.*

Victim number sixteen was Roger Trator. The verse was from Spenser, *Is not short pain well borne, that brings long ease, and lays the soul to sleep in quiet grave? Sleep after toil, port after stormy seas, ease after war, death after life does greatly please*. The killer used the same M.O. in both slayings and the handwriting on the verses is the same as the others."

Doctor McGowan jotted down some notes, then said, "Our killer seems to think she has a calling to punish these men. We're seeing her perception of the avenging angel. This is where the honor comes in, she's convinced she's doing what must be done. She must know those men in order to write the verses. It's possible she gets whatever information she feels she needs in advance of the murders and decides what the judgement will be. So maybe your sighting of Suzie with the latest victim was nothing more than a fact-finding mission, a gathering of information, so that she can weigh the possibilities and execute the sentence."

"Do you still think the killer has a multiple personality?"

She nodded. "I'm afraid so."

CHAPTER 22

September passed into a mild October but the streets remained unsettled as did the people who had to live there. The friendship between Max and Ned survived but Max's feelings of love cooled. Occasionally Ned stopped by her office to talk with her but he made no effort to visit her at home, nor did she invite him.

Hank spent most of her time now on her book. Writing had become extremely difficult because she realized she could no longer write it objectively. The past year had brought about many changes in her life and she had to learn to deal with them.

Storm let himself in to the apartment and waited. When Hank finished the segment she was working on, she turned and smiled. "Hi, sweetheart. I never thought I'd say this, but I miss being on the streets. At least I was out in the fresh air and the walking was the best thing I ever did. I was tired much of the time, but it was a good tired, I felt alive. Cooped up in the apartment, chained to the computer, isn't rewarding like I thought it would be."

He kissed her and walked to the kitchen counter and poured them each a drink. He said, "I talked with Max today. I'm always afraid I'm going to say something that will catapult her back into that catatonic state. But Doctor McGowan says she's much better and can handle the questioning as long as it isn't prolonged."

"The doctor seems to be doing a marvelous job with her. She looks so much better now, younger too. Molly's leukemia is in remission and she does the cooking for Max and makes sure Max is getting the proper food. Every now and then I have dinner with them and of course they know who I am. There didn't seem to be much point in hiding it any longer. Shrewd old Molly was amused and said she wondered where I always got the money to buy the brandy. She was also very grateful that I did. I'm not sure how Max took the news. I think she had mixed emotions but she was happy to know I had a place of my own to stay. Initially, she wanted me to stay in that little apartment with her and Molly. Once a week, I bring some food over to them and brandy for

Molly. I know Molly's in remission but she looks terrible." Hank studied Storm's face and knew instinctively he had something to tell her. She asked, "Any new developments on the serial killings?"

"I got a copy of the coroner's report on Julian Grant. The medical examiner thinks he was murdered."

"What? I thought you said he drowned."

"That's true. He did drown but now it appears that he might have had some help. The M.E. found a crack in his skull. There is a possibility that he was hit on the head and knocked unconscious. He was probably pushed into the water. Since he was unconscious, he was unable to yell for help."

"Could he have been knocked out accidentally at the time he fell?

"Sure, that's always a possibility. The question remains, what was he doing on the waterfront alone, late at night? I think he might have been lured there by a party or parties unknown. The strange thing is no one has come forward to claim the body."

Hank shrugged. "Not so strange. His parents were dead. He was an only child and I can't remember hearing him talk about any other relatives. Do you think there was a connection between his death and the other deaths?"

"I don't know. We spoke with a few dockworkers who were on the dock the night he drowned. They saw a man and woman, it could have been Suzie. The stevedores gave a fairly accurate description of her, but nobody remembers what the guy looked like. For all they know, it could have been the President of the United States. When you have as much showing as our friend, who's going to look at a guy? Maybe that's the way she planned it. She knew nobody would be able to identify the guy." Storm picked up his glass and drained it.

"Why would she do such a thing? If she is the killer, why would she change her selection of men from Streeters to non-street people? Why would she change her mode of killing? It doesn't make sense."

"Will you tell me one thing that has made sense since these killings began? Yet there has to be a pattern. Damn it. Why can't I see it?"

"Have you had any luck with Max? Does she remember the night of the attack?"

"She's blocking. I don't know if she'll ever be able to face that night. In the meantime the murders continue."

"There hasn't been a murder for about six weeks. Maybe it's over."

"Wishful thinking, my love. I think our killer enjoys killing. When the itch begins again, she or he will be on the prowl looking for the next victim. Once the victim is selected, the killer must experience a euphoric high. The killer is like a stalking cat, hiding, waiting, ready to pounce as soon as the opportunity presents itself. No. Our killer isn't going to get that kind of high any other way. The murders will continue until we catch the killer. Doctor McGowan has been very helpful with a profile of the killer."

"Doctor McGowan? What does she have to do with it?"

"She's the psychiatrist the police department uses. I thought I told you that."

"No, you didn't, or if you did, I don't remember it. When I saw her at the hospital, I thought she was smart. This just confirms it. Is that why she was called when Max had her breakdown?"

"She wasn't called. Max became her patient when she was brought to the emergency room. I understand the psychiatrists work on a rotation basis. Other than private patients, the psychiatrists take the patients on the nights they are covering emergency care. When Maxine was brought in, it just happened to be Doctor McGowan's rotation. Why are you so interested in Doctor McGowan?"

"She's very pretty, isn't she?"

A smile tugged at the corners of Storm's mouth. "Yes...very pretty. She is also very...married." Storm's laughter rang throughout the apartment. "I don't believe you're jealous." He took her in his arms. "I love you, Hank. You're what I want, not Doctor McGowan, not Suzie Bimbo or anyone else."

"I feel like such a fool. I know you love me. I just have this awful feeling that I'm going to lose you...that I'm not going to be here to enjoy our love."

"You're making the Bimbo's threats get to you. I told you I won't let her hurt you. Don't you believe me?"

"Of course I believe you. But you can't be with me twenty-four hours a day. She knows where I live."

"I have men on stakeout. She won't be able to get in without being seen. If she's spotted, my men are instructed to take her into custody. Frankly, I hope she does show up. It might put an end to the murders and free up that magnificent spirit of yours. You weren't afraid of a bull like Mike Shaye but you are terrified of a prostitute because she threatened you."

"It wasn't just the threat, there was something about her that turned me inside out. I think we're dealing with someone with a very serious mental problem."

"We agree on that one. That's why Doctor McGowan has been brought in on the case. She's convinced Suzie Bimbo will stop at nothing to get what she wants. She's completely lacking in morals and that alone makes her dangerous. But when you combine the fact that she is amoral with her thirst for blood, she could be considered as criminally insane. Where did she come from? We think she came to this city last December or January. Some of the street people saw her as far back as January. Nobody knows where she stays and nobody knows where she goes. We know her name is Suzanne Hoffman. She doesn't have any friends that anyone has ever seen. She never talks to women and the men she has been seen talking to usually end up dead. It seems the one exception is Ned. That's the real puzzler. Why not Ned?"

Hank said, "Maybe it's a bond of two poets."

"What did you say?"

"I said...my God, do you think that could be the link?"

"I guess I never thought of her as a poet. Poets are gentle people, generally. I wonder...?"

"But she tried to kill him, didn't she?"

"I think if she really wanted to kill him he would be very dead. I think it was Max she wanted to frighten. She knew how fragile Max's ego was and all she had to do was draw a little blood. Seeing the blood on the man she loved sent Max into a tailspin. That eliminated Maxine."

Hank shook her head. "But he already told Max he wanted Suzie. Max would never push herself where she wasn't wanted."

"It could be that she wanted a message to be sent to you and she sent that message through Max."

"What a horrible thing to do to another human being."

"I think she hates you, Hank. We have to find out why. Do you think she feels threatened by you?"

Hank threw back her head and laughed. "Threatened by me? Could be. I have what she wants. You. I guess nobody ever said no to her before. She hates me because you won't go to bed with her."

"There has to be more to it than that. Where does she get her information? We can't find any traces of her. It's like she appears at will and disappears the same way."

CHAPTER 23

Maxine's surprise showed in her smile when Storm Andrews walked in to the city office building to see her.

"How are you, Max?"

"I'm doing well, thank you, Detective Andrews."

"We're friends, Max. At least I hope we are."

"Yes, of course we are."

"Then don't you think it would be all right to call me Storm? I haven't seen Molly recently, is she okay?"

"She has good days and bad days. Recently, she has been having more bad days than good ones. Lucky for us, her medicaid card came in so we can get her some treatment. She's at the hospital today for a blood transfusion. They said she should feel a little better. They wanted to give her some chemotherapy. She asked the oncologist if it would cure the disease. When they said no, she refused to have it done. She said if they were going to prolong her life only to have her live in misery then she didn't want it. I don't think anyone realizes how good a person she is. I wish there was something I could do to make her life more pleasant."

"You've already done it. You care. You accepted her the way she was. Now in the final phase of her life you gave her a place to live and the chance to take care of someone she loves. She thinks she's taking care of you."

"She is. She has taken care of me since my first day on the streets. I wouldn't be here today if it wasn't for her. Enough about me, was there something you thought of that you wanted to talk to me about?"

"No. I just wanted to be sure you were all right. I'm on my way to see Doctor McGowan. Any messages?"

"Just tell her how grateful I am to be working and to have her as my doctor. Somebody up there must love me to have blessed me in so many ways."

"Take care of yourself, Max. See you soon."

She waved. "Good-bye, Detec— Storm."

The walk to Doctor McGowan's office was invigorating. Autumn was beautiful, but wet. It started to turn cold and Storm pulled his collar up to keep the wind off his neck. When he arrived at the medical building, he took the elevator to Doctor McGowan's office. The receptionist looked up when he entered.

"Top of the morning to you, Detective Andrews. Looks like it might be getting colder outside."

Storm Andrews smoothed down his hair. "And the balance of the day to you. Looks like I blew in from another planet. How are you today, Megan?"

"Great," she said, and looked at her watch. "Doctor McGowan will be out in about five minutes.

The door to her office opened and she walked over to him with her hand extended.

"It's good to see you again, Storm. Please come in." When the door closed, she said, "You seem troubled. Has something happened?"

"Not yet. I have a gut feeling that says our killer is getting restless. I wish you were also a psychic, maybe you could tell me where the killer will strike next."

"You seem certain the killer will strike again soon. Why?"

"It's nothing I can put my finger on. Like I said, a gut feeling. You must think I'm a couple of cards short of a full deck." He walked over to the window and looked out at the city.

"No. I have a lot of respect for gut feelings. There are times when that's all I have to go on too. We learn to listen to those feelings and if we're not afraid of them, we even learn to channel them where they can be most useful."

"I've been thinking about our discussion. If our killer has a multiple personality, can the destructive personality take over?"

"Not necessarily the destructive personality but the dominant personality can emerge and take charge. Usually, the stronger personality will emerge in an effort to save the weaker personality rather than have that one threatened to the point where none of them can function."

"Let's say, the weaker personality is given a lie detector test, will that test show what the other personality is responsible for?"

"Not if the weaker personality is unaware of the stronger one. That personality can only answer for itself. The other personality is like a separate and distinct person, with no tangible connection to the weaker personality. In most of these cases, only the stronger personality knows about the other and what those personalities do. You're getting closer to the identity of the killer, aren't you? The mind will react in strange ways to protect it from a truly threatening situation." She looked at her watch. "Afraid I have to bug out. I'm expected at the hospital. Keep in touch."

"Thanks, Pam."

"For what? For telling you what you knew already? I hope you catch the killer soon. I would hate to see you become a patient."

"Don't worry about me. I saw Maxine earlier. She sends her love." He picked up his jacket and waved.

He stopped at the precinct and sat in front of the board he had prepared on the murders, and conditions surrounding them. On the map above the board he checked the areas where the bodies were found. They almost formed a circle. There was only one area left to complete the circle. He stared at the map. "God in heaven." He called the weather bureau to get a forecast for the next few nights. Tonight would be foggy. The fog was due to lift by ten o'clock in the morning. "Well, Storm, my boy," he said aloud, "you know where, but you don't know when or who." He arranged for a stakeout. The police involved in the stakeout would dress like the Streeters. The fog would be a definite problem if the killer picked that particular night. He knew he would be there all night so he phoned Hank.

Hank smiled when she heard his voice. "I was just thinking about you, but that's not strange, I think about you all the time."

"Hank, I'll be on stakeout tonight. I want to be sure you don't let anyone into your apartment, for any reason. If it's me, I'll let myself in with my key."

"Storm, I don't feel right about this stakeout. Please be careful. Let me know as soon as it is over. I love you."

"I love you too." He hung up and looked at the board again. Pieces of the puzzle were beginning to fall into place. He laid out the verses left by the killer. The common thread running through them was vengeance. But why? It was still light, there was time. He walked to Nick Andros' restaurant.

"Storm." Nick Andros came toward him with outstretched arms. "Where have you been hiding? I missed you." He looked behind Storm. "Where is Hank?"

"She's back at the apartment. I'm going on stakeout. Thought I'd get something to eat first. It's going to be a long night."

"Sit down, I'll cook for you myself. How about a drink?"

"Not tonight, thanks, Uncle Nick."

Storm picked at his food.

"Something wrong with the food? You want something else?"

"No. I'm sorry, Uncle Nick, I thought I was hungry. The coffee is great. Strong, the way I like it. Maybe I'll take some of this along with me."

"Sure. I put some in a thermos for you. You want me to make you a couple of sandwiches?"

"No, but do you have an empty liquor bottle? Good. Fill it with tea and put it in a paper bag. I'll take the thermos with coffee in a separate bag. Thanks, Uncle Nicky."

Nick Andros watched his nephew walk up the street. He had the strangest feeling he was seeing him for the last time.

Hank was restless. She walked to the window and looked up the Parkway. Fog was rolling in from the river. She closed the draperies and sat in front of the television without seeing the picture. She stretched out and felt the blessed relief of sleep overtaking her. Maybe not so blessed. The nightmare started again. She was running as in all the other dreams. Then she heard it. The deep-throated laugh. The fright started somewhere in her stomach. The faster she ran the louder the laugh became and the ground kept slipping away so that she was always in the same spot. The specter came up behind her and cast a long shadow. She looked for her own shadow but it was gone. The laugh grew louder. She looked over her shoulder and the laughing specter was holding her shadow captive. She tried desperately to wake up. In her dream, Hank was sure, this time, she would not awaken, she was sure the captivity of her shadow was symbolic. Whatever this specter was, it had taken possession of her soul. The specter leaned closer, laughing, taunting her with her own shadow. It lifted its free hand and pulled the hood back from its head. It was the same skeletal head with the perpetual grin. Like brief flashes, another face was superimposed on the laughing skull. It happened several times, but it was too quick, it was impossible for her to determine the identity of the other face. The specter reached out and touched her. She felt the icy fingers slide across her face and down her arm. Its hand reached up and pulled the black hood over its head again. It threw back its head and laughed and turned and started to walk away. Suddenly, it turned back to her, raised both arms over its head and brought them down with a force that caused a hefty wind. Hank kept looking up at a black object being hurled at her. It landed on top of her. She screamed and rolled away from it. She stood up and looked down at the object. It was only then did she realize the black object was her shadow. It lay at her feet, trampled and lifeless. The specter had killed her shadow. She put both hands to her mouth trying to stifle a scream. The specter was death and it was coming for her. This time, it played with her shadow, but the next time...the next time...it was coming for her. She heard a loud noise and the sound of glass breaking. She opened her eyes to a feeling of complete exhaustion. She saw shafts of light as they worked themselves under the draperies. She was still stretched out on the sofa. She rolled into a sitting position and winced. That had not been a good position for her back. She stood up and staggered to the window and pulled the draperies open. The glare from an overcast sky forced her to shield her eyes. She had all the symptoms of a hangover without having had anything to drink. Her head pounded and her stomach did flip-flops. She looked at her watch. It was seven forty-five. She realized the television had been on all night. She picked up the remote control and turned it off, felt her way into the kitchen, poured a large glass of orange juice and sipped it. She held the cool glass against her forehead and took a deep breath. Her mouth felt like an army had walked over her tongue with muddy boots. She made her way into the bathroom, brushed her teeth and swished the blue mouthwash between her teeth before spitting it out. She looked in the mirror and studied her face. There were deep, dark circles under her eyes. "You look like hell," she said to the reflection. "If you're going to look this bad in the morning, you should at least have had a good time the night before. Breakfast and hot coffee, that's what you need to make you feel human again, Hank, my girl." When she walked out of the bathroom, she noticed the lamp that had been on the table beside the sofa was broken, and the pieces strewn over the table and on the rug. "That must have been the crash I heard," she said, as she bent over to pick up the pieces. She straightened and rubbed the back of her head. "But first, Hank, old girl, you had better take some aspirin." *Strange,* she thought, *my head feels like it's ten times the normal size, but it doesn't look any different.* She popped four aspirin into her mouth and downed them with a swallow of orange juice. She turned when she heard a key in the lock.

"Storm?" Her look of concern made him smile. "You look as bad as I feel."

"I was chasing a murderer all night, what's your excuse?"

"I was chasing a shadow."

"Same dream?" He held her in his arms and kissed her. "I'm really beat. Think I'll take a hot shower and crash."

"I'll make some breakfast while you're showering. How about some creamed chipped beef on toast?"

"Sounds good. I won't object if you make a pot of strong coffee."

"You've got it." As she headed for the kitchen, she called over her shoulder, "How did the stakeout go last night?"

"I'll tell you about it over breakfast."

Hank enjoyed watching him eat. "It's a pleasure to cook for someone who enjoys food." She poured a second cup of coffee for each of them. "Was the stakeout successful?"

"Yes and no. The fog was so dense at the waterfront that visibility was zero but we did get to see the killer. Albeit not close enough to make a collar. But now we're certain as to the identity of the murderer."

Hank gasped. "You could have been killed."

"But I wasn't."

"Storm," she shouted, "you could have been killed."

He shouted back, "But I wasn't. Hank, listen to me, I wasn't." His voice lowered and his eyes softened. "I'm here, with you." He held her until the trembling stopped. "Aren't you even a little curious about the identity of the killer?"

"It was Suzie Bimbo."

It was his turn to gasp. "How could you have known that?"

"It's no big thing. She's the only one it could have been. There are only two people who can find their way around in the fog without getting turned around. Molly and Bimbo. We know it can't be Molly. She doesn't have enough strength to pick up a glass, let alone scamper through fog so heavy you could cut it with a knife and then have enough energy left to stab the next victim. That doesn't take any logic, all you need is common sense. I told you all along she was the killer. You wouldn't believe me. Who was the victim this time?"

"James Lassiter, age forty-six. He was recognized by one of the stakeout detectives. Until a few years ago he was a professor of English Literature at one of the local universities. He was also an alcoholic. He lost his job at the university then dropped out of sight. I think Suzie Bimbo knew about him too. The verse was very apropos. I don't know the author but the verse goes like this. "*The winds and clouds, now here, now there, Hold no such strange dominion...*"

Hank finished the verse for him, "*As woman's cold, perverted will, and soon estranged opinion.* John Clare's When Lovers Part."

"You're almost as good at this as Ned. How do you remember all these verses? I have a problem remembering the first line and that only after I read it over at least ten times." He saw the troubled look on Hank's face. "Did you know him...this James Lassiter?"

"Yes. I was in one of his classes."

"What kind of person was he?"

"He was good at what he did. The females in the class weren't too happy with him. He was hard on grades unless you let him seduce you. He loved getting the girls behind his desk during class so he could put his hand up their skirts. He rarely called on a girl if she was wearing slacks."

"Did he ever do it to you?"

"He tried. After that attempt I wore nothing but jeans to class for the rest of the semester. I don't think anybody liked him. He was just a dirty, lecherous old man."

"But he was only forty-six."

"So, two out of three isn't bad."

Storm smiled at her and tilted her chin to get a better look at her face. "You look tired. Are you trying to double for a panda? The circles under your eyes are so black I thought I was looking at a raccoon when I walked in."

"Really? I had better check it out." She looked in the polished chrome of the sink tap, took a paper towel and wiped her face. "Hmmm, just as I thought, my mascara ran," she looked dumbly at the blackened paper towel. "I fell asleep on the sofa and didn't wake up until this morning and I haven't washed my face yet." To herself, she said, *When did I put on mascara? I never use that stuff anymore.* To Storm, she said, "If you could see Bimbo, how come you couldn't catch her?"

"The crime had already been committed when we saw her. And you're right, she knows her way around this city better than anyone I know. The ground was wet and this time we got a clear footprint. Before anyone else came into the area, we cordoned it off."

"How did you know where she was going to strike?"

"I told you killers follow patterns. When I looked at my map of all the places the murders took place, they formed a circle. There was only one blank spot in that circle, and that was where we stationed ourselves."

"That sounds far-fetched. How could she orchestrate these murders so that they would take place in a circle?"

"We've been thinking the strikes were random but that wasn't true. Since she was the seducer, she picked the spot where she would meet her men, thus the pattern. Last night she closed the circle."

"But you don't know any more about her now than you did months ago. She closed the circle. What does that mean? Does it mean the crime spree is over? Does it mean we go on like nothing happened? Is she going to leave me alone now?"

"I told you, she likes the feeling of killing. She's not going to stop. There will always be one more. I think she gets her sexual jollies out of knowing when she finishes with the sex part, she's going to get her thrills. She's a black widow spider. Once the news media hears what we've got, they'll probably label her 'the black widow.'

The phone rang. "It's probably for me. I told them at the station where I'd be." He picked up phone. "Hello." He bit his lower lip as he listened. "I see. Are you sure? It's okay, I'll be there later." He hung up.

Hank said, "You can't continue on like this. You need to get some sleep."

"I'll sleep tonight. I worry about you when I can't be here."

"I'm fine. Stop worrying about me."

"Sure, you are. That's why you keep having that nightmare. Tell me about it." He pulled her onto the sofa in his arms.

"Tell you about what?"

"The nightmare. Was it the same as always?"

"It's never really the same, there is always an added nuance, subtle, but there." She related the dream to him as she remembered it, including the dead shadow and what she thought it meant, symbolically. "I must have been extremely restless, I knocked the lamp over. It broke into a hundred pieces."

"Don't worry about it. I'll get you another one."

"The lamp isn't important. What matters is that I'm doing things and not remembering that I did them."

His arms tightened around her. "If I had all the things happen to me that happened to you, I probably couldn't remember my name. Stop being so hard on yourself." He looked at his watch. "Got to go."

"Will you be back tonight?"

"Don't know yet. Depends on how things mesh. I'll give you a call late in the afternoon. Why don't you crawl into bed? Pretend I'm there with you."

"My imagination isn't that good."

He kissed her lightly on the mouth and left.

Storm looked around at his stakeout crew, as well as Doctor Craig, the medical examiner, and Larry Carson, who had been handling the inside work while Storm was on the streets.

Storm stood and put another black pin on the map to indicate the latest murder. "Let's take a good hard look at this and see what we've got."

"We've got a walking time bomb. That's what we've got."

Storm looked at Doctor Craig. "What are you saying to me, Doc?"

"James Lassiter didn't have to be killed. He would have died soon anyway. He had AIDS."

"You're sure?"

"Absolutely. The problem is we'll never know all the intimate contacts he had since he became HIV positive. We don't even know when that was. Now, we have a known prostitute, who has been screwing every male between here and Cairo, who has had sexual relations with our AIDS victim. How many more men is she going to infect before we catch up with her? Believe me, Storm, this is every physician's nightmare. The permutations are staggering. If he was bisexual as I suspect he was, single-handedly, he could wipe out a good portion of this city."

"Did you test the other victims to see if they were HIV positive?"

"Yes. If I had found anything you would have known about it ten seconds after I did. That doesn't say they would not have become HIV positive if they had lived."

"Okay, what else have we got?" Storm Andrews was worried.

Larry Carson took a card out of his pocket. "Remember when you brought in your belt buckle with Suzie's prints? We checked our files, FBI files, the national file, everything, but couldn't come up with a match. I was about to give up the search, when I looked in my file where we had Molly's fingerprints that we took off the bottle you lifted from your friend. We found a match. Suzie's fingerprints and Hank Castle's fingerprints are a match."

Storm stared at the young detective. "Are you certain?"

"I checked them several times, just to be sure."

Daryl Jenkins was the youngest member of the team on stakeout in the tower of Hank's apartment.

"Miss Castle left her apartment by way of the tower stairs at about eleven o'clock. She stopped in a storage area and pulled out a miniskirt and top and changed into these clothes before she left the building. She was heavily made up and her hair was somehow different. Maybe she wore a wig. She carried a shoulder bag. She passed less than ten feet away from where I was hidden. She checked the outside before she went into the fog. Dave Barry picked her up outside but lost her a few blocks away. She didn't come back to the tower until four o'clock. She went through the same procedure, changed her clothes, then went back up the stairs to her apartment. I didn't want to touch the clothes unless we had a search warrant. But I did get pictures. They should be developed by now." He picked up the phone and dialed four digits.

"Harry? This is Daryl Jenkins. How are you coming with the pictures? Great, could you run them down to us? Thanks."

Storm picked up the phone and dialed an outside number. "Doctor

McGowan? Storm Andrews. How tight is your schedule? Yes, it is vitally important. Thanks, I'll see you soon."

When the pictures arrived, they were passed around. Storm's throat felt like someone had shoved a basketball down there. He stared at the pictures. "How many copies do we have?"

"Three of each. Why don't you take a set. You'll probably need it when you talk to Doctor McGowan."

"I'll be back. Then we're going to the apartment."

Pam McGowan was sitting at her desk when Storm arrived. "You sounded tense on the phone. Are things starting to break?"

"That's a good word for it, Pam. But it would be more like splintering than breaking." He pulled the pictures out of his pocket and handed them to her. He almost choked on his words. "This is our killer."

She looked at the pictures then looked into his eyes.

"Do you think she knows about the other personalities?"

"No, I don't...and I don't know how I'm going to tell her."

"You realize, of course, that the shock of such news could bring out the other personality, the one that's homicidal."

"I wish it would. I think I can deal with that one. She's hard and shrewd and calculating. But what's going to happen to the sweet, loving, trusting woman? She's going to die along with the whore."

Doctor McGowan's eyebrows shot up. "Isn't she innocent until proven guilty? Chances are she'll be found to be criminally insane and confined to a psychiatric institution for the rest of her life. I don't think a court will sentence her to death."

Storm slumped in a chair. "No, the courts won't have to sentence her to death. She did that to herself. The latest victim that she seduced had AIDS. Doc Craig said he would have been dead soon, anyway." He walked to the door and turned. "We're going to pick her up. Will you be available?"

"Whenever you need me."

Storm posted two men outside of Hank's apartment and two on the tower stairs, and two in front of the building. "I'm going in first. Give me ten minutes, then come in."

CHAPTER 24

Hank sat across from Storm in the living room, listening but not believing what he was telling her.

"You're wrong, Storm, that's not possible. I would have known if there was somebody else living in this body."

Storm felt like he was betraying Hank. He said, "Remember the nights when you had your nightmare, each time another victim showed up on the streets."

"But that's not true. You said Suzie was the murderer."

"Your other personality is the woman you fear most. Suzie."

"No," she said in a low voice. "No. I'll never believe what you say." Hank slid off of the chair and crawled over to where he sat on the sofa, she wrapped her arms around his legs, crying and begging him to tell her he was only teasing. "You know it's not true. Please, Storm, tell me you know it's not true. You couldn't love me if this was true.... And you do love me. I know you do."

"Yes, I do love you." He reached into his pocket and took out the pictures Daryl Jenkins had taken and handed them to her.

She looked at the pictures. "These were taken in the basement of the tower. But that's not me. It can't be me." She moved away from him. Her voice that was so charged with emotion and panic, suddenly became harsh, emotionless. Her upper lip curled in disdain. "You're trying to frame me. You're doing this because you're in love with that shrink. You're trying to throw me over but I'm not going to let you do that." She paced back and forth behind the sofa, shouting obscenities at him, when suddenly he was aware the tone of her voice had changed. He could feel the hairs on the back of his neck bristling. Slowly he turned to face her.

"I wondered when you were going to make an appearance, Suzie."

She laughed a deep, sensuous, throaty sound. "I told her the day would come when I would have everything that was hers. She didn't believe me that good guys finish last. You're not as dumb as I thought you were. You're a much better detective than you are a lover. Although I guess you were adequate for Henrietta. It never really took much to satisfy her. The evidence for that was in the fact that she was stupid enough to marry that fish face."

"You mean Julian Grant? I'm interested in knowing how you got to him? How did you get him down on the waterfront, at night, by himself?"

"How do you know I did?" Her smile was taunting.

"I think you're a very intelligent woman. If you killed him the way you did all the others, we would have been suspicious. He would have been the only non-Streeter to be murdered with your particular brand of horror. Instead, you played on his fear. You knew he was deathly afraid of deep water. As long as he was dead, it didn't matter if it had your signature on it or not. You knew if we arrested Hank, you would also be incarcerated and that would ruin your plans to take over her body, her book, her life. It's not going to work."

"I think it will. You can't put me to death without putting Miss Innocence to death as well. She would pass any lie detector test you can devise. She simply doesn't know anything about me and as you have seen, she is not going to believe you."

"When did you come into existence, Suzie?"

"When Henrietta was eight years old. Then she got divorced from Julian on August 8, 1988. Get it? The eighth day of the eighth month of the eighty-eighth year in the twentieth century."

"So that's the significance of the number eight."

"That dumb Henrietta told you. You just weren't listening."

"Why don't you let Hank come out again so I can talk to her."

"Do I look stupid to you? You think I don't know what you're trying to do. I'm never going to let her out again. You're going to have to deal with me. Baby, I can show you a time like you've never had before. I can carry you to heights beyond your wildest expectations. I can make every fantasy you ever had come true." She started unbuttoning his shirt. There was an animal appeal about her.

Storm took her hands in his and pulled them away from his shirt. "It's not going to work. You have nothing I want."

"I've got what every man wants." Her sneer was unsettling. "I'm what every man dreams about, I'm what every man fantasizes about when he can't make it on his own."

"No you're not. Hank is the dream. You're the nightmare."

She walked behind him. He heard the low growl begin deep in her throat but before he could turn around, he felt something cold hit his back. He dove onto the floor and she was all over him, the bloody stiletto poised to strike again. Her knee entrapped his right arm and he was suddenly aware that his left arm was almost useless. He watched as the blade came down and penetrated his left shoulder, again and again. Darkness closed in.

He rallied briefly. Suzie was writing furiously at the desk. He pulled his gun from the shoulder holster and fired a shot out the window. The noise startled Suzie and she picked up the stiletto and slowly walked toward him, when the darkness closed in again.

CHAPTER 25

An attendant unlocked the door and Doctor McGowan walked in. "Good morning. Did you sleep well?"

Suzie Hoffman pushed the print button and the finished page came out of the printer. "Can't you see I am trying to finish my book?" She snapped.

"Well, Suzie, you can continue with your writing after I leave. I think we should talk."

"Listen, shrink, you think I don't know you're trying to get Henrietta back again? Well, that's not going to happen. I'm here now and this is where I'm going to stay. Now why don't you bug out?"

"There is no reason why you and Henrietta can't live in harmony."

"That's what you think. Have you ever met her? No, of course you haven't. The only one you know is me."

"Not true. I met Hank at the hospital when Maxine was a patient."

Suzie looked up without lifting her head. "Is it true that I could be HIV positive?"

Doctor McGowan frowned. "Where did you hear that?"

"Damn it. Will you give me a frigging answer instead of asking questions all the time?"

"That possibility exists. It could be several years before it shows up in your system."

"Where did I pick it up?"

"James Lassiter."

"Ah yes, the professor. He liked his sex kinky, the kinkier the better. Damn, I almost regretted doing him in because he was a good sex partner."

"How many times did you have sex with him before you killed him?"

"Once, that same night. Then it was over. He couldn't go twice in one night and time was running out. I had already told Henrietta I was going to take over. I couldn't wait for her to figure out who I was. She might have tried to stop me from coming out again. I was surprised when Wally Stockheim told her I had been in her apartment, that she didn't tell Storm Andrews. She had her chance and flubbed it. Now, she's trapped forever in my body." She laughed, "However long…forever is."

"Is there any remorse on your part?"

"Absolutely not…. Well, maybe one regret. But what the hell, we all have soft spots. Now why don't you get the hell out of here so I can get back to this book. Who's better qualified to write this book? But for me, there wouldn't be a book. Except for me, the plight of the homeless would never have had so much attention. By reducing their numbers, I raised the public's awareness that there is a forgotten society out there. What did you do to bring that problem to the attention of the world?"

Doctor McGowan nodded. "Yes, you did bring the problem of the homeless to the attention of the world but you could have done it in a much less destructive way. Let's talk about Julian Grant."

"He's another one I regretted killing."

Doctor McGowan's shock showed on her face.

"Gotcha, Doc. You didn't think I would feel remorse for anybody, isn't that right?" She didn't wait for a response. "He died too quickly. I really had some special plans for his death. But…he was late meeting me and those dumb dockworkers were hanging around. I would have enjoyed seeing him die by inches. Well, at any rate, he can't screw up the lives of any more kids. I'll bet a lot of mothers would be grateful to me for eliminating that bastard who preyed on kids. Know what, Doc? Julian was the lousiest lay I ever had. He wasn't circumcised and he always had a stink about him and the stink stayed in my nostrils for days after he and Hank had sex. Down on the waterfront, he didn't recognize me right away but his level of excitement was so high, he would have screwed a snake if somebody held its head. He was begging me to finish it for him, so I did. Not in the way he would have wanted. Just before I hit him with a pipe, I told him who I was. I never saw anybody look so scared. I hit him just hard enough for him to know he was drowning and I watched him go under. Henrietta slept better that night than she had in a year."

"Did Henrietta ever know about your escapades?"

"Are you kidding? I wouldn't even be here if she had learned to look out for herself. She was a good reporter but it ended there."

"How long have you been around?"

"I told you, since we were eight. After Bruce raped her, it looked like she was going off on the deep end, that's when I was born. She needed protection. I was there. The strange thing is I had to protect her from Bruce but I loved having sex with him."

"What about Storm Andrews?"

Suzie turned from the computer, her face afire with hate. "You'd better get out of here, Doc. I'm not going to talk about that man to anybody. You hear me?" she shouted.

Doctor McGowan stood and walked toward the door. "Maybe you should let Hank back in your life.... She was the writer. I've read the trash you're putting out. It will never be published. If you want that story to get published, you'll have to bring her back. You see, Hank really did have a purpose in this life."

The attendant unlocked the door and locked it again after the doctor left.

* * *

"Hello, Doctor McGowan," the nurse on the surgery floor smiled her greeting.

"Hello to you too. How is Detective Andrews today?"

"He's doing well, considering. He should be discharged in a day or two. He could use some company."

Pam McGowan opened the door to the private room. Storm sat in a chair with his back to the door. In his hand was a piece of paper with a handwritten verse on it.

He looked up as Doctor McGowan entered. "Hello, Pam."

"Hello, Storm. You look much better today. I talked to your doctor and he tells me you're doing quite well."

"I'll be going home soon."

"I know. How do you feel about that?"

"I'm not sure. It's going to be strange not having Hank to look after." He handed her the piece of paper. "This was the verse Suzie prepared for me."

Pam McGowan took the paper from his hand and read aloud the verse from Alphonse De Lamartine's "Meditations Poetiques."

. *"Man, it seems is not able to bear the languid rest on Nature's bosom, and when the trumpet sounds the signal of danger, he hastens to join his comrades, no matter what the cause that calls him to arms. He rushes into the thickest of the fight and amid the uproar of the battle regains confidence in himself and his powers. What is life but a succession of preludes to that unknown song whose first solemn note is sounded by Death?"*

EPILOGUE

Storm Andrews sat facing Doctor McGowan in her office.

"Why won't you let me see Hank?"

"Storm, she's not Hank Castle anymore. She's Suzie Hoffman, the same Suzie who tried and almost succeeded in killing you. The only thing this woman knows is that you were responsible for her capture. She has had the taste of blood and now she craves it. Suzie is so consumed with hate that she has no memory of Hank's love for you. Remember, it was Hank Castle who fell in love with you. It was Hank Castle who was capable of giving and receiving love. But it was that very love that got her into trouble. It was her love for Julian Grant, then being rejected by him, that brought the protective Suzie back into being. Suzie saved Hank's psyche but took her life. You don't know this woman, Storm. She is incapable of civil human emotion and given the chance, she would carry out her vendetta on men for the rest of her life. A locked ward is the only place for her, for whatever time is left to her. The only regret she has is being caught. This personality she has become has no empathy for the street people and no love for anyone and that includes Hank herself. After a while, Hank became a means to an end. That end was the annihilation of all men, because every man's face was that of Bruce Dickinson, whom Hank hated, or Julian Grant, with whom she had a love-hate relationship."

Doctor McGowan walked to the sideboard, poured coffee into two cups and handed one to Storm before she continued. "I talked with Doctor Craig. He gave me a copy of the autopsy report on Julian Grant. The irony of this whole unfortunate situation is that Julian Grant was riddled with cancer and the primary site was the prostate. Julian would probably have been dead in six months." Pam McGowan put her cup on the desk. "So, Suzie went to a lot of trouble to kill a man who would have been dead in less than a year and she ended up with Lassiter a victim of AIDS and she'll probably die because of it. The State doesn't have to try her and come in with a guilty verdict. They don't have to condemn her to death. She did that for herself." Doctor

McGowan studied the man before her. "Storm, she feels no remorse…not even for herself."

Storm sipped his coffee. "If she had known Julian Grant was dying of cancer, would it have made a difference in the outcome? Would that knowledge have assuaged her compulsion to kill him?"

"I don't know. My personal feeling is that it would not. She had to have her pound of flesh…her way."

"What happens now? To me, I mean."

"The emotional wounds will heal, just as the physical ones did. It'll take more time. The healing process at times will be painful, as only memories of a lost love can be painful. Time is a great healer."

She reached over and put her hand on his. She said, "There's an old Italian saying; L'amore fa passare il tempo, Il tempo fa passare l'amore. Love makes time pass, and time makes love pass. You're grieving over the death of someone you loved. That's what it amounts to…. Hank died when Suzie attempted to kill you. When your period of mourning is over, the sun will shine again and hopefully, you'll find pleasure in the company of someone else. In the meantime, take solace in the thought that you prevented more murders. The streets will be safer now, at least as safe as inner-city streets can be."

* * *

Printed in the United States
59717LVS00004B/154-171

9 781424 124947